D1455656

THE SHADOW LINE

Also by Laura Furman

THE GLASS HOUSE
WATCH TIME FLY
TUXEDO PARK
BOOKWORMS: GREAT WRITERS AND READERS
CELEBRATE READING *(WITH ELINORE STANDARD)*
ORDINARY PARADISE

THE SHADOW LINE

Laura Furman

WINEDALE PUBLISHING
HOUSTON

Library of Congress Cataloging in Publication Data

Furman, Laura.

The shadow line.

Reprint of the edition published by The Viking Press

625 Madison Avenue, New York, N.Y. 10022

I. Title

PS3556.U745S5   813'.54   81-24089

ISBN 0-965-7468-6-0   AACR2

The author would like to thank the Texas Institute of Letters and the University of Texas at Austin for the generous grant of six months at the Paisano Ranch outside Austin.

Grateful acknowledgment is made to the following for permission to reprint copyrighted material:

Doubleday & Company, Inc., Withers, London, and the trustees of the Joseph Conrad Estate: A selection from *The Shadow Line* by Joseph Conrad. Copyright 1917 by Doubleday & Company, Inc.

Helga Greene: A selection from *The Long Goodbye* by Raymond Chandler.

Printed in the United States of America

For my family

One goes on. And the time, too, goes on—till one perceives ahead a shadow-line warning one that the region of early youth, too, must be left behind.

Joseph Conrad

... you can never know too much about the shadow line and the people who walk it.

Raymond Chandler

THE SHADOW LINE

I

She was running through a brilliant light whose walls billowed like the hull of a ship. He moved forward steadily in pursuit. If she looked back, she would lose momentum, yet more than anything, almost more than escape, she wanted once again to see his face.

David pulled Liz closer to him, as if in sleep he could feel her leaving him. Stirring, she remembered morning and running. Morning was the light that slipped over the edges of the white shades into the chocolate-brown room. She opened her eyes and could barely see the silhouette of the palm tree outside their window, the winter fronds straggly and stiff. She was in the house on Graustark with David. His touch was the surface of her dream, his smooth skin the walls of the ship. Running; she had promised to go running with David in Memorial Park.

"Time?" David asked.

"Four-fifty-seven." She read the numbers off the clock radio. In three minutes KTRH would come on: international headlines, national and city news, sports, and weather. Slowly, deliberately, David disentangled himself from Liz, the sheets and blankets, the pillow he held against his neck to ward off breezes (and, Liz thought, bad dreams) and reached in the direction of the clock. He would be too slow, she thought, and she lunged across his body for the clock, grazing his head with her elbow. They reached the OFF button at the same time.

"Sorry," Liz whispered, and she lay back against the white sheets, pulling David with her. "So sorry," she said, stroking his tough gray curls.

"I had it," he said. "On the nose."

For another moment they lay together, listening to the click of the refrigerator downstairs, to the slap of a passing car on the pavement, and then, "Okay," David said. "Let's hit it."

David left the bed first and Liz lay on her back, watching him dress quickly in the chilly room. He put on gray gym shorts and T-shirt, a white sweatshirt and his silver-rimmed glasses, sneakers and white socks. The first time she'd met David Muse, he'd been playing tennis and was dressed in white. He'd looked large, modest, and cheerful, not a contender but someone who was doing what he liked. Liz had always felt prickly around people in skiing outfits, tennis whites, running suits—as if they were showing off a superior state just by their costumes. They had been lovers for seven months now, and Liz was still surprised when she reached to hold him at how tall David was, at his warmth when he slept and she cuddled against him.

The house they rented was owned by a rich boy who'd grown up in Houston and who lived now on an island off Georgia. When he bought it, the house had been a plain yellow two-story house with a garage apartment out back and a porch running around three sides. The owner installed elaborate beveled glass windows in every opening, distorting the views in and out. He'd covered the lawn with a wooden deck that extended from the porch to the fence, and he'd had the house painted chocolate brown with white trim, inside and out. The only exception was the kitchen, which was entirely apple green. The floors were sanded and polished. There were shiny white ceiling fans in every high-ceilinged room.

The garage apartment had been converted into a small cottage with shiny shellacked pine paneling in every room. The yard between the house and the cottage grew wild, a jungle uninterrupted except for a limestone path that went between them and continued around to the front gate.

The owner had enclosed the house, deck, jungle yard, and cottage behind a wooden stockade fence that he'd planted with bamboo, now grown higher than the fence in back of the house. Then he'd left town for good.

Cal Dayton, Liz Gold's friend and editor, friend from New York, editor in Houston, had moved into the cottage when he'd come home to Houston a year and a half ago. David had moved into the house after his divorce in the summer. Liz was the newcomer, new to the house and to Houston. She'd moved in with David a month before, in January.

Liz had moved in but not quite unpacked, and she intended, some empty weekend, to unpack the summer clothes folded in cartons that were stacked in an unused bedroom along with books, folded director's chairs, and a bare bed. She would get to it, she kept thinking, but they'd rented a town house at Walden, a resort on Lake Conroe, an hour and a half north, and weekends were never empty.

She thought the colors of the house made it seem like being inside a very smart piece of luggage and maybe she didn't have to unpack. Neither she nor David owned much furniture and she'd left the most substantial pieces at her old apartment, now her office. She'd come to David's house with two Oriental rugs and her down comforter, her clothes, and a few watercolors in polished hardwood frames. She thought it was just as well that the walls were chocolate brown. They took up space that might have made the house seem too large for her and David.

Silent, sipping coffee, David drove down Alabama to the empty cross street that led to the bayou and the parkway. The bungalows along Dunlavy were varied by width of siding, vintage of paint job, whether the yard was a decorous flat green or a rubble of old cars. One or two of the houses were painted in neutral shades, and the numbers on them were in bold tasteful decals, easily visible from the street. Other houses hid behind fences as high as Liz and David's.

"I guess the street's turning around," Liz said.

"I guess," David said. "Spinning its wheels. Have you ever been there?"

He pointed out a charity thrift shop with bars on the windows and door and a plastic sign hanging from the front announcing the days and hours it was open.

"My former mother-in-law used to clean out every spring and give her stuff to that place. Her ladies did too."

"Ladies?"

"You know about ladies. The club. Old friends."

"I'll stick to the Blue Bird," Liz said. "It has unplumbed riches. Also it's right between home and the magazine."

"A word to the wise," David said. "Direct pipeline to River Oaks."

At Allen Parkway the vista opened. The neighborhood ended and they could see the skyline of downtown Houston and the parkway curving east to it. The sun was up, giving backlight to the oil company and bank towers. David turned the car away from the city, toward Memorial Park. Allen Parkway was the most tasteful road in Houston, leading briefly past green hills and an old cemetery, past anonymous office buildings and motels and Old South apartment complexes with columns and domes. The YMCA was built to look Old Spanish. Liz liked the rougher freeways better, especially at night—the Southwest Freeway and the Gulf Freeway that led south to Galveston, north to the house at Lake Conroe. At night the red neon emblem of the Baroid Mud Company could be seen as a landmark, and closer to town, a white neon grand piano revolved slowly above the speeding crowds.

Her idea, before she moved to Houston, was that all of Texas was empty and dry. But Houston was wet, a city whose economy was based on a fifty-mile ship channel dug between it and Galveston; no hurricane would destroy the serious business of Houston's port as it had Galveston's. Instead of a high dry place, Liz found Houston to be semitropical, a city constantly oozing liquid into its bayous, and what was not yet firmly moist enough to flow into the bayous, or to form sudden downpours of rain as solid as a river, stayed as air, heavy and laden with fragrances. When the wind blew from the southeast and Pasadena, it smelled industrial and chemical. After a norther, when the wind swung around to the east, came the smell of roasting coffee from the Maxwell House plant east of downtown. At other times came the odor of jasmine, ligustrum, and waxy tropical flowers she'd seen only in books and had never smelled or touched before.

Above the city were the coastal plains, to the east the piney woods of East Texas, to the west the Hill Country and San Antonio and Austin. Below the city, stretching east and west, all along the Gulf Coast as far as Brownsville and Corpus Christi, were small towns with names like Blessing and perhaps one café to their credit.

David turned onto Memorial Drive, and Liz saw a sign she hadn't noticed before and a builder's crane peering over a stand of thick trees. A high-rise apartment building was to go up, overlooking Buffalo Bayou and Bayou Bend, the house and grounds the oil heiress Ima Hogg had given to the city along with Memorial Park. Three houses were for sale along Memorial Drive. Liz wondered if it was the road and the building people were objecting to—Memorial was heavily traveled and promised to be more so—or was it that they had moved up and grown beyond houses that could be seen from the road?

"I may not get back from New York Thursday, if the meetings go on and on."

"And you leave Tuesday? Tomorrow? When would you come back?"

"Friday. Saturday morning. How about coming up on Friday and we'll spend the weekend in New York? See your parents. I'd like to meet your father."

"I don't know," she said. "I'm getting an assignment from Cal tomorrow. . . ."

"Okay," David said. "We can make up our minds later."

"Will you see Lucy this time?" she asked.

"If I'd wanted to see Lucy," David said, "I'd still be married to her," which was a polite answer, Liz thought, since they both knew Lucy had left him. "I don't know who I'll be seeing in New York. Probably the board will be fellowship enough for me."

Liz reached over and touched his bare leg. "Sorry," she said.

She hated running but she liked going to the park with David. When they were both suited up and riding in his old black Oldsmobile Cutlass, she felt amazed. Nothing in her previous life had prepared her for being so normal, so American. She felt both a relief that she could be inconspicuous and a panic that she had lost herself in something large and powerful.

The morning was gray and chilly. Late winter was an especially moody time in Houston. It could be sunny and blue by noon or there might be a bone-chilling winter rain.

David pulled into the park and drove to the grassy inlet where they liked to stretch. It was an opening in the woods, a clear lawn with a giant magnolia and a ninety-foot loblolly pine that dwarfed it. The hardwood trees were still leafless, but the magnolia was deep green. Unlike other mornings, there was an absence of smell and sun and mosquitoes. It would be another six weeks or so before the mosquitoes came with the hot weather.

"Which is the tree with the asp?" Liz asked, thinking of Cleopatra's end. What light came through the woods was filtered and old, as in a primeval forest.

"Pines are okay," David said. "It's the live oaks that have the asps. Don't put your hand on a live oak without looking first."

He'd grown up in and around Houston, in and around everywhere there was oil. His father worked for Shell; his mother was a native Houstonian. They'd moved every few years of David's childhood and adolescence. College was his first stable time, he told Liz, four years in one place. He'd lived in Texas, Oklahoma, Louisiana, and Vancouver and for two brief and exotic periods in New York and Japan. When they lived in New York, his parents sent him to boarding school in Massachusetts because they were afraid of the public schools in New York. Otherwise, David saw to himself in the new places and figured out a method of making friends quickly but not deeply. He kept the next move always in mind. He'd spent his college and law-school years in Austin at the University of Texas, and when he married Lucy Williams and moved to Houston, David thought he'd found the deep well of stability. Liz's childhood in Manhattan—same apartment all her life, same walk down West End Avenue to elementary school, buses to high school—had the same ring of permanence to him, almost romantic. But he'd fallen out of love with places, he'd told Liz the first night they spent together.

"You can stay in one place always—which looked like heaven when I was a kid—and be restless as a flea. I wasn't unhappy, mind you. I just had my eye on something else. My dad loves the moving. I did learn that owning a house isn't any worse than owning a car, especially in a good market. Look at that house I bought for me and Lucy. On the market one day, sold a week later. Now it's on the block again. Big deal."

"I grew up in an apartment," Liz had said. "Buying a house is a big thing."

David's parents lived in Europe now. In a few years, his father would retire. "Maybe they'll move back to Texas. My mother has relatives all over the Gulf Coast. Or to Florida." Liz had been shown pictures of them—his father big and lean like David, his mother slight and blond. They were on a golf course, their clubs in front of them as if they were putting. In another snapshot that David kept on his dresser, he was twelve and wearing a tight dark suit and tie. His parents were dressed up also, his mother wearing a print dress and a hat with a small veil. They were on their way to church in Tokyo, David said. A house servant had taken the photo. The background was bland, and Liz thought they might as well have been in Kansas.

Liz leaned against the pine, stretching her tendons, one leg at a time. She was more stretched naturally than David and had less patience with warm-up exercises. She did as many standing stretches as she could think of, then lay on the damp ground for sit-ups and leg raises. She held David's feet for his sit-ups and then he held hers, praising her for the number she was managing to do, reminding her of how few she'd been able to do when she'd started running with him seven months before.

"I can't believe I did this in August," she said.

"You were trying to impress me," David said.

"Well, it worked."

There weren't many people out yet on the running path, only a few regulars they recognized from evening runs.

"I'm not doing more than a mile," Liz said as they started on the dirt path.

"Do a little more. You should always do more than you did your last run."

"Just a good mile," she said. "And you? Three? Six?"

"I'll go around once—three miles. If you'd stay with me, I could do more."

"Them's the breaks," Liz said. They'd jogged slowly about a quarter of a mile and were coming up to a curve at the baseball field and the Catholic church. "That's the thing. When you're with someone like me, it isn't any fun without me."

"Is that so," he said. "I was wondering."

They ran then in silence along the golf course. One man was out practicing his swings in a languid fashion. David ran steadily and easily; it was all genetic, he'd reassured her. He was built for it—a little tall, perhaps. She wished she'd told him first thing in the morning that she loved him better than she'd ever loved anyone, and that he gave her more steadiness than she'd ever thought possible. She was too out of breath now to make it sound convincing. It would come out as a ploy for attention or for stopping the run.

They were on the small up-and-down approaching the tennis courts. She was almost home free, her mile complete.

"Do a little more," David urged again. "Up to the big pine past the courts."

"Nope."

"You'll be smarter and write better if you run longer."

"Don't want to be. Couldn't stand it."

At the four portable toilets they breathed in gingerly going past. The post marking the mile was in sight.

"Try it," David said.

"No. You do the extra mile for me. Run one for the gimp."

They reached the post and Liz stopped trotting. David jogged in place for a moment, looking puzzled or disappointed, she couldn't tell. She almost started moving toward him to please him, but he said, "See you back at the car," and jogged on without her.

Liz knew she would get more benefit from a rapid, concentrated jog-walk, but she dawdled as she went along, studying the trees and the light, the texture of the running path. A plane flew overhead, momentarily visible against the gray. She didn't like it when David went away. His business trips usually lasted one or two days and took him to Austin or to Dallas. The anticipation of his absence became at times so painful that his departure was a relief, but then another vulture appeared. What she thought of as the luck that had brought them together might just as easily allow them to part. His trips were quick, yet at times during an absence she wouldn't have been surprised to get a call saying he wouldn't be back. Never mind his ties to her, his choice of her. When he left, David was whole in her mind. When he returned, so did a more fractured sense of their life together. In the phone call of her imagination, David was able to say goodbye, and she was left facing a life without him. Their daily time offered no such clean-cut options. She couldn't imagine a life without him once he was home.

At a distance she could see how different they were. She had never taken a vacation—planned ahead, reservations at faraway hotels, books read in advance of great ruins. David had traveled with Lucy on a European honeymoon that Liz imagined as out of Henry James, a stately and educational tour of the capitals and important points in between. David was used to the idea of having money to spend. He was planning to buy a house in Houston to save money on taxes. He rarely bought clothing, but when he did it was expensive. He could buy a weekend in Massachusetts if he liked and silk shirts for Liz. In back of this material freedom were the real goods Liz could barely imagine: stocks, bonds, and the expectation of a modest inheritance; money to play with and money to invest; money in the future and the present. Her only resource beyond the fees she was paid for stories was the money from her husband, Willy. Against her father's advice, she whittled away at the capital.

Willy had been a hundred times richer than David but he hadn't known how to be. Even before he inherited the bulk of the money, when he was only well padded, they could never figure out how to spend it. When Liz and Willy decided to eat at an expensive restaurant, they were setting up for disappointment: the dressing up, the astonishment at the prices, the conviction that they were in the wrong place. The food was never good enough, the restaurants never pretty enough to match their guilt at spending money that way. Afterward, they were always relieved to be home. She remembered the shared relief as among their happier times.

Liz turned around rather than make the complete circle around the path. The mockingbirds were singing loudly. The morning had changed. The sun was now visible in a pale blue sky.

Back at the tennis courts, three men were standing on an exercise platform, stretching. They weren't runners. They were muscle men. A man ran past her who resembled Willy, but Willy had never been one for sports. In New York, Liz met people on the street she'd known all her life, from elementary school, high school, camp; teachers, friends of her parents, parents of friends. In the ten months she'd been in Houston, everyone was new to her. Only recently had she begun to recognize people she'd seen before, at press conferences, parties, at the magazine where she freelanced; people she'd interviewed and people she'd met through David and Cal.

A runner was coming toward her, a sandy blond man her own age, in red shorts and a white sweat-filled shirt. He was staring at her, not with the glazed look most good runners had but trying to get her attention. She stepped aside, as he approached, and pretended to be interested in the trees. There was so little street life in Houston, Liz had become unused to being looked at. When she was home from college, wearing miniskirts, she'd walked a gantlet each time she'd gone from her parents' apartment on Riverside Drive to Broadway. Once a man called out, "Oh, you have beautiful knees." When she was younger still, in seventh grade, a man had followed her into the building, into the elevator. When the elevator lifted off, he'd exposed his erection and grabbed under her dress, tearing the elastic of her underpants. Liz had screamed and hit all the buttons on the panel in the elevator and run out when the elevator stopped. A neighbor had searched the building's stairs for the man, but he was gone, back to the street. Sometime she'd buy a car with air conditioning, Liz thought, so she could ride with the windows closed.

She hadn't planned to stay in Houston. She'd come because Cal had started *Spindletop* and he'd called her often to say she should get into her mother's old Chevy Nova and get going south. She'd come thinking she would probably keep moving, maybe continue west to California. But she'd stayed this long, and now there was David.

Two black runners passed her at a steady slow pace, moving their legs at the same moment, their limbs loaded with muscles. Liz picked up her pace. She didn't want to keep David waiting, and she thought of his departure the next day and how little time they seemed to have together. They would have the weekend at Lake Conroe, at Walden. Maybe Cal would come. They'd spend their time eating and walking and reading some of the piles of magazines, papers, and books they brought with them. They'd drink too much wine, and when it was time to go to bed, she'd have David to herself.

She was past the church now and the ball field, almost at the sign for Showers, a quarter of a mile to the car. Sometimes at night when she looked out at the cottage and saw that Cal was home, most likely alone, she was surprised to feel envious. She wouldn't have wanted to be Cal or to be alone, but still, she felt the envy and she drew conclusions from his solitude she would have resented when she was single—it seemed simpler to be alone, at least looking out across the yard.

She was standing at their bedroom door, still in her shorts and sweatshirt. David emerged from the shower, the air from the warm room hitting their bedroom in clouds, and was drying himself quickly and roughly. He had bright positive brown eyes, deeper chocolate than the walls of their house. His broad nose had been broken in high school when he'd run into a wall playing basketball. He kept his hair cut short but it wanted to burst into waves and curls. David's mouth was wide, and his skin the color of honey, Liz thought, a pale filtered honey, waiting for the sun. She was a northern child, in the sun a few days a year on a summertime weekend at the beach, red nose in the winter, bright cheeks in the fall. Her skin was pale, and her long thick hair surrounded her face like a dark halo. Her blue eyes made her look more Irish than Jewish. They were the one feature from the Hungarian side of her family. She was small-boned and compact and, before she'd started living with David, exercised fiercely once or twice a month when she looked at herself in a full-length mirror and thought she was getting old.

When she was a teenager in New York, Liz had sought boyfriends who matched her. Her husband had been redheaded and skinny as spaghetti. David was her opposite. Cal Dayton looked like her but they had never been lovers, only the best of friends.

"What time do we have to be at Clarice's?" David asked.

"Seven," she said. "Seven-fifteen. Come home early."

"Okay. If I can."

He put on his dark blue trousers and a white shirt.

"What are you doing today," she asked, "suing someone?"

"I thought I'd try to avoid litigation today. I'm getting my act together for the folks in New York. I have to report to the board what the foundation's doing."

"Well, I'm going to have a day to myself. I'm going to wander around like someone without a job."

"Does Clarice have a house for you to look at?"

"Not this week," Liz said. "She hasn't called."

"Phones go two ways in Houston," he said. "Don't worry. I'll do the looking when I get back."

David glanced in the mirror, touched his hair, then took his jacket from the closet and put it on. She went over to him and smoothed his collar over his red-patterned tie.

"Nice," she said. "A real grown-up man."

"Thanks. What's a gimp?"

"A cripple," she said. "Someone who's lame."

She glanced at the clock. It was eight, time for David to go to work.

"Why did you say that before," he asked, "about running one for the gimp."

"There was some old movie," she said, impatient with him for asking. "Jimmy Cagney. He's in prison or something and someone says to him, 'Run one for the gimp.' "

"I don't mean to stick you with the looking," he said. "Don't worry about it." He kissed her on the forehead and said, "It's not Jimmy Cagney, it's Pat O'Brien. And it's not prison, it's football. And it's the Gipper, not the gimp. Win one for the Gipper, the coach says."

"Details," Liz said. "Stick with me. I'll never steer you wrong."

"Lois Lane," he said.

When she stepped out of the shower, she stood for a moment, listening to the empty house. He was gone. She'd watched him drive away, then she'd turned back into the house and taken a shower. She thought she heard a step downstairs, but it was nothing. She opened the window and watched the steam wash out, leaving her chilled. She would be glad to get the next assignment from Cal, she thought.

She had an hour before her haircutting appointment, so Liz drove straight down Alabama to the Blue Bird Circle Thrift Shop. Rainy days made her feel like thrift shopping, and so did being with people too much. Sometimes it was only a small crack in time, like this hour, that made her long for the Blue Bird. It was a keen desire, akin to a piercing yen for chocolate or a drink. She had a natural clock and rarely lost track of where she had to be next and when. The occasions when Liz forgot time—it is seven years since I left Sweden, nine hours until I see David, two days to deadline—took place at the Blue Bird, where often she would look up at the large round clock above the front door and realize that she had let time slip past her.

It was empty when Liz walked in. The long white building took up half a block in width. The other half of the Blue Bird property was a two-story brick house, not unlike David and Liz's house on Graustark, that the Blue Bird used for selling furniture. The neon fixtures on the ceiling of the Blue Bird gave a white flickering light that Liz had learned not to trust for color. But whether it was the light or herself, she couldn't tell—sometimes a shirt or jacket that looked one way in the shop, jaunty perhaps or antique, only looked tired and faded when she got home. What had been red was maroon or, worse, what had been royal blue was shocking purple.

She recognized the Blue Bird volunteer behind the cash register. She was short and broad, and her gray hair had been curled in regular screws, then flattened by a nearly invisible net. The volunteers at the Blue Bird wore royal blue uniforms with blue birds at the breast pocket, and their hair was trimmed, waved, and controlled. There were no dark-haired volunteers, Liz had noticed, only blondes and shades of blond and gray and white. Behind the gray-haired volunteer at the cash register was a rack that held the choicest items in the store, the fur coats and bridal gowns, designer gowns and dresses—Pucci one day, Ungaro the next. At the central wrapping counter there were usually two more volunteers and an old black man dressed in dark slacks and a white uniform jacket to whom the ladies deferred when he complained that there were no hangers or sacks or clothespins.

She started at Better Dresses, the section that offered polyester dresses with matching bolero jackets and imitation Chanel suits with heavy braid. Once in a while she found something there: an Anne Klein wool suit for $8.00, jacket, skirt, and trousers; an all-cotton blue jacket with a full skirt to match. Liz spent some time each Blue Bird visit at the evening gowns and cocktail dresses. She owned a black silk cocktail dress and a long navy blue dress, which she'd bought new, like uniforms, hoping they'd last her lifetime for the rare occasions she had to dress that way. She liked looking at the bridal gowns, their stiff satin turning yellow, and at bright-colored full-length dresses with collars and cuffs heavily crusted with sequins or jewels, at a white satin rose pinned to the dropped waist of a long red dress. Sometimes Liz tried on toreador pants and strapless gowns, clothes she would never include in her shy wardrobe. She looked like herself in the strange clothes, never like another woman.

Better Dresses offered nothing, and so Liz moved across the room to the other racks of dresses. She liked checking the labels to see the parade of stores—Neiman-Marcus, Foley's, Sakowitz, Joske's, and the Dallas store Sanger-Harris. There were obscure labels as well, from manufacturers and stores she'd never heard of, and there were famous labels, custom labels, and no labels at all, only the careful seams of a homemade garment. Not every piece of clothing had been bought for life, she saw. Some exuded their choice for a special occasion, a new job, a treat. She didn't like to think of the feelings of the women when they gave up on their clothes.

In her size, Liz found an English dress, a black and white knit that looked as though it was from 1967. She held the dress up to her. The skirt reached five inches above her knees. The neck was jagged as a jack-o'-lantern's grin, and the sleeves were cut away to reveal diamonds of flesh. The black and white pattern was dazzling, a piece of Op Art, a kind of design she hadn't seen in years.

She'd worked her way near the back room of the Blue Bird, where the volunteers sorted and priced the clothing. Two white-haired ladies in blue uniforms were standing at Coats, and one said to the other that she'd just been to visit with Mary Elizabeth Summerwell and that she was suffering. "Oh," said the second, "what a shame. I didn't know you were going. I have a card right here for you to sign for her. It's from all of us."

"I was just there," the first woman said, proceeding. "She's suffering terribly. They still don't know what it is; they're waiting for the doctor to make up his mind," and then the voices lowered and all Liz could hear was "exploration." The first said, "Bye now," and took off, a little bowlegged woman whose stockings were wrinkling around her ankles. Liz heard her call out cheerfully to the ladies behind the wrapping counter, "Y'all be good now," as she left the Blue Bird. Liz decided against trying on the black-and-white dress. It wasn't one hundred percent wool. She had to draw the line somewhere.

She left Dresses and Coats and drifted to Blouses, looking in all sizes because she never knew what she might find. Most of the time the Blue Bird volunteers summed the clothes up accurately—size, price, and worth. But sometimes they slipped up and it was necessary to be patient and leaf meditatively through all the blouses in all the sizes, past plaids, checks, flowers, Hawaiian styles, embroidered windmills, and faded loud colors, past crepes and rhinestones, cowboy snaps, polyesters, blends, satins, to see if the blouse she might want to take home had been hidden and was waiting for her to find it.

Liz looked up at the clock. Forty-five minutes of her hour were gone. She had only a few more racks before the women's section was finished. She found the pale pink blouse by chance then. It had a long collar and buttons that rose from the wrist halfway to the elbow. It had been a perfect blouse in 1970. She was sure of the date because she'd been in Sweden then, and just such a blouse had been a gift from Willy.

She'd arrived in Sweden with two suitcases, not knowing if they would stay a month or all their lives. He'd found them an apartment near Stockholm and told her he was giving her an allowance of sorts. Each month, he would deposit a certain amount of money in her bank account. She didn't have to tell him what she did with the money. Then they'd chip in to pay for rent and food together. He said he realized he was depriving her of income by taking her to a place where she couldn't earn her living as she wanted to, as a journalist.

"When you're fluent in Swedish," Willy said, "you'll get a job on a newspaper."

Sometimes in the afternoon after Swedish class, Liz walked around in central Stockholm instead of going straight home to an apartment that might be empty if Willy was at a meeting, or occupied by a stranger or by Willy and his boys' club of deserters and resisters. She looked into restaurants whose tables were set with white dishes, pink tablecloths, and brass candleholders; into the king's palace, into the modern museum, but most often into clothing stores. She was in Europe for the first time, she reminded herself, land of beautiful clothing. She should be able to find clothes that would fit superbly, fashioned of cloth she'd never touched before, in colors she'd only seen in Renaissance paintings. But the clothing she admired was out of the question. How could she walk into Swedish class wearing a cashmere sweater? She didn't want to be envied by the other immigrants, who'd come with nothing. She didn't want to be in the same category—bourgeoise, well-dressed—as the teacher, who was Liz's age and lived with her mother and was engaged to a doctor. What did a person wear to a meeting of exiled soldiers and politicos and their wives and girl friends? How did one dress in a classroom of Portuguese men who had left their army because they refused to fight in Angola, of stocky Poles who'd come for a better life, of skinny Greeks who couldn't read the alphabet and were hoping for a factory job in this northern industrial country? The clothing of all the Americans she knew, and the Swedish wives, was as tired as the people themselves. Even the garments the babies wore, the layers of padding that protected them from the cold darkness, seemed limp.

Liz saw the pink blouse in the window of a shop on Sveavägen, a pale pink blouse with a big fashionable collar. She had nothing to wear with it; in her fancy for it, the blouse stood alone and made her happy. If she had the blouse, she thought, it would be all right.

Christmas was coming. There were decorations strung from lampposts, and at school they were taught about the Festival of Lucia. The deepening darkness told her it was almost the solstice. At home they'd celebrated Chanukah and Christmas. Here they would do nothing. When Willy wasn't at meetings or with the boys, he was reading: Kim Il Sung, Marx, Lenin. *What Is to Be Done?* The news of the war was that it was getting stronger and that nothing they or anyone else did seemed to be touching that bright steamy place or the pain it enclosed. She felt ashamed when she asked Willy for the blouse for Christmas, but he smiled and said he hadn't known what to get for her. She half expected him to give her the money for it, but Willy went downtown and got it himself. He gave it to her Christmas morning. Who was she to have this blouse, she'd thought, when there was this fire in their lives, when they might never get home? The boy from Connecticut gave her the pink blouse, and Liz wore it that night at dinner, then put it away for a special occasion. It hung in the closet with Willy's work shirts and flannel plaids, with her wool jacket and pants. Sometimes if she was alone in the apartment, Liz held the blouse up to different skirts and trousers, trying to make a match. Always before when he'd bought her presents, Willy apologized and reassured her they could be returned, even before the ribbon and fancy paper was off the package. The night he gave her the pink blouse, they'd lain together in bed inventing names for their children, names Liz couldn't remember any longer, some American, one or two Swedish. Until Willy died, Liz held dearest, sweet as the pink of her blouse, their shared illusion that they could follow their plans through if only they chose to, and that in time the plans wouldn't change or be changed for them by time.

She was the only customer at Tito's. Rose and Sharon, who worked upstairs giving makeup lessons and manicures, had gone to Cancún for the week. The other hairdresser with whom Tito shared the house on Westheimer was off for the afternoon. The room—usually so open-looking and stylish with a cheerful and inventive flower arrangement or odd plant from the florist next door—looked derelict. A pile of brown smocks such as Liz was wearing now, as she sat in the big padded chair, lay by the front door, waiting for the laundry pickup. Don, the other hairdresser, had left curlers and bobby pins and brushes all over his table, as if he'd gone somewhere in a hurry.

The afternoon was warm, the cool morning in the pines a dream. Sunlight beamed through the picture window where Tito had his mirror, table, and chair. When she'd first come to Tito, Liz hadn't liked the idea of having her hair cut out in the open where anyone passing could watch. But no one ever looked in, and Liz, in the three or four times she'd been there, had grown used to sitting in the window. Westheimer during the day had the quiet of a circus before showtime. At night the street would be crowded with tourists for the topless places, customers for the gay bars, crowds of people driving around looking for pickups or parking spaces or walking off their dinners.

Tito stood behind her, slim and small, his own black hair cut in a rough, street-urchin style that became him. His neat blue oxford shirt was tucked into starched khaki trousers, and a comb and a pair of scissors protruded from the shirt pocket.

"What do you think," Liz said, her eyes meeting his in the mirror. "What would you think of taking it all off?"

"All? You want me to shave your head?" He spoke softly, a faint Chicano rhythm to his speech.

"I want to see the bones rattling in my head. Really short. Otherwise, I'll be back tomorrow wanting it shorter."

He began combing her hair, slowly and gently, and when it was combed he lifted it and let it fall in heavy luxurious waves. He held it up to and away from Liz's cheekbones and eyebrows, frowning.

"Maybe," he said. "You may be right. It would be wonderful—this very dark hair clipped very short. You're sure?"

"Oh well," she said. "I'm never sure of anything. But it was short once before. When I went to Sweden."

"Sweden! You've been so many places. I've been nowhere."

"Brownsville. I've never been there."

"I've made up my mind," Tito said. "I'm definitely moving to New York. I have a job there. And a sublet."

"I'm so sorry," Liz said. "I'll miss you. You're sure?"

He laughed and said, "As sure as you are about this cut."

When her hair was wet and combed through again, lying flat and obedient as it never did when dry, Tito divided it and clipped sections back from her face.

"Did you ever cut so much hair off at once," she asked.

"Once before. When I was doing my school. This woman came in with bright red hair. I mean, long. It came within a foot of the floor. She wore it wound up in a bun on top of her head. Every week, she went to her mother, who washed it for her. She had to sit on the bathroom floor and drape the hair over the edge of the tub."

"Why couldn't she wash it herself?" Liz watched Tito cut away on the left side of her head, wanting to say, Stop. A mistake.

"It was too heavy when it was wet," Tito said. "She couldn't stand in the shower if it was wet. At night, her husband took the hair and draped it over the edge of the bed so she could sleep. She had her hair long like that because when she was a child, her mother took her to a hairdresser and the woman cut the child's hair too short. A pixie cut."

"I don't want one of those," Liz said. "Nothing cute. I'm too small."

"Don't worry," Tito said.

"How did you cut this poor woman's hair? Didn't it take hours?"

"I didn't do it like this. Your hair is short enough to work on gradually. I put hers in a ponytail and just cut straight across. Then I shaped it. A very simple cut. She put her hair in a bag she'd brought for that purpose."

"What did she do with it?"

He shrugged, concentrating on Liz's neck.

"Maybe she sold it. Maybe she kept it."

"Why did she do it? I mean, what decided her at that moment to have it cut?"

"I never asked her, Liz. A whole crowd had gathered around my chair when they saw she was getting it cut. It was a school, and people always watched each other work. Their interest faded completely after that first cut across the ponytail. . . . How do you like this?"

Her hair was shorter now, and it seemed that a different face might be emerging.

"Do you mean, should we stop now?"

"Oh, no," Tito said. "I'm going to continue. I just wanted to know how you felt about it."

"It's all right," she said.

"Trust me."

"If it's a mistake, I'm stuck with it."

"Be more positive," he said. "You have to believe in yourself. I used to want to put a paper bag over my head and hide. I needed a shopping bag with two eyes cut out. Oh, I used to freak out, all right."

By evening, it was raining and cold. The silhouette of the palm tree outside their large bedroom window looked sad, its dried fronds beating a wintery tattoo in the breeze. The gas fire at the corner of the room gave off a sweet smell. Near the heater, it was warm and dry, almost too warm. Across the room where Liz lay on the bed, the air was chilly and damp. The water fell in thin sheets along the beveled glass.

"I can't get used to it," Liz said. "Not so much living here. But the simplest things about being with you. I can't take them for granted."

"I don't want you to," he said. "I like to see you thrown off base by being—"

"Happy? Don't say it so loud. That's part of it. But this feeling of waiting for the end. I'm sorry. I shouldn't talk like this."

"There's nothing wrong in saying it. It doesn't make anxiety valid or true or prophetic just because you say it."

David was knotting his peacock-blue silk tie, looking in the mirror of the oak dresser. Liz lay behind him, on their bed, propped up against the pillows, her dark green wool dress spread around her like an irregular flower. Her new haircut made her look like a Shakespearean boy actor, healthy, ready to deliver a sensible speech on justice. She wore her pearl earrings and matching necklace, a gift from her father. On her small head, the dark curly hair rested like a cap, and her features looked larger and better defined. Her lips were painted a shade that was almost pink.

"You didn't tell me you were going to get your hair cut off," David said.

"Don't you like it?"

"I like it fine," he said. "But you didn't tell me."

"We'll be late," she said. "How much longer will that tie take you?"

"No doubt," said David mildly, "someone will be later. You're not quite ready yet, are you?"

"The guy who cut my hair is moving to New York," she said. "Next week. He's the nicest man. He's from Brownsville. He thinks New York's the big time."

"It is," David said.

"They'll eat his lunch," she said.

"Maybe he'll enjoy it. It's an old American custom—everyone's got to try New York once."

"I didn't know until I got there that I was going to have my hair cut so much." She touched the hair behind her ears. "Who's going to be there tonight?" She stirred, thinking she would do something else to make herself ready.

"Clarice and Doug. It's their house, so they have to be there. You and me. Doc. Cal. Helen was coming, but she's gone somewhere for the week for some sun—Mexico somewhere."

"Are you driving Cal or is he driving us?"

Liz reached for the white phone by the side of the bed, but David said, "He's got plans for after dinner, so he's driving by himself. I talked to him this afternoon."

"Aha. What's he doing after dinner?"

"That's his business," David said. "I didn't ask. I think that's all tonight. Just family."

"Family and me," she said.

David turned from the mirror and took his jacket from the back of the peach-colored armchair. He looked at Liz, whose hand still rested on the phone as if one more call would complete her day. One dark-stockinged foot was off the bed; a silver and bronze leather sandal dangled from her big toe.

"We can skip dinner," he said. "Tell them we have encephalitis."

"It's okay," she said. "I want to see everybody. I'm just being a brat. But let's not stay all night. You're leaving so early tomorrow." She reached out her hand, and David helped her up. "I'll just brush my hair and then we're gone."

"I'll get the car started," David said. "And bring it to the door."

She stood and walked to the dresser.

"Wait," she said. "I'll go with you. I'll be ready in one second. I can't get my hair to stop sticking together."

"It looks fine," David said. "Very emphatic."

"Okay," she said, setting her brush down. "I think it takes hair a while to get used to being cut. I'm coming."

It was warmer in David's car as he drove toward Clarice's house. The windshield wipers sounded reassuring and solid against the rain.

"I thought when I moved to Texas, I'd never be cold again," Liz said.

"You're not as cold for as long."

"True. Did Cal mention anything? He said something was happening about the magazine."

"No," David said. "He hasn't said a thing about it. Maybe he's going to change the name. I never did understand why he called it *Spindletop*. Spindletop's out by Beaumont, almost a hundred miles from Houston."

"Well," Liz said, "but it's a symbol of Houston for Cal, a symbol of the whole deal." They drove past a brick house where, Cal had told her, Howard Hughes lived as a boy. "I'd never heard of Spindletop until Cal told me about it."

"I'll bet you thought gas came from those pumps at service stations just like milk comes from bottles."

She and Cal had been at a dinner party in New York, she told David. A friend who was a painter had set up a banquet table of sawhorses and plywood in his studio, and he'd covered the wood with white sheets. Liz couldn't remember what they'd eaten, but there had been plenty of food and wine. One friend was dieting, eating only oysters from a can or orange juice and yogurt, and she'd brought a rubber chicken to the party with her, which she held by the feet and banged on the table for emphasis when she spoke.

"Sounds like fun," David said.

"It was all right. Anyway, Cal told a story about two young men who were sharing a bunk at the one boardinghouse there was in Beaumont."

"Feeling lucky to get a bunk, I can imagine."

"I guess. One was a rich boy from New Orleans, the other older. They liked each other, Cal said, and they decided to throw in their lots together. If they made it, they'd make it together. If not, not. Have you heard this story?"

"No," David said. "Go on."

"I don't know how you've missed it. Cal's told it a couple of times at dinners and things. Well, they had to think of a name for their company—everyone there was naming these three-minute-old companies after their mothers or girl friends. But these two wanted a really good name. They didn't want to be braggarts or anything. They wanted a modest name for their company, so one of them suggested—at this point there's a big pause, Cal has everyone really quiet, even the rubber-chicken lady—one of them says, 'Say, how about Humble?' "

David grunted. "I see what you mean. It's a swell story, of its kind. It should be in the oil museum."

"It is a swell story. I'm glad you like it. Of course, it sounded different in New York. Less heroic, just a story about money and not so moving."

"What's moving?"

"The adventure. The fact that they took a chance and did well, I mean big, off the chance. And the way Cal told it, too. That's what I like about hearing the story."

She looked out as they turned onto Kirby and passed Jamail's, the city's fanciest grocery store. She would have to go there at the end of the week to gather food for their weekend at Walden.

"David. Don't you ever get tired of all this Houston stuff?"

"Houston stuff?"

"The heroism. The frontier. Texas."

"You run into it more than I do," David said, "in your line of work. Cal likes those stories more than I do. I got enough of hearing about the oil business when I was growing up."

"That's what I mean," Liz said. "But I was almost in tears the first few times I heard Cal tell about Spindletop and Humble. I guess he always tells it when we've been drinking."

She was talking too much, she thought, and taking out her usual edginess at going to Clarice's house. She liked Clarice and Doug all right, but Clarice was the cousin of David's ex-wife, Lucy, and her house was next door to the white cottage where David had lived with Lucy. The cottage lacked only red roses climbing over the doorway to make it a picture-postcard setting for a marriage.

Clarice's house was from the same vintage as the brown house on Graustark, but it had been made modern. Exterior walls had been replaced with glass, making the lower floor of the house a showcase, and on the upper story, windows removed or replaced by modern slits of glass. The house was protected from the street by a gray wooden fence even taller than the one around the brown house. The front yard was a landscaped garden of rocks: white pebbles in amoeba-shaped beds were kept in check by larger black rocks.

David rang the bell at the door in the gray fence. He reached out and touched Liz's neck, then bent down and kissed her.

"Who?" Clarice's daughter, Jessie, had answered the bell, and her nasal seven-year-old voice was made tinnier by the loudspeaker.

"It's David and Liz," David said. "Push the button, Jessie."

They waited for the sound of the bell and Liz said, "Damn. I hope it doesn't start raining harder while she's making up her mind if she remembers who we are."

David said, "She probably can't reach the button."

They opened the gate when they heard the buzz, then walked up a pink stone path to the layers of front steps. Wooden tubs of brilliant red geraniums rested on either side of the glass entrance door.

"My, my," Clarice said when she opened the door, "isn't this weather the worst. What a darling haircut. Pixieish. You look so young."

"Spring flowers, February showers," Liz said, watching Clarice and David touch cheeks. She kissed Clarice, feeling wrapped briefly in a perfumed embrace.

"Douglas couldn't make it back from New Orleans in time for dinner," Clarice said. "So we'll have to make do with each other, and Doc will be host."

"We're not such bad company," Liz said. "I won't worry. Hi, Jessie."

"Say hello," Clarice instructed her daughter. "Shake hands with Liz."

Clarice clothed Jessie in expensive dresses that looked like costumes for a drama set in England between the wars. The big-eyed, sandy-haired child looked uncomfortable in the frills, white tights, and Mary Janes. Clarice always wore what Liz had at first assumed were thrift-shop muumuus and formal tent dresses. Then she realized they were purposely dowdy, of a variety only an overweight rich person could afford. Clarice had curly blond hair and very fair skin that grew pink easily with emotion or fear. She was Lucy's cousin and her best friend. Liz was always careful never to say anything to Clarice she wouldn't want reported to Lucy.

Liz took Jessie's small limp hand and raised it once, then let it go. The child looked up at her mother, panicked that she would be asked to stay with the company. But Clarice said, "Go find Maria, honey. It's time for your bath and beddy," and Jessie left them standing in the wide foyer.

"Before we go in," Clarice said, standing between them and the living room to their left, "I wanted you to know Helen wants me to take you both on as my exclusive clients. I'll be able to devote more time than she. I'll find you the best house—if that's all right with y'all."

"Fine," Liz said, and David nodded. Cal's mother, Helen Dayton, and Clarice had gone into the real-estate business together the year before.

"I'm glad to hear you're so busy," David said, "that you're dividing the client list."

"Well, just," Clarice said. "I may have something for you, but I won't know until tomorrow."

"I'll be at the magazine," Liz said. "David's going to New York. But call. We'll see."

They walked into the living room. Across the couch and large Bokhara, Liz saw Cal and Doc, Lucy's father, standing at the plain green marble fireplace. There was a low fire burning that reflected in the heavy glass and steel coffee table before the white linen couch. The men turned at the sound of Clarice's voice at the doorway, and Doc came forward to greet David and Liz. His kiss brushed Liz's cheek lightly; then he squeezed David's hand in a warmer embrace. He was as tall as David, with bright white hair.

"How are you, boy," Liz heard him say to David, and she excused herself and went to Cal.

Cal had the bluest eyes in the city and thick, short hair that was seal brown, turning sun-gold and pale gray. He was the smallest man in the room—Doc and David towered over him. Cal was built like Liz, compact and small. He kept his weight down through nervousness, and his energy both annoyed her and reassured her. She hated it when Cal answered the phone by saying "Speak to me," as he did during deadline, but she spoke each time, quickly and to the point.

"You look like an ad for Scotch," Liz said, "leaning so casually against that mantelpiece."

"Very expensive Scotch, I hope. A blend of exclusive clans. And your hair," Cal said. "Let me guess. Audrey Hepburn in *Funny Face.*"

"Guess again," Liz said. "Try Giulietta Masina in *La Strada*. Are those new boots? I'ver never seen you wearing cowboy boots."

"I always liked them and I had a pair in my closet the whole time I lived in New York. But they've gotten so chic I vowed never to wear them. I was downtown today near Stelzig's and feeling snappy. I saw these and I thought, Why do I think I'm so different from the rest of the world—so I bought them. I love your hair, Liz. It's so emotional."

Doc brought Liz a gin and tonic, the drink she'd asked for the first time they met and the one he'd bring her always. She thanked him and he turned to get David's bourbon and water, which David drank only with Doc.

When they were alone again, Liz said, "What's the big surprise? Are you still going to pop it now that Doug's not coming?"

"It's Doug's tough luck to miss the announcement. And it isn't a big surprise. Just big enough."

"Well, cheers," Liz said. "I'm coming in to the magazine tomorrow for an assignment, right?"

"You sure are."

"David thinks he'll be back by the weekend."

"Great."

"When will you come to Walden?"

"I didn't know I was invited," Cal said.

"Well?"

"Try and keep me away."

They joined the other three, who were talking about the Oilers, and the conversation drifted from football to taxes. Liz drank the gin. The chill the cold glass gave to the bones in her hand, even through the cocktail napkin, reminded her of winter where she'd come from. She tried to imagine her father in this room or Willy. These people were probably Republicans, she thought. She'd never wanted to know for certain. When she'd told Clarice her father was a lawyer, Clarice had commented that it was nice that David and her father were in the same business. Liz's father's practice was mostly civil liberties. During the Vietnam war he'd taken on many draft cases and the only clients whom he and David might have had in common were those on drug charges. David's practice tended toward intellectual properties—like Austin musicians—drugs, libel, and foundation tax law.

They moved across the entrance hall to the dark-blue dining room, where the food was laid out on a pine side table, and filled their plates with slices of roast beef, spoon bread, and a salad of red tip lettuce and endives, then sat at Clarice's oval English table that was big enough for twelve people. When Liz first met Clarice, before she'd seen her house, they'd commiserated over a lunch about lack of money. Once Liz had seen Clarice's setup, she learned that lack of money meant to Clarice that she hadn't yet come into the majority of the trust that waited for her fortieth birthday, that Doug's salary from Exxon didn't cover her wishes. Liz held the conversation against Clarice, but she also realized soon enough that Clarice saw something glamorous in Liz's financial precariousness, which she probably understood as little as Liz did her stability.

"Have you decided where to go for Easter, Doc?" Clarice asked. She'd put herself between Doc and David, while Cal and Liz sat opposite them. "We may take you up on the invitation to Wimberley, if that's still on."

"I may find myself in Karnes County," Doc said. "I have a friend who's living out on his ranch nowadays, mostly. He's called to ask me over. But you're welcome to the ranch. Just let me know and it's yours."

"It isn't the same without you," Clarice said. "Not as much fun for Jessie."

"That's kind of you to say it," Doc said, "but the bluebonnets will be there if I am or not. Y'all go on. Maybe I'll be there, I can't say just now."

"And I get the wrong horse if you aren't there," Liz said, then regretted that she'd spoken. It had come out like a complaint and was meant to be a compliment to Doc's hospitality. It wasn't clear to her, now that she'd spoken, if the invitation included her, David, and Cal, or if Doc's "y'all" had been directed only at Clarice.

"Do you, Liz?"

Doc turned his pale blue eyes to her. She knew he didn't like her, but she'd always liked the old man, perhaps because he reminded her of David. There was something physically similar, and there was an indulgent kindness in them toward others that she admired. The truth was, she had gotten the same horse both times she'd been to the ranch, an old trustworthy mare, and Liz's fear was that she'd be dead next time Liz arrived in Wimberley. It had surprised Liz that Texas held at its center the beautiful Hill Country—no more rocky or desolate than parts of New England—and that Doc owned what seemed like such a large hunk of it. He'd bought the ranch in the golden age of Texas real estate, he'd assured her, when his seven hundred acres—not even large by Texas standards—cost less than a house in River Oaks.

When she was newly arrived in Houston and went to Clarice's for the first time, Doc had welcomed her as a friend of Cal's. He'd said, "I'm glad you've come. It's a good sign for Houston when people like you move here. It shows we've become a real city." Liz had thought of his words later, trying to hear irony or sarcasm beneath the surface. No one would have welcomed her to New York or pretended she would do anything for the city but try to survive in it.

"No," she said. "Don't mind me, Doc. I get the right horse. Four legs and a flagging metabolism."

She picked up her empty wineglass, and David reached across the curve of the oval to fill it from the bottle in front of him. He smiled at her in a way that reminded her of waking with him and of making love, a quick warm gesture. He looked comfortable here in Clarice's house where every piece was just right. The small oil of a shipwreck behind David was more violent than she remembered it—the moment of the waves breaking on shore, the boats out beyond reach.

"Cal," David said, "let's have your surprise."

"Is it something to eat?" Clarice asked.

"Sorry," Cal said. "It's a surprise about *Spindletop.*"

Liz felt David's shoe against her foot, only a touch, a kiss in passing. She moved her foot under her chair. In public, with these people, she needed to feel upright and she tried not to look at David with too much warmth or to advertise by any physical gesture that they were lovers. If she married him, she thought, it would all be simpler.

"You've sold it for a huge profit," Clarice guessed.

"I only own fifteen percent," Cal said patiently. "So unless I want to spend my days in Huntsville, I'd better not sell it. No, this is a surprise in two parts and I'll tell you as soon as you let me." They shuffled and smiled and waited for Cal to speak. He took a sip of wine, then said, "It isn't such a big deal. Really. But the first part is who really owns the magazine."

"Aha," David said. "Now my secret fantasies can be revealed. It's Ross Perot. I knew it all along."

"Forget it," Cal said. "It's a home-grown money. The mystery majority owner is—Hunter Corrigan."

"I would never have guessed it," Doc said. "I didn't know he took an interest in Houston-based businesses. He's in California most of the time, isn't he?"

"Well, his interest has been distant for the two years we've been in existence. That's why he never wanted his name revealed. It was—"

"A condition," Liz guessed. "Reveal my name and you turn into a pumpkin."

"Something like that," Cal said. "He didn't want to be bothered."

"And now he does?"

"Now he thinks we can start making money. He's going to be publisher, pump some money into the magazine. We're going from tabloid format to a slick magazine next issue. Lots of color. Bigger budgets for art and editorial—"

"Anything would be an improvement," Liz said.

"Better salespeople," Cal said. "Business is joining *Spindletop.* We'll get a little help from competent people."

"I had no idea you could keep secrets so well," Clarice said. "I'll have to remember to tell you more of mine."

"This wasn't very hard," Cal said. "Don't press your luck. No one's really tried to find out who owns the magazine. We made up a corporation name, and that's all the state of Texas cared about."

"This will be a big difference to you," David said. "I'm pleased for you, Cal."

"Oh, well," Cal said, "it's never easy. I don't expect it to be."

"Your mother will be so pleased," Clarice said. "But she must have known all along. I wish she were here instead of languishing on a Mexican beach."

"Why will Helen be pleased?" Liz asked. "And who is Hunter Corrigan?"

"Well, Helen was Hunter's father's secretary forever. Gus Corrigan was—" Clarice glanced at Doc, and Liz guessed that she would have continued differently had he been absent. "He was the man she most admired in the world. And she'll probably be pleased that Hunter's involved in the magazine."

"The Corrigan Corporation is one of the biggest corporations in Texas," David said. "It has international interests now, of course. But it started out as the family business in East Texas—what was it, Doc, cotton? Timber?"

"Both. Timber from their own land. Cotton from land they leased or bought up. Gus Corrigan's old man was at Spindletop. He made a small fortune and then pulled out. He went into shipping, bought some leases in West Texas that did better than the ones he'd sold at Spindletop. And he hung on to the leases between Houston and Beaumont. He had a well that came in a few days after Spindletop, but it never got the attention."

"So this all means that Hunter's rich," Liz said.

"Honey," Doc said, "he's rich beyond your wildest dreams of avarice."

"That's rich."

"We did a little work for them," David said. "A Corrigan cousin wanted to set up a foundation, and we helped her with it."

"The Corrigans are so lucky," Clarice said. "Remember the partner?"

"That was just an unfortunate accident," Cal said. "So I was always told." He turned to Liz. "The only partner Gus Corrigan ever had— aside from family members who own stock and didn't have much say except as employees and minority stockholders—the only real partner died in a private plane crash. They found the plane and the body eventually somewhere in the Big Thicket. And Gus bought out the wife and sons shortly after that."

"It was a generous settlement," Doc said. "But it happened mighty conveniently, from what I heard at the time. They were in some kind of struggle and Gus won by default. But he was always a lucky man. Lucky in his father. A fortunate man at business. Liz needs some wine, David. The widow remarried, as I recall. In short order."

"So it's a happy story for everyone but the partner," Liz said. "Thanks, David. Or does he turn out to have terminal cancer?"

"No," David said. "He's the requisite loser."

"Well, I hope the magazine is a winner, too. What did Hunter do before he decided to be a magazine publisher?"

"He tried producing records," David said. "A few clients of mine had run-ins with him. A fellow of infinite whimsicality."

"That's putting it kindly," Cal said. "He's a hard man to pin down."

"But you've done it," Liz said.

They carried white porcelain bowls of strawberries to the living room, which had been cleared of glasses in their absence by the invisible Maria. Clarice poured coffee from a tray that had appeared on the low table before the couch. The cups were tiny and porcelain, and Liz watched the men grappling with the gold handles. The fire had been renewed, and Doc brought from the bar a decanter of brandy and five snifters. The men lit cigars, and Liz leaned back to listen to them talk.

The first time she'd gone to Clarice's, she'd been elated by the pretty house and the ease with which everything was accomplished. She'd talked and laughed for hours and the next day couldn't remember anything she'd said.

"What did we talk about," she asked Cal, and he replied, "Now, let's see. We asked about each other's health, business, aging parents, new acquisitions—those of us who acquire—and if there was anything we missed at the week's previous lunches and dinners."

"But it was so comfortable for me," Liz said. She would have said it was like family, but it didn't have the hard edge her family's dinners did.

"Thank the Lord you were there," Cal said. "You're so interesting. You kept it all going and you gave everyone something to do—ask about you, where you're from, what school, what have you done, why you're in Houston."

"No wonder I can't remember," Liz said. "It was all about me."

She couldn't recall anyone in New York saying someone else was interesting, and she wondered when Cal had started to think of people as such. People might be called boring but rarely would they be labeled interesting. She wondered if interesting always meant outsider.

"We'd better go home," David said. "Before we get much more brandy in us. I have a seven o'clock plane, and Liz and I are jogging before that."

"How cruel," Clarice said, rising as they did. "Both to leave and to jog. But go right ahead. Disgrace me and get thinner. See if it bothers me." They said good night to Doc and Cal, and Clarice walked them to the door.

"Thanks, Clarice," Liz said. "This was lovely. Tell Doug he missed a good time."

"I'm just as glad he didn't fly on a night like this," Clarice said. "I'll bet it's thick in New Orleans. I hate it when anyone I love flies. Well, isn't that a bright thing to say when you're taking off, Cousin David. Just forget I said anything—"

"Don't think of it," David said.

"—and Liz. I'll be calling you. I think I may have the right thing for you."

In the car, Liz leaned back against the seat cushion and said, "Did we leave too early?"

"No," David said. "It's ten o'clock. Besides. I am leaving early in the morning. They'll do just fine without us."

Clarice reminded her of girls she'd gone to college with, as had Lucy. Nothing bad had happened to them yet, or if it had they didn't let it show. They didn't question the way the world was run, nor did they worry about their place in it. At the end of college, people began being aware of what was taking place in Vietnam; the year Liz married Willy, Clarice was pledging in a sorority in Austin, the same one her Cousin Lucy belonged to. Liz had envied girls like them in college because they seemed so sure of their futures, a time ahead with peace at the dinner table, children attending the same schools they had, the same husband all their lives.

When she moved to Houston, Liz assumed she'd be friends with Cal's friends Lucy and Clarice. Before Liz had much furniture in her apartment—a foam mattress on the bedroom floor, the rugs in the living room—Clarice and Jessie had dropped by. Liz invited them in, apologizing because she didn't have any food or drink in the house— would they like water? Clarice sailed into the apartment, past Liz, and began opening the closet doors where Liz had hung her clothes, stacked her old files and books; she looked out the windows, parting the white curtains Liz had just bought at Sears; she pulled the doors to each room to and fro, as if testing to see if they'd been hung correctly. Was it the bareness of the place that made Clarice act as if Liz were a client who wanted Clarice to sell the place for her? Or was it that Liz was a stranger and therefore—no men present, no antiques and silver and old oil paintings—Clarice could do what she wanted? She'd looked hungrily into the closets, as if there were something there she needed badly.

"I think Clarice has lost some weight," Liz said.

"Nice of you to think so," David said.

Outside in the dark she watched the street roll by. They passed a new French restaurant which was next to a Chinese grocery, two strip shows with XXX on neon signs and the cutout silhouettes of Amazons set along the flat roof lines. She saw the all-night grocery with cars parked at random in the parking lot, the empanada stand across from it, and an icehouse on the opposite corner, its benches empty, the concrete parking area in front slick and dark.

"I don't know what's worse," she said, "being too fat or too thin."

"Clarice always talks about losing weight," David said, "but it doesn't get her as far as a diet would."

Lucy had been thin. By the time she left David, her blue veins stood out on her arms. A few nights before she left him, David and Lucy came to dinner, along with Cal, at Liz's apartment. They were the first people she'd cooked for in Houston, and Liz had spent the day preparing the meal, which included a duck in the style of suckling pig. She was worried because the place smelled so of duck fat and green peppercorns. When they were getting ready to leave her place, Liz went into the bedroom to get David and Lucy's jackets. A small package dropped from the wide cuff of Lucy's satin Chinese jacket. Liz found a piece of duck and sausage stuffing, a sprig of broccoli, half a lemon cookie, and a small white dinner roll, all wrapped in a man's white handkerchief. She quickly rewrapped the secret meal and hid it again in Lucy's jacket.

"Is Doc over at Clarice's a lot?" Liz asked.

"I think so. I don't really know. Clarice's mother is all the way in Corpus, and now with Lucy gone, Doc's in need of family. So he goes there."

"It's good of Clarice," Liz said. "I always feel guilty about Doc. He's so nice to me."

David was driving smoothly and quickly, making all the lights and turns in an easy practiced way, never hesitating or losing his way as Liz did on Houston streets.

"Don't worry about Doc," David said. "Other women wouldn't want me spending time with him or the rest of my old friends. Or at least wouldn't be friends with them herself."

At the brown house, David offered to let Liz go inside while he parked the car up the street, but she said she'd go with him. It began raining in earnest when they got out, and they ran down the dark block together, wet from the rain, and climbed the deck steps up to the house.

Liz stood under the hot shower, trying to warm her bones. She breathed in the chlorine smell of the city water as if it were an elixir. The chlorine she washed in, the coconut oil she rubbed on her body afterward, were confirmation that she was in Houston. When she'd arrived in the summer and lived for months in a nearly empty apartment, knowing no one but Cal, the smells in Houston had been the first things to become familiar to her, to become her own in the new city. She wrapped herself in a towel, then stood before the closed door to the bedroom, shy for a moment, wishing she were elsewhere or wearing her oldest flannel nightgown. Sometimes she couldn't face David. When she opened the door, she saw that he was under the comforter, reading by the bedside light. He looked up at her and smiled.

"You'll get chilled all over again standing there," he said. "Why aren't you wearing your long johns?"

"I almost did," she said.

"Well, come here," he said, laying his book on the floor beside the bed.

"Do you want something to drink? To eat? Are the lights off downstairs?" Liz looked out the back window and saw that Cal's lights were out except for his yellow porch light. "Cal's not home yet."

She went to the dresser and, letting the towel drop, put on a T-shirt and a pair of knee socks, then walked to the bed and climbed under the comforter with David. There were complicated moments when she saw him as a stranger, when the sound of his soft voice with its slight Texas accent was the sound of a cover-up to her; as if, should she listen hard enough or ask the right question, she would detect hostility to her, the opposite of everything he said and did.

David pulled her close beside him. She lay back, her head on the pillow, and kissed him on his lips and neck, on his ear, then put her hands on his arms, moving along his skin. There was nothing for a moment but the touch of him and his warmth, his hands taking off her shirt, her laugh as she took off her socks. We always have this, she thought. It will smooth everything else. She thought of Willy and felt a hand on her throat, her throat closing on itself. Liz opened her eyes and saw David next to her, looking at her, pushing back the soft curls above her forehead.

"What is it?" he asked.

"Nothing," she said. "Only the light. It's so bright."

II

Liz drove past the Blue Bird and Pasternak's Grocery, past an orange sign on a dark-gray building: GIRLS, GIRLS, GIRLS, *Hostesses* $365 *per wk.* Sometimes when they passed by on the way from Graustark to the magazine, Cal and Liz saw light-haired women coming and going beneath the sign. "Retreads," Cal called them. They'd never seen the women do anything erotic or incriminating; they were just women walking into a dark-gray building. A gold Camaro was parked on the sidewalk in front of the building today, AM country music streaming from it.

Past a 7-Eleven, past a mansion about to fall, under the Southwest Freeway, and down two blocks was the magazine.

When she'd first come to Houston and Cal had given her directions to the building on Winbern, she'd been sure he'd said Windburn. It was a narrow two-story building across from a boarded-up Masonic temple, down the block from the all-day all-night magazine and news store on Main. A vine grew across the bottom story, blocking the art department's windows from the sun, cheap burglar protection, Cal said. The entrance was set into the building under an arched entryway. The lobby was tiled in ancient blue and white octagonal tiles, with smaller tiles spelling out THE CARLTON. A new sign hung above the big glass and wood door, also in blue and white. The magazine's logo spelled out Spindletop Magazine, the d and l leaning toward one another to form the angle of an oil well.

In the tiled foyer, where once there might have been a mirrored oak umbrella stand, was the receptionist's white Formica desk, which Cal had bought at Office City along with all the other furniture. The building had once been divided into two large apartments, one up, one down. When Cal started *Spindletop,* he rented the top floor of the Carlton and the whole staff—Cal, Graves the business manager and ad director, Mary Alice and the art department, Cheryl the receptionist, the writers, and the salespeople—was crowded together. When the downstairs tenant moved out—the miracle was that he'd lasted so long, Cal said—the art department and Cheryl moved downstairs with the salespeople. Graves, Cal, and the editorial department remained upstairs. The Carlton wasn't ideal. The salespeople wanted more space. The two staff writers, the researcher, and the copy editor wanted partitions for privacy and complained they were distracted by the sound of each other's phone calls and typewriters. The art department wanted more space, better equipment, and a louder radio. For the time being, Cal said, it was fine. Everyone liked the Carlton, they just wanted more of it for themselves.

"Hi, Liz," Cheryl said. "I love it. It's fabulous. You look so adorable."

Liz put her hand to her head and patted her hair down.

"Adorable," Cheryl repeated. "I have a whole bunch of messages for you. Your phone's broken?"

"I forgot to change the tape on the machine last week. Thanks, Cheryl."

"Spindletop." Cheryl answered the phone. "May I help you? . . . Thank you. . . . Don't go away, Liz."

Cheryl was younger than the rest of the staff by at least ten years. She'd come to Houston straight out of a junior college in Wisconsin because she heard there were jobs. She could have been making three times as much typing at a law firm. She'd done secretarial work for three months before she saw Cal's ad in the paper. Cheryl wanted to write someday, and meanwhile, Liz noticed, she acted as if *Spindletop* were a pageant at which she was lucky enough to get a front-row seat. Cheryl wore her nails long and painted them blood red. Her curly brown hair was shoulder length, sometimes pinned back with small metal bows the shape of her mouth. At night she went to cowboy bars.

Once Liz and David had seen her standing alone in the parking lot of an all-night grocery on Richmond. She was leaning against a Volkswagen, crying. They'd stopped and driven her home to her apartment. They hadn't asked what had happened to her. Liz called her in the morning to see if she was all right and still didn't ask. Later Liz wondered if that omission was really as kind as she'd hoped.

"How's David?" Cheryl asked. "The doll."

"Flying away on a little dollie airplane. He's going to New York for the week. Who's this who called this morning? Clarence Man? Clarice?"

"I'm sorry. It got real crazy here about an hour ago." Cheryl turned once more to answer the phone.

"I'll just go up," Liz mouthed.

Cheryl waved a piece of paper at Liz, which she took and read as she started up the stairs to Cal's office. It was a list of questions from Martha, the researcher, about a profile Liz had just completed on a Houston society beauty. Liz had described the woman as having skin stretched surgically to the tautness of a trampoline, and Martha wanted to know when the surgery was performed, who was the doctor, and what was the exact procedure. The face, Liz thought, if left to its own devices, might have had the character of a worried woman in a Walker Evans photograph. As it was, the woman looked merely hungry and, as Liz had written, stretched.

Cal's office was at the top of the stairs. He rarely closed his door, and sometimes there were log jams of people waiting for him.

In New York, she'd wondered what kind of editor Cal would make. A start-up enterprise needed someone with taste and talent. He had those qualities. It also needed a leader whom the staff would turn to and trust. Cal was as kind to the staff as he was to her and his other friends. He talked to Cheryl with as much attention as he gave Liz. He was less sharp than he'd been in New York, even under pressure, and he was fair. The writers trusted him with their copy and trusted him to give them the best assignments for their skills. When he passed along a dull task, he didn't pretend it was anything but what it was. The magazine reflected Cal's excitement at being back in Houston. He printed what he liked, what he admired, what he thought was funny and interesting.

The stairwell and the hall were empty now. Along the stairwell were hung framed awards won by the tabloid for investigative stories and for layout, and *Spindletop*'s first issue. Cal said the awards belonged where everyone could see them, not just to cover the cracks in the walls of his office.

She knocked on the doorjamb and said, "Hey. You busy?"

"Hey yourself," Cal said. "Did you get those questions from Martha?"

"My notes are back at my apartment. I'll call it in this afternoon. I'm hungry. Can we talk over lunch?"

He looked at the calendar on his desk. Cal had too much work for one person, and there were times when the surface of the desk was hidden by precarious piles of papers and files—queries on stories, drafts from writers Cal was editing, research he had to read, magazines he kept up with, memos from the staff, proofs. At the worst times, the floor was covered also. Cheryl had pinned a note to Cal's door: *Please clean up your room.* Liz suspected that some of the piles remained constant—letters to answer, greetings from old friends.

Next door, Graves's office was immaculate. He had traded out ads for a carved Mexican desk, a leather swivel chair with a high back that made him look small, though he was over six feet, and a thick shag rug in orange and brown designs that he told Liz came from the Northwest Indians. Northwest of the Loop, she concluded. Graves had always been a mystery to her. He was rail-thin and fast-talking, with limpid eyes like Charlie Chaplin's. His thin layer of hearty mannerisms made Liz nervous. He was nervous himself, Cal said, more eager to please than she could imagine. He wore Western clothes and boots from a reptile she didn't want named. It didn't matter if she loved him or hated him. He sold ads and hired people who sold more. For the rest of the business management there was Cal, and, she supposed, there had always been Hunter.

Cal had told her in New York that he wanted his own magazine someday. She'd put that desire in the category of things that might happen, something to keep in mind, like wanting to see the Northern Lights or Venice in the spring. But Cal had pulled it off. After almost two years—Cheryl had begun talking about where they would hold their second anniversary party—Cal had solid advertising, a growing readership, and he was breaking even. In Houston he looked like someone who had found his work, a different look from someone who was in love or a winner in the Irish Sweepstakes. He looked full of himself, as David had said, and the scared look that had been in his eyes in New York was gone.

"I'm free for lunch, but we have to make it quick. Close the door, Liz. I want to talk to you for a few minutes before we go."

She settled into the red easy chair Cal kept by his bookshelf, across the small room from the desk. On the desk was a framed studio portrait of Helen as she must have looked when Cal was in high school, and, in a Lucite box, a snapshot of Cal, Liz, and David taken the previous September on the limestone veranda of Doc's ranch house. A huge prickly-pear cactus was in back of them, and they lifted their coffee cups in salute at the camera.

"I have a Bad Old Days for you. It's not big enough for a feature, but it's a good story. You shouldn't need more than a couple of weeks on it, at the most."

The Bad Old Days was a department Cal ran every few months. It was primarily a research piece on a Houston scandal or historic event. Writing a Bad Old Days involved a certain amount of time in the library or Metropolitan Research Center, then interviews with survivors, if there were any. He'd run pieces on past mayors, on Houston during the civil rights movement of the 1960s, and on dead or less conspicuous citizens of the city—surviving wildcatters and professional characters, retired news writers, and eccentric collectors. There were new people pouring into the city each week, and most of them couldn't have cared less about Houston's history. They would get their money if they could and leave when they did. Few, if any, of them had a clue about Houston's past.

Maybe no one expected to stay in Houston, Liz thought. Every day on the call-in shows on KTRH, she heard people preface their remarks by saying, "I've been in Houston thirty-five years now. Never thought I'd stay to spend my life here."

Bad Old Days might be the evening-out ground, Cal hoped; and it was, in any case, a good place to tell old stories. Since most of the people written about were dead, there was less worry about libel suits, and juicy gossip could be included.

"I thought you wanted me to start on the Iranian exiles story."

"Not yet," Cal said. "It can wait. They aren't going anywhere." He leaned back in his chair and said, "I wouldn't kid you, kid. This is a good one. It happened twenty years ago in Galveston."

"I've only been there once," Liz said, "when we all went to the Buccaneer Club."

Cal straightened an already straight pile of papers that lay in front of him. "This happened the other end of the island. A woman and her four-year-old child were killed, and it's never been solved. Her name was Carolyn Sylvan. This was April 1959. Rumor was, she was the mistress of a man named William O. Osborne. He owned a public-relations firm, William Osborne Associates."

"Great name," she said.

"One of the first in the city. He was married and had one child."

"Sounds complicated and sordid," Liz said. "All the elements, but—"

"Someone got Carolyn Sylvan a big house out on the west end of the island. It was hunting land then except for shacks and a few houses."

"Doesn't sound like standard mistress behavior."

"I'm telling the story," Cal said. "Listen up. She was from the Panhandle. Maybe she liked wide open spaces. In any case, Osborne claimed that he got a phone call one night telling him to get out there, and he found her shot dead and the little girl run over. She was dead too. But the police couldn't pin it on Osborne. The gun wasn't found nor the car that ran down the kid. He was released a few nights later. Maybe the next day. And that was the end of it. Osborne died about fifteen years ago, around 1963."

"We must be very hard up," Liz said. "It doesn't sound worth exhuming. Sell it to me, as editors so often say."

"It was a very big deal when I was sixteen," Cal said. "Everyone remembers it."

"How big? Like Joan Hill?"

"Big enough. It was colorful. And remains unsolved."

"How come you remember it?" she asked.

Events in her childhood and adolescence had gone by her like water. The Army-McCarthy hearings were her parents arguing and friends shouting at parties; the coronation of Queen Elizabeth was the starchy pages of her cousin's scrapbook; the election of John Kennedy was the first event to emerge from the gloom. The late sixties in Vietnam was the first time Liz thought carefully about a public event or followed it with any interest. That was because of Willy, just as earlier she'd gone to demonstrations against the bomb because her best friend was going.

"You were a real teenager, you said, Cal. Shouldn't you have been polishing your car? Perfecting your tennis game? Worrying about your complexion?"

"I've always had skin like a rose," Cal said. "And my mother worked in the same building as Osborne. I met him once."

She stood and walked behind the easy chair.

"I'm not going to do it, Cal. I'm sorry. I have my reasons. Murder gives me the creeps. I don't even read mysteries anymore. Get Warren to do it. He's the investigative whiz. Or Amy. She'd love to do a high-society murder and tell how bad the rich folks are."

"This isn't exactly high society," Cal said. "It's more middle class. I want you to do it. They're busy on other things. I'm asking you, Liz."

She walked to the window and looked out over the freeway. Her back to Cal, she thought quickly over a list of editors she might query about articles. The trouble was, the only stories she could think of were outside Houston, and the ones the editors might assign her to were outside of Texas. She didn't want to travel just then, she thought. "Okay," she said, turning to face Cal. "You twisted my arm." She went to her pocketbook and took out her notebook. "Tell me all the names again and the dates. And when does Helen get back from Mexico? She could be helpful. Tell me the places."

They stood in the foyer, looking out at the day, which had turned crisp as autumn.

"Your car or mine," Liz asked.

"You must be kidding," Cal said. He looked across Winbern at Liz's 1965 Chevy Nova, which had once been brown. Cal drove a 1967 yellow Lincoln convertible whose top tucked into the trunk space at the press of a button. "I'm parked down the street. There's a new place in the River Oaks center. Chrysanthemum. Brioche."

"Dahlia? I know what you mean. Clarice mentioned it."

A car pulled up in front of the magazine, an old blue Delta 88.

"I haven't seen Amy for ages," Liz said.

Cheryl called out, "Cal. Pick up the phone. You've got a call. It sounds serious."

Liz went out the door and waited for Amy to get out of her car. She was a pale, sandy-haired woman who'd come to *Spindletop* from a small West Texas paper. She was doing a good job writing features, Liz thought. No one could have worked harder. She had expected to be friends with Amy, but it had never worked that way. Liz was older than Amy by about seven years but that wasn't the difference. Rather, she thought, Amy resented her for coming from the East. New York, Amy had said a few times; it must have been wonderful in New York. Liz had advised her to try it. It was just another place, she'd said, echoing David. But perhaps Amy had thought she meant that she wasn't good enough for it.

"Nice day," Amy said. "For once."

The two women stood on the steps of the Carlton, their faces to the sun.

"How's it going? Anything interesting?" Liz asked. "And how about lunch?"

"I just had a grotburger. To my regret. I have to make a million phone calls," Amy said.

Cal joined them outside and said, "Sorry. I can't go to lunch, Liz. Something's come up. How about dinner tonight? I'll take you anywhere you want."

"Okay," Liz said. "Well. I'll be on my way. I'll start working on this thing. See you, Cal. Amy."

They walked back into the building, and Liz walked slowly across the street to her car. She had the day to start the story, time to go downtown and do some research. She unlocked the Nova and got in, then sat for a moment, thinking she was a fool to take the assignment. Away from Cal, she felt how much she didn't want to do it. She touched the door handle, about to go back in and tell him she'd changed her mind. Then she started the engine and drove away, back under the freeway.

Cal had found the apartment for her. It was only four blocks from his place on Graustark, one of four apartments in a gray building overlooking an empty green that was to be built on someday. In the meantime it was used for baseball and picnics, for Frisbee playing by the St. Thomas students from the university down the street. On sunny weekends, the place was covered by people lying oiled on beach towels.

Liz's apartment was white, newly painted just before she moved in. The floors had been sanded and waxed, and in all the rooms—living room, kitchen, and bedroom—windows overlooked trees and lawn. It was on the corner of the block. The rooms opened one into the other through French doors Liz kept ajar. When she'd lived there, she'd slept on a foam mattress on the floor. When the mattress was covered by her fat down quilt and she was propped up against four large bed pillows, Liz felt as if she were Heidi, tucked by her doting grandfather into an Alpine bed. She felt secure on the floor, which wouldn't, as she said to Cal, go anywhere without her knowing it first.

She'd come to Texas with a car full of books, rugs, clothing, her quilt smashed into a wad, and one pine blanket chest. Helen Dayton contributed a bamboo couch that had been on her back porch. Clarice loaned her a wicker armchair and some cushions. When she'd moved to David's, Liz had left the borrowed furniture at her own apartment and taken the down quilt, most of the rugs, and the blanket chest with her. She'd left her largest rug in the apartment, over by the living-room window. It was a rose-colored Caucasian rug, with a hard blue ornament in the center that looked like a flower's face.

She had also left her writing table and chair and her files, the magazines she'd accumulated since she'd moved there, and piles of notes, research, and clippings she intended to file sometime. The papers had gotten away from her, and though she meant to take a day and do nothing but file, sort, and discard, she never did. David had bought her two white file cabinets for her birthday. The gift certificate for them was pinned to the bulletin board in the kitchen along with postcards from friends and bumper stickers—LA TREMENDA! 1010 AM, *Have You Hugged Your Motorcycle Today?* Liz ended up sleeping in her apartment more often than not when David was away. She didn't like sleeping in the brown house alone, even with Cal across the yard.

Without Cal, Liz wouldn't have come to Houston, and her present life, which seemed remarkable to her, would never have taken place. Outside her bedroom window, instead of the palm tree and the stockade fence, she would have twelve stories of air and a courtyard that was light for two hours a day of northern sun squeezed past the surrounding buildings.

Her apartment in New York was the apotheosis of New York apartments. Even as she moved in, Liz knew that if she left this apartment, she left the city forever. The apartment had off-white plaster walls and shiny floors, twelve-foot-high ceilings, light from the north, and enough room—bedroom, living room, kitchen, bath, and a foyer wide enough for her thick round oak table. It was her fourth apartment in the six years since she'd left Willy in Sweden. She had vague memories of the building from her childhood. She might have visited a friend from elementary school who lived there, but she was never able to pin down which friend it was or what had happened during the visits, if indeed they'd taken place. Sometimes in the cavernous marble lobby, a woman moved in a certain way or stood in the shadow of one of the Corinthian columns that divided the open space, and Liz was sure she'd seen the woman before. She might have been a glamorous mother twenty-five years ago, dressed in an angora sweater set and a tight skirt, spike heels, serving chocolate chips and milk to the little girls.

When she returned from Sweden, her parents found her a job at an afternoon paper. A friend of theirs was the managing editor. She spent months clipping articles from fashion magazines for the files. After work, she wrote her own stories. A few were published, but she didn't get a byline.

Willy came home. She heard he came home when the war ended. He was still wanted for skipping bail, so he'd made his way from Sweden back to Canada and then turned himself in at the U.S. border. He didn't bother getting in touch with anyone from the movement, and the judge, perhaps relieved at the quiet in his courtroom, sentenced Willy to only six months, and he served every day of it.

When she'd been at the paper a year and was beginning to cover fashion shows and the occasional rock concert, Willy called her. They hadn't spoken twice in two years since she'd left, and she was sorry at the symptoms of excitement she felt at hearing his voice. She was sweating, her palms were wet.

"What was it like," she asked, "coming back home?"

"It was like throwing a party and nobody comes. I walked across the Peace Bridge—I wanted to walk back into America. So I did and then I asked for the nearest cop shop and turned myself in. They yawned and arrested me."

"I'm sorry I didn't come visit you in jail," she said.

"I'm sorry I didn't answer your letters," he said. His voice sounded gruffer and more businesslike than she remembered. "It wasn't as if I had a whole hell of a lot else to do."

"You didn't write your autobiography?"

"There's something you can do for me now," he said.

"Anything," Liz said.

"A couple of years ago, some people bombed a big Brown & Root construction site, the beginning of a bridge in Louisiana. Brown & Root was part of the consortium that was building South Vietnam—airfields, prisons. They made a bundle on the war."

"I remember it vaguely."

"I want to connect you with those people. They're still underground and they want to talk."

"Are they turning themselves in?"

"No."

"Then what's the story? You know better than I—no one wants to hear about this anymore."

"I thought you'd want the story," Willy said. "I don't notice you writing such hot stories. These are people who've been hiding for years, Liz. Remember what it was like for two months in Toronto? *Years.* Have a heart."

"Okay, okay. I will, but I can't vouch for the paper. They don't have to go for it just because I write it. And Willy—this isn't like writing for the *Rat* or something. I can't be a mouthpiece."

"This will work for you," Willy said. "I know it."

He picked Liz up before dawn two mornings later and drove with her in his white VW van to a large metal building that might have been in

Brooklyn or Queens. He had gained weight in prison, and for the first time she realized how much time had gone by since they met. Had her skin coarsened as his had, and were her features now so much more prominent? His thick red hair was cut short and stood out from his head at irregular intervals. He was dressed as always, in layers of T-shirts and long-sleeved shirts, now in winter with a big sweater over the load of clothing. His jeans were torn at the knee, and she could see his bony flesh and golden hair through the tear. Then he blindfolded her, telling her it was a requirement and that they'd go nowhere until she put the cloth around her head and tied it. When she'd done the red kerchief around her eyes, she felt his finger, checking that she hadn't left any gaps to see through. It was the only time Willy touched her that day.

Liz could tell only that they'd gone over a bridge to get there. She sat at a long table and took her notebook, tape recorder, and pens out of her shoulder bag. The subjects sat in back of a screen.

"We can't let you get away with the tape," one woman said. Her silhouette showed short, frizzy hair and, when she turned to one of the others, a large nose and jutting jaw. She told Liz to call her Selma. "They can hear traffic and background noise, from anything—they'll trace where we were."

"But you won't be here anymore," Liz said. "You're moving on, right? I can't go to my editor and tell her to believe me on this. Cross my heart. I won't give the tape to the police. Ever heard of confidentiality, freedom of the press?"

They talked for four hours and she taped everything. She insisted they answer her questions as well as reciting their stories and justifications in their own rhetoric. There were three women and a man— Selma, Harriet, and Joanie, and Rob. Joanie had a crackly, friendly voice and reminded Liz of the political people she'd most admired, the ones who were natural and unforced both in their speech and actions. She was modest about the possible good or bad that could have come from their action, and honest about the personal cost to her.

The story didn't belong precisely on the women's page and it wasn't hard news. The political line was uninteresting, her editor informed Liz, but she gave Liz time off to write the piece. Liz spent three days making portraits of each of the bombers and putting together what they'd been willing to say about their lives underground, which sounded unbearable to Liz. The constant fact of their lives was that they moved on and had to depend on and trust a network of strangers for their safety. They had lost themselves, given themselves over to their outrage at the war and the iron logic they had developed about the politics of their country. She thought they were most brave not to have taken permanent refuge in one of the disguises they wore—waitress, health-food store worker, any occupation that didn't require much identification or fingerprints.

Liz's story was well received. It came out on a day when nothing much was happening. She was surprised that so many people read it and remembered her for writing it. She waited for a message from Willy, some recognition that she'd done a good job and hadn't gotten anyone in trouble. Her father warned her not to talk when the FBI came, and she didñ't, saying she would speak only with her lawyer present. She didn't hear from them again and didn't understand why she didn't. Her lawyer was her father's partner and he'd dealt with the FBI many times, but he couldn't explain why they didn't come back.

Her parents asked why she didn't try to move to the news side of the paper or push to get away from the women's page. She explained to them as well as she could that she didn't have the ambition other writers her age had. They worked harder than she and wanted nothing more than to be at the top, wherever they gauged that to be. She didn't want to do that, she said. She didn't want daily deadlines and she didn't want to be responsible for too many facts. Eventually, she thought, she'd work for magazines, and probably it would be the same kind of thing: fashion, design, celebrity interviews, fluff.

Cal lived on the other side of the building, three floors down, in an apartment that faced east over the courtyard. If Liz leaned very far out of her living-room window, she could see into Cal's kitchen.

They first met in the marble lobby on Thanksgiving morning. On one wall there was a wallpaper mural, a scene out of Watteau, Liz thought. Small gentlemen and ladies with sharply pointed toes were landing on an island in the middle of a lake. A small gazebo could be seen in the distance, at the edge of the woods. She stood gazing at the mural, wishing the doorman would appear so she could tell him to hold her mail. She was going with her parents to northwest Connecticut for the weekend.

"Do you think the whole building's in East Hampton." She heard a voice behind her.

"Or Great Neck," she said.

"I wouldn't know," Cal said. "I'm just learning about East Hampton. Great Neck must be next."

She had seen him before, across the lobby, waiting for the elevator on his side of the building.

"Going away?" he asked. "I'm waiting for Duffy myself. There's something odd happening in my pipes."

She hesitated. She knew you were supposed to take care whom you told your plans, but what was there to be stolen in her apartment, she reasoned, and this man—bright eyes, a lion's mane of white, brown, and gold hair—didn't look like a burglar.

"My parents are taking me away for a few days," she said. "Now I wish I had brothers and sisters."

"I'm an only child myself," he said. "Cal Dayton. And you're . . ."

"Liz Gold," she said. "And how will you celebrate Turkey Day, as my father calls it?"

"Oh, some friends who live on the East River are having a big bird, and we're all taking a little something."

"What are you taking," she asked, feeling left out of a good time. Her parents made separate retreats to the workshop and the living room during country days and were company only at night, for meals which her mother insisted must be simple and no trouble. Liz wanted some trouble, elaborate holiday dishes that would take all day to make. Once she got to the country with her parents, she knew, she would have lost the impetus toward food and would retreat to her corner with a book or take solitary walks if the November weather permitted.

"Cornbread," Cal said. "I use Helen Corbitt's recipe. Marvelous. Sour cream."

In time, they got into the habit of calling one another after work to see if they would get together. "Chinese?" he'd ask. "Chicken," she'd reply.

Cal worked at the *Village Voice*, writing, editing, lending a hand on production. He was learning everything he could, he told her, storing it up for the time he'd return to Houston and start his own magazine. He'd edited a technical magazine for McGraw-Hill, copyedited for Random House, and worked briefly at *Vogue* and *Glamour.*

"Help me," Liz said a few days before Christmas. She'd been to a preview of early fall clothes from a designer who worked out of a loft downtown. "I liked the clothes fine. I liked the designer. But how many ways are there to say blue silk? Green jacket? Beige shirt?"

"No problem," Cal said. "Just hard work."

They'd finished an early dinner and Liz was going back to the paper to write the story.

"I mean it," she said. "I'm not afraid of hard work. Just failure. Help me."

"All right," Cal said. "Tell me about the clothes—one outfit you liked."

"Okay. There was a kind of very soft silk deal—a tailored shirt, not military, just plain. And pants in the same silk, cut very plain also."

"Bell bottoms? Flairs? Man-cut? Loose?"

"Stovepipe. Straight up and down. And over the silk she had a very blousy kind of cardigan jacket—it was wool. I have it written down. But it was a wool cloth, not a knit. And it was green."

"Green? By green you mean—"

"Light green."

"Mint? Seafoam? Celadon? Gray-green?"

"For God's sake. It was green. Light green. In fact, I had to look twice to be sure it was green, not beige."

"Never say beige. And how about—" Cal closed his eyes and thought for a second, then said, "A greeny oatmeal blouson jacket over—what color is the silk job?"

"Violet. Lavender. Lavender more than violet."

"Greeny oatmeal blouson jacket over simply cut lilac silk shirt and trousers. It's not great, but it gives a picture. Don't just think in terms of one perfect adjective you have to find. That doesn't work. Try to describe the texture, color, and cut of every piece, then put them together to create one picture. And bingo."

"I'll be up all night," she said.

"The designer had to do it, you know. She picked out the fabric, the cut, and the colors and put them together. Just follow her lead."

"Okay," Liz said. "That makes it sound better. I just feel so silly writing about clothes."

"Why?" he asked. "Don't you like clothes? You seem to spend enough time and money on your own."

"Of course," she said. "But I feel guilty about it the whole time. Which makes it all right."

"Does it?" he asked. "Not where I come from. Would you feel less guilty about clothes if you were planting a bomb in Bendel's while looking for that simply cut silk shirt?"

"Oh, Cal," she said. "I'll be late to work."

If either had a date—rare for her; she didn't know about Cal—the evening call would be brief. It was policy never to interfere, never to ask to be taken along. They were invited places, by his friends and hers, almost as a couple, but she knew the same group of men met and went places they would never take her, just as her friends didn't include Cal at certain occasions. She thought this friendship on eggshells was unnatural. They were not lovers, of course. Cal had told her early on that he was gay. Still, she felt closer to him than she had to anyone since Willy, closer in fact than she had to Willy in Canada and Sweden. Once, late at night, she came home alone from a date. She had listened too long to her date telling her about himself. She had waited the whole time for him to ask one question about her. If he had, she would have spent the night with him. As it was, she took a taxi home alone. She'd drunk too much gin, and when she locked the door and turned on the lights in her apartment, she made herself another drink. Cal had a guest for dinner, she knew, but she called anyway. He answered, asked how her date had been, said he was sorry it had been so bad, and that he'd call her in the morning. Liz went to her window and leaned way out to see if the lights were on in Cal's place or if he and his guest were in bed. Then she pulled herself back in quickly from the darkness and cold winter air and shut her window.

They both grew melancholy that the winter took so long to be done. Cal told her during the February nights and dark afternoons about Houston, about the early oil discoveries and the pranks of politicians and millionaires, but mostly the stories were private, about Cal's first car—a '49 green Plymouth he bought for $50 when he was sixteen—and about his mother and father, the little towns they'd come from in Texas and Louisiana and the lives they made in the city.

Cal's first memory was of the opening of the Shamrock Hotel, Glenn McCarthy's white elephant. Every room in the hotel was painted green for the occasion, and celebrities were brought into Houston from Los Angeles, New York, New Orleans—all over—for the opening party. Cal remembered something green and the big swimming pool. He was in a stroller, pushed by his mother, Helen, to the edge of the crowd to watch.

Cal kept a picture of Helen in the kitchen, and one of his father, who'd died of a heart attack when Cal was twelve. "High-strung," Cal said, "and overweight, which proved fatal. I don't think he and Helen got along. She didn't think he really had it. I don't remember precisely. There were fights. Well, there always are fights. It's a mystery I don't care to solve. He was a salesman, always selling something." After his father died, Helen went to work full-time, leaving Cal to get his lunches for himself, and leaving him with unaccustomed freedom, an ambiguous gift.

For her part, Liz showed him her elementary school, only five blocks from where they lived. They walked to the playground in Riverside Park where she played stickball and took moody adolescent walks—"Still do," she said. She took him over to her parents one night for dinner. They got along, but not brilliantly. Her parents were so serious, he said as they walked back down Broadway to their building. "I can't imagine what it would be like to have parents who argued over whether a book review in the Sunday *Times* is accurate. Or fair."

"They're serious," she said. "But they like their seriousness in small doses. They never liked Willy. He was too serious about politics. My mother said he was effete."

"Did she think he was gay?"

"No. I don't think she thinks about whether people are gay, except if they're being oppressed. She just didn't like her generation of leftists being blamed for letting the country get into the situation it was in. That's how she heard him. She compared him to the students at Oxford who were pacifists and refused to fight against Hitler. Of course, in the end many of them did and they were killed, just like everyone else. She and Dad always considered the antiwar movement too sectarian and narrow. They worked against the war, of course, but they didn't think it would amount to much in the long run. It was a single-issue movement that would die when the issue died. Willy never saw beyond the war. Who could?"

"He led their little darling a merry dance," Cal said. "They probably didn't like that much."

"Just to Canada. Sweden. It could have been worse. He could have gone underground and spent his life in drag. No. I'll never forgive myself for leaving him in Sweden. I should have stayed a year. I owed him a year."

"You think it would look better on your résumé," Cal said. They'd reached the front door of their building, and Liz stopped. She didn't like saying anything personal in the lobby, where words echoed from column to mural to chandelier.

"He told me to go. He told me to, because he knew I'd go anyway."

"Deserting a deserter," Cal said. "What's the just deserts for that?"

"A life sentence," she said. "He wasn't a deserter, anyway. He was a resister. And bail jumper."

"And what do they think of Willy now that the smoke has cleared."

"My father tells me to track him down and get a divorce before something else happens."

"Still and all," Cal said, "Willy did you a good turn. This way you won't go and marry someone on impulse."

One afternoon in the very early spring, Liz was working at home, completing a profile of Bud Baker, a color-field painter from Arkansas who was renovating a flophouse in Soho.

Cal called and asked what she was doing.

"Writing. I'm trying to figure out what looked so great and exciting when I was with Bud and what looks so dull now. I don't have anything but figures on how much money he's spending. But there's something else there, something more interesting. Vital."

"How would it be if I came over?" he asked.

"What are you doing home in the middle of the afternoon? Of course, come over."

She kept working, trying to weave the staggering amount of money Baker was spending in with the reasons he was spending the money, some frivolous, some for his work. When Cal arrived, she said, "One more page and I've got it. Grab a beer. I'll be right there."

He waited for her in the armchair by her desk, looking through a magazine and sipping his beer. When she finished, she turned off the typewriter and said, "So what is it? Are you in love?"

He stood and stretched. He was dressed in a white T-shirt and gray and white baggy trousers which emphasized his tweedy hair and colorful eyes. The week before, an old friend of Liz's had tried to seduce Cal, saying that she'd save him, as if being heterosexual meant you were that much closer to heaven.

"You know my poker game," he said.

"Every Thursday. Rain or shine." He played at his friend Sandy's house, a small three-apartment brownstone along the East River that had not yet been knocked down to make way for a more profitable structure. Sandy's grandfather had owned the building, and Sandy lived off the income from the rents.

"I went there last night," Cal said, "and everything was fine. Then we all left. I wouldn't have left but I don't know. I didn't feel like staying."

Liz hadn't known that he ever stayed at Sandy's. If he did, did it mean they were lovers and, if so, were they in love or just together? She nodded, as if she knew everything.

"What's wrong, Cal?"

"Someone broke into Sandy's apartment after we all left. He killed him. And Sandy killed the burglar. They both had guns."

"What was Sandy doing with a gun?"

"He had lots of guns," Cal said. "A collection. Sandy was a champion. He used to drive to some shooting range in Connecticut and practice every weekend."

"Oh, Cal. Do the police know how it happened?"

Cal sat down again and held his face between his palms, massaging his cheeks and forehead.

"I have a really grotesque headache. I think I've swallowed a bottle of aspirin today. The kid broke in—the door's popped open—and he had a gun. Sandy kept a gun by his bed. You know, he was so isolated over there. He kept the building looking so nice, the kid probably thought he'd hit the big time. It doesn't take Sherlock Holmes to figure it out. They shot each other and they're both dead."

They finished half a bottle of brandy Liz had gotten at Christmastime, then walked across Broadway to a bar that served steaks. Cal kept drinking brandy. Liz switched to beer. By the time they left the dark bar, she could hardly talk and she held Cal's arm for support. Broadway smelled like spring, warm air and people out for strolls, getting the late paper early or just taking a look after a long closed-in winter. For a moment on the esplanade, they clung together, waiting for the traffic to clear so they could cross. She could feel Cal's chin against hers, his body stiff in her arms.

"Liz." His voice was close to her ear.

"Hmm," she said.

"We had just started being lovers. He was a sweet person. He wanted to get to know you better. He said you should come out this summer to a place he has in New Jersey and we'd all have a good time together. I told him all about you." He let go of her and straightened himself up, passing his hand over his eyes.

"I'm sorry," Liz said. "I never knew him well."

"You know that billboard you can see from the West Side Highway, right after Twenty-third Street? The man smoking a cigarette and those nasty green mountains? That's Sandy. A few years ago. They keep that billboard up there."

"You're right," she said. "Isn't that funny. I didn't recognize him. We can cross now."

At the door to the building, Cal stopped and said, "Life doesn't care who lives in it, does it? Think of all the real stinkers who made it through the day."

She walked with him to her elevator. "Come stay at my place tonight. Or I'll stay with you. You don't want to be alone, do you?"

It was the first time she'd made the offer, and she hoped he would let her care for him. "I think I'd better cry this one out alone," Cal said.

"But, Liz. Are you going away this weekend? I wish you'd stay. It would be a big help."

Cal went across the empty lobby for his elevator. Liz's elevator came first and she held the door open for a moment, to give Cal a chance to change his mind. He looked so hunched up. But he gave no sign, and Liz went upstairs.

In her apartment, she didn't stop to turn on the lights but walked straight through to the living-room window. She hadn't planned to go away that weekend but would have canceled any plans she might have had. She would stay and watch over him, stay as close or as far as he liked. Liz opened the window and leaned out, and she waited there until she saw the lights go on, then off in Cal's apartment, to show her that Cal would sleep that night.

The phone was ringing when she walked in.

"I made it to New York," David said. "I just checked in, and I have a half hour before the meeting. How's it going? Did I wake you when I left?"

"No. I woke up and you were gone. I wish you had woken me. Anyway, Cal assigned me a story. Other than that, Bayou City is much the same."

"What's the story?"

"Nothing big. A department. A Bad Old Days about someone named Carolyn Sylvan who went and got herself killed. It happened about twenty years ago in Galveston."

"What's the idea?"

"My question exactly. That it happened. What happened. Who were the people. Why it was never solved."

"Maybe it was solved but they didn't prosecute."

"No one was arrested for it."

"That doesn't mean it was unsolved," he said. "They just didn't have sufficient evidence to prosecute."

"Cal says everybody knows about it. Have you ever heard of it?"

"It's a really dim memory, if it is a memory. My grandmother always sent my mother the juiciest stuff from the Houston papers. But I don't recall it really."

"Where are you staying? I can't imagine where you are."

"Essex House," he said. "You have the number."

She touched an airplane ticket that lay by the phone, a round trip between Houston and New York, an open fare good for a year.

"Cal says everyone thought her lover did it."

"Maybe he did," David said. "I have to go. I'll call late tonight."

"Bye," she said, and when he hung up she said, "David."

He'd started the custom of giving her the airline tickets when they'd been together two months. He'd been packing to go on a two-day business trip and Liz had sat in his peach-velvet armchair, trying to think of last-minute things to say that would be entertaining or pleasing, something that would make him come back to her. Just before he snapped shut the suitcase and left, he took an airline ticket folder from his jacket pocket and threw it to her. She looked at it. It was a Delta ticket to Chicago.

"Come with me," he said.

"I'm working on that health spa story."

"Join me tomorrow. Join me unannounced. Surprise me."

"That's a nice way to put it," she said.

"I'm trying to nip this jealousy in the bud," he said.

"You just don't want to be in Chicago alone," she said. She smiled and crossed the room to David and held him as close as she could. The system worked for a while, though now when she looked at the pile of unused tickets, Liz thought she'd better come up with a more permanent solution. David had complained that his American Express bill looked like the Versailles pact, charges and cancellations covering pages.

Pinned to the wall above her telephone was a photo taken one night when Liz and Cal, Lucy and David went to Galveston. It was just weeks after Liz moved to Houston, days before Lucy left David for good. The four sat at a round table that was covered by cans of beer and platters of fried shrimp and condiments. In back of them on the mantel of a fake fireplace was a plastic chest sprayed gold. Pouring from the chest were plastic beads, coins of unknown origin, gewgaws, all gold, the treasure of the Buccaneer Club. They'd walked through a festival on the Strand and had been drinking beer all afternoon in the sun. Then Cal took them to the Buccaneer Club.

Cal led them away from the Strand for a few blocks, then stopped before a door that had been painted red. He knocked and waited, knocked again, and after a time a small window in the door was opened. A middle-aged black man with soft, handsome features looked at each one of them.

"Wade," Cal said. "We're awfully hungry. Any shrimp today?"

Wade let them in, greeting them with a cordiality that Liz thought was impartial, probably impersonal. He settled them at the table before the fireplace, then disappeared to get them their first round of beer.

"If I ever completely lose my mind," Cal said, "and become an invalid—a Howard Hughes kind of guy—I want Wade Swan to come take care of me."

They drank more beer, ate as much shrimp as they could, and then it seemed to be a good idea to take a picture. Cal was taking a photography course and had in the back of his car a camera and tripod, and he proposed taking a portrait of the four. In the photo, Cal was the only person in focus. He was the most still and casual, though he'd just run back to his seat after he set the camera. Lucy looked frizzy-haired and pretty, a little blank. She stared past Cal and Liz at the kitchen door. David's mouth was set in a cheerful smile. His eyes were on Lucy. Liz looked pale in the photograph, as if the day in the sun had bleached her.

After that day in Galveston, Liz was sure she'd made the right decision in coming to Texas. Many of Cal's stories about his time in Houston and Austin had been remarkable to her because they sounded like fun, and Cal was remarkable to her because he could describe an event as fun with complete unself-consciousness, as a statement of plain fact. Fun was a word that among Liz's New York friends had been used only for irony, to indicate a pitiable naiveté or a hopelessly suburban attitude. It was never a goal toward which to shape one's experience. But here she had spent a whole day with other people, laughing and talking, looking at things together, having a good time, having fun.

She liked Lucy better than she had during a brief meeting in New

York. Lucy meant well and obviously admired Liz. She was genuinely glad Liz had moved to Houston, and maybe they would be friends. Lucy and David had a good marriage, Liz thought, complete with white cottage and two-car garage. They played tennis together and ran, had family dinners at the holidays during which no one argued about the war or anything else, Liz was sure. They'd been married nine years. Lucy was thirty, two years younger than Liz. Why hadn't they had children yet? Liz wondered, then figured they would, and she'd spent a moment imagining a child as pretty as Lucy, as large and strong as David.

It was one o'clock. There was still time to go downtown and get started on the Carolyn Sylvan story. She would call Martha at the magazine first with the information she wanted, and then she'd go to the library. Sometime, she thought, she'd clean up her apartment, take down the Galveston photo and her calendar of Texas wildflowers and her bumper stickers and postcards. If she was so worried about David seeing Lucy in New York, why did she want to look at a picture of Lucy each time she used her own phone? She liked the photograph for its historic value, and for evidence that there had been a time not very long before when it would not have been a body blow if she'd never seen David again. She would hardly have noticed it.

She found the name in the phone book. William O. Osborne was listed in Houston on South MacGregor Way. She checked the map. The street was across Brays Bayou from the University of Houston. Liz considered calling right away and setting up an appointment with his widow—if she still was there—and decided against it. She'd wait until she had more on the story.

Neither the *Houston Post* nor the *Chronicle* allowed writers for *Spindletop* to use their morgues, so Liz drove downtown to the Houston Metropolitan Research Center to read their files and microfilms of the now defunct *Houston Press*. When she went to Galveston, she'd check the morgue of the *Galveston Daily News*.

The downtown branch of the Houston Public Library was housing the research center until its own building was ready across the plaza.

The library was a glass cube that looked, when lighted at night, like a diorama of a library. The research center would eventually be in the original library, a Moorish building with a broad staircase, high ceilings, ornate wooden shelves, and murals from the WPA. Liz had done a small story on the research center, and she'd met one of the curators then, Ross Taylor, a short dark man from Nashville. He'd shown her the center's collection—some of it catalogued, some not—of photos, maps, letters, diaries, postcards, magazines, and newspapers, all to do with Houston history. He was working on an oral history of the city, taping interviews with elderly wildcatters, Mexican Americans, former slaves, Chinese, and grandes dames.

Ross was at his desk when Liz arrived. His area was back among the metal shelves that held the collection.

"Howdy," he said. "We haven't seen you for a while."

"I was doing a story on a fancy lady," Liz said. "How's the center going? Do you move soon?"

"Well, we haven't made much forward progress but not much backward, either. Looking on the bright side. How may I help you?"

"I need to look at newspaper microfilm for April of 1959. I'm doing a story on Carolyn Sylvan's murder. In Galveston. Do you know about it?"

"Only vaguely. Galveston? Let me set you up with the microfilm, and I'll try to locate some other stuff. I seem to recall running across the subject sometime."

Ross left her at the microfilm machine and, quickly, Liz saw that the newspaper accounts followed the general outline of Cal's version.

Between eight-thirty and nine on an April night, William "Fast" Osborne received an anonymous phone call, which instructed him to go to the house off Twelve Mile Road on the west end of Galveston Island, the house he'd rented the previous autumn for Carolyn Sylvan, a young blond woman, and her four-year-old daughter, Rose. He drove to Galveston and found the bodies. The child was on the driveway. Carolyn Sylvan was inside the house, near the front door. Osborne immediately called the Galveston police.

He was detained as a material witness and stayed overnight in the Galveston jail, a guest of the county. He was then released and was never arrested.

The *Press* accounts dwindled from headline news to back-page filler, then ceased.

There had been one other witness, and her testimony wasn't useful. Blanche Long was a neighbor of Carolyn Sylvan's. She told the police that she heard two cars going to Carolyn Sylvan's that night. She was sure they were going there because the house was located on a lane just off Twelve Mile Road. One car had come and gone. Then another—presumably Osborne's—had come and stayed.

"It's not much," Liz said to Ross when she'd finished reading. Her eyes ached from staring at the microfilm. "The bare facts are grim but they don't lead anywhere. They never found out who was in the first car. I'll bet they tried to pin Osborne down about who called him, but he didn't budge."

To be thorough, Liz had scanned the paper for the week before and the week after the first and last accounts of the murder. It was April and starting to get hot. There was nothing much else going on. It was the last year of the Eisenhower presidency. Liz looked at the ads for dresses and hats, remembering when women had dressed like the models in these drawings and blurry photographs. Her mother had looked that proper only on the rare occasions when she went out with Liz's father. He was very social and loved giving and going to parties. Her mother didn't like either. Most days of Liz's childhood, her mother had vaguely embarrassed her by not dressing like other mothers, by wearing dungarees or plain suits with oxford shoes, good enough clothes for the park or marching. As clearly as the embarrassment, Liz remembered her shame that she should think about such things in connection with her mother, who was more than good, better than Liz ever hoped to be. In 1959, Liz was fourteen and in Manhattan. In 1963, she would go to college in New Hampshire and meet Willy. What she thought of as her real life would finally begin.

"Have you ever seen a picture of Carolyn Sylvan?" Ross asked. "I ran across one in a bunch of old letters we got from a Mrs. Debevec who lived in the Heights. When you came, I got it out."

Ross handed Liz a newspaper clipping in a plastic sheet. She'd seen the same picture on the microfilm.

Carolyn Sylvan wore her straight thick hair nearly waist length. She was sitting on the front steps of a bungalow that might have been anywhere in the South, and a little girl was draped across her lap like a limp cat. Carolyn had a high forehead and deep sunken eyes. Her nose was narrow, and her mouth was small. The lower lip protruded slightly, as if she'd just finished eating something sweet and might soon lick her lips. The child, Rose, was pretty, with the same broad forehead and a softer face than her mother's. Unlike most women, whose beauty might be diminished by a younger representation of themselves, Carolyn was so adult and likable, so sturdy and beautiful, that she made her child's face look unformed.

"You want to talk to her," Ross said. He looked at the photograph over Liz's shoulder. "I guess old Mrs. Debevec liked her face. She's dead now and we got her scrapbooks. She clipped pictures of people she liked the looks of, from the papers and magazines she collected. She took a bunch of pictures, too, of her neighbors in the Heights. When I ran across this clipping of Carolyn Sylvan, I asked the natives around here. They remembered the murder."

"Carolyn Sylvan must not have had family here or a single friend," Liz said. "No one to keep the case going in the papers or with the police."

"No money either," Ross said. "If she'd been a rich girl, who knows. Some murders never get solved, though, no matter what."

There were two Esperson buildings, side by side; Niels was finished in 1927, Mellie opened in 1941. Both had been built by Mellie Esperson, widow of Niels, who had prospected gold in Colorado, struck it rich in oil in Humble, then invested in Houston real estate. The ceilings in Niels had been dropped and the bronze ornaments removed to make it look more placid and modern. But Mellie retained the original deco lobby, with polished metal and glass doors and fine angular bronze-work over the fire extinguishers, the shining metal framing the lobby directory and the prisonlike elevators. The floor was green marble, cool, dark, and luminous.

Liz stood at the directory. She recognized a few names of older people she'd met at parties or receptions, friends of Doc's. She'd read in the newspaper account of the murder that Osborne had his public-relations business office on the fifteenth floor, and so, feeling idle, thinking she should go home and make arrangements to spend the next day in Galveston, Liz had walked the few blocks from the library. She'd only been inside the modern downtown office buildings—Pennzoil, Tenneco, Shell Plaza—and was surprised at the Esperson Building, which could have been on lower Fifth Avenue and had for Liz the same commercial solidity the East Side had when she was a child going downtown on the bus to Best & Co. for a haircut.

She took the elevator up to the fifteenth floor and stood in the wide hallway. This was the workaday part of the building, less ornamented than the lobby or the elevator. To her right were unlabeled double doors. When she opened one of the doors, she saw an empty carpeted space, with marks showing where there had once been a receptionist's desk. Across the floor, she could see other marks where there had been partitions and desks. She heard a sound. A man stood behind her. He was tall and gray-haired. He wore thick horn-rimmed glasses and a blue suit and a red bow tie.

"May I help you?" he asked.

"I'm from *Spindletop* magazine," she said, "and I was wondering where William Osborne's offices were. You probably weren't here when—"

"I've been in this building twenty years," he said. "Mr. Osborne died in sixty-three. Sixty-four, maybe. Of course, his company went bust long before then. These weren't his. These were Corrigan's. Down the hall was Osborne, but there's nothing to see. The people who took over, they took over."

"Did you know Mr. Osborne?"

"I knew him to say hello to. And if he needed anything, he called me."

"And Mr. Corrigan? Gus Corrigan?"

"He was a character." The man's pale round face opened in a smile. "A character. He'd ask the birds in the trees for their wings. But these offices haven't been Corrigan's for years. They built their own building. This wasn't the main branch for years. Just spillover. Little stuff."

Liz walked down the hall. One newspaper account had recorded that Carolyn Sylvan had worked for Osborne, a later one said that she had met him in the building. The hallways for Niels and Mellie were connected. Carolyn Sylvan might have met him anywhere in the two buildings. Liz looked at her watch and saw that if she wanted to be able to get out of downtown, she had to leave. Rush hour would start soon.

Her next step was Galveston: the Rosenberg Library, clips from the *Galveston Daily News,* and her friend Jeff Bryan, who owned a small biweekly paper. If she was very lucky, she might be able to get what she needed from Jeff and skip the library and the newspaper.

Back in her apartment, she sat by the phone, letting it ring up to a dozen times at William O. Osborne's house on South MacGregor Way. When she was ready to hang up, a woman answered. Her voice was soft and hesitant.

"This is Liz Gold from *Spindletop* magazine. I'd like to speak with Mrs. William Osborne."

"This is Virginia Osborne."

"Hello. I was wondering, Mrs. Osborne, if you might have some time for me this week. I'm doing a story—"

"There was a young man here from the *Post.* He wanted to take photographs of the house for a story on our neighborhood. I told him it was out of the question."

"I'm afraid I'm not doing a story on the neighborhood," Liz said. "I don't know if you're familiar with our magazine, but we have an occasional department called the Bad Old Days."

"I see," Virginia Osborne said. "And I qualify as a bad old day?"

"It's a story on the Sylvan murders, Mrs. Osborne. I wanted to talk to you for background."

She paused so long Liz was afraid she would refuse, but she waited her out. Liz had learned to overcome impatience during interviews and phone calls, and to squelch her instinct to make the situation easy and polite. She let the other person bear the burden of the uncomfortable silence.

Virginia Osborne said, "Have you spoken to anyone else?"

"Whom would you suggest?" Liz asked. The other obvious people were dead.

"Oh, I leave that to you, Miss Gold. I'm sure you know your business better than I."

"Possibly." Liz waited for the other woman to ask her to call back, giving herself time to phone a lawyer. Or perhaps she might offer an appointment so far in the future it would be useless. But Virginia Osborne said, "Thursday would suit me fine. Two o'clock. You have my address?"

Liz stood before David's dresser mirror, noticing the deepest line on her face, a crease between her eyebrows, that had been there since high school. By her mouth there was another, one that had become more evident since Willy's death. She opened her bottle of Dramatically Different Lotion and started to massage it into her skin. It was comfortable in the bedroom at twilight and warm inside the blue terrycloth robe David had given her. She'd told him she'd always wanted one but couldn't face washing it or paying for it. The next day he'd arrived home with the robe and told her she should have more faith in herself.

In the mirror, she could also see Cal, who was sitting in the peach armchair, leafing through a magazine. On the table by his side were two drinks. He looked up at her and said, "This drink is so cold you can't see the lime. Want yours yet?"

"Sure. You'd think in a climate like this I wouldn't have dry skin. That no one would have a wrinkle."

"Stop jogging," he said. He put her drink on the dresser and returned to the chair. "It makes the day too long. Brings on wrinkles and tiny complaints."

"Maybe." Liz took a sip of the cloudy gin and tonic. "In New York, I drank these only in the summer. Winter was Scotch. Or red wine."

"Welcome to the Wild West," Cal said. "Here, my dear, it used to be considered gauche to wear white before Memorial Day or after Labor Day. I mean. By Memorial Day in Houston it's been in the nineties for months."

"Not the nineties. Surely not."

"The eighties. Depends on the spring. People out on ranches used to wear woolen suits and ladies dressed in layers of crinolines and underwear. Civilization."

"Where should we eat?"

"Ouisie's. It's so close." He set the magazine on the table and turned to face Liz, his legs dangling over the arm of the chair. "Did you love the Esperson Building? I used to meet Helen down there for a treat. She'd take me to James Coney Island right down the block. Maybe we should go there."

"Let's go to Ouisie's. I liked the building fine. But it's all gone, you know—the offices. Corrigan's. Osborne's."

"I wish you'd seen Corrigan's offices. They had two floors. What you saw on the fifteenth was reception and clerks. Files. That kind of thing. The upper floor was Corrigan and Helen, and an outer office for a secretary for my mother. Helen used to take me in to see Gus."

"And how was that? Before the hot dog or after?"

"Before. It was always scary. Even after I was grown up, he remained scary. Formidable, crude. Explosive. You never knew what he'd do or say next."

"And your mother—she was with him a long time, wasn't she?"

"From the time my father died to when Gus died. She closed up Gus's affairs—the corporation was bought by a conglomerate—and then she retired. She adored him and did everything for him. His wife was useless, a real fading genuine Southern type, not tough like Helen. She died when I was about thirteen, after my mother had been a year with Gus. Helen saw to it that the household was run right for Gus, here in town and out at his ranch. But she didn't spend any time there."

"She didn't act as his hostess?" Liz picked out a silk shirt and a pair of woolen trousers from the closet, then stepped into the bathroom to dress, leaving the door ajar.

"She wasn't his mistress," Cal said. "If that's what you mean. Not that I didn't wonder. Not that she wouldn't have done it. But I think he went for another type, or he saw that Helen was more useful to him as an employee. She saw to it that Hunter was kept in one school or another and covered up for him, so as not to bother Gus."

"Why did he go to one school or another? Why not one?"

"He couldn't find a school that would keep him," Cal said. "He got into . . . boyish scrapes."

"Pulling the wings off flies? Stealing cars?"

"Some of each. A little of everything."

She stepped back into the bedroom and saw that Cal was finishing his drink. He seemed distracted and tense, a mood she attributed to the change at the magazine.

"Hunter's a lucky man, isn't he," Liz said. "Rich father. Helen around to clean up his messes."

"It seems that way," Cal said. "He's always had everything, or what most people want—looks, money. But his family was a mess."

"Well," she said. "No doubt publishing a magazine will clear his head of cobwebs. Distract him from his childhood troubles. Is he easily distracted?"

"Very," Cal said. "It's his specialty. You have to know how to talk to him to be sure he's getting what you say. It makes some people think he's dumb, plain and simple. But he's so rich, he don't mind. Let them talk."

They drove to the restaurant in Cal's convertible, and as they passed over the Southwest Freeway, Liz looked down at the jam of cars heading west for the Loop, south toward Galveston. They passed streets with names of shortbread tins—Castle Court, Bonnie Brae—and then Cal's favorite streets, North and South boulevards. When she'd arrived from New York, he'd borrowed two bicycles and they'd taken a quiet Sunday ride beneath the arch of live-oak limbs that almost met over the center of the wide streets. She saw Spanish moss for the first time and brilliant shots of sunlight breaking through the trees. Cal pointed out a pink stucco mansion that was the one he wanted.

The restaurant wasn't crowded, but they were told to wait. The waiting area was also a shop that sold soap, crystal bunnies, English tins, potpourri, terracotta armadillos. Sometimes when she came to Ouisie's for lunch, Liz succumbed and bought something small, though she tried to resist the goods, which would collect dust and be lost with the rest of the souvenirs she owned. Cal wandered across the room to look at the candles in the shape of Texas and cowboy boots. Liz noticed a red heart-shaped bar of soap identical to one she'd had in college. Willy brought it home from a summer in Europe. It was the last easy gift he'd given. He found it less trouble to give away money than to pick out a gift. "You find it," he'd say, "and then let me give it to you."

They were seated at a corner table at the plate-glass window looking out on Sunset Boulevard. Liz turned and looked up at the menu written on the blackboard behind them.

"Stay away from the cream sauces," she said. "Too rich. Too thick."

"I always liked their cream sauces," Cal said.

The waiter took their orders for food, and another gin for Cal, white wine for Liz.

"I wish I had your capacity," Liz said.

"I wish I didn't." Cal looked around the large room that was slowly filling with people. Moroccan rugs were hung on the wall and moved with the breeze from the ceiling fans. "There's Gerald," Cal said, waving across the room to a tanned, white-haired man who waved back and raised his wineglass to them both.

"I thought Gerald said Ouisie's was a nest of harpies and he'd never come here again."

"Nevertheless," Cal said. "When does David get back?"

"Friday night. If you're going up to Walden Friday, maybe you could meet his plane and bring him with you. And I'll go earlier and get things all cozy for us."

"We'll see how the week goes," Cal said. "Don't count on me." He waved to a woman across the room who was dressed in a bright orange robe. "So Virginia Osborne said she'd see you. That's good, Liz. She's a recluse. She used to keep livestock or something and scandalize the neighbors."

"Isn't that illegal within city limits? Along with drilling for oil?"

"When I was growing up, all through Galleria and even nearer to downtown, it was country. People kept chickens and cows, and no one thought a thing about it."

"I saw a goat the other day when I was driving along Richmond. I thought I was going to run it over."

"That florist on Westheimer and Buffalo," Cal said. "There's still two cows in the next pasture. Used to be a herd." Cal's hand was smoothing the same place on the shellacked table over and over. "I had cousins who lived near the Osbornes—the bayou was great for exploring. Finding relics."

Their drinks arrived, and then the pasta with pesto and salad.

"How are you doing?" she asked. "Are you worried about him being in charge at the magazine?"

"Yes," Cal said. "But it's the price of money. I don't think Hunter's going to do anything dangerous yet. A few adjustments. He gets bored real easily by too many details. He may not stay long."

"And his money?"

"He's always been able to sell the magazine out from under me. I have a small percentage, but minority stock is minority stock. It's always nerveracking when someone takes over. He could do anything he wanted—I don't have a choice if Hunter decides to make it into a fashion magazine or a business rag or . . . I'd have things to say, but I don't have the weight to make the decision go one way or the other."

"You have the moral weight," Liz said. "It's your magazine—your idea and style. The staff is yours, they're all loyal to you."

"He could dump them," Cal said.

"Just like that?"

"In a New York minute. And that's how long he'd give to considering my moral weight. You haven't met him. I wish David were around."

"Do you have a legal problem?"

"No. Not yet. I just feel like an orphan when he's out of town and Helen is too."

"I rely on you that way. On David too."

"What do you rely on me for?" Cal asked.

She didn't know how seriously to take the question.

"Friendship. Support. You know what I owe you, Cal."

"You don't owe me a thing," he said. "Don't ever do anything thinking that. It's just . . . friendship. Right?"

"But we've gone through things together," she persisted. "I don't forget that. That's what I mean."

The restaurant was full now, and the noise bounded off every surface. They smiled at each other and pushed away their plates.

"How is it with you and David?" Cal asked. "You seem content."

"It's better than I ever imagined it could be with another person. A man. He's my friend and he's everything else to me besides. It's just that I feel so stupid, Cal. I should be jumping at the chance to marry him. I jumped at the chance to marry Willy and he wasn't a prize. Though I sure thought so."

"I don't know a thing about marriage," he said. "From my point of view—if you love David and marriage means something to you, why not do it?"

"It can be undone. Is that what you mean? Okay, but he wants a house. Not for sentimental reasons. We have to live somewhere and he wants the tax advantage. He wants marriage because that's the way David is. He loves me in a way that means marriage. But it's too soon. It's only February. Lucy left just last May."

"Who's making the rules?"

"No one, Cal. I go around asking people when they married. Was it two months after they met, four months? Ten years? In New York there would have been answers. My friends would have been saying, Wait and see. Be careful. You never know." She finished the last drop of wine, then asked, "You talk to Lucy, don't you? How is she?"

"Lucy's fine. She's just getting settled in an apartment. She's taking acting lessons."

"An actress? She's starting to be an actress at age thirty?"

"Now, Liz. It's something for her to do, and she always wanted to be an actress. She had wanted to leave David for a year before she did. They weren't getting along."

"I know. David's told me. He said if I wanted to be picky about when his marriage ended, I could start counting two years before she finally left. But it's more than the real estate, buying a house. Or the time he's been married or unmarried. Let's order another round."

When the drinks came, Liz said, "I'm being stupid, aren't I? Going over and over it. I should just say it's equally wise to do it and not to do it. No guarantees. Tell me, Cal. I need your advice. I want it all with him, but when I think about actually moving into a house that's ours or getting married, it seems impossible."

"Gus Corrigan used to say that free advice was worth every penny you spend on it."

"You're tired of hearing about it. I know. It's hard to be married twice, Cal. It's unsavory. And we're fine as it is."

"Well, if you're fine, let it roll."

"David doesn't let it roll. Neither do I."

"Love troubles sometimes seem so willed to me," Cal said. "People expect security out of the very thing that's the most insecure. Marry him to please him. You love him and it's what he wants. He isn't going to change. People don't change. He's not going to give up on you."

"Give up on me?"

"He'd probably still be married to Lucy if she hadn't left him. He doesn't give up on people. And he likes being married. So you could be happy married or unhappy. But it's the next thing if you want to stay with David. Well, listen to Auntie Cal."

"You're telling me not to screw up, right?"

"Liz?" A small, thin man dressed in khaki pants and a blue shirt stood next to their table.

"Tito. I'm glad to see you again. And so soon. This is my friend Cal Dayton. He's the editor of *Spindletop*. I've talked to you about Cal."

"I adore your magazine," Tito said earnestly as he shook hands with Cal.

"Sit down," Liz said. "Do you have time?"

"I can't. My friend is waiting for me at the cashier." He was silent for a moment, then said, "I'm staying."

"But yesterday—" Liz explained to Cal, "Tito cuts my hair. He told me he was leaving for New York."

"I was almost there," Tito said. "I found someone to take my apartment and my car. I even had a garage sale."

"That's a sincere move right there," Cal said.

"But I didn't want to leave Houston, you see. I felt like a real pioneer when I came here from Brownsville, and I didn't want to go to New York and be nobody. You know? It's all so fabulous there, but—"

"You always make it sound more fabulous than I've ever seen it," Liz said.

"It's fabulous to *visit*," Tito said. "But it's all pressure, pressure, pressure up there, and I thought, Wher₁ would I have a chance to have my own place?"

When he'd left them, Liz looked around the room at the people and the tables of food, the glasses and the rugs on the wall, and the pale pink walls that flattered everyone's complexion.

"This looks pretty civilized to me," she said. "The frontier?"

"Eye of the beholder," Cal said. "He has a shop. I have a magazine. For however long."

The freeway was clear when they drove over on their way back to Graustark. An occasional car made a gentle moving sound along the road.

"I lived in a place one summer that was right on the freeway," Cal said. "It was like a great mother river that never stopped flowing. It was like living in the rain."

III

Liz followed the curves of the bayou, watching the houses for the right number. The houses were large and echoed the architectural styles of other times and places: an English half-timber, a stone castle with turrets and a tower, a plantation house with columns as wide as Liz's car. Each stood close to the next, though a vista of a hundred clear miles wouldn't have dwarfed them, and looked out over the deep bayou that was groomed and wide, cemented over and civilized. On the other side of the wide bayou was the University of Houston and smaller, more suburban houses. The neighborhoods on both sides of the bayou had been great estates at one time, then were developed for wealthy Jewish families and others who weren't allowed to live in River Oaks or Shadyside or couldn't be bothered.

Virginia Osborne lived in a white chateau with windows overlooking the bayou. Her land was bordered by white split-rail fencing. The lawn was bright green. A cattle guard and a locked gate barred the driveway. There was an intercom fitted in the pillar of the wrought-iron gate.

Liz slowed down, then continued around the block and saw that all of it was edged by the white fence. At the back of the house was a grove of trees. A white mare and her foal were grazing alongside another white horse. She continued around to the front gate again and rang the buzzer. A woman's voice asked who was there, and Liz identified herself. She was buzzed through and left her car about fifty feet from the house at a sign that read GUESTS PARK HERE.

Liz walked to the door and hesitated a moment. Then she pressed the bell and waited, looked away at the broad blue sky and the generous expanse of green. There was a steel framework of a large building going up across the bayou. The trees were covered with new leaves. It was warm in the sun and hard to tell that it was only late winter, except by imagining the heavy lushness of the summer to come.

The door was opened by a woman who wore jodhpurs, riding boots, and a white shirt. On the hand she rested on the door was a thick band crusted with small diamonds.

"Miss Gold? I'm Virginia Osborne. Come in."

The hallway was small, with large black and white squares of marble covering the floor, but it opened onto a generous foyer. A curving white staircase rose gradually and ended out of sight. To the right was a cavernous yellow living room and beyond that, at the back of the house, a deep green conservatory where plants crawled up the walls and hung three feet deep from the ceiling. It was a house someone had lived in for a long time, thought Liz, a house it would be impossible to leave. Her own reluctance to buy plants was bolstered by the sight of the green room.

Mrs. Osborne guided Liz to the left of the foyer and through a dining room which held a long table and chairs, all swathed in white cloth. The kitchen had been planned with care, probably in the fifties. The appliances were avocado green and built flush to one another. The electric clock was set into the gray wall above the refrigerator and hummed as the second hand went around.

"Would you care for anything?" Mrs. Osborne asked. "We're alone in the house today, so I'll make whatever you like."

"Tea," Liz said. "Or coffee. Whatever's handy. I hope you don't mind if I tape the interview. I have a terrible memory and worse handwriting."

"Do you? Are you sure that's all you'd like? I have something of everything."

Mrs. Osborne's smile was out of place, shy and pleading. She looked in her sixties, which placed her in her forties at the time of the murder. Her hair was wispy and colored somewhere between sand and wheat. Her skin was leathered, not in the way of a woman who goes to resorts but like a farmer. The armpits of the white cotton shirt were wet. Her forearms were strong and muscled under soft aged flesh.

"A beer?" she suggested to Liz. "An apéritif?"

"I'd fall asleep. Thank you. Coffee would be fine."

"Then coffee it is," she said, and turned away to the sink.

Liz felt she'd failed her in some way she couldn't define.

"Are you new to Houston, Miss Gold?"

"I came last June," Liz said.

"I hope you'll stay with us awhile." She spoke in a formal way that rendered her statement impersonal.

"I probably will," Liz said, trying to match her for blandness.

When the coffee was ready, Mrs. Osborne loaded the tray with a cup and saucer for Liz, a china coffeepot edged in tiny gold leaves, and a blue-flowered plate on which she arranged cookies that she took from a jar shaped like a fat policeman. She carried the tray into the conservatory.

The room had been painted a milder shade of yellow than the living room, though the color was obscured by the plants. There was a circle of white wicker chairs with worn chintz covers which reminded Liz of the living-room couch in her apartment. A white wicker bar stood to one corner, a silver ice bucket and glasses on a tray on top of it. Mexican tile covered the floor, giving the room an additional chill.

Liz turned on the tape recorder, tested it, then set it next to the tea tray on the thick glass coffee table.

"You understand," Mrs. Osborne said, "I don't mind the machine going. To answer your question of a while back. But I don't wish to be quoted on anything. If this is unacceptable, then . . ." She spread her workman's hands in a gesture of armistice.

"I'm not even sure there's much of a story," Liz said, as gently as she could, in order to reassure Virginia Osborne that the attention wouldn't be focused on her.

"I wonder what you're doing here in that case," she said.

"Basically," Liz said, "just collecting background. Have you read the magazine? We have a department that appears every few months, the Bad Old Days, and we try to write up pieces of Houston history."

"History," Virginia Osborne said. "My. History."

"So many people are new to Houston, and they don't know the old stories."

"So you'll turn them into old Houstonians with old gossip?"

"Not gossip," Liz said. "Our researcher verifies every statement we print. And we don't have a mission, Mrs. Osborne. Except to be a good magazine and sell copies." She thought she had the other woman's sympathy now, and she went on. "We're trying to retell the story of the Sylvan murders. And while I can understand that you wouldn't want to be overly involved, I do assume that you'd like your point of view included in the story. We try to tell all points of view and to be objective."

She stopped herself from talking anymore. The woman's silence and poise were dense as a Buddha's.

"This may be a short call," Virginia Osborne said at last. "You see, I have no point of view on this story, as you call it." She poured a cup of hot coffee for Liz and asked, "Cream? Sugar?"

Liz accepted the cup, then waited for her to begin talking again.

"There were so many accounts in the papers," Virginia Osborne said. "They nearly all got something wrong."

"What kinds of things?"

"Bill's age. And one said I came from Georgia. That's absurd."

"I've read some of the papers," Liz said.

"I was out of town when it happened. My father—he did live in Georgia; he'd retired to be near my sister in Atlanta—I was visiting my father. I came back to Houston the next day, and I tried not to read the newspapers. They got so many things wrong."

"I'd be interested in what they got wrong," Liz said, "so that I can get it right."

"My daddy had a heart attack," Mrs. Osborne said, "the week before she got herself killed, and I was in Georgia seeing to him. I wasn't from Georgia."

She looked around the room and pointed through the open doorway into the yellow living room to a dark wood Chinese chest with metal fittings. A white bowl holding yellow tulips was centered on the chest's polished surface. The tulips looked as if they'd died the day before.

"My grandfather was a missionary," Virginia Osborne said. "He brought the chest home with him to Charleston."

"It's beautiful," Liz said.

"Bill never liked it." Mrs. Osborne fell silent again, looking at her hands.

"Then you didn't call him by his nickname? 'Fast,' wasn't it?"

"That foolish name. It was supposed to give the impression that Bill was some kind of wizard, a fast-thinking, fast-talking man. He was in a fast-talking business, but that's as far as it went. They're all little boys at heart. They think if they call one another funny names it covers up their games."

"You had a child?"

"My son lives in Boston. He was away at school when this happened, and we kept him away after."

"Did you ever meet Carolyn Sylvan, Mrs. Osborne?"

"Not what you would call a formal introduction. I noticed her once when I was downtown shopping and I dropped by Bill's office."

"She worked for your husband?"

"Who told you that?" She seemed amused. "She worked in the building. If you call it work."

"I'm sorry," Liz said. "I still don't understand."

"She was just a girl from the country working for some company in the building, and she wanted to get as much as she could as quickly as she could manage."

"Maybe she got more than she bargained for," Liz said.

"People always feel sorry for victims," Mrs. Osborne said. "There's more ways than one of being a victim."

"Were you aware that the affair was going on?"

"After a fashion."

Liz waited for her to expand the statement, but she only stared again at her hands and then the tray, as if the coffeepot were of great interest.

"Maybe you didn't want to know," Liz said. "Sometimes—"

"No. I meant what I said. I knew in a way."

She moved the coffeepot around so that its spout pointed in the same direction as the smaller spout of the creamer, then she placed the sugar bowl between the pot and the creamer. She stood and walked to the window. A ceiling fan was doing a good job, but the humidity imposed itself from the outside and made the room seem close, aided by the earthy odor of the plants. Looking past a camellia and a wandering Jew,

Liz saw a hedge of oleanders outside between the fence and the conservatory, which blocked the view to the street. Looking out, one saw a quarter acre of short Bermuda grass and a pecan tree. No other houses were visible, no evidence of life beyond Virginia Osborne's pasture. The tape machine was still running, recording the silence with hums and breathing of its own.

"Your husband's public-relations business," Liz said. "Who were his major clients? In the late fifties—was that a good time to be in the P.R. business? I mean, did corporations automatically hire public-relations firms as they do now?"

"Bill did all right. He had one or two big clients and the rest were people who wanted their names in the paper or out, for one reason or another."

"And did he do well, Mrs. Osborne? This house—"

"He should have been in real estate. He had sound instincts for a real-estate deal. After the murder, he was ruined. Who would want a public-relations man whom everyone assumes is a murderer who got away? Not that there aren't murderers running around loose, but they've all gone to trial and been acquitted these days. Or they have money." She stood and walked to the window, looking out at the hedge. "He died of heart failure, just like my daddy. Bill tended to fat."

Virginia Osborne would never get fat, Liz thought, nor would she have had a messy affair.

"For whom did Carolyn Sylvan work?" Liz asked. "I went up to the building the other day—"

"I haven't been in the Esperson Building in years. I haven't been downtown in years. She came from the Panhandle, some little town." She turned to face Liz. "Believe me, Miss Gold, I didn't spend a lot of time talking to my husband about Carolyn Sylvan. Even if I'd thought they were having an affair, I would never have mentioned it."

She would have held everything in, Liz thought, and she probably made it easy if not cozy for Osborne to come back to her and stay with her until his death.

"And when did your husband die?"

"Nineteen sixty-three, Miss Gold. You'll find obituary notices in the papers, if you care to."

The tape recorder clicked shut, signaling that one side of the cassette was filled. Virginia Osborne looked startled, then relieved, as if the noise meant the end of the interview. Liz felt tired. Mrs. Osborne hadn't even admitted that her husband and Carolyn Sylvan had had an affair, nor had she denied it. She was practiced at evasion, and Liz didn't feel up to following her through another maze of questions and answers to the possible prize of new information. Liz hated such confessions, hated receiving them or probing for them. Afterward, she was left to decide what was good for the story and what secrets she could leave hidden. She never betrayed a confidence, but even when she didn't reveal what the subject wanted hidden, the people Liz interviewed had resented their stories being told at all. This time, for this story, it didn't seem worth the effort. She would leave the machine off, put away her notebook, and go home.

Virginia Osborne was watching her, as if she might pull out a concealed weapon. "Have I helped you?" she asked, as Liz put the tape recorder into her bag.

"You have. For today. I'd appreciate being able to call on you again, if I need to, Mrs. Osborne. As I said, I only want to get your point of view."

"My point of view, Miss Gold, is that it's over and past. I suppose that makes me a rather dull interviewee."

She gave a social laugh, then breathed in deeply and let out the air in a slow controlled stream.

"Now that you're not working"—she stood and moved toward the bar—"perhaps you'd like a drink."

She went behind the bar and set on top of it a glass pitcher and wand and a stemmed martini glass. She opened the ice bucket and looked inside, then smiled as if the sight pleased her. Liz understood then. She should have had a drink to start with. If Liz had consented to drink, Virginia Osborne would have been able to start or to continue drinking that much sooner.

"Do you have some white wine," Liz asked, "or vermouth?"

"I have some Lillet," Virginia Osborne said. "Someone gave it to me." She pulled an unopened bottle from behind the bar.

"That's lovely," Liz said. "Lots of ice, please."

The ice bucket must have been kept full at all times so there wouldn't be pauses during which Mrs. Osborne could consider if she should have another. She filled the pitcher halfway with ice, then poured in a lot of gin and a little vermouth, swirled the mixture around, and filled the stemmed glass. Then she filled a glass with ice and Lillet and carried both drinks on a small round tray to the glass coffee table.

"There," she said. She took a sip. "I'm surprised anyone's interested in that old story. There have been better ones in Houston."

"It's unsolved," Liz said. "That makes it seem more intriguing."

"Whatever are you doing here?" Virginia Osborne asked.

"What do you mean?"

"What are you doing in Houston? You're not from this part of the world, are you?"

"I'm from New York," Liz said. "I might as well be here as anywhere else. I'm just part of the great migration. Have you always kept horses?"

"I started keeping horses around the time of Miss Sylvan's death." She emptied her glass and went to the bar to refill it. Her posture was very good and her voice was firm, but Liz could feel her relaxing. She was a very disciplined drinker, then, one who made rules and kept them like law. If she didn't like to drink alone, Liz wondered, whom did she corral into joining her of an afternoon? Perhaps she stayed on a horse or clipped the azaleas or polished the silver until it was unbearable or five o'clock.

"I rode when I was a girl," Mrs. Osborne said, when she sat down again. "I've been around horses all my life. When the old Pin Oak stables were functioning, I rode there. Now I have only the two mares and the foal. I don't ride, really, just up and down the bayou. Traffic. The foal goes in two weeks. Her mother too. Do you ride, Miss Gold?"

"I grew up in Manhattan. I was afraid of the cars between the stable and the bridle path, even if the horse wasn't. So I only took a few lessons. I ride when we go to a friend's ranch, but it's transportation, not sport."

"Of course, it's different now," Mrs. Osborne said, "but I used to be in a group who met and rode together. We were in shows. Wives of men who did business together."

"When did you first come to Houston?"

"We came just after the war. Bill was from Chicago originally. We met when he was in the service. He was an officer, and so we met. He was stationed near my home for the duration. I thought he'd be something fine. We got married and drove down to Texas in a black Studebaker. It was hot. It got hotter. The closer we got to Houston, the hotter it got, and I remember thinking in Biloxi that it had to get better. I thought the same in New Orleans. But the first time I saw this city, my heart sank. I never dreamed we'd stay here. I never wanted Bill to do that public-relations work, but he couldn't make a go of anything else. He was meant to work for other people. He did fine if there was someone else calling the shots. I was only twenty when we met.

"Are you married, Miss Gold? It's hard to tell these days, with women not going by their married names."

"Yes," Liz said. "I'm married. I met my husband at college."

There was something in Mrs. Osborne's words—"He was an officer, and so we met"—that made Liz want to join her in the reconstruction of a polite world. There's a war on but people meet and marry; there was a murder and I went riding; there was a war on and we went away from it; I came back alone. And yet Liz disbelieved the other woman's calm and wanted to see beneath it. Another afternoon, she thought.

"My son met his wife when he was at Harvard. They're very active in the Sierra Club," Virginia Osborne said, and gestured toward a large picture book on the table.

I should go to the magazine, Liz thought, just to check it. I can get to the Blue Bird if it isn't too late.

"And your husband?" Mrs. Osborne asked. "Today women don't take their husband's names. I like that. Another Lillet? What does your husband do in Houston."

"He's not in Houston," Liz said. She might have let it go at that, but she stood and walked to the bar, poured herself another Lillet, adding more ice. "My husband died two years ago, before I came to Houston."

"It's an awful thing to lose a man," Mrs. Osborne said. "It's awful when they do it. But there's no stopping other people." She stood and refilled her glass, as if to illustrate her point. The two women walked back to the couch together and resettled, then Mrs. Osborne said, "Bill got himself cut into some terrible deals. He had his own way of finding the most complicated situations, then making them worse. Or finding some that weren't so complicated and making them so. The worst was that murder."

"Not the affair?"

"That was the simplest part," Mrs. Osborne said. "For all of them."

"All of them? You mean Carolyn and your husband?"

"There's always others."

Her words were not so much slurred as slowed. The relaxation and numbness Liz was feeling was probably a tenth of the effect of the gin. She regretted talking about Willy. Why should Virginia Osborne care. Liz put her glass carefully on the table.

"Others? Do you mean there were other men involved?"

"Marriages aren't just between two people, or love. Even the most simple. No. But that's not what I mean." She looked over at the glass pitcher on the bar as if it were a crystal ball, then turned to Liz and smiled. "My husband was a clumsy man, Miss Gold. People who knew him well weren't at all surprised when that girl died, or the child. He had good qualities. I'm not denying him his due. But he was a terrible manager. A worse businessman. He had a talent for messing up the simplest ideas. The most felicitous arrangements."

"Would you call the affair felicitous?"

"Profitable in ways you couldn't imagine," she said, looking Liz in the eye. Liz was shocked at the clarity of Virginia Osborne's gaze; then it clouded over. Mrs. Osborne smiled politely and sighed in a general way, showing that their time together was finished.

As she drove slowly down MacGregor Way, sleepy from the drinks, limp in the sticky air, Liz thought, It looks as foolish to be sneaking around in an adulterous affair as to be the one betrayed. If Virginia Osborne meant it and if Carolyn Sylvan had other lovers, Osborne was a fall guy, for the murder and in the affair. In his widow's estimation, it wasn't unlikely he would be twice a fool.

Liz remembered her father at dinner one night describing a hapless client—a nice fellow but greedy, and his greed made him a perpetual victim.

"It's the difference between a schlemiel and a schlimazel. You know what the difference is, Lizzie?"

She shook her head solemnly, trying to memorize her father's words.

"A schlemiel," he said slowly, building to the punch line, "spills chicken soup on a schlimazel."

She had waited for an argument from her mother—don't oversimplify, don't make fun of people—but her mother had only laughed and asked if Liz was ready for more string beans.

One February morning, Liz woke early and waited by the phone, more awake than asleep, until it was eight and people could be called. Sandy had been dead three weeks, and after the first night Cal had spent his time quietly, with Liz or alone, then took a week off and flew to California, where there were old friends from Houston. He would be back any day now. At the first number Liz called, a woman answered and said she hadn't seen Willy for months. She was indifferent but awake and gave Liz another number. After two more misses, Liz gave up on that chain and dialed Willy's cousin Joey, who gave her a number with an upstate area code.

Willy answered the phone, and it took him a minute to recognize Liz's voice. Then he asked how she was, how the job was; was she still living in the same place?

"I'm calling because I'd like to see you," Liz said.

"Oh? I'm living a pretty quiet life these days," Willy said. "I never come to the city. I can't help you with any hot leads."

"It doesn't have to do with that. I just felt like I wanted to see you. An old friend. We're still married, remember?"

He was silent but she could hear him breathing, considering. Then he said, "It's been a long time since we talked. Can you come this weekend? Do you have a car?"

"I can't come until Saturday and then I have to be back Sunday. But it's okay. I'd rather not drive."

"That's right," Willy said. "I should have remembered. You're afraid of snow."

"It wasn't the snow that got me in Stockholm," she said, angry at herself for tracking him down and for thinking she could go to him. "The snow was the least of it, and you know it."

"Take a bus to Saratoga," he said. "I'll pick you up."

He read off the bus schedule for her, and they settled on the one she'd take. Liz asked, "Can I bring you anything? Wine? City supplies?"

"That won't be necessary," Willy said formally. "We have what we need."

She fell asleep on the Thruway and woke outside of Albany, clutching a pamphlet handed to her in Port Authority. Liz uncrumpled the green paper and read: WHO GAVE YOU THIS PAMPHLET? She remembered the gray hair and sallow skin, the face of a man no older than she. SOMEONE WHO TURNED TO JESUS AND FOUND THE PEACE AND JOY THAT HE PROMISED US.

She set the pamphlet on the floor beneath the seat, carefully, as if it might hurt her if it shifted from where she placed it.

Willy was there to meet her, standing outside the silver diner, shifting from one foot to the other. He was dressed warmly in a bulky down jacket, but he was blowing on his cupped, gloveless hands to give them life. Each year Liz had been with Willy, he lost the expensive Christmas gloves his mother gave him, usually by Lincoln's Birthday.

Liz got off the bus and let the other passengers walk past her before she went up to Willy. They looked at each other for a moment, smiling involuntarily; then he kissed her cheek and bent to pick up her small overnight bag.

"You look great," Willy said. "I like your hair long."

He motioned her across the parking lot to a red van. She followed him slowly, feeling a reluctance to get into another vehicle after the long bus ride. She looked back at the diner and the statue of the rearing horse on the snow-covered roof.

"Wait," she said. "Do they sell papers and magazines in there?"

"What do you need a paper for?"

The question sounded odd to Liz. Willy used to read all the New

York dailies and the Sunday papers from New York and Boston. In Stockholm the greatest discontent he expressed was at the thinness of the *Herald Tribune* and his inability to read Swedish papers.

"I have a story that should have been in yesterday, but they bumped it. I want to see what they did to it."

She turned and walked to the diner. It was dim inside, and the air was filled with smoke and the mixed odors of coffee and tuna fish. The floor was streaked with melted snow and dirt. Liz stood before the magazine display by the cashier and reached first for a *Vogue*, then replaced it; then for a *Harper's Bazaar* and replaced that. She picked up the paper and folded it under her arm, then replaced that on the pile on the counter. The red-lipped blonde on the cover of *Vogue* and the cover lines across her cheek promised Liz a look to summer by, and she turned and went outside again.

She looked over the gray and white parking lot, thinking he had left her, and then saw the van by the road. Willy was waiting inside, hunched forward, his hands resting on the steering wheel.

"Where's the paper?" he asked when she climbed in her side of the van.

"I decided I was addicted to news and I should taper off slowly."

He started the van and pulled them into the mild traffic going into Saratoga.

"I figured you were calling someone," he said.

"Why would I be calling anyone?"

He shrugged. "If you want to make a call, you'd better do it now. It was Ruby's turn to pay the phone bill this month, and she didn't have enough money. So we can't make outgoing calls."

"I don't have anyone to call," Liz said. "I thought you'd left without me."

"Why would I do that?" he asked.

It was after four, and the winter light was failing as they drove through Saratoga Springs. Liz noticed the thoroughbred stables and the elegant track, now shrouded in snow. She'd always wanted to come to Saratoga during August and stay in a swell hotel and understand which horses to bet on. The shadows on the snow-filled fields as they drove away from town looked melancholy, and Liz felt the city dweller's panic at the prospect of the absence of people and traffic and stores. She wished she'd bought one of the magazines and were holding something expensive and silly and unlike the pure, serious landscape they were riding through.

"Well," she said. "Why did you move up here?"

"After jail, I felt burnt out on people and planning. Ruby and I wandered around. We drove across country. Then we drove back east. She kept leaning out the window, saying, 'That place is for sale. No. Too close to the road.' But I didn't think about buying anything until I got here."

Who was Ruby? Liz thought. How long had they been together? Of course Willy would have someone by now.

"Why here?" she asked. "I mean, why come back east at all?"

"We're from here," he said. "Why would we live anywhere else? And anyway—we didn't find a place. Ruby knew Dick from a long time ago. He was in Vietnam and came back a mess, stayed with his mother for about a year not doing much of anything. Then he began organizing in Boston. He went home again last summer and we visited him. His family doesn't have money, but their names are on all the streams and hollows and roads."

"A pedigree person," Liz said. "You used to dislike those people."

"He doesn't trade off it," Willy said. "It's just interesting."

He lapsed into silent driving, and she regretted she'd spoken. They had never done anything together since their early days at college that sounded as easy or companionable as his trip west with Ruby. What she remembered about her time with him was what she felt now, herself outside a window, nose pressed to the glass, looking in on Willy.

"So you came to visit Dick." She prompted him.

"He was staying with his sister by then. She's in the next farm over from ours. Then the old man who owned our place decided he'd give it up. He sold us the farm and his furniture. Some of it. He moved to an old people's home in Springfield. That was just October. So we couldn't do much, just plow up the garden before the first frost. Spread manure. Get the place sealed up for winter."

"Manure," she said and laughed. "And politics, Willy? What are you doing?"

"You ask that as if you thought I'd lost my faith. Something will come up in time, and I'll get up and out and do something about it. But the war's over for now. I'll just tend my garden."

Since she'd known him, he'd been involved, first in the civil rights movement and then in the antiwar movement, and it was odd to contemplate Willy without a political focus. He painted a picture of himself from the Lifestyle page, former activist opts for quiet. Liz leaned away from Willy and felt the chill through the window glass.

"How's the job," Willy asked. "Still telling the people where they can find a croissant at midnight?"

"You sound like my parents," she said sadly. "They think I'd be better off doing hard news. They think I'm silly. Selfish. But the truth is, Willy, I feel guilty—I feel morally obligated to feel guilty—but I don't want to do much else. I'll never get a Pulitzer Prize, and I won't save the world. But I'm not bad at what I do. I don't hurt anybody."

The van traveled along a high flat road, and then the hills began. Though it was early evening, it was dark enough to see the lights glowing inside the farmhouses as they drove past them, and the houses looked smug and warm against the still mounds of snow.

"Ruby's sister is still underground," Willy said. "So when we lived in Boston they bugged the phone and read the mail, and they hassled her at work. She was working at a communal health-food store where they really took their tofu to heart."

"What do you mean," Liz said, feeling like a straight man, dreading what was coming as if the joke he was to tell would reflect badly on her.

"One clique firebombed another clique to settle a big theoretical dispute right after Ruby left. Goodbye health-food store. Anyway, Ruby has a niece who has cerebral palsy. Her parents were taking care of the kid, but they don't have any money and they work at jobs all day. So the FBI offered to put the kid in a special school where she could learn a few things, where she'd get the best care, if Ruby would turn her sister in."

"I know. I know they do things like that. Where's the child now?"

"I pay for the school," Willy said, and he grinned. "They were right. It's a very good school. My parents couldn't block the money my grandfather left me, so I be fat. I bought the place and keep Sarah in school. We're going to do a lot in the spring. Plant herbs and vegetables. We read a lot of garden books."

"How do Dick and Ruby make a living?" She was always interested in the answer to that question and always asked it, just as she looked in the medicine cabinets of people she was interviewing. She never reported what she found, and she drew the line at searching drawers.

"I support Ruby mostly. She does substitute teaching now and then. Dick sells a little dope. Picks up carpentry work when it's around. We always keep the house clean because of Ruby's sister."

Liz wondered if she'd changed as much as Willy had in appearance. His features had always looked too large for his slender bony face, but something, age or experience, had made peace and given him a rougher and handsomer look. She couldn't see his old face inside the new, blander mask. In a few years, she thought, she wouldn't recognize him if they met in the street.

"It must be nice to live with people," she said, and was surprised at the wistfulness she heard in her voice. "Sometimes a week goes by without anyone touching me. I don't mean sex, just touching. I have one good friend. He's the most companionable person I've ever known. I never get bored or restless with Cal."

She was trying to get Willy to ask her sympathetic questions or to respond to her like the old friend she'd said she wanted to visit, and she felt absurd, as if she were begging him to recall the name of a person he'd met once at a party years before in another city and whom he could recall only a portion of—the curve of a neck, the sound of a laugh.

"Who is he," Willy asked, "anyone I know?"

"No. He's a Texan. From Houston. He lives in my building."

"And why isn't he touching you? Sounds like a setup to me."

"We're not lovers," Liz said. She hated saying that Cal was homosexual. She'd been brought up to believe that it was wrong to explain away a person's complications by a crude fact of religion or race, although in this instance a fact would have turned the trick. "There are boundaries in the relationship. In every relationship. But since Stockholm, the thing is, Willy—no one expects anything of me. There's no one waiting for me, no one I can let down or make happy. And don't say it's what I wanted."

"You always had so many friends," Willy said.

"I do have friends," she agreed. "And living in the same neighborhood I grew up in, I can't walk down Broadway without bumping into someone from camp or sixth grade. I even know the bag ladies."

They rode slowly through a small town—she saw an Agway feed store, a few gas stations, a bar, the Episcopal church, and the Ford dealership—and then they passed under a railroad bridge, out of town, and up a steep, sharply curving hill. Willy turned suddenly to the right and they coasted downhill, then on a flat road along a river.

"The Battenkill," Willy said.

"Good for trout fishing, isn't it?"

"I don't know what to say," Willy said. "I don't know how to help you."

"That's all right. You're afraid I want something from you, aren't you?" She tried to speak with a neutrality she didn't feel.

"I let you come here, didn't I? I didn't have to do that."

She was surprised that she felt hot tears coming, warming her eyes.

Willy turned up a hill that rose to their right and said, "We'll be at the house in a few minutes. The others are there. We can talk more later. Or tomorrow."

"I have to be on a bus at noon," Liz said.

Willy pulled into a driveway and stopped the van. The front of the white house was cupped by a curved Victorian porch, all fretwork and coziness. On the porch, a wooden rocker was covered with snow that had blown up the hill. The rocker moved slightly in the wind. They were very high up; Liz could see out over an emptiness that must have been a valley, the darkness broken only by a few lights. At the end of the darkness, also high up, she saw a radio tower and a group of lights that could have been a town. On the driveway ahead of them were a black VW Bug and a red pickup truck with a wooden cap.

Liz put her hand on Willy's arm to stop him from getting out of the van immediately.

"I never thanked you for setting me up with those people," she said. "And I never got to tell you—"

"It's cold, Liz. We can talk in the house."

"I never got to tell you how much I disliked them, Willy. Or how it scared me that you were involved with them."

"I wasn't involved. I was on a committee that chose me as a go-between because I said I knew you. It could have been anyone with a contact."

"I'm glad you're out of it," Liz said. "I didn't like them. I don't know who they think they are or why people should look up to them. I didn't let this into the story. I tried not to. I let them speak for themselves. But I'm glad it didn't have anything to do with you, past or present."

Willy looked at Liz. Their eyes met and stayed together for a moment. Then Willy nodded and said, "Okay. Now we'd better go inside."

The first room looked empty until Liz noticed a coatrack draped with jackets, sweaters, hats, and mittens and a large basket filled with boots. The wooden floor had been painted at different times and a mustard-colored rectangle at the center of the room, surrounded by a dark blue border, testified to this. Rag rugs were scattered around the basket to absorb melting snow. Liz put her overnight bag on one of the rugs and unzipped it, looking for the oxford shoes she'd packed that morning. As she crouched by her bag, setting aside her quilted soap bag, her flannel nightgown, an extra shirt and sweater, Willy took off his down jacket and hung it on the rack, then started to take off his boots. Liz heard footsteps at the door that opened into the house, and looked up.

Ruby stood in the doorway. She was shorter than Liz. Her hair was a peculiar shade of henna red, showing brown at the roots, and it was cropped like Willy's, short and uneven. Her eyes looked unnaturally blue. Contact lenses, Liz thought.

"You're Liz," Ruby announced. Her voice was low and grating. Her accent had the echo of New York in it, possibly the Bronx. She was wearing old jeans, steel-tipped boots, a down vest, an Aran sweater.

"Yes," Liz said. "Thanks for your hospitality. It was nice of you to have me."

"I've been curious to meet you," Ruby said. "And it's a long winter."

She looked at Willy, who now looked domestic and mild in sheepskin slippers he'd taken from the basket and a down vest he'd found on the rack. It was cool in the house, and Liz reached for her extra sweater.

"The walls," she said. "What happened?"

The wallpaper looked as if it had been unsystematically ripped away from the plaster wall, leaving streaks of paper—half a magnolia blossom, a green leaf torn at the stem.

"There was an accident with the furnace," Willy said. "We were in Connecticut and Dick didn't come home when he thought he would. There was a storm and a power out. The furnace didn't come back on and the pipes froze. Then burst. It was a sauna in here."

"We were thinking about new wallpaper anyway," Ruby said. "Have you ever peeled wallpaper? It makes you think you've lost your mind. How about some coffee? Dinner's going to be a while."

The kitchen was a large white room with windows all along one wall and five doors along the opposite wall. The knobs and hinges of the cabinets and doors had been touched with shiny red paint. A small green stove was the source of the intense dry heat in the room. The appliances looked new. The kitchen table and chairs were old and worn, an assortment of Windsor and ladderback chairs, some painted, some shellacked, some with small cushions, others bare.

Ruby moved between the stove and refrigerator, then turned to the table where Liz and Willy were sitting and carried a tray with hot coffee, cups, sugar, and milk to them. She waved her hand to indicate that Liz should pour for herself. The aroma of strong coffee filled the room, and Liz pressed her fingers around the thick brown cup, letting her fingers warm. She almost imagined that this was an ordinary country weekend during which she would at first wonder why she didn't live always in the country, and at the end wonder how she'd stood it so long in the stillness.

"Willy doesn't have any pictures of you," Ruby said. "So I've always wondered what you look like."

"I've probably changed in nine years," Liz said. "Where did you two meet?" She immediately regretted this direct question and said, "You don't look like a Ruby to me."

"What do I look like?"

"Charlotte. Sharon."

"Well, call me Ruby. It's my birthstone."

One of the five doors was half glass and was, Liz could see, a door to the outside. The next was blocked by a refrigerator, and the third bore a handwritten sign: DO NOT FALL DOWN STAIRS.

"What does that mean?" Liz asked.

"That's the dungeon," Ruby said, and she laughed. She was very pretty; Liz could see it now. When she smiled, her coloring made sense and the indigo eyes looked warm. "You don't think we're making bombs down there, do you?"

"I hadn't thought of it," Liz said. "If you are, I hope you know what you're doing."

There was another deeper silence in the kitchen now, and Liz wondered if she'd taken a joke seriously and betrayed she was outside such jokes. She felt like a sullen adult among laughing children. Willy was frowning at Ruby, warning her off, but he was smiling.

"You see," Ruby said, touching the corners of her eyes as if she were moved to tears, "I told you we needed someone here from the outside world. We get so steady here, so all-American, I wonder sometimes if we aren't dead already."

"It is quiet," Liz said. "I feel as if I've been carrying a transistor to my ear and someone shut it off."

She heard a sound behind her, turned, and saw the fourth door opening. She moved her chair away from the door, though it wasn't really blocking the path, and looked up to see a man in his late twenties coming down the stairs. He was short and looked muscular. He was tanned dark the way men get when they work outdoors year round. He wore his black hair long, tied back neatly in a ponytail. There was one small gold loop threaded through the lobe of his left ear. With his long hair and tan skin, Liz thought he must be an ambassador from warmer places, but his eyes looked cold to her, so dark that pupil and iris were one. They were hard and glittering eyes, as if made of glass.

He sat at the table next to Liz without a word, and Ruby stood to bring another cup for him and to refill the kettle with water.

"This is Liz," Ruby said at the stove. "And Dick—Liz."

"Hi," Liz said.

"You got here," he said. His voice was smaller than she would have imagined, and the words sounded begrudging. He spoke as people farther west in New York State do, the beginnings of the midwestern twist to his words.

"Me and Greyhound. Right on time."

"No lunatics? There was a crazy guy last time I took the bus."

"I slept a lot," she said.

"You would have noticed," he said.

"Dick had a bad ride up last time he went to New York," Willy said. "He may never leave here again."

He smiled at Dick as though he were revealing an endearing trait, and Dick looked up to meet his eyes. For an instant Liz thought he was angry with Willy, but he smiled.

"Willy tells me you're from here," Liz said. "He said your family came straight over on the *Mayflower.*"

"Not quite," Dick said. "My dad was Polish, worked in the mines in Pennsylvania. He brings down my social standing a peg or two around here."

Ruby returned to the table with a pot of tea. Its herbal sweetness fought with the now stale aroma of the coffee. Liz felt a surge of acidity in her stomach.

"Oh, I forgot," she said. "I brought something for you." She reached into her pocketbook, which she'd hooked to the back of her chair, and brought out a small paper bag. "It's black cherry tea," she said, handing it to Willy. "I had it once, and it's delicious."

"Caffeine?" Dick asked. He picked up the package and opened it, waving his hand over the open bag to bring the smell to his nose.

"Excuse me?"

"Does it have any caffeine in it?"

"It's only dried black cherries. Why would it have caffeine?"

"But you don't know," Dick said. "You don't know for sure," and he tossed the small package on the table.

"I didn't think to ask," she said. "Black cherries . . ." She looked at Ruby and Willy, who were sipping coffee, eyes down. Her gift remained untouched on the table. "Remember strawberry soup, Willy?"

He looked up at her, and his eyes brightened for a moment. "We never fixed any, as I remember. We ate a lot of sardines."

"I once tried to make a sardine and rice casserole," Liz said. "Pretty disgusting."

Ruby looked at her, poker-faced, and said, "That's right. You were with Willy in Sweden."

"For a little while," Liz said, thinking of Cal's remark about deserting a deserter. At Arlanda Airport when she said goodbye to Willy, she thought she would never see him again in America.

"Sorry about the cherries," Dick said, and she looked at him, surprised. "It's the moon. It's in the worst possible position now for me. Another degree one way or the other and I'll fall over from everything being so wrong."

"I'm sorry," Liz said. "That's a delicate position to be in."

"It doesn't matter," Dick said. "It changes all the time."

She looked at Willy, who'd always scorned astrology, and he said, "Would you like to see your room, Liz?"

"No rush."

"It's no trouble," Willy said politely, as if she were a maiden aunt come to call. "If you've finished your coffee."

Willy led her through a chilly dining room (one wall was patterned in log cabins and maple trees, the rest bare plaster) to a narrow hallway and up a flight of shellacked wooden stairs. Halfway up the staircase was a window with a view down the long hill to a wooded area and beyond to the line of lights and the radio tower. Willy took her past two closed doors and opened a door into a small blue room furnished with a scrollwork iron single bed painted hot pink and covered by a patchwork quilt, blue sheets, and lofty pillows. On the quilt was a pattern of little girls watering flowers from watering cans as big as themselves.

"It's like a child's room," she said, thinking of Ruby's niece and her missing mother.

"There's more blankets in the chest. You'll probably need them tonight." It was colder upstairs, and the room smelled musty.

"Have your parents visited?" she asked, sitting on the bed, feeling its coldness sink into her.

"When they get back from Africa they'll visit."

"What are they doing in Africa?"

"She always wanted to go there." He walked to the window and pulled back the white lace curtain, revealing the window frozen into a lacy pattern of ice.

Liz looked down at one of the little girls on the quilt, a pink-sprigged child, and asked, "Should we talk about a divorce, Willy?"

"Is that why you wanted to come here?" He shifted from one foot to the other, back and forth in a slow dance step.

"No. I could have written you a letter. I wanted to see you. I felt adrift. My friend Cal. The one I told you about in the van. A friend of his was killed by a burglar, and it scared me. It made me want to see you again."

"Before we die," and Willy laughed.

"I guess that was it. I didn't think it through. But it made me feel very lonely, this guy getting killed. I don't know why."

Liz rose and walked to the window. Close up to Willy, she could smell a faintly perfumed odor, a deodorant or a fragrant oil. She wanted him to hold her and to tell her it was coming out all right, better in some ways than they'd ever expected. He stood looking at the white landscape inches from his face.

"It made me feel as if we were all people standing in a big open white space," Liz said, the words coming now from dreams she'd had in the weeks past that had gone unrecorded and unremembered. "And we can look at each other and lean toward each other so that our shadows might intersect. But we never touch and we never move from our spots."

"We probably should get a divorce, Liz. Tell Joey when you get back to New York. He takes care of things for me."

She looked at Willy and their eyes met. She'd get nothing from Willy, she thought, and had forfeited all right to expect anything.

"I always thought grown-ups were people who were resigned," she said. "People who could accept the worst and not piss or moan about it."

"And what does that make us?" Willy smiled at Liz fondly, as if she were a bright child who'd stumbled on an ancient and wise maxim.

"Not grown-ups yet," she said. "Speaking for myself. I'm not there yet."

Before dinner, Liz went to the bathroom. She washed her face with cold water when the hot didn't come on, and dried her face on a boardlike towel that must have dried outside on a line. An October issue of *Woman's Day* lay face down on the floor, its surface puckered by water stains. Liz leafed through the magazine, judging the layout, skimming over what to do with tuna, how to arrange food on an autumnal table, how to hem napkins on your own zigzag machine and preserve autumn's bright leaves in glycerine. There was a paper covering available that looked like cloth, and a sweater that could be crocheted for $6.98. She replaced the magazine on the floor and inspected herself in the mirror. She looked as drained as Willy, and she wondered if it was her presence dragging on him, making him seem older and quieter and beaten, or if jail and exile had accomplished that, and she was only the icing on the cake. He was probably beyond caring about her either way, and she was left to remember her half of their mutual experience alone. No one else would want to hear about it, she thought; why should they?

The dining room was cold, and Liz put on her extra sweater again.

"You're going to wear that thing out," Dick said, "putting it on, taking it off."

They sat around a wooden table that someone had started to strip. Flecks of white paint clung in the indentations and bruises on the wooden surface.

They passed their plates to Ruby, who filled them with a venison chop, a potato, a broiled tomato, and one large spoonful of peas and onions. She studied each plate carefully before passing it back, and she made the plates look like the ones in the magazine. It was Ruby's magazine, Liz realized. How old was Ruby, she wondered, and how strange to be living here with these two men, worrying about how the food looked on the plate.

Liz cut into the meat and saw that it wasn't done. In the center, there was a line of dead raw meat. There was no fat on the chop, only lean meat that tasted dense as fudge.

"I've never had venison before," Liz said. "Where do you get it around here."

"Dick got the buck," Ruby said. "We dressed it together."

"Was it hard to kill?" Liz asked.

"I tried during bow and arrow season," Dick said, "and I didn't have any luck. I sat in those woods down the hill for days." He cut his meat and chewed slowly and methodically. Willy, though silent, seemed distracted to Liz. Dick had the countryman's ability to absorb silence undisturbed. "I got this buck we're eating here at my mom's house. I was helping with the dishes one day. He was standing in the field, eating stumps of corn. We brought in the corn weeks ago."

"And then what?" Liz asked.

"I grabbed my dad's rifle and ran out and shot it. Then I had too much meat for our freezer and I gave most of it away." He looked at Liz's plate. "Don't you like it?"

"I like it fine," she apologized. "I just can't finish it. It's really rich. I usually only eat chicken or veal."

"Don't get much veal around here," he said.

Liz watched Willy eating. He had always been fussy about whether meat was done just so and which vegetables he'd eat, and he wouldn't touch hamburgers from certain chains. He put a piece of meat in his mouth and chewed slowly over and over, as methodically as if he were counting the chews. Then he'd swallow and rotate to the next food—potato, tomato, peas—and then he repeated the round. Once she saw him gazing at the plate as if he couldn't remember the next move.

After dinner, Ruby said they should go for a walk.

"It's a full moon," she said. "It's so light you can read a newspaper by the moon."

Liz borrowed a wool hat and mittens from Ruby. They walked past the cars down the drive to the icy road. The sky was clear and black with a great white moon beaming a cold piercing light on the white fields and the ribbon of black road. They walked down the long steep hill. Liz almost fell at one point but Dick steadied her. She felt the strength of his hand through her sweaters and jacket. At the woods, they stopped and Dick pointed his arm to the center of a thin bare-treed grove.

"That's where I was sitting with my bow and arrow," he said. "There's an old truck in there, you can just barely see it. It's got no engine or guts, just a shell. It sits in a circle of trees. Whoever got it in there isn't going to get it out ever."

"Like an enchanted princess," Liz said.

"Or like an old wreck of a truck someone dumped," Ruby said. "I found the hind end of a deer there once. I guess the people just wanted the antlers for their wall."

They turned and started the climb back up to the house, which looked festive lit up against the sky.

"If I'd stayed hunting much longer," Dick said, "that's what would have happened to me."

"You'd have been cut in half?" Liz asked.

"No," he said. "Like the truck. I could hear the trees growing around me while I sat on that rock."

"It must have been miserable," Liz said. She couldn't imagine going hunting at all, for misery or pleasure or food.

"I like hunting," Dick said. "I go every year because it makes me sit still in the woods. I could almost think I was part of the rock."

"Real country virtue," Willy said.

"I'm taking you hunting next year, Willy boy," Dick said. "Target practice all summer and then just as soon as the season opens—maybe sooner."

In bed, shivering in her clothes under four thin blankets that were damp with cold, Liz thought the warmth would leave her body and be distributed onto the sheets and mattress and that she would die. She wondered why Willy had let her come. She hadn't disturbed anything. There was nothing to disturb but a rural torpor and a touchy native. Willy lived as though he were serving time. Maybe the years in Sweden and the months in jail, the years since he'd done such a simple act and burned his draft card, had eaten his youth and left him passive and silent. It seemed preposterous that she'd come to him for help.

She heard footsteps outside her door and a scratching that could have been a mouse or a signal. She lay still, breathing evenly. It could have been Willy or Dick. It could have been Ruby. It was nothing, she thought, and before she heard the footsteps leaving, she was asleep.

Her room faced east and the sun, rising at seven, shone into her face. She turned and covered her head with the mound of blankets and quilts, and one dream later looked at her watch. It was eight, and the bus left at noon. It would take an hour to get to Saratoga. She would be safe if she went downstairs in another hour, sat around with them, and then left. She smelled bacon and coffee and heard the low murmur of voices downstairs, but it wasn't until nine, as she'd resolved, that she got out of bed and put on her oxfords. She could hear a scraping noise outside her window and looked down over the driveway to see Dick and Willy shoveling snow. The wind in the night had blown drifts against the three vehicles, but the sun had melted the ice on the glass and she remembered that in the city the snow was mostly gone. She assembled her bag and carried it down the stairs with her. Ruby was at the kitchen stove, dressed again in boots, jeans, and vest, but this morning she wore a fuzzy pink wool sweater that made her hair look chic and frivolous rather than a mistake.

"They'll have the driveway clear soon," Ruby said. "Do you want some tea?"

"Do you have anything with caffeine in it?"

"The jury's still out on your black cherry tea," Ruby said. "And we just ran out of coffee. There's some instant somewhere."

"I'll take it," Liz said. "I'm not proud."

The morning sky was unbroken as the night sky had been and looked as purely cold. She thought about Ruby's sister underground and wondered if they kept in touch.

"It's a long winter, isn't it?" Liz asked. She accepted the cup Ruby handed her, and the taste even of rehydrated coffee made Liz relax for a moment and feel as expansive as if she'd had a glass of wine. "You should come visit me in the city. There's room for you and Willy. I have a friend in the building, and when we have guests—"

"We never go to the city," Ruby said. "In fact—" She stopped speaking and looked at Liz, who felt she was being measured and filed away. "If we can get passports, we're leaving the country in the spring. I hear there's warmer places."

"It must be nice to be so free," Liz said politely, but by free she meant in possession of Willy's money. "Why is it hard to get passports?"

"Oh, one thing and another," Ruby said. She turned her back to Liz and then faced her again. Liz had the feeling she'd been laughing at her. "Willy's record. My record."

"Dick's record," Liz said.

"Oh, Dick's one of those people who never get caught. You know people like that, don't you?"

"I suppose. I don't know. Everyone gets caught sooner or later."

"You just believe the old myths about the police. Or do you mean he'll feel remorse? Not for anything he's done so far. Not that I know of."

"It's been generous of you to have me here," Liz said.

"That's okay. I didn't have anything to do with it. Why did you want to come? Reunion with Willy?"

"No. I just wanted to talk. About personal things."

"That was tough, your friend's friend getting killed by accident." Liz looked at Ruby, searching for sarcasm in her bland expression. "Willy told you?"

"Willy tells me everything," Ruby said. "As far as I know."

Liz looked at the clock on the wall and asked, "Do you think the drive to Saratoga will take longer than an hour? I have to get back to the city."

"Don't worry. They'll be finished on the driveway in a minute. You don't think we want to keep you here, do you?"

"No," Liz said. "I don't suppose you do."

Ruby went outside to see how Dick and Willy were doing, and Liz stood up when she left the room, suddenly curious. The three were so smug, as if they had a secret that they were keeping so well it was bursting. She went into the dining room and opened the closet door. It was a deep closet, reaching back beneath the staircase. She saw some mounds of clothing, possibly bedspreads, and three rifles leaning against the side of the closet. The closet smelled of an acrid oil, and Liz closed the door quickly, looking behind her to see if anyone had caught her. She returned to the kitchen.

Dick and Ruby stood on the porch and waved goodbye. Liz looked at them and gave a flap of her hand. Once they were around the curve in the road, she asked Willy, "Why do you let Dick live with you?"

"Ruby and I thought it would be better for the relationship not to live just the two of us. She and Dick are old pals. They used to go out."

"He doesn't strike me as the buffer type," Liz said. "Like having a time bomb living with you."

Willy laughed. "Dick minds his own business."

Liz looked out the van window and became absorbed in the passing spectacle of snow piled on tree limbs, snow on the hills, mounds of snow by the roadside, houses covered in snow, and cows standing in snow, their plumed breath hanging for an instant in the blue air before disappearing. She looked over at Willy, trying to find a common memory that would make him even for a moment what he'd been when she first knew him—defiant, denying borders and boundaries. He'd once looked like a man who threw rocks at the sky, not to stop the sun or bring the rain but for the pleasure of defiance. Yet she'd always wanted him to slow down and even might have stayed with him in Sweden if he'd been willing to promise her they would stay there; there they would live. He'd said it was only temporary, just exile, and she'd thought the exile would become their lives. And now, like a joke, he was settled more than she, living in a house he owned, on land that was his, planning on hunting deer in the faraway autumn. Probably all country people had guns, she thought. What did she know about it?

At the bus station, Willy parked by the diner and waited in the van while Liz went inside and bought her ticket, a *Vogue, The New York Times,* and a Snickers bar. She walked around to Willy's side of the van, her bag weighing down her shoulder, her purchases clutched under her arm.

"Goodbye," she said. "Thanks for letting me visit. I'll call Joey on Monday and we'll get it settled." She wondered if she'd ever see Willy again. She felt there was something she ought to have said to settle the past between them, to inspire a conversation in which she would explain and he would understand why events turned out as they did. She felt afraid for Willy's future and for an instant wanted to beg him to leave those two and the cold peeling house and come back to New York with her. She imagined his drive back to the house, the night with Ruby and Dick and the quiet of the countryside around him. "Anytime you want to stay with me in New York, I have room. I'd do anything for you, you know that," though this wasn't strictly true.

"I'm fine," Willy said. "You don't have to do anything for me."

"Thank Ruby for me again. She did all the cooking. I don't want to do anything in particular. Just to let you know I'm there."

"I've known that all along," he said. "Here's your bus. Bye. I hope things cheer up for you in the city."

Liz was almost at the door of the bus, waiting behind five other people in an unorganized line, bundles and suitcases and skis to be loaded, when she heard Willy call her name. She turned and saw him driving the van slowly toward her, and Liz stepped out of the crowd of travelers to meet him.

"Liz," he said when he'd pulled up beside her. "I meant to tell you. I'm really glad we're getting divorced. This way—maybe sometime we'll be friends again."

Liz fell asleep as soon as the bus cleared Saratoga and woke as it pulled into Albany forty minutes later. She waited on the bus during the rest stop before the run to New York. She skimmed the paper and turned automatically to the women's page. There had been no revolutions overnight, not on the women's page. The Snickers bar rested on the fashion magazine beside her and obscured a portion of the model's creamy smiling face.

The greater part of the Thruway was unbroken road. An occasional billboard or restaurant intruded on the landscape. From the height of the bus, other cars looked insignificant. Liz closed her eyes and tried to sleep, but she thought too hard and too sequentially about what she had to do when she got back to the city. Cal might be home. Maybe they'd have dinner. She had lied to Willy and Ruby, as if they'd care, pretending she had to get back. She imagined the peace she would find in her apartment and the first few minutes—the only ones she dreaded—of returning to the quiet of an unshared home and putting away the dishes she'd washed on Friday night and Saturday morning, unpacking her suitcase, resuming her life.

She tried to picture her dresser at home. The silver mirror, stuck in one corner a picture of herself and Cal before the Christmas tree in Rockefeller Center. A yellow ceramic box made to look like basket-weave, containing hairpins and buttons. Her jewelry was in a maroon leather box, and Liz imagined being inside the box, next to her pearl earrings. She thought of her Nova, her mother's gift, parked in the garage below her building, usually behind other tenants' Plymouths and Lincolns and Porsches. Then the car was crushed and sat lopsided and dented beyond repair. The top of the leather box fell off and the earrings rolled away and fell over the edge of the dresser, disappearing into cracks on the parquet floor, swallowed by ancient dust.

Horror movies come to life, she thought. Objects and people have a life of their own, witnessed by others only in passing. Willy never wanted to see her again. He had made sure to present himself as another person, no longer one whom she'd loved but one in a zombie life with strange companions and a secret schedule. He had never said he'd forgiven her or written her off for leaving him in Sweden. She had always reasoned that the marriage had died before she left; that was why she could leave, after all. It had been a successful weekend from Willy's point of view. She would never try to see him again and she doubted she ever would, accidentally or with intent.

Once she was in her car and outside Virginia Osborne's gate, Liz decided to go straight back to her apartment. She stopped along Almeda at a light and watched two men who seemed at first to be repairing an Olds Cutlass just like David's. They were stripping it, she realized as she drove away. She drove up Montrose, past white-brick two-story apartment houses with drab curtains flopping out the geometric thirties windows, past the Mecom fountain and the traffic circle—the two upside-down water flowers of the fountain flowing as steadily as the traffic—and past the white Warwick Hotel with its Mercedeses and Cadillacs lined up neatly outside the entrance. At night the blue neon sign on top of the hotel could be seen all over town—WARWICK THE WARWICK.

When Liz got upstairs to her apartment, the phone was ringing and she fumbled with the keys, hoping she would catch the phone before it stopped.

"Where have you been?" David asked. "I've been calling all day."

"Earning my living. I was interviewing the widow Osborne."

"Is she still alive?"

"She didn't strike me as the type to throw herself on her husband's funeral pyre," Liz said. "There may be more to this than meets the eye."

"There may be less," David said. "A married man kills his mistress when she gets too demanding . . ."

"There's no evidence so far that she got demanding, excessively or otherwise. I don't even know that she was his mistress."

"Oh, come on," David said. "You don't have to invent the wheel every time you take a drive. He never denied it."

"Well, Carolyn Sylvan never got a chance to defend her honor. Mrs. Osborne implied something funny was going on, funnier than you'd think. Anyway—when are you coming home?"

"I was wondering," David said. He sounded nervous to Liz and more tense than usual, but being away and in New York at a series of meetings with a cranky foundation board seemed reason enough to her for nervousness. "Why don't you fly up here tomorrow? We can spend the weekend in the real Walden."

"But it's a suburb."

"So's our Walden. It's just a more spacious suburb. Or we'll go to Boston or to Martha's Vineyard. I've never been there. A nice empty weekend."

"Do you mean it?" she asked. She leafed through the pile of tickets and found one to Boston. She could go there tonight and wander around on her own until David arrived from New York. She'd been in Boston only a few times. Willy had burned his draft card there and had been arrested at a rally. She'd traveled to Cambridge once to interview a Harvard professor.

"Don't think about it," David said. "Don't brood on it. Yes or no."

"We've never been in the east together," she said. She hadn't been back since she'd driven down in May, all alone, her car packed with what she'd decided to keep. "Is it cold?"

"You'd need a coat," he said.

He was waiting for her reply, being patient and not pushing, hoping she'd say yes. But instead of seeing them together at a cold winter beach, she saw herself in the Nova driving south past red earth and pine trees, dead armadillos by the side of the road in Mississippi, past flatland with clusters of plain buildings and flashy neon signs, along the Gulf that looked nothing like the blue Atlantic she'd left. She hadn't liked traveling alone for so long, hadn't been sure she liked the sumpy world she'd found or the glances in restaurants and gas stations at the sound of her northern voice. She didn't think then of what she'd left behind or of what was ahead in Houston. The world was the road in front of her, good or bad, and if bad she knew she would soon be out of it.

"I'm sorry," she said. "I can't do it. I don't want to go back east fast just like that. And anyway, Cal's coming this weekend."

"If you don't want to come," David said, "or if you're still jerking yourself around thinking I'm with someone else up here, fine. I'll be happy to come home, though I might have to get back up here some-time next week. But don't make up feeble excuses. Cal has great inner resources. He can spend a weekend without us. When did you invite him?"

"I don't know. Yesterday. The day before. When he gave me the story."

"Liz, ask me next time. I like Cal fine. But ask me."

"You're right. I'm sorry. I shouldn't have done that. Now it sounds tempting. The beach?"

"Skip it," David said. "Don't start worrying about this."

She held tight to the phone receiver, listening to the air ebb and flow between them. Her ear hurt from pressing the receiver close to her head to catch what David might start to say, to try to sense how he might be looking and feeling.

"I'd rather never suggest anything to you than to think you'd feel diminished by the offer, or by refusing. Fair's fair," he said. "I've got to go now. I love you. I'll see you in a little bit. Tomorrow night. Will you be home?"

"I'll be home waiting for you," she said. "Come back to Houston and I'll make some offers . . ." but after they'd hung up, she sat by the phone, wondering if she'd made a mistake.

When the phone rang again, she considered letting it go. If she went quickly, she could get the weekend food-gathering over with and be free all tomorrow. It had started raining during David's call, and the rain was coming down furiously. She could stay in, she could hide.

"Great," Cal said. "You're there. Two things."

The sound of Cal's voice gave her new energy. He sounded excited and in a hurry.

"Just two?"

"There's someone I want you to meet, Liz. So can you get over to the magazine now? Fast. Before he goes."

Before she left the apartment, Liz ran her fingers through her short hair, trying to slick it down. At a red light on Alabama, she put on lip gloss by feel, then checked her aim in the rearview mirror. Then she was at the magazine.

"Go right in," Cheryl said. "It's going to be great." She snapped fingers on both hands and waved her hands around her head. "We've been saved."

"Is it Santa Claus with Cal?" Liz asked as she climbed the stairs, but Cheryl was busy with the phone and didn't answer.

She knocked on Cal's office door and it was opened by a stranger, a man of medium height who looked too muscled to be comfortable in the narrow sports jacket he wore. He was built like a fighter, with broad shoulders and chest, and a face that had been revised since its beginning. He was dressed in gray with a silver tie. Past him, standing at the window, looking out at the last of the rain and the traffic on the freeway were Cal and another stranger.

He was about Liz's age and had pale hair and a broad open face and clear glasses that had slipped halfway down a slender nose. His mouth was red, like a child's, and he wore colors that were soft and sweet—a sand-colored jacket, a plum shirt, cloud-gray pants. As she moved across the room, Liz saw that his skin was as smooth as the skin of a much younger man or a child. He might have looked this way always and perhaps would never change, looking neither old nor young.

"Liz. Honey," Cal said. "This is Hunter Corrigan." Cal was smiling broadly as he did when he was very excited or happy, as if he'd been waiting to introduce Liz and Hunter for a long time.

"Hello," Liz said, and she took the hand he offered.

"One of our principal assets," Hunter said. "Cal's been telling me all about you."

His voice was light and uncertain, a tenor who would be asked to mouth the words. He had no real accent or intonation but that of an American, a Six O'Clock News talker. His eyes were pale, a celadon green with flecks of gold. He took Liz's hand and held it. On his left pinky, he wore a band of three kinds of gold, twisted together. His skin was warm and dry.

"I hope I'm an asset," she said. "Are we out of the woods now?"

"I'm prepared to support the magazine," Hunter said. "As I've been doing all along. And more. I hope we'll all work hard on it together."

"I always think having a net helps you work," Cal said. "We can do more of the stories we've wanted to do but didn't have the wherewithal. And Mary Alice is working on a new layout for slick paper. Color spreads, Liz."

The man in gray at the door cleared his throat and said, "Time to get it, if you want to make the plane. It's waiting on you."

"Harrison," Hunter said, "this is Liz Gold. The star reporter."

Harrison looked at Liz and gave a quick smile. She felt dismissed by him. Any interest she might hold was limited to the fact that Hunter had taken the trouble to remember her last name.

"I'm sorry to have to leave now," Hunter said. Liz moved past him and stood next to Cal. The rain was continuing. She noticed a silver Mercedes across Winbern, its orange hazard lights blinking patiently in the downpour.

"We've covered the main points, haven't we, Cal?"

"The lawyers will settle that one matter, and we'll go ahead with our plans," Cal said.

"It shouldn't be long. I'll be in touch," Hunter said. "You know where I'll be."

He took a pack of cigarettes from his jacket pocket, then found a gold lighter in another pocket. He offered the pack around the room, pausing at Harrison, who raised his eyebrows and gave a subtle turn of his chin to the window and the waiting car. Hunter smiled and lit his cigarette, blowing out his smoke with a leisure that acknowledged that everyone in the room was watching him. Harrison looked at his watch.

Liz wished they'd leave. She hated people missing planes. At last Hunter said, "I'll be back. We'll have time," and then they were gone.

Cal and Liz stood at the window, watching Harrison open the car door for Hunter, then run around to the driver's side. They watched the car until it vanished in the line of rush-hour traffic. Liz wondered what Hunter would do to Harrison if he did miss the plane, or perhaps Hunter had an acute sense of time and liked to cut it very fine.

"I could sleep all weekend," Cal said. "Trying to get a contract out of him was like pulling teeth. It had better go through."

"He sounded eager for it to work."

"His lawyers can break knees with their bare jaws."

"He's interesting," she said. "Ever married?"

"Never has. Never will."

"Why?"

"It would take a really big negotiation for a marriage settlement."

"Unless he found someone he believed loved him. Don't laugh at me that way."

"You don't understand that kind of money," Cal said. "Rich people get married but—it's the same thing. Him. His money."

"How much money could it be? Oh, never mind. I'd love to stand around talking about other people's money, but I'm getting stuff together for Walden. Do you have any preferences? Will you drive up with us Saturday morning?"

"I have to work Saturday," Cal said. "I may not be up until late Saturday night. I'll have to see how it goes."

"Oh," Liz said. "In time for dinner?"

"Maybe. Maybe not. Look, I hate to be so indefinite. If it matters to you and you have to know, we'd better make it another time."

"No," Liz said. "That's all right. I'll just fix something and it'll be there."

Liz could barely make out the street. Five o'clock and the traffic was thick all over town. Near the Loop, it would be at a halt, a parking lot, as the traffic reporters on the radio said. Liz passed the Blue Bird, now closed, and thought ahead to Jamail's, miles across Montrose. Maybe it wouldn't be crowded in the rain. Maybe the young matrons like Clarice and the older people like Doc and Helen Dayton would either skip it or had sent their maids earlier in the day. Liz had the feeling, when she shopped in Jamail's for all the special foods she knew David and Cal liked, that she was in the wrong store. She should be at Eagle, the big ordinary supermarket next door, not in the food enclave of Houston's rich, waiting her turn with lithe matrons and retired millionaires for a consultation with the cheese lady on the perfect cheese accompaniment, after a meal of veal roast and steamed vegetables, for a dessert of mixed berries, all out of season.

Willy had gone to Sweden six months before Liz, telling her he wanted to get a place set up for them. She hadn't done well in Canada. The fear that made Willy feel more lively made her feel like hiding. The danger was to Willy, not to her; she knew that the chance of the United States sending police into Canada for one more draft resister and bail jumper was slight. Still, he talked in his sleep about jail or slept like a dead man for eighteen hours at a time. Days, he sat at the window of their boardinghouses—they moved every week or so—and wrote long tracts; Lenin in Switzerland, Willy in Canada.

Three moves is as good as a fire, Liz had heard, and each time they changed rooms, she left a little something behind in the garbage—a shirt once prized as the favorite, now frayed and stained; a washcloth; a book she'd finished. He didn't like her leaving clues, Willy said, and he would have wiped each room clean of their prints had she not been there to say, "Willy, for Christ's sake. Stop playing Dick Tracy."

"It isn't Dick Tracy," he'd answer gently, "it's real life," but he stopped trying to eliminate their traces, and she continued to leave crumbs behind.

Then his passport came through, a blue-covered Canadian passport in the name of a Canadian male who had died in infancy in the year Willy was born and whose name Willy had selected from the obituaries in the paper's morgue, on whose identity Willy built his own—driver's license, social insurance number, and, best of all, the passport that would take him to Sweden.

Then he sent her home. He wanted to have a place she could come to, he said, and it would be better for them to be apart for a while.

They'd been too close, he said, but she didn't think so. They hadn't made love for the last month in Toronto, each hugging pillows, curled apart at night.

Before she left for New York and he for Stockholm, Willy asked her to go for a walk with him through Cabbage Town, the neighborhood they lived in most steadily. He told her that he had been thinking for a month of going not to Sweden but to the Mideast for training.

"Training for what?" she asked, thinking that the war would be over sometime and what would Willy do then.

"It's a training camp for guerrillas. I guess you would call it that."

"You mean, plastique first thing in the morning? Kidnapping seminar at noon?"

"I turned it down," Willy said. "Don't be sarcastic. You know me better than that."

When the six-month absence came, during which Willy wrote that he was going to Swedish-language class and looking for an apartment while he lived with a Swedish lawyer who did liaison work between the American deserters and the government, Liz began to wonder about Willy. His letters came from Sweden with Swedish stamps or on yellow and blue Swedish air-letter forms. But perhaps Willy was really somewhere else, and instead of being indignant about the baby Swedish they were teaching him and the other immigrants, perhaps Willy was learning about weapons and tactics.

In the meantime, Liz lived like the war wives she'd seen in old movies. She moved back into her old room at her parents' apartment. Her mother was active in the Women's Strike for Peace. Her father did draft counseling and had draft resisters and activists as clients. Liz wished the war would end. She tried to remember what Willy was like and remembered early things, before the war: naming their babies, yet unborn; the first time they slept with each other, first for each; the first and only time she was unfaithful to him, when they'd quarreled and hadn't spoken for two weeks, which seemed forever; and their reunion, his forgiveness. Now their tears seemed silly, as did her rebellious infidelity. If the war ended in time, she thought, they would have their babies and live in a house somewhere. Not in Darien, a place that made her nervous. Not New York. They would go someplace else and do exactly what they had planned to do.

Willy's check from his parents arrived each month, with a letter from his father, typed by his father's faithful secretary, Gertrude, who usually sent a small handwritten note, full of encouraging phrases and exclamation points.

Willy had found a large apartment, four rooms facing north. The living-room windows were double-glazed, floor to ceiling, and curved in a bow. There was a large imitation Persian carpet in faded shades of green and wheat covering most of the floor. At the center of the wall that faced the windows was a white-tiled stove that was their only source of heat until one winter day when Liz ran the hot water too long and something popped in the kitchen with a loud explosive noise, and the radiators started heating the high-ceilinged rooms.

They lived a bus ride away from the center of the city in a neighborhood that was being demolished. Liz had gone alone one afternoon to the historical museum and walked through an exhibit of old photos of their neighborhood before the Gothic wooden two-story cottages, so fancifully carved and painted, had been torn down. The exhibit's captions, written in a Swedish elementary enough even for Liz, called the neighborhood the heart of Stockholm. It had been a place where an ordinary worker could own a gingerbread cottage. The heart of Stockholm was alive now in the hearts of Stockholmers, as the neighborhood was destroyed to make way for apartment blocks and new cities for the new Sweden.

At one each afternoon there was blasting that shook the windows of their apartment, setting off who could say what tremors. The rubble from the blasts yielded firewood for their stove. They gathered the scraps of wood at night when the demolition crews were gone. They burned curves which might have decorated porches, thin columns that might have supported gazebos, and sticks charred beyond recognition but still worth carrying back. It was a wartime scene, Liz and Willy wrapped in layers of clothing, searching in smoking rubble for firewood. Sometimes when she was tired, Liz realized that it was all Vietnam to her—the strange language, the darkness that extended so far into daytime.

Their block was the only one standing whole—their three-story apartment house huddled around a dark courtyard, the cottages next door, the stone carver's shop at the corner, and in back of them the spacious open cemetery with its pruned and stunted trees, and the occupations of the dead carved larger than their names: worker, mechanic, teacher, socialist. The reason their block stood whole was that one of the neighboring cottages was owned by an artist who'd been born there and intended to die there, one way or another. If they tore down his house, he announced to the Stockholm papers, he would kill himself. He was old and had no wish to be relocated.

Willy was busy every day with meetings of the deserter community and with his guests. He was a genial host, who smiled and offered shelter and food to anyone who needed it and to some who didn't, Liz thought. The newcomers and drifters came first to Willy and Liz and then found their own way. There were not many newcomers, though. The big problems were the Americans who refused to settle in to the quiet Swedish ways and who could not leave Sweden.

Americans in Stockholm for an international peace conference stayed with Willy and Liz. Not one washed a dish or cooked a meal or lifted a finger for the six-day visit except to point warningly in the middle of a discussion. After that, an American came who'd been jailed in Israel for a year on charges of spying for Egypt. He didn't eat food Liz set in front of him until he saw Willy start to eat. "Jail," Willy told her. "He doesn't do anything unless he's given permission to." When he'd been there two weeks, the prisoner trusted Willy and told him he mistrusted all Jews, even Willy, but it was Jewish women who were the real betrayers. He stayed another week while Willy looked for another household willing to take him. "Out in the street," Liz said. "Maybe the Israelis were right about him." But she continued to serve him meals until he was shunted off elsewhere.

They entertained an undersecretary from the Chinese embassy and held negotiations with a jovial West African diplomat, trying to persuade him to work toward the acceptance of deserters by his country. Late in another night of drinking, when they were alone, Liz asked Willy, "Why would they want deserters? When you think of it, they have no skills; they're young and untrained and mostly white. Don't the Africans have enough of their own troubles?"

"Maybe they want to make some political hay from it," Willy said. "It might be useful," but the negotiations broke down.

Liz knew two dishes: a rice casserole with some pieces of chicken, and a kind of omelette wrapped around peas and onions. Willy made rice and beans. She took a weekly trip to the central branch of the library and meant to look for a cookbook in English, but always forgot.

Every weekday for six weeks, Liz went to language class, taking a bus into the city, watching the sun rise at eight-fifteen and set as she rode home at one. A classmate—a Polish refugee who'd been granted political asylum and was set for life in Sweden—taught Liz to crochet, and she made first a misshapen blanket barely large enough to wrap herself in, and then place mats for the enamel kichen table. None of the Americans was granted political asylum, only a temporary permission to stay for humanitarian reasons. Most of the discussions among the Americans centered on how temporary was temporary and how much time they'd do in jail if they went home, as compared with a life of Swedish time.

Liz thought all exiles must sleep the long drugged hours she and Willy did, until one of the younger boys in the clubhouse Willy made in their living room announced he couldn't sleep longer than three hours consecutively and hadn't for a year, the stretch of his time in Stockholm. There was a deserter from Oklahoma who said he didn't mind so much what had happened to him—he'd never expected to see the world anyway and now he'd seen Germany and Sweden and he'd learned another language. A deserter she heard about but never met shot rat poison in his arm one weekend and survived it.

She waited for them to be able to go home. When she met the Swedish wives of the older, more settled deserters and resisters, Liz felt she was masquerading. They discussed day care and baby allowances, and the American fathers spoke a heavy Swedish to their babies. They'd crossed a shadow line and would stay in Sweden for their lives, though their friends were still mostly Americans and though they talked about going home. They were immigrants now, not exiles.

If she never heard another word of Swedish, it would be all right with Liz. She was stupid at languages, she discovered. She'd always thought that in a pinch she'd do better at another language than she had at high-school French. She could hardly do more than point at items she wanted at the grocery and the butcher, and more frequently than not bought odd packages of food with directions for preparation neither she nor Willy could translate, food that waited on the kitchen shelves for fluent friends.

At the edge of spring, when the seasoned ones talked about the hours of unbroken daylight ahead, Liz saw that her marriage came down to a single fact: she was free to go, Willy was not. There was nothing in Sweden for Liz but Willy, and increasingly Willy wasn't there. She was extra baggage he should have dropped on one of his previous moves.

Her mother sent her a ticket back to New York. When she told Willy, he looked as if he would cry, his face contorting into a sharp and disappointed grimace. Then he'd hung his head and cleared his expression, looked up at her, and said, "Okay. You should go. It's my trip, not yours. You can't build your life around my legal troubles."

"I'll be back," she said. "After a rest. I'll be better then, you'll see."

She promised again and again that she'd return as she spread her clothing and books in the middle of their still-bare living room and held up pieces of clothing, asking what she should take, what she would need. They were alone in the apartment now, for Willy's boys were leaving him with her at last.

When he came across the room to her, Liz thought he was going to help her fold a sweater she was holding up, or perhaps they would embrace, as they hadn't for a long time. Instead he grabbed her by the shoulders and shook her so that her head bobbed back and forth, slapped her back and forth across her face, saying, "Go. Go. But don't keep asking me questions. And don't ask me to make it right for you. Damn you. Damn you. Don't keep pretending. Just go."

IV

On Saturday morning, Liz woke before David and went, barefoot and naked, across the bedroom to the window to look out past the palm and the fence to the blue sky. The windows in the room were closed, and she couldn't tell from the fractured blue patch if the day would be warm or cool.

She dressed quickly, careful not to disturb David, who had returned exhausted from New York in the middle of the night. Liz had intended to stay awake for him but had fallen asleep, her book across her chest, the light on over the bed, seduced by the pull of sleep and dreams that were like black water. When he came into bed, she turned to him and they made love without speaking very much, fitting together easily, and Liz lost track of being awake or asleep. A vague feeling persisted through the night, the feeling that there was something else she should be doing.

In the kitchen she started water for coffee and took from the cabinet over the sink a thermos she'd given David for Christmas. It was burnished metal, silver in color, capacity two quarts, and was to her a sign of solidity and domesticity. If they were to travel in a recreational vehicle, she would want it to be a silver Airstream. If she had a suitcase to wander with, it would be hard as the thermos, silver as the Airstream. If she could choose how she would be buried, it would be in a silver coffin, sealed with careful flat seams and covered with small bolts, like the thermos.

The porch light was still on at Cal's, a sign he'd spent the night away. She checked at the living-room window—his car couldn't be seen on the street. Liz thought that she would leave a note on his door, telling him what he knew—that he was welcome at Walden any time and that she'd be making dinner—and was annoyed with herself for wanting to tell him, why hadn't he bothered to call her, and for being so eager for assurance of his presence. Would she be making stuffed loin of veal if he weren't coming? She went back into the kitchen and looked at the white package of expensive meat, the brown bags of tiny carrots and potatoes, watercress and tomatoes, the thick cheesecake for dessert. On the kitchen counter were two avocados and a cantaloupe, material for a special salad, Helen Dayton's recipe. The lady at Jamail's had told Liz they'd be ready for tonight, but they felt like hardballs still. If Cal wasn't coming, he should call. She wondered where he was and whom he was with. She had not come to understand any better than at the start of their friendship that if he spent the night with a man it didn't mean that they would have a relationship, only that they'd had sex. He told her she made it too complicated. The few times he let her in too closely on his freer life—bringing an unsuitable nineteen-year-old to Walden once—she had been unsettled by her reaction of envy and disgust.

She answered the phone on the second ring, thinking still of David trying to sleep, sure that it would be Cal.

"Liz? Too early?"

"No, Clarice. We're about to drive to Walden as soon as David wakes up. How are you?"

"Oh, much the same as always. Liz, I have a house for you. I think this time it's the really right one. It's near us, only a few blocks away. Which I would dearly love."

"Close enough to borrow cups of sugar?"

"Not quite that close. It's fairly old but the owners have put a lot into it. There's a new kitchen and a bath and a half."

"Expensive?"

"Within the range David wants," Clarice said.

Liz guessed that Clarice was deciding whether to ask for David.

"How about Monday," Liz said. "I could come see it Monday."

"They're showing it today. Honestly, Liz. I wouldn't advise anyone ever to rush into a house deal. But look at it while David's here. He'll be gone next week again, won't he?"

"Just to Austin for a day or two, most likely. He'll be around. Honestly, Clarice, I don't want to wake him up."

"I know," Clarice said. "I know." She used the same words and the same tone as when she spoke of going on a real diet: I know it's the right thing, I know I won't do it. "Monday, then," she said. "Monday morning?" The house would go to someone else, Liz thought, and then she'd have to explain why to David. "Love to David. How are y'all?"

Between the city and the airport, I-45 North was bounded by neon signs and shopping centers, discount Western clothing stores and warehouses of surplus goods, trailer camps that waited for a tornado to hit, nude dancing clubs that were dingy and mean-looking, their entrances flanked by the spread and muscled haunches of painted cutout women. Many of the signs along the way announced three times: *Bar-b-cue*, *Bar-b-cue, Bar-b-cue*; MATTRESSES, MATTRESSES, MATTRESSES. Beyond the shopping centers and bars were flat open fields or stands of straight tall pines, and the new housing developments that had spawned the stores.

Once they'd driven nearly an hour and were past the airport, the landscape grew more refined. The shopping centers were newer and the signs were designed to be tasteful: gold lettering on olive drab, white on navy blue. They were out of the city.

"Clarice called this morning," Liz said.

"I heard the phone ring," David said.

"She's got another house she wants to show us. It's near her."

"When can we see it?"

"Monday," Liz said. "If you're busy, I'll take a look. What's her neighborhood called?"

"Shallow River Oaks," he said.

"Oh, good. I'll bet we're the only people at Walden this weekend. It's so in between."

They'd begun renting the townhouse on Labor Day weekend, the only time they'd seen Walden crowded. The two-bedroom townhouse was owned by Vinnie, one of David's partners, who was separated from Cookie, his wife. At Thanksgiving things had thickened up, but most weekends they had the place to themselves, which was what David wanted.

"Did you miss me?" she asked.

"Of course. Minute to minute." David laughed. "I'd hate not to miss you. But I was only gone a few days."

"It's weird when you're away," she said. "I'm always on the edge of adjusting to it. But I'm sad." She looked over at a passing Mercedes. "By the way, I met the great Hunter Corrigan on Thursday."

"What's he like?"

"Hard to tell. I guess you could say he's enigmatic. A secret. I don't know why Cal dragged me over there. What was old Gus Corrigan like?"

"Never met him. Cal would know."

"I hope Cal's mother's in the mood to be interviewed tomorrow. He told me he'd soften her up. She's a tough one."

David grunted in agreement. "I talked to Vinnie. He and Cookie aren't going to make it. She's filing for divorce."

"I'm sorry to hear it."

"So the place is in divorce, as Clarice says. They want to know if we want to buy it."

"Buy Walden? I don't know, David. It's your money, I guess, but . . . Walden? It's such a comfortable joke."

She turned from David and looked out the window. They were passing the Woodlands, a giant conference center, and would be at Walden within thirty minutes. The promise on the Woodlands billboard was green privacy, stretches of pine hiding stretches of real estate. People have to live somewhere, Liz thought, but what a fuss there was about it in Houston. People lived in their money, folded into and sheltered by their dollars.

"Let's just keep driving," she said.

"North to Dallas?"

"More." He wasn't smiling, as if he might take her suggestion seriously. "Where would we end up?"

"If we stay on 45—Minnesota. Or we could take a left at Dallas and go to New Mexico."

"I'd like to pack a cooler and just drive around Texas someday with you. Go to all the little places."

"Texas is at its best when you stumble across it, so you can be surprised. You can't go looking for it. Vinnie will honor the lease at Walden, but he wants to sell. I don't want to hold him up."

"We just don't see anything we like in Houston," she said.

"I'm not accusing you of anything, Liz. I'm saying we should both stop paying rent and bring our taxes down. The whole country's tilted toward ownership."

"It's depressing to look at houses."

"It must be something terrible," he said. "You've so far rejected Tudor, Spanish, Colonial, Moderno, hideous, not-so-terrible, motel style. We'll buy sometime in the Hill Country or New England if you want a dream house, or if you want to be closer to your parents."

"I don't think I want to own anything," she said. "I can't believe you're so casual about it."

"Don't make too much of it," David said. "It's simpler than getting married, and we're going to do that sometime, aren't we?"

He turned off the Interstate and they traveled along the wide two-lane blacktop to Walden. Liz liked the swing off the highway. She liked country roads and not being sure what lay ahead. David was right—in between their present and some mutual dream they'd develop of country or travel or the right city, they had to live. He had a greater capacity than she for daily life. She lived gingerly in their comfort and company. David wasn't the ideal of her early life, and she wasn't his. But they could care for each other and preserve each other, hoping the care would make them last together, the way women treat their cashmere and silks with extra attention.

Once inside the big Walden gates, they drove along the deserted golf course, and at the corner of Emerson and Thoreau they took a left and went slowly past a three-story condominium, heading for the marina. Had it been a holiday weekend, 280-Zs and shiny BMWs might be parked outside each townhouse in their row, teenagers draped over the newly washed hoods. The place was impeccable—streets clean and swept, lawns clipped and edged, a stage set that waited for no one in particular.

Walden was a planned community built on Lake Conroe, an hour

and a half north of Houston, on the edge of the piney woods that divide
Texas and Louisiana. There were small hills, tall pines, single-dwelling
townhouses like the one they'd rented, three-bedroom houses, and an
apartment building, a marina for sailboats and motorboats, a golf course
and tennis courts, a country club and swimming pool. Many Walden
owners bought for investment, and this was their third or fourth choice
for a weekend out of town. The place suited Liz just fine. She liked the
effect that the underpopulation gave of an immaculately kept ghost
town or a community that had survived an unpredicted, sobering disaster. Weekend to weekend, it was pristine and untouched.

Their townhouse was at the end of a row of five identical two-story
structures that occupied a peninsula across the water from the marina.
From the brick patio and their small lawn that joined with the other
lawns without a break, they could see the marina packed with boats and,
in the other direction, a large block of apartments, each with a balcony.
These were places for young couples, single people, or families yet unable to afford larger quarters. The neat rows of apartments reminded
Liz of Sweden, a place for everything and nothing extra. From their
patio, Liz and David could also see across to the country club, which
resembled an elaborate suburban synagogue, the clerestory lighting
Saturday-night Country and Western dances and special beef buffets,
attended by people from other parts of Walden.

David carried in the bags of groceries, and while he unloaded the
food into the refrigerator, Liz started the laundry. They collected their
laundry week to week for Walden, where there was a washer and drier,
saving them a trip around the corner in Houston to the laundromat next
to Studz News. Clarice told them she'd never believe they wouldn't
catch diseases from those machines.

David opened the kitchen windows and slid open the patio doors.
Upstairs, Liz smoothed down the red cover on the king-sized bed and
slid open the door to the balcony in their bedroom. At the threshold of
the guest room, Liz hesitated to go in. It had been the children's room,
almost every inch of the small room occupied by two sets of bunk beds,
which had bedspreads showing cowboys and rodeo horses. Cal was their
most frequent guest. Sometimes he slept in an upper bunk, sometimes
in a lower. She'd wondered often if it made him feel lonely to be sleep-

ing with three empty beds, but he spread out his clothes on the other beds and never complained. She wished he would call and tell them when he was coming. She felt caught between his indifference to their plans and David's wish, spoken too late, that they be alone.

"There's something satisfying about laundry," Liz said. "So permanent. So together."

"You're just suffering from too many years of expecting the worst. A few years of laundry and the glow will fade." But she could tell he was pleased, and she didn't contradict him.

On the patio, David sat facing the sky and the country club, a new book open and ignored on his lap. Liz turned her chair to contemplate the living room through the screen doors.

Cookie, Vinnie's wife, had taken subscriptions to three decorating and gardening magazines. Each room at Walden had a united color scheme with strict coordination among the drapes, furniture, rugs. Even the pictures on the wall had been chosen to go along with the scheme. The living room was in shades of tan, rust, and yellow. There was a brown shag rug beneath the glass and steel coffee table, and an imitation teak bear that matched the stained wooden floor in the kitchen. The walls were off-white, and behind the bar Cookie had hung baskets and straw hats she'd collected during Mexican vacations and at import stores. The kitchen had a trash compactor, freezer, washer and drier, large refrigerator, ceramic cook top, and microwave oven, as well as a conventional oven. There was a cutout in the kitchen wall for a lunch counter, and a breakfast nook that looked out front to an enclosed ivy garden. The stockade fence blocked the view of the garbage pickup hole immersed in the front lawn and of David's car.

On the kitchen wall, above the counter, were posters in deep orange, bright ochre, and electric blue, Cookie's accent colors. The posters had been mounted on cardboard but they were warping. 24 DE JUNIO: DIA DEL CAMPESINO. Heroic images of Bolivian miners, the lights on their helmets shining. SOMOS LIBRES, LA REVOLUCION NOS ESTA DANDO LA TIERRA. And across the room, in the corner where Vinnie's little sailboat was stored, TIERRA SIN PATRONES.

"Are the posters in divorce too?" Liz asked.

David looked up from his book. "I think Vinnie could be persuaded to throw them in. He might even pay us for taking them."

"So we wouldn't have to do anything but pay up every month."

"You've got it." David stood and stretched. "I'm considering running or drinking beer."

"Wait until tomorrow to run," she said. "I'll come with you."

"I've heard that before," he said.

"Someone has to stay and watch the laundry. And I have to start the veal roast. I got enough for an army. Tomorrow."

Alone in the house, Liz went upstairs and put one of Vinnie's tapes on the stereo. The music was the haunting kind played in department stores at Christmas, bland and hypnotic. She wondered if Cookie would move back to Indiana. She'd confided to Liz at the two dinner parties where they'd been together that she traced all her troubles to the move to Houston.

Once the wash was in the drier, Liz took her veal cookbook and went to lie on the couch. She read through the recipe twice and all the chopping, sautéeing, stuffing seemed like a lot of work to her. She picked up a magazine and tried to read, but she couldn't concentrate. The type of article she wrote for *Spindletop* wasn't interesting to read, and she looked through other magazines only to see the layout and if there were ideas Cal might want to use with a Houston angle. She fell asleep with a corduroy pillow pressed against her cheek, feeling the soft ribs embedding themselves in her skin, too lazy to move.

When David woke her, she asked, "Is it late?"

He was kneeling by the couch, still wet from running, and she moved so that he was half holding her up. "Not late," he said, and kissed her cheek where the corduroy had imprinted itself.

They carried the laundry upstairs for folding and sorting, and Liz felt drugged and sad, looking around at Cookie's handiwork, wondering what they were doing there.

"What time does Cal come?" David asked.

"Around dinner, I guess. I haven't heard from him. Maybe he won't come."

"He'll call," David said. "Why wouldn't he come?"

"Should we buy this place?" Liz asked. She walked around the bed where David was leaning over a rumpled pile of sheets. She put her arms around him, pressing into his firm back. "It would make it so simple."

"Maybe," David said. For a moment she thought they would make a decision, and it didn't matter to her if the decision was right or wrong, so long as it moved them past the present. "Maybe," David said again. "We have time to think it over."

When the sheets were folded neatly, when their clothes were sorted and stacked on the long dresser, she wouldn't let David take a shower but pulled him down onto the deep red cover with her. They made love, slowly, distractedly, she thought, listening for the sound of Cal's car or for the phone. Only when she was near orgasm was she concentrated fully on David, closing her eyes and noticing the smooth thickness of his skin, the places they made with each other that didn't exist otherwise, as if her body was made for him, for them, a separate matter when they were apart.

The evening was cool enough for them to wear sweaters as they sat outside with their drinks. They'd stuffed the veal roast without a recipe, filling it with sage, garlic, and black pepper, tying it and putting it in the oven to cook slowly until Cal arrived.

David sat on a redwood chair and Liz lay back on a matching chaise longue. They held gin and tonics, the cold glasses freezing their fingers, the lime clouding the clear liquid. It was starting to be spring in earnest, and the evening had the tentative coolness of spring or fall, of a change. She tried to think what kind of New York evening it was—May or late September—and felt a momentary dizziness, the insecurity of the ropewalker who looks down.

When the phone rang, she was startled but leaned back deliberately and said to David, "You get it, darling." She listened as hard as she could, hearing only the low murmur of David's short replies, the silences of Cal's explanation. He would come. He wouldn't come. Why had he said yes in the first place, only to let his refusal go so long, and why did she want him there with them? Liz wondered. If they hadn't expected him they might have slept longer after making love, might have made love again or gone out to dinner. Then she thought, It's a short drive. He might still come. And she imagined Cal arriving, cheerful, holding a gift bottle of something special and telling them what a breeze it was up the freeway, how he'd just turned on his tape machine and the next thing he knew he was here.

"He's not coming," David said through the screen door.

"I guessed as much," she said.

"He says his mother can see you at two tomorrow. Is that all right?"

"Do you mind going back so soon?"

"Fine with me. Do you want to talk to him?"

She tried to see David's eyes through the gray screening.

"No," she said. "I'm too lazy to get up."

"I'll tell him that," David said. "He'll be surprised to hear it."

They drank more, maybe too much, Liz thought, and by the time the roast could be eaten, they were too hungry to set it on the table, carve it nicely, and eat the salad they'd cut up and put in the refrigerator to keep cool. So Liz sat on a stool by the lunch counter and David carved pieces off the end of the roast, then cut slices of French bread which he buttered lightly. He made a plate for Liz and handed it to her through the hole in the wall, then made a similar plate for himself. She glanced over at the table by the door, set for three with place mats and wineglasses, cloth napkins and stainless.

"Would it be awful if I made a sandwich?" she asked.

"I won't tell anyone," David said, piling up the salad and meat into a sandwich of his own, eating it standing up and telling her it was better than any New York food he'd had all week.

After dinner they put on jackets and walked to the marina. The moon was half full and gave them enough light to see the pebbled road in front of them curving around unoccupied houses and clipped lawns, all the way to the wooden paths of the marina. The piers were lit at ankle height, and as they walked Liz listened to the water slapping against the moored boats, to the rhythmic clanging of halyard against mast, as regular and sad as tolling bells.

They stopped at a mahogany Chris-Craft that was docked under a long sheltering roof. It had dark puckered leather seats and shiny fittings. The bow was generous and the boat looked both sturdy and graceful.

"I wonder how long this has been here," David said. "It shouldn't be out in the open like this. The wet air will get to it sooner or later."

"How old is this thing," Liz asked. She'd never liked boats particularly, nor the water.

"At least twenty years," David said. "Maybe fifty-eight, fifty-nine."

"Was it expensive?"

"It sure was. We couldn't have bought one. I love this model. It's a big fat old boat, like an old Cadillac. A real tank."

"Why do you think Cal didn't want to come," Liz asked. "Did he sound all right?"

"He sounded a little rushed, a little hassled. I couldn't tell much about his mood. We don't do much talking, you know. Just shoot the breeze. You're his real buddy."

"I know," Liz said. "I was just wondering what you thought because I don't know either."

Before they walked away, they stood for a moment longer, David kneeling by the boat and running his hand along the smooth side. Liz wondered how Carolyn Sylvan might have looked at the wheel of such a boat, her blond hair pushed back by the wind, grim-faced and defiant, not listening to the instructions of the man who owned it. It would never be hers. She wasn't the kind who'd own a Chris-Craft or any other expensive thing that couldn't be packed and taken along or ridden in for a getaway. She couldn't have afforded a boat like that, Liz thought, never in her short life.

Helen Dayton lived in a white brick house with black shutters, a narrow portico, and modest columns near the Rice University campus. The houses on her block were kept tidily, and Helen had large terracotta pots with geraniums on either side of her front door, an extra touch Liz admired. It was the kind of gesture she always intended to make but rarely did. Pots of orange flowers would look good at the house on Graustark, but she never got around to getting the soil, pots, and plants. When she saw easy chrysanthemums in the supermarket, Liz remembered that they were flowers of mourning in some Eastern nation— Japan? China?—at least when they were white, and she passed them up.

Clarice had shown Liz and David a house a block down from Helen's. It had been painted tan with brown trim—"Rent house colors," David said—and the rooms were small. They'd imagined breaking down walls, adding windows and a deck. One of the bedrooms, the child's room, smelled of urine and perfume. Had the people intended to stay in Houston, Liz wondered, or had they painted the house in a hurry and poured perfume on the carpeting for themselves?

"Liz," Helen Dayton said. "Come in and sit down. The weather can't decide what it wants, can it?"

She was a shockingly beautiful woman, the more so because she looked as though she hadn't lifted a finger in her life to make herself look any better. What would makeup or a fancy hairdo do for a woman with the uprightness of a breastplated Roman goddess and a handsome face out of a Renaissance portrait? Her eyes were her best gift to her son—the clear and startling blue—but unlike his, her hair was one color, a strong white, straight hair twisted back into a loose knot low on her neck. As far as Liz could tell, Helen's only vanity could be detected in her slimness—she ate as carefully as a model—and in her shoes, which showed off her legs and long narrow feet to best advantage. Only the tight small lines around her carved mouth betrayed any tension greater than a person might have over deciding on one teaspoon or two of superfine sugar in iced mint tea. She was wearing a wheat-colored line shift and gold sandals with a slight heel. Her toenails were painted a dull shade of bronze, a little sexy, Liz thought, for a woman in her sixties, the mother of a man in his thirties. But she was a woman who lived alone and pleased herself, a woman who looked after herself well.

Cal had told Liz that Helen hadn't redecorated since his father's death. Once a year she took down the white swag draperies and transparent curtains to be cleaned. The room was formal. The walls were painted a Wedgwood green with white trim at the base and ceiling line. The furniture, a couch and matching armchairs, was soft and upholstered in a textured pale green cloth with a silver sheen. Liz, who didn't smoke, noticed that the ashtrays in the room were gold and minute, set on inconvenient and fragile end tables, and imagined Cal during his weekly night with Helen, tapping ashes and sweeping them into his palm. The coffee table in front of the couch where Helen indicated Liz should sit was covered by a protective piece of glass. She handed Liz a coaster for her glass of iced tea. Liz recognized Cal's cautiousness in his mother's preservation of the decor, but she wondered what it had been like to be a child in this room or, worse, a teenager, all limbs and gawky movements.

"Cal told me you were doing a story on Carolyn Sylvan," Helen said. "I don't understand why you would bother, to tell you the truth. There wasn't much to her, and I don't think being dead these years has increased her interest."

Liz wanted to tell her to take it up with Cal, but she shrugged, then took a sip of tea. "I'm going to have to tape this, Helen, with your permission." She took the tape recorder from her bag and settled it on the glass-covered table. "I have a terrible memory and worse handwriting."

"Fine," Helen said. "It doesn't bother me."

Helen would never speak impetuously, Liz realized as she tested her machine. Nor would she confide anything to Liz she wouldn't have wanted published in the morning paper.

"There," Liz said. "We can start."

"I do have great hopes for you now," Helen said.

"Now? Because of Hunter being out in the open?"

"It's a chance to have real success, something you all deserve. You've worked so hard."

"Cal's worked hard," Liz said. "I'm a newcomer and I work medium to zero. I don't know about Hunter. He may be rich, but he doesn't know zip about publishing."

"It's the chance, you see," Helen said. She sounded more involved than Liz had ever heard her before. "Hunter's been blessed with more money than a person could want. But he's had troubles that have meant—he's never learned to manage for himself. Cal has. They'll be able to help one another now, and it will be a great success. You'll see."

Her tone was convincing and prophetic. Liz could almost imagine a new, dependable Hunter who caught his own planes. Then she thought how hard she found it to be too sympathetic to the problems of extraordinarily rich people, though she knew this was shallow and prejudiced—they bled, they got their feelings hurt.

"He certainly looks like a fortunate fellow to me," Liz said carefully.

"I wouldn't have wanted his childhood for Cal. Hunter lost his mother when he was a child. Gus Corrigan tried as hard as he could, but he was so busy."

They both looked down at the moss green carpet, as if in contemplation of the business that so occupied Gus Corrigan.

Liz said, "The Corrigan money came from oil? Doc was explaining it last week."

"That's the good part," Helen said. "It started with oil, with the big well east of Spindletop. But Gus's father had the sense to buy other leases and simply keep them in mothballs until the price got to where it was worth it to drill. That was real foresight, and Gus learned from his father to be patient, to take his opportunities when he wanted them."

"Gus was second-generation money then," Liz said.

"You might put it that way," Helen said. Liz could hear in the older woman's voice a tenderness for a story closer to her than her own past. "He was the one who made the whole business work, you see. There have been other fortunes, larger fortunes, not so well handled. There have been other sons who tried to do what their daddies did. They failed for not recognizing the times they lived in. But Gus diversified. Before Corrigan Industries was absorbed, he owned cotton and timber and was very deeply involved in banking. What there was to do that was reasonable but had real potential, Gus invested in. You see, Liz, he wasn't a small-timer. He could wait for profits. He could see when to cut his losses. He supported Houston when there was nothing much here and all anyone could think to do was laugh when you suggested this could be a great city. Opera. Ballet. Houston was just a big joke to the world. But Gus knew."

"And Hunter's mother?"

"Mary Frederick was from Louisiana. She had enough money to stay completely independent of Gus, financially. She had her money in the most conservative investments."

"So she didn't lose or gain much?"

"That's the idea, Liz. You have to know the size of your risk, of your gain, Gus used to say. Sky's the limit only meant the ceiling was out of sight. But it was somewhere."

"Did she give the Mary Frederick Room to the museum?" It was its most distinguished collection, including two paintings by Velásquez, a Goya, and a small Cézanne, the only modern work in the room.

"She had her activities," Helen said. "Of course, Gus finished up that project after her death."

"What did she die of?" Liz asked. "She wasn't very old, was she?"

"In her forties. It was a swift kind of cancer, a terrible thing. She died in 1956, when Hunter was thirteen."

"So his father took care of him after that?"

"They don't live the way you or I do, Liz," Helen said, a note of patience in her voice. "I took care of Cal when his father died. It was different for Hunter. Would you care for more tea?"

While Helen was in the kitchen, Liz looked at the display of photos in silver and mirror frames on the painted mantelpiece. She recognized Cal as infant, walker, sturdy Little League outfielder, frowning adolescent, smiling college graduate. The most recent photograph was a snapshot David had taken that summer. Helen had put it in a plastic frame. Next to the pictures of Cal was one of his father, from whom Cal had inherited his full lips and strong lantern jaw. The photo in its silver frame seemed to be fading, and when Liz looked away she couldn't keep an image of the man's face.

There was one photograph of Gus Corrigan, larger than the rest, a formal studio portrait. The first time Liz had come for dinner to Helen's house, Cal said, "There's the old man," pointing to Gus's photo, and Liz had assumed he meant it was a likeness of his father.

Gus was more squareheaded than Hunter, less fine-looking, with a brow a Roman emperor might envy. He looked determined and strong, and it seemed to Liz that the softened lighting was trying to make him look contemplative and kind. He looked stubborn and hard to her. Unlike Hunter, he looked his age. Wrinkles showed around his eyes and on his brow; a cleft of a line had formed between his eyes, as though he were for eternity figuring the best odds.

Helen carried in a tray from the kitchen loaded with full glasses of iced tea and a plate of cookies. Neither she nor Liz ate a cookie.

"When did Mr. Corrigan die," Liz said, when they were settled and she'd turned the tape recorder back on. "I won't take up much more of your time talking about him, Helen. I've really come about the Sylvan murders."

"Don't worry, Liz. He died five years ago, and I retired then. He would have been seventy this year. I've told Cal and I'll tell you, I don't see why this has to be dug up."

"Didn't Cal explain why he wanted me to do the story?"

"He said it wouldn't be right to protect any one group of people in *Spindletop*. He's offended people in the chemical industry, on the police force, in the oil business—so he won't hesitate at an old and minor scandal."

Liz was never sure how close Cal really was to his mother. In New York, he'd spoken of her with admiration, telling Liz how long and hard she'd worked. Now she was well set up—she had a hunk of Corrigan stock left her by Gus, enough not to have to worry about money, enough to maintain her real-estate business at a genteel pace. She lived within her means, but, Liz guessed, she'd always lived that way, never expecting what was impossible, an artist at making the best of things. She probably had her hair done once a week, a manicure once in a while as a treat. Her nails would be trimmed, filed, and painted weekly in any case. She did volunteer work at one of the hospitals in the medical center. She had Cal, who came once a week to dinner and with whom Helen subscribed to the ballet and the symphony. She went to the opera with friends. But what kept her going, what she thought about late at night when she was alone, Liz couldn't guess. She had been young enough to remarry when Cal's father died. She never had. If she'd been in love with Gus Corrigan, she must have decided that he was out of reach and that she would be close to his life as his secretary, as close as she would ever get.

"Everyone knows Osborne did it," Helen said. "What's the fuss?"

"He was never brought to trial. The case was never solved."

"That wasn't his fault," Helen said. "There was never the slightest breath of another suspect. And who else would want to kill that skinny little girl? She barely knew anyone in Houston. Of course, it could have been someone she found in Galveston. It was a rough place then."

"Did you ever meet her?"

"Of course I did," Helen said. "I knew all the Corrigan employees, at least the ones here in Houston. Gus found her up near Amarillo, and he was kind enough to give her a chance to make something of herself. He gave her a little job in a subsidiary, Panhandle Industries."

"And Panhandle Industries had its offices in the Esperson Building?"

"It was one small room and a telephone. Some stationery. It was a paper company."

"I went to the building the other day, to see what it looked like inside."

"I prefer that building to those Erector sets people work in now. We had the floor to ourselves—Panhandle included."

"Could Osborne and Carolyn Sylvan have met in the building?"

"They did," Helen said. "No question about it. He had his offices on our floor; Gus made space for him. He did most of his work for us. He wasn't much, public relations or anything else. I never knew why Gus Corrigan bothered with him. I really think Cal might have filled you in on these details, Liz. Not that I mind."

"I've just started on the story, Helen. You're only the second person I've talked to."

"And the first?"

"Virginia Osborne. I saw her the other day."

"Grain of salt."

Helen set her iced tea carefully on the glass-covered table. Liz had seen the same expression on Cal's face before he confided in her, a moment of quiet reconsideration of her trustworthiness.

"Carolyn didn't have any skills, you see," Helen said. "I tried to help her. She barely knew how to answer a phone properly and take messages. She was taking typing lessons, but she skipped classes. Gus never called her in for dictation because she couldn't do that either. I had to make up chores to keep Carolyn busy: envelopes to address, carbons to file. She got so bored and restless. She had no real work to do, and she'd come into my office and sit in the chair next to my desk, humming away and looking at me with those bright eyes of hers. I never knew what Carolyn was really thinking."

"What was she humming," Liz asked. "Did she like popular songs?"

"No, it was some little song about a bunny that her child liked. And then a tuneless horror she used to test my patience. During lunch hour we sometimes walked around. We went to Foley's if we felt like it. I never had a daughter, and Carolyn was only seven or so years older than Cal. She never talked about her past, where she came from, who her family was. Nor who was the father of her little girl. She used to get me to go to dress departments in Sakowitz and Foley's, to show me the dresses she liked."

"What kind were they?"

Helen laughed. "Very grand. All wrong for her. They would have swallowed her alive. Her charm was that she was so like a little girl herself. She would have looked wonderful in white cotton piqué."

Liz wondered if Carolyn Sylvan came and hummed on purpose, trying to rattle Helen. Perhaps she'd wondered what she was doing in Houston and where were the bright lights. Or perhaps she knew perfectly well, perhaps she had a closet full of dresses and only played a part with Helen, to string her along to some end Liz couldn't guess. She wasn't surprised that Carolyn and William Osborne had both worked for Corrigan. They had to have worked for someone, and it was probably no different from finding that three people she'd met in different places in Houston all worked for Tenneco.

"Did you ever meet her daughter?" Liz asked.

"Pictures. Just pictures. She liked dressing the child up and having her picture taken. And she came by with her for the Christmas party, right before she moved down to the coast. She'd only been with us a few months when she announced she was going, just like that, to live in a big house out on West Beach, near where Pirate's Beach is now, off Eleven Mile Road. Cal asked me to get you directions, Liz."

"Yes, I think I'll go there tomorrow. I have to look up some things in the library in Galveston anyway. Pirate's Beach?"

"Once you get over the causeway, take the Sixty-first Street exit and go straight to the Seawall. You have to turn then, right or left, because the Gulf of Mexico's in front of you. Turn right and continue on out and you'll come to the turnoff for Eleven Mile Road. Follow the sign for the church out there, then go along Twelve Mile Road to Pirate Lane. Go down to your right. You'll see the house. It used to be yellow. An old house with columns. Lord knows if it's still there. Used to be on its own land, but there's a development across from it now, Lafitte's Acres." She looked up at Liz and smiled, letting Liz know it was the end of the interview. "I hope you like the house Clarice has found for you. She said you're going to look at it tomorrow."

"It would be nice to be near Clarice," Liz said. "One more thing, Helen. Did you ever visit Carolyn Sylvan in Galveston?"

"No, Liz, I didn't. I saw the house years later, but I never saw her again after she left Houston. Why should I? It wasn't a nice story, and it doesn't have an ending. There's enough ugliness going on right now. With Hunter at the magazine, y'all might try to accentuate the positive. I've told Cal what I think."

Liz took a shortcut across the Rice campus on her way home. She hoped David would be waiting for her. He'd said he might go running or watch the Rockets game with Doc. The parking lot of the Rice football stadium and the art museum was deserted, leaving an unbroken and flat emptiness until the brick classroom and dorm buildings rose ahead in a curving Spanish cluster. The Texas sky was darkening for a spring rain. What was she doing here? Liz thought, and for a moment she felt dizzy, as if she'd looked up too long. It was a form of agoraphobia she'd suffered since coming to Houston. Once in a while it still came over her that she was in a strange place where she couldn't read the signs for people or the weather. Yet it was for the strangeness that she'd come. She drove past the quadrangle and the dorms, under an archway of live oaks, out to the Main Street gate, then down the esplanaded street, past the Mecom Fountain and the bright Warwick Hotel, on to home and David.

There was a rustle of the newspaper from the kitchen downstairs, the click of a spoon against china. Liz dressed quickly and went downstairs, still sleepy, chilled in the morning air. David was sitting at the table eating cold cereal and bananas, the morning paper propped up against the fruit bowl in front of him. The apple green of the kitchen made these borderline days—a little sun, a few clouds visible through the fractured window—even dingier than they turned out to be. Liz always felt shamed by the cheerfulness of the colored walls.

"Coffee," she said, and David gestured to the stove. "Thanks."

When she'd had a sip of warm milky liquid, Liz went to the drawer where they kept the hammer, saw, picture hangers, tape, plastic bags, and maps, and withdrew the maps of Texas and Houston. She arranged them on the other side of the big round table, smoothing the city map until it was flat, folding the Texas map until only the point of the Gulf Coast showing Houston and Galveston was visible.

"What are you doing today," David asked.

"Driving to Galveston."

"You don't need a map," he said. "Get on 45 at San Jacinto and don't stop until you see oleanders."

"This time of year?"

"They may not be at their best," he said, and returned to reading the paper.

"I can never find San Jacinto," Liz said. "I'll get on 59 at Shepherd and merge."

"Jesus Christ," he said. "You live here. You're a journalist. Why can't you just accept the fact that there's an entrance to the Gulf Freeway closer than the one to 59—you have to go all the way across town in the wrong direction to get to 59."

"Who cares?" She'd meant it as a joke, but it was what she would do. She couldn't find the entrance at San Jacinto, though when David drove it looked easy enough. A few turns here and there and then pass Sears, pass Main Street and a district of rambling derelict houses and crisply designed two-story apartment houses now falling into shabbiness, clothing hanging from the windows, never drying in the humidity—there was San Jacinto.

"It's easy," David said. He came around behind Liz and pointed out the route on the map. "Take San Jacinto. It's one way. You can't go wrong."

"Is my charm wearing thin?" Liz asked. She turned and looked up at him. His shirt smelled from laundry starch and freshness.

"It isn't charming to play dumb," he said.

"I'm not playing dumb. I get lost. I've carved my little routes around this city. I get most places." David didn't answer but returned to his chair and propped up the paper again. "I'm better than I was," she said.

"Okay, Liz. Okay. Let's just drop it."

Liz went into the living room, found the book she'd been reading the night before, returned to the kitchen, and prepared a bowl of cereal, slicing the bananas chunkier than she liked. She settled at the table with her bowl of cereal and her book.

David said, "Be careful driving on the Gulf Freeway. It's all cut up. Don't bother leaving before nine, you'll just get stuck in traffic."

"I like looking at maps," she said. "It makes Houston seem more manageable."

When David left for work, Liz pushed aside the bowl of cereal, took her bowl to the sink and washed it, then looked at the map of Houston spread over the table. Standing above the map, she tried to see some shape to the city—the elongated almond of Manhattan Island, the three rivers meeting in Pittsburgh—but Houston on the map was nothing but roads. The only natural configuration was the path of the bayous that wound through the city—Buffalo, Brays, Greens, White Oak—and the Houston Ship Channel, the reason the city existed. In her story on the Houston Metropolitan Research Center, Liz had quoted from an old diary: "Galveston's downfall will be Houston's greatest fortune." This entry was written on the September morning the news reached the one-horse town of Houston that Galveston Island had been all but destroyed by a hurricane. After, the Gulf of Mexico was moved fifty miles inland to create the Port of Houston. There was no reason to put a city in that place other than the need for a safe port and the fact that enterprising developers wished it to be so. There were still people in Texas, Cal had told her, who wanted the Corps of Engineers let loose to dredge a 260-mile channel from the Gulf to the dry plains city of Dallas.

The map was printed in white and pastels. The 610 Loop was not a real circle, though it was the connection from road to road and place to place. Traveling around Houston meant playing hopscotch or making the jump over the cracks to avoid the childhood curse—break your mother's back or worse, unspoken worse. The highways were red, the bayous blue, and the streets were a pale green grid that told nothing, the names of founders and heroes, obscure past Houstonians: Ella Lee, Dismuke, Binz. Signs on Houston buildings made promises, but the facades were indecipherable. Who would guess, seeing a two-story cube covered with vines, that the magazine offices were inside? Who could know, passing a high wooden fence and a chocolate-brown house, that inside was a woman with pale skin and short black hair, who gazed at the map of the city she lived in, trying to figure the way out, the way in, dreaming over the map like a child with an illustrated book of dragons and witches hidden in the trunks of trees?

When the snow was gone from the New York streets, Liz quit her job and worked freelance. She quit because she saw she wasn't getting anywhere. She would never be made an editor, nor did she want to be; neither would she be transferred to another department or even to the Sunday magazine. There were younger, more ambitious writers working at the paper. They would stay forever and succeed best of all. But, as she explained to Cal, she didn't know what would be best for her. It was time to move on. The job had been a lifesaver between Sweden and the present. Now it was time to quit because it was too safe for her life.

Cal took her to dinner at the Ginger Man and they ate coeurs à la crème for dessert, indulging in an Irish coffee after that and walking uptown in the promising wet spring air. They parted in the marble lobby of their building.

"Happy trails," Cal said. "I think it's great that you're quitting. We all need a kick in the pants now and again."

Liz was sure he was seeing someone new. He'd been quiet for a while after Sandy's murder, and they'd seen each other almost every day. Now he went away on weekends, and some weekday nights when she phoned he didn't answer. She could see figures moving in his apartment but never clearly enough to know who it was. He gave her a gift of avocado sun oil packaged like fine machine oil, and when she asked where he'd gotten such a clever gift, he named a store in Los Angeles. He'd been there for a weekend, he said, but didn't say why and Liz didn't press him.

Working freelance left Liz with time on her hands. She was either very busy or, for the first time since Sweden, unoccupied for days at a stretch.

One day in late July, when she'd just finished a profile for a magazine in Atlanta and a quick article on French cooking classes for children, Liz was facing a period of empty time. One editor said Liz should come in and talk at the end of the week. Another wanted her to cover a seminar that would take place in ten days. Liz thought of going to the country, but she didn't want to want to visit her parents and didn't want to go elsewhere alone. Cal's windows were closed and curtained. Since Memorial Day he'd been sharing a house in East Hampton with friends. Work was slow at his office, and Cal talked about quitting his job and going back to Houston. He seemed cheerful when she saw him and talked about his future as if there was something fine in store.

Down in the courtyard two redheaded kids played basketball. It was only a matter of time before a tenant called the superintendent to make them stop throwing the ball against the wall so close to the apartment windows. It was Saturday, July, Manhattan. Everyone she might have liked to talk to was elsewhere, and her occasional summer pleasure in the closed-up shops and emptier streets was diminished by restlessness and the feeling that she was trapped.

She was happy when the phone rang, thinking it might be a better offer than pacing her apartment.

"Liz." The voice was vaguely familiar. "Joey here."

It was Willy's cousin and lawyer. She hadn't talked to Joey since February, immediately after her weekend with Willy, when she'd arranged to have an uncontested divorce. She'd seen Joey briefly when she'd gone to his office to collect some papers, including one depriving her of any financial interest in Willy. She showed the papers to her father, and he said, "It isn't so much that I would want to see you taking money from him. But you did right. You didn't sign it. I taught you that in your cradle. Never sign anything unless a lawyer's seen it first."

"Joey's a lawyer," she said.

"Joey is Willy's cousin and Willy's lawyer. Never mind. So long as you didn't sign anything."

"I didn't expect you to be home," Joey said. "This being a summer weekend."

"My yacht sprang a leak," Liz said. "Actually, I was going to rent a beach house. Everyone panics about weekends in the city. So I decided not to, but I don't know if I've made the right decision or not."

Joey was silent, and Liz wondered why she was telling him this and why Joey was calling. She had the papers on her desk, still unsigned, but he wouldn't call on a weekend about that. Perhaps he wanted to ask her out, she thought. Joey? Me and Cousin Joey?

He cleared his throat and said, "I have some very bad news, Liz. There was an accident up at Willy's house."

Her first thought was that Ruby hadn't been kidding. They did have a bomb factory in the basement.

"He must have been fooling around with a rifle," Joey said, "out in a field. Hunting out of season."

"He didn't know how to load a rifle," she said. She tried to think of something to say, quickly, to put off the specific information Joey had.

"Liz, he died two days ago of a gunshot wound. There's a memorial service at the temple in Darien tomorrow at two o'clock. Do you know where it is? Do you need a ride?"

"Tomorrow? How did it happen? Tell me again."

"He's been cremated," Joey said. "There won't be any burial, just a short ceremony at the temple."

Liz looked around her living room, surprised the furniture and rugs were still so peaceful, still in place. She touched her right arm with her left hand, gripping hard to be sure this was happening. The news had the bad ring of truth. There weren't mistakes about bodies and bullets. This time Willy was gone for good.

Joey sighed. "There's no way of knowing what really happened. The coroner upstate said it was a clean shot through the chin. His words, not mine. It was the kind of thing that might happen if you didn't know enough not to point a loaded rifle at yourself. And I quote. Or if you didn't know the gun was loaded and you were checking. I don't know much about guns myself. There were no signs of anyone having been with him. Willy was living alone. A neighbor found him."

"But he wasn't living alone. There were two people with him last winter."

"Whoever those people were, they're gone. Willy's been using large sums of cash. Five thousand and up to ten thousand at a shot. Over the last few months Willy withdrew fifteen thousand in cash."

"Withdrew from where?"

"He sold stocks. Cashed bonds. His trustees couldn't stop him up to that limit. Don't jump to any conclusions, Liz. I don't think they ran off with his money. I talked to him last week. He seemed happy. Peaceful. The coroner's conclusion is that it was an accident and there isn't any reason to contradict him. Liz?"

Joey sounded tired, and Liz realized he must be calling a long list of people, gathering them for Willy's service.

"I'll be there," she said. "I won't keep you on the phone. I'm sorry, Joey. I know you loved him."

"You did too," Joey said.

After they hung up, Liz listened to the shouts of the boys playing basketball in the courtyard. Joey was trying to absolve her. If she'd loved Willy, then however badly their marriage had gone there was still a justification for the amount it had taken of Willy's short time.

Cal came back from Long Island and drove her to the memorial service in Connecticut. For brief moments along the green-lined highway she was happy simply to be leaving the city and to be alive, as if she and Cal were on a holiday together.

The service was short. A speech was given by one of the men who'd visited them during the peace conference in Stockholm. Willy's parents looked rigid. Joey stayed by their side. Afterward, Liz kissed his parents, held their hands briefly. She hadn't seen them since her return from Sweden, when they'd had an awkward dinner together, and now it was too late to talk and not the right place. She stood in front of them, wordless, until Cal touched her arm and took her away.

On the road home, Liz said, "What do we do now? I can't cry anymore today."

"When my father died—" Cal said and then didn't finish what he started to say. "Sometimes it felt as bad as you feel now. Some days it got a little better."

"Joey said I should expect some insurance money. I think I should spend it on a detective to find out what happened to Willy."

"That's a kind thought. But you won't see the money until the insurance company investigates. If they don't turn up anything, you won't either."

"How do you know?"

"I watch TV like everyone else. Now, Liz. I have a dinner date tonight, and you're more than welcome to come. My friends from Houston are here, Lucy and David Muse. Some foundation David works for has board meetings in New York, so they spend a week or two here."

"Maybe I'd like New York more if I lived in a hotel."

"You'd like it more if you didn't come from here. Try eighteen years in Marfa, and Broadway would look good."

"Willy wore everyone down, didn't he? His mother looks as if a steamroller would do her good. Joey looks limp. I feel worse than I've felt in my whole life. I can't remember ever feeling like this, so frustrated. I feel as if Willy's alive somewhere, looking at us and feeling superior. That's unfair, but it's been one thing after another. The war's over. I thought it would be better now. You know, Cal, I never really bought all that goody-two-shoes country-living stuff he was handing me."

"Why not? It's been reported in *Time* and *Newsweek.* It's the tail end of a trend."

"People don't just disappear the way Dick and Ruby did. They don't turn up dead like Willy did unless something's going on."

"People do turn up dead," Cal said. "It's in the nature of things."

"But the money. And the lack of politics. What was he doing with the money? How could he just stop politics? It was all he had."

"Maybe he played the horses. Maybe he gave to the March of Dimes. What gives you more rights over Willy dead than alive?"

"But it's my fault," she said. "It's my fault. I told him I didn't want to know what he was doing, I told him I didn't like those people I interviewed—"

"Let it go," Cal said. "You left him a long time ago. You told me yourself. It wasn't your fault. It wasn't even any of your business."

They ate that night in an Indian restaurant that overlooked Central Park. Cal had arranged to meet Lucy and David Muse there when the sun would be starting to set. The restaurant was in a small building, on a floor just above the level of the trees, and New York looked like a verdant city with stars and park lights glowing in the trees.

The maître d' was dressed in a red tunic and black pants that lashed around his calves. He wore a black turban that permitted a wisp of thin black hair to curl down his neck. He led Cal and Liz to a rounded red-plush banquette, bowed, and left them. A waiter materialized quickly, took their order for drinks, and left. The black-covered menus resembled small dictionaries. Very soon they each had in front of them, on the round and padded white-clothed table, a gin and tonic, the lime bobbing on the bubbles, kissing the ice. They were the only people in the restaurant.

"Cheers," Cal said.

"To friendship," Liz said. "God knows it's more reliable than anything else so far."

"There's Lucy," Cal said. He waved an arm and called out, "Hi, sweetie."

For a moment Lucy Muse hesitated by the arched doorway, then she caught sight of Cal and waved back. She was medium height and very thin, her frizzy blond hair cut in a thick Buster Brown that framed her face and emphasized her fine nose and small lips. Her eyes were wide and blue, her brows almost invisible. She wore a white silk sailor shirt and billowy white trousers. She held in one hand a bag whose clasp looked like a pink rosebud. Liz became aware that she was still wearing the black linen skirt and dark plaid silk shirt she'd worn to the memorial service, all the miles there and back. She wished she'd been less lazy and had changed clothes before coming out to eat.

Cal and Lucy hugged, and Lucy said, "I'm so happy to meet you, Liz. Cal talks about you all the time."

Liz held out her hand. "I can't believe we haven't met already."

Lucy settled into the banquette, next to Liz, facing Cal.

"We don't get to New York often enough. Just for board meetings."

"But then you get a suite in the Plaza," Cal said.

"I wish we lived here all the time. There's never nothing to do. We walked all around Washington Square this morning and had some really strong coffee at a little Italian place."

The waiter floated up to them and Lucy ordered a white wine with soda water. "I don't drink much," she told Liz. "It goes right to my head."

"Does it linger like a haunting refrain," asked Liz.

"What? Oh, the song. No, it sits there just like a headache."

"I'm so glad you're finally meeting," Cal said.

"We'll have to go ahead without David," Lucy said. "He was very disappointed because he's afraid he'll never get a chance to meet you again. He always turns to the women's page to read your stories when he's in New York."

"That's very flattering," Liz said. "I'm sorry he isn't here."

"It was Erica," Lucy said. "It's her foundation, and when she says jump, you do."

"I'll see him another time," Cal said.

"You'll be seeing him all you want soon enough. The more I think about it, the happier it makes me. It will make a real difference to Houston, I know it will."

"I haven't told Liz yet," Cal said. He looked as if he was sorry Lucy had spoken, and then she started to explain what she'd meant, he raised his hand to signal that he would talk. "It didn't seem like the right time, Liz. But things are working out." He lit a cigarette and blew the smoke upward. "I found a backer for my own tabloid magazine in Houston. He promises to keep me going for three years. It's a real dream deal."

"It's a good investment," Lucy said firmly, as if Liz would argue.

"You'll move to Houston?" Liz felt like crying then, a more pained and quick response, she noticed, than she'd had the day before to the news of Willy's death. This loss was more believable, more of a blow to her daily life. But why should things have gone on the same forever, she reasoned, her and Cal and the apartments, growing old across the courtyard from one another?

"I'll move in September. I have to wind things up here, and I'm getting in touch with fabulous people in Houston. Mary Alice—she's a designer. I met her at St. Thomas. And a few writers. There's a woman named Amy Monroe I've been talking to on the phone. She's in West Texas and says she'll move to Houston and live on beans."

Cal had wanted his own magazine for so long. Liz had listened to his plans, his criticisms of other publications, but she had never imagined that he would overcome the obstacle—money. It had seemed insurmountable, so his talk about his own magazine had been like talk about football or baseball to her. She wished she still smoked. She wished she hadn't finished her drink.

"We'll orient the magazine to people," Cal said. "One feature a month that's hard news, investigative stuff. There's enough water, air, and chemical pollution stories to keep us going for a while, and Houston's always good for political scandals. All kinds of profiles, one major one a month. Then some Houston history. Most people haven't heard the stories yet, so we'll call it the Bad Old Days. Gossip. Parties. The neighborhoods. All the lifestyle stuff. Education and business. It's a rich city in every way, Liz."

"There's all that money," she said. "What will you call the magazine?"

"I thought of *The Raven*, after old Sam Houston, but it sounds too gloomy. *Buffalo Bayou*. It's the prettiest combination of words in the city. There's nothing else but the Loop to define the city geographically, but I thought calling the magazine *The Loop* would make it sound like a planned parenthood newsletter."

During dinner, Cal and Lucy talked about people in Houston. Lucy seemed old-fashioned to Liz, and she was sorry Lucy's husband hadn't come. She imagined him as a businessman in a gray suit, uncomfortable with his wife's arty friends. Lucy and Cal were talking about real estate and who'd bought what where. Lucy had the odd combination of being very specific about sums of money and very vague about her own standing. She pouted if Cal teased her too hard and almost flirted with Liz, courting her responses to questions, asking her about her life in New York. Liz noticed that Lucy didn't really eat. She ordered a Seafood Biryani and spread one spoonful of it over her plate, separating the rice from the scallops and shrimp, cutting the shrimp into smaller and smaller pieces, then finished by piling it all on one side of the plate and pushing the plate away from her. If she had more than two bites, she'd taken them while Liz's head was turned.

"Where will you live," Liz asked.

"My cousin Clarice owns some property," Lucy said, "and she just got her real estate license. She's going to find something for Cal to rent."

"Something cheap," Cal said. "If Clarice knows the meaning of the word."

"It'll work out," Lucy said.

Liz thought of Willy and felt the loss of their years together. Had their marriage worked, she thought, there would be friends, maybe children, something in her life that would set the absence of one friend, Cal, in perspective.

"I'll have to give you a big party," Liz said. "But my life will be insupportable without you."

"Haven't you told her?" Lucy asked.

"No, smartie, there hasn't been time."

"I know where you've been," Lucy said. For a moment Liz thought she meant Toronto and Sweden and then realized she was talking about the funeral. "Cal told me. Why don't you come to Houston. I feel so foolish telling you—I don't know you and I'd rather be living the way you do, an apartment in New York. But it might be the right thing for you to move along."

"Come to Houston?" Liz asked. "You mean, for your magazine?" She turned to Cal and smiled. "Where would I live? What would I do?"

"You'd write whatever you wanted to," Cal said. "You could work freelance or be on staff. It's chancey. I might not last three issues."

"Will you give up your apartment," Liz asked, "or are you subletting?"

"The telling question. I'm going all the way and giving it up."

"That's a big commitment," Liz said. "I won't rule it out. What a funny idea. Houston."

They said goodbye to Lucy in front of the Plaza.

"I hope you don't think New York is all like this. Real people don't live like this." Liz pointed to the Pulitzer Fountain. "I always think this is a stunt for outsiders." She'd meant to joke but she had trouble finding the right tone to take with Lucy, who was so earnest and probably, thought Liz, nicer, more honest than she. The fountain was fine and she should leave the fountain alone. What she really felt when she saw it was not that it was a fake for tourists but that she was in a real place, the place she'd grown up in, and that anything might happen around the corner; she was uplifted, the city was justified. "I'm tired," Liz apologized. "I should be asleep with a tape over my mouth."

"I hope I see you in Houston," Lucy said. "Even if you come just for a visit. We'd have a lot of fun. Lunch tomorrow, Cal?"

"Great," Cal said. "Give David my love. Tell him I'm sorry I missed him."

"He's sorrier than you," Lucy said. "He didn't get to see that view of the park. Or Liz."

By September, Liz was accustomed to the idea that Cal would soon be gone. She considered moving. If she didn't go to Houston, she might go elsewhere. She hadn't been to Europe since she left Sweden. She'd never been to California. She pinned a map of the United States over her desk and looked at it while she talked on the telephone.

"Houston!" Her father had been to a conference once in Houston. He'd gone to a hamburger stand across the street from his motel and witnessed a murder. One of the carhops was shot by a jealous boyfriend. "Even if I'd seen nothing but Quakers," he said, "it's a violent city. It'll choke on itself in ten years. It's going to be the biggest urban disaster in the country. No zoning. Crummy social services. And the climate! Go to San Francisco if you have to go somewhere."

The insurance money would come through, Joey told her, confirmation of an official acceptance of Willy's death as accidental. It was more money than she'd ever expected to have. Invested conservatively, she could live marginally on it for the rest of her life. Against her father's advice, she signed away all further claims to Willy's estate.

September had always seemed the best season in New York to Liz, even when it had meant returning to school. It was dry and sunny, a gentler version of summer with the melancholy promise of winter. She was walking to the liquor store on Broadway and Eighty-sixth Street one evening to select wine for the party she was giving Cal the next night. She had already gone to the best butcher in the neighborhood and bought a leg of lamb and had ordered a cake for the dinner guests and the other twenty people who were coming for dessert and champagne. The cake in the shape of Texas would be delivered the next day. The salad greens were in her refrigerator, the bread was on order. The wine was the last chore for the party.

Liz stopped to admire the displays of fruits and vegetables at the Korean market. She looked up from the eggplants and saw Ruby across Broadway, standing in front of a hardware store. The window display of steel saucepans and pots twinkled in the setting sun. Ruby stared across the four lanes of traffic at Liz and made a gesture that might have been a greeting, or perhaps she was only brushing her hair away from her forehead. Then she turned and walked up Broadway.

I should do something, Liz thought. She doubted if it was Ruby—the same hair? the same stature? Why would she be in New York, on that street at that moment? And what would Liz ask her, what was there to say about Willy except why did he die, how had he lived? I should follow her, Liz thought, grab her and shake the story from her.

She watched Ruby disappear from sight, then turned and continued the few blocks to the liquor store. She stood before the large window and looked at the display of wines from France and California, at the bunches of dusty plastic grapes scattered among the bottles. The reason she hadn't followed Ruby was the reason she hadn't done anything while Willy was alive. Liz didn't think she had any right to know anything he didn't tell her. She was afraid of what she might hear.

If traffic was moving, the Gulf Freeway was fast. Liz had to jump in. There was no time to hesitate: north to Dallas, south to Galveston. Liz made the right move and she was in.

No sooner completed than obsolete, the Gulf Freeway, I-45, was being widened and rebuilt with new exits and entrances, wider lanes. In the meantime, it was a hazardous road, daytime or night, a roller coaster with cement walls and pickups that loomed inches in back of you, pushing you off your lane whether there was a place for you to go or not. It was a dance, a continual motion, agitated and helter-skelter for almost thirty miles until Houston ended and the flat marshes of the coast began, edged by housing developments and the refineries at Texas City but still a fragment of a clearer time.

Meanwhile, though, the signs kept her moving: the billboards announcing vasectomy services, birth-control clinics, and Winding Oaks, an apartment complex that looked like a motel. A pickup passed, wearing a bumper sticker: LUV YA BLUE, LUV YA JESUS. The sky was open, with flat white clouds billowing in from the Gulf. The Harmony Wedding Chapel was a dirty white building with a small spire. Nearby was a store with a sign bigger than its building: BRIDAL CENTER OPEN SUNDAY. There was an emphasis on religion, Liz thought, on the beginning and the end: birth control, Earthman Funerals, the Harmony Wedding Chapel, Park Place Baptist Church with its looming modernist spire, so like a child's iron toy church. There was the Taj Mahal, Indian restaurant and memorial to great love, and nearby slimming studios and Hobby Airport. She read mysterious messages on the sides of warehouses and on billboards and bumper stickers: Kirby Eureka Hoover; Creek Is Potential Country; Onward Thru the Fog; Hitler Was Mad Too, Eddie; I'd Rather Be in Texas / Horseracing at Delta Downs / Fishing / Playing Tennis; I Pause for Paws; Marry a Cowboy We Need More of Them; Atchafalaya It's Not for Sale. There were bumper stickers for Christians, Democrats, Republicans, oil-field workers (We Do It Deeper); for bowlers and patrons of kicker bars. Liz had once bought a bumper sticker that urged women to pick up women hitchhikers, but aside from that (she'd never put it on her car bumper) she had never felt strongly enough about an issue to risk getting into a discussion, much less a fight, with someone who disagreed with her choice for president, her stand on nuclear power or Vietnam, or racial and sexual equality. She'd never wanted to attract attention to herself in that way. Now when she thought back to demonstrations during which she'd helped push over barricades or fling stones at the window of Pan Am (the airline that took men overseas and flew them back in body bags), she found it hard to recall where she'd gotten her daring. From Willy, it had to be from him and from not caring about what might happen to her.

Past the big shopping malls—Gulfgate, Almeda, Baybrook—the land started to show its hand. There were still billboards that promised beauty and peace under a sturdy roof, but more often the land looked as it might have before NASA created a city between Houston and Galveston Island, before people had spilled over from the city into the little towns and empty grassy marshland between Houston and the coast. On flat green fields, broken only by an occasional pecan or live oak, Liz could see a barn, half fallen, or a tin shack, one side open to the weather. She saw a marsh, an egret standing on one foot, and in the distance a windmill. In the marsh was a stand of live oaks, a pond, and cattle—Brahmas and Herefords—standing heads down, chewing. It was possible that they heard the continual roar of passing cars as the wind.

Once she'd driven over the causeway, the bay a flash of deep blue on either side, Liz stayed on the freeway until the Sixty-first Street exit, passing John's Oyster Resort and Smitty's Bait Shop and a sign that warned LAST STOP SHRIMP. She drove up Sixty-first Street, over the public pier—a narrow trashy beach, opening onto the bay and the houses on stilts across the water—then drove on, as Helen had instructed, passing one-story shops and gas stations, apartment complexes and doughnut shops, until she was at the Seawall and the Gulf of Mexico, broad, gray-green, and endless. The tops of drilling rigs out in the Gulf looked like substructures for the beginning of a new city on water.

She drove along the Seawall until the road divided and turned inland on Eleven Mile Road. Square houses stuck up on stilts were grouped together on the gulf side. Some were painted bright colors but most were gray or graying, each with a deck and the same number and shape of windows, the same air conditioners sticking out. She found the uniformity depressing. The houses on stilts were odd-looking. If they were odder it would have brought some gaiety to the small developments, and Liz wouldn't have imagined people on family vacations, drinking too much beer and fighting behind the thin walls.

At the sign for the West Isle Presbyterian Church, Liz turned onto a narrow shell road, thick on either side with oleanders. There were a few houses on the road, more beat-up and personable than the newer houses on stilts. Old bait buckets and fishing poles, brooms and ropes, a car with flowers growing up through rusted fenders, decorated the yard of a pink shack with black trim.

She turned on Twelve Mile Road and drove past the church. There was a small sign for Lafitte's Acres, a large open field with gray-shingled cottages. FOR SALE signs were sprinkled in front of the houses, but the general air of the place was more prosperous than the houses on the main road. Liz slowed down and let an ancient pickup pass her, then turned into Pirate Lane. There was an opening for a driveway in a tall wild hedge of oleanders and palms. Liz turned into the U-shaped drive and drove slowly along its curve, noting the fruit trees placed between the high hedge and the two-story house. There were two fig trees, a persimmon, and another she couldn't identify. On either side of the broad yard a row of live oaks taller than the house lined a tangled barbed-wire fence.

The house was grand. She hadn't expected anything so fine or memorable, assuming that the merchants and bankers of Galveston would have saved themselves for the east end of the island, the historic district Cal had shown her the day they'd come to Galveston with Lucy and David. But even in the historic district the house would have been worth a nod. Alone, within walking distance of the Gulf, on more land than the narrow lots of all but the greatest town mansions, Carolyn Sylvan's house stood symmetrical and sturdy, thick columns rising to support the deep portico that ran along the front. There must have been rockers there once, porch swings and strawberry baskets, great terracotta pots on either side of the big front door and at the windows that were nearly as tall. Now the porch was scattered with dead leaves from the large magnolias that stood at either end of the house. A few beer cans and Coke bottles lay with the leaves. The house had been yellow once and now was graying. The paint had been eaten from the narrow clapboards by the sun and salty air.

Liz left the car and went to the porch. A NO TRESPASSING sign was tacked onto the front door and the shades were drawn inside. The windows of the second story were bare. The air smelled good there by the beach, wet like Houston air but missing the chemical content.

The garage was built for four cars, each double door padlocked, and Liz stood on tiptoe to see through the grimy glass. The space was empty and looked as forsaken as the house. Someone had trimmed the lawn. Someone looked after the trees. Liz turned, hearing a noise that was like a slow rattling. It was only the live oaks, shaking in the breeze.

Though she felt foolish doing so, Liz knocked at the door of the house, then tried the knob. The door was fastened shut. She walked all around the house, trying to see into the windows. Only on one window was the shade askew so that she was able to see the central foyer and staircase and, past it, what might have been a living room on one side and on the other a dining room with a half globe hanging from chains in the middle of the ceiling.

The staircase with its hardwood risers and wood banister faced the entrance door and curved up to a stained-glass window with a design of a shepherdess and her flock. The living room was empty, with windows on three sides and a ceiling fan at the center. It was an old-fashioned fan with wooden leaves around the stem in an attempt to make the fan blades look like part of a flower. Liz craned her neck and looked up the staircase, imagining large bedrooms upstairs, one over the living room with a white bed and white curtains. She imagined the windows raised as high as they'd go and a ceiling fan pushing the west gulf air over and around bodies resting on a hot afternoon. She saw the bed covered with white cotton, mosquito netting draped over the bed. Why would Carolyn Sylvan want so much white in the house? Liz thought, and then said to herself, I would in this house with the sweet smell of the Gulf and the constant sound of the wind.

Liz turned, startled to see a pickup truck pulling into the driveway and stopping in back of her car. It was the truck that had passed her earlier. The truck was army green with a white steel cap, newer than the rest of the body. The driver's door was decorated with decals of ducks and fish. There were four black stripes underneath the decals, obscuring the name of the previous owner. The window of the truck was rolled down, and Liz looked at the driver. They stood staring, she on the porch, he in the truck. I'll be damned if I'll talk first, Liz thought.

He looked away and left the truck, walking slowly toward her. "Morning," he said. His voice was high and tight. "May I help you, ma'am." He looked her up and down, and Liz wondered if she looked eastern and strange or only like a woman trespassing. His tone was proprietorial.

"I was hoping someone would be here," she said. "My name is Liz Gold and I'm with *Spindletop* magazine in Houston. We're doing a story on Carolyn Sylvan. And this house."

He was close to her now, and she saw that he was taller than David and very fit. He wore a pink T-shirt with a blue pocket. Above the pocket was spelled out M-A-R-I-N-E in deeper pink lettering. He wore a cap made of dungaree material. On the cap were four stars. He stopped walking and stood between Liz and her car. Slowly, she began to move sideways to be able to get to her car. A grackle screamed above her in the magnolia.

"Woody Cordell," he said. "I'm the caretaker here."

"Pleased to meet you," she said. "I wonder if you might answer a few questions and then show me around inside. This is really a piece of luck, you turning up like this."

"Sorry to disappoint you," he said. "I'm afraid I can't help you."

"Who owns the house? Who do you work for? Really, my questions are very simple."

"Simple or complicated," he said, "I don't answer questions. If you have questions, you'd better ask Mr. Kelly Kilgore."

Liz took out her reporter's pad and wrote down the name, spelling it aloud slowly for confirmation and receiving only a steady country gaze in return.

"Does Mr. Kilgore own the house?"

"He's a lawyer. His office is on the Strand."

"But who owns the place? It can't hurt to tell me that. Do you take care of it? Do you mow the lawn?"

He stood and looked down at her. She received his blank and practiced gaze as long as she could, thinking that in another time he might have been a cowboy looking out to the big horizon, or maybe he was only dumb and there was nothing behind his gaze.

"Okay," she said. "Thanks a lot." She stood for another instant, thinking he might relent, but he stood firm. He couldn't have been more than a teenager when the murder took place; he might not even have been in Galveston then or might have had his mind on other things.

"Are you from Galveston?" she asked.

"You talk to Mr. Kilgore."

When Liz was in her car she looked back at Cordell. He was standing on the porch, arms folded like a cigar-store Indian, and he was still there when she drove away and lost sight of the house and the hedge in the rearview mirror.

On the Seawall, she thought it was still too early to return to Houston, still a young day. She could go to the library and read the local reports of the murder. She would call her friend Jeff Bryan and see if he could come up with anything from the police for her. She would make an appointment with Kilgore. She would do what she could in an afternoon.

She drove slowly along the nearly deserted Seawall. If she kept her eyes on the Gulf, she could capture a feeling of openness. A jogger went by her, breathing hard. Two gray-haired women in Bermuda shorts pedaled by, glancing around for possible obstacles—skaters, children, a motorcycle gang.

Liz stood at the wall phone, at the back of the empty restaurant. Giant models of crayons floated gently from the ceiling, wafted by the breeze from the ceiling fans. The place still held remnants of the nightclub it had once been, an elegant place in 1958, a curved black Formica bar with a mirror covering the wall in back of it; curved vinyl booths with small round black Formica tables. The floor was covered with beat-up black and white linoleum.

"I'm at a place called Burt's, on Postoffice," she told Jeff Bryan. She had spent a week in September in a small town near Austin, covering a rape trial. The defendant was from Galveston, and Jeff had covered the story for the small biweekly newspaper he owned and edited. They'd played gin rummy and hearts at night, for lack of anything better to do, and she'd come to like Jeff. They'd both said they'd get together when they were back home, but this was their first talk since the trial ended.

"I'm on deadline," Jeff said. "Do you want to come over and see the office? Watch us go crazy?"

"What about if I come back day after tomorrow? I just made an appointment to see a lawyer Wednesday morning, and don't want to do the drive three days in a row. Jeff, I have a favor to ask. What do you think are my chances of getting the police file on a twenty-year-old unsolved murder?"

"If you go through regular channels and talk to the DA and the police chief, there's no way. It's still an open case and therefore isn't public record."

"How about you? Being a native and all?"

"I could try," he said. "Give me the information and I'll see what I can do. Meanwhile, we'll have lunch on Wednesday."

Liz gave him the names and the date of the murders, thanked him, and hung up. She should go to the library, she thought, or stay and have a sandwich and a glass of iced tea. The pace in Galveston was half the Houston rhythm. There were junk shops on the island, also, but she decided she wouldn't try the thrift shops. The rule on thrift shops was to go where there were rich people, not where poor people finally let go of their worn-out goods. She looked at her watch. If she lingered very long, she'd run into rush hour. Even if she was heading in the opposite direction, she didn't want to see it.

The ride back was smooth until Almeda Mall, when the traffic grew thicker as it neared the Loop. Liz remembered she hadn't called Clarice that morning as she'd promised and, much worse, hadn't gone to see the house. She didn't know how she would explain that lapse to David except to say that she'd forgotten, which she had until that moment when she was trying to move one lane to the right to avoid a van that pushed her along at seventy miles an hour, one foot to her rear.

She thought again of Carolyn Sylvan's bedroom, the white netting moving in the sultry breeze. For all she knew, it had been a pink bedroom or peach and gold, but as she stopped and started in traffic, Liz preferred to keep in mind a shadowy white bedroom, the hot air surrounding a white cotton bed.

When she left Sweden and Willy, she took with her a conviction that she'd better not try marriage again with anyone else. In the years in between Sweden and Willy's death, she'd had patches of sleeping with men whom she'd picked up at parties or who happened to be houseguests at the same country weekends, or men she'd known a long time ago and had never really noticed before. With some of them, sex was ecstatic and never to be repeated. The only bad times came when she saw the man too many times, when she came to expect him or to wish that he would—for her—swerve from the path he was on when they met. If she spent a few hours with them and left, it was fine, better than fine. Otherwise, it soured, and Liz had to spend time mourning the loss and the waste of whichever man had turned sour. It took a while for her to get started again with someone else.

Once Willy died, the chance encounters ended. She stopped missing sex, she told Cal, though he said she was too complicated about sex and that "Missing is something you can always do." But she stopped wondering what would happen next, stopped worrying about looking right just in case. It was nothing she did on purpose, just the next turn of the wheel, she told Cal.

When she met David, he was with Lucy and she saw him whole with Lucy, both dressed for tennis and looking like examples of the things money can't buy—youth, health, stability.

The Saturday of Memorial Day weekend, three weeks after Liz arrived in Houston, Cal had invited Lucy, David, and Liz for a picnic on the Bottoms, the banks of the Brazos River about thirty miles southwest of Houston. A friend of Cal's owned land there that was leased for oil and cattle. They'd driven out on the Southwest Freeway, then in past the tiny three-shack town, onto dirt roads and miles back into the fields. They parked their cars—David had driven his in case he and Lucy wanted to leave early—then walked a mile down a dirt road through a thick wood of live oak, cottonwood, pecan, and pine. An armadillo scooted past them, and they saw strange birds flying through the forest.

They'd carried their food and drink with them. Cal and Liz contributed a smoked turkey breast and a cooler of beer, French bread, and some pickled tomatoes. Lucy had a bright Mexican basket which she set down on Cal's green wool blanket.

"It's nothing special," she said, and unpacked half-full jars of tarragon and lime mustard, a jar of green olives stuffed with almonds (only six or so olives were left in the brine), plastic bags of nuts and broken crackers, morsels of Brie and cheddar.

"This is like having lunch with a classy bag lady," Liz said.

"I cleaned out the refrigerator," Lucy said.

After the picnic, they walked down to the river and the women waded in the muddy water. They found oyster shells and Liz was surprised the water was so warm. She was expecting the shock of a northern river.

On the walk back to the cars, David and Cal trailed behind.

"I've been cleaning house," Lucy said, "trying to pare down." She seemed nervous to Liz, but then Liz didn't know her very well. Perhaps she was like this all the time—slightly jumpy, glancing behind at David. Liz had noticed that he looked at Lucy in a way she found hard to define, as if he was making sure she was there and forcing her to look back at him. Once his eyes rested on hers, he seemed able to relax and ignore her. When he failed to catch her eye, he became distracted from the conversation.

"I did that when I moved here," Liz said. "I really liked getting rid of most things. I made a rule—anything I hadn't worn for a year went. Of course then it immediately comes back into fashion."

"I have a bag of clothes with me," Lucy said. "Most of it's old T-shirts of David's, but there's some stuff of mine you might like. I was just going to dump it in a Salvation Army bin."

"Okay," Liz said. "I like old clothes."

When they reached the car, Lucy opened the trunk and took out a green plastic garbage bag. There wasn't much in it that Liz wanted; it was the kind of clothing she'd let go of too recently to start acquiring it again: a severe and proper business suit (when had Lucy worn it?), a yellow shirt with pink clown heads. Then she found a brilliant green silk shirt that looked new and asked, "Why are you giving this away?"

"It doesn't look right on me," Lucy said.

Liz held it up to the other woman. "It would look beautiful on you. The color."

"No. It would look better on you. Your dark hair."

"Keep it," Liz said. "You'll wear it. You're just in a mood, and you've gotten carried away."

"Take it," Lucy insisted. "I won't wear it. Anyway, as I was looking through my closet, I thought to myself, Why do I deserve to have this silk shirt? I already have silk shirts."

Before Liz could answer, Cal and David reached them at the car and Cal announced he was ready to get back to town. Liz couldn't remember saying goodbye to Lucy or David. On the way back to town, Cal drove past his high school, about which he still had nightmares, and by the house of his first and only girl friend.

Cal had waited downstairs to be sure Liz got into her apartment. She'd stood at the living-room window and waved to Cal, then turned back to the empty apartment to find a hanger for her new silk shirt.

The next day, Lucy left David and flew to New York. For the next two months, as far as Liz could tell, David did very little but think about Lucy. He flew up to New York for one weekend, and when he came back he told Liz it looked hopeful and confessed that he found it impossible to believe their marriage could end. Lucy would change her mind. He drank a lot and started in late July to pack up the little cottage in order to sell it. He talked to Lucy every day, sometimes several times a day, long conversations Liz sometimes overheard when she was visiting him. When the phone rang at the cottage, she wondered if she should leave. She was humbled to know that nothing she could say or do there in the flesh would mean as much as Lucy's voice on the phone. It was humiliating but instructive.

Liz called David first, about a week after Cal told her Lucy had left. That day, Liz wanted company for lunch and thought of David, telling herself that he was a friend of a friend and might want cheering up. She dialed his number at work and was told that he was in a meeting and wouldn't be available until four-thirty. Liz left her name and number with David's secretary. She hung up and sat quietly, noticing that she felt bereft and that her hands were trembling, as if she'd done much more than ask a friend of a friend to lunch.

Liz, Cal, and David spent a lot of time together, and David referred to them as "you guys." He said a few times that he'd call Liz and take her to dinner or the movies, but he didn't. What he did was stay at home and drink, and between them Liz and Cal took turns sitting with him, listening to him realize that it made sense that Lucy had left—they'd been unhappy for so long—and then accommodate himself to the idea that she would never come back.

Much of what David said was repetitive and not always interesting to Liz, so she took the time during his talking to watch him and to think about him. While he listed his faults and flaws, the problems he and Lucy had, she thought that this was probably the worst thing that had ever happened to him, the greatest contradiction to his feeling that the world could swing relatively his way if he didn't make any sudden moves. He'd been an athlete in high school and college. He'd always done well at school. He'd gone to Vietnam and had an easy, safe hitch as a supply officer. Now he didn't trust himself any longer and stayed late at the office going over contracts and deals, hoping he would reach a breaking point and convince himself that he could once again feel self-confidence. He could hardly see straight when he left the office, but he would pause by the elevator and wonder if he should return, if he'd overlooked something important.

For Liz, who often returned once she'd left the house to check the stove, the lights, the door, this didn't seem so terrible. But David had never before been visited with such anxiety, and it was wearing him down. He told Liz that things hadn't been good for two years and that he should have expected this. While he talked, Liz thought that Lucy was a fool and imagined her in New York, dating the feckless men Liz had known there.

When it came down to divorce—and it did quickly, within two months—David moved out of the cottage and into the brown house on Graustark, where Cal lived in the jungle yard. The three of them spent time together, and Liz wondered if David liked her. When she mentioned her past life or Willy, or made references to men she met in Houston on business, or when she hinted that she might be feeling about David in a new way, David's expression emptied into politeness. "Hmm," he would say, and Liz knew he was waiting for her to change the topic to something neutral or his broken heart.

Cal told her to stop seeing David alone if she was falling in love with him, or to come out and tell David what she was feeling. Cal said that it tainted the quality of her sympathy to be falling in love with him and not expressing it. But she didn't take the advice. She couldn't imagine telling him now any more than she could have told him the first time she met him at Clarice's. She started keeping to herself and seeing David less. He seemed to her as happy to be with Cal alone as in her company.

The nights she didn't see Cal or David, Liz watched TV. Once she saw a woman she'd heard Willy had dated after he returned to the United States, an actress with straight hair, flawless skin, large white teeth, and a high waist. She had been in a political phase when she knew Willy. Now she played nurses uniquely sensitive to the problems of patients, or insane old maids with too many secrets. Liz felt comforted late at night to think of Joanna in Hollywood and of herself in Texas. It spread them out and diminished the pull of New York and the past.

One night she was watching TV and heard a knock on her door. It was David. He'd been walking, he said, and saw her light. Was it too late to talk?

He stood in the doorway, bent slightly to the left from a knocking he'd taken playing high-school football, and Liz saw that he was over being miserable. He had recovered somehow, and she felt a twinge of envy for his resilience. She also felt sad, as if, recovered, David would have no more use for her and would return to a world of friends and family and old Houston.

"You look cute in that robe," he said.

"It's a cute robe," she said.

"May I come in?" he asked, and she stepped out of the doorway and gestured him inside. He started to walk into the apartment and tripped on the doorstop, stumbling toward Liz. She reached out to steady him, and then they kissed and kissed again.

"Would you like a drink?" she said. Her voice was shaking.

"I suppose," David said. He wouldn't let go but held her and looked at her until she was embarrassed. She broke away and went into the kitchen. She brought two gin and tonics to the living room where he waited for her on the wicker couch.

"It's like Key West in here," he said. "All this white and this porch furniture."

When they made love that night, Liz felt sure. She felt something click into place when they were together. David was with her at last, and she knew it would be all right once they made love. He wasn't a frivolous person. She wondered if she would be able to match him.

V

He was waiting in front of her apartment exactly at the time he'd promised when he'd called to ask her to lunch. He sat at the wheel of a silver Mercedes, his wrists resting on the steering wheel. He was staring straight ahead with a concentration Liz wouldn't have judged that he had. The window by his side was rolled down, and the breeze moved his pale hair. The other windows were up, and Liz saw that they had been treated with a silver that was not as opaque as a policeman's sunglasses, not as transparent as stained glass. Hunter looked blank as a boy waiting for a birthday treat, not stirring because movement might ruin his luck.

"Hi," Liz said. "I'm sorry I came down late. I got stuck on the phone."

Hunter got out of the car and walked around to the passenger side. Liz followed and when he closed her door felt enclosed within the car. The car smelled of leather and cigarette smoke.

"What a nice car," she said, when he was back in the driver's seat.

"It's okay," Hunter said. "It's reliable." He started the engine and pressed buttons and levers. The window rolled up, the air conditioning came on. He drove slowly down the block, past a neighbor who sat in a long Mexican dress, watching her toddler stagger down the sidewalk; past a fat black dog who never stirred from her place on the porch with the two-seater.

"Are you enjoying yourself so far," she asked, "now that you're a publisher?"

"It's more interesting than I thought it would be. It hasn't gotten boring yet."

He was intent on his driving, not on the street signs, not on the stores, restaurants, bars, and nightclubs they passed, nor on the houses on the outskirts of River Oaks, but on his views out of his mirrors and windows. He played one view against the other, refusing to slow down for a yellow light, though his timing was off and he was a second or two behind where he should have been. He sped up to get into the right lane and slowed down, but he never stopped completely and never got it right. Liz thought of telling Hunter to stop at the yellow, not to jump into every red light and squeeze into all available openings. As he wove in and out of the paths of other cars, pickups, and vans, Liz saw that he would make it so long as the other cars remained constant factors. He drove as if he were part of a pinball machine, and if there were a collision, there would be a consequence in numbers only, a lowering of his score. He never looked at her. He didn't speak. By the time he turned onto Post Oak Road, Liz was clutching the door handle. He reminded her of boys she never went out with in high school, who looked as though they were waiting for jail or for a street corner, some dull fate. In the meantime they simmered. He reminded her also in his concentration and sadness of Willy, who at one time watched TV the way Hunter drove, spending hours of his life on beauty contests and game shows, changing channels as if his swift moves could create a program he wanted to watch. She wondered if Hunter was a professional bad boy, like Willy, or if he was only a hard case, untouched even by his own failures.

"Where did you learn to drive," she asked when he pulled up in front of the Chinese restaurant. Next to the restaurant, on the ground floor of a curved glass skyscraper, was a health club. The green-tinted window revealed a pool three lanes wide and Olympic length. She had never seen anyone in the pool or, indeed, the club. At night, the pool glowed like a sapphire in the artificial light.

Hunter smiled at her question and got out of the car, coming around to her side and opening the door for her. He held her elbow and guided her to the restaurant. His hand felt warm on her arm after the air-conditioned car. His pale jacket brushed against her. She couldn't tell if it was wool or cashmere, or some fabric she'd never hear of.

"My father taught me when I was twelve," he said. "Don't you like the way I drive?"

"It's fine," she said. "It makes you grateful to be alive. I like it fine."

Over the red and gold pulpit where the maître d' stood, there was a Chinese ideogram that took much of the deep red wall. Liz wondered what it said or if it was in fact authentic or decorative. The maître d'—tall, thin, Chinese—said there would be a very short wait for a table and perhaps they would like a drink. He gestured toward the cocktail bar, crowded with people sitting at small bamboo tables looking hungry and bored.

"My name's Hunter Corrigan," Hunter said. "There must have been a slip-up in our reservation." He gestured to the large book that rested at a tilt on the pulpit. The maître d' scanned the list, then looked at Hunter and said, "Of course, sir. I remember you now," and led them to a table that had been there the whole time. It was in a corner where they could watch everyone in the restaurant and view the sea of people, pink tablecloths, and shining glassware against the bisque walls.

When they were seated and had opened the menus, Liz said, "I guess that's what's good about having your name in Houston. You weren't on the reservation list. I can read upside down."

"Smart girl," Hunter said. "I can barely read right side up. How do you like your food? Hot? Mild?"

"One hot dish. The rest bland. And I'd like you to order for me. Whatever you like."

"Smart and obliging," he said. "I was hoping you'd order for me, but . . ."

While Hunter looked over the menu, Liz looked around the room. She was surprised to see that she knew several people. One was a friend of Cal's, the director of a small museum in West Texas, brought in to revamp the collection of an oil family and get rid of the fakes. He'd been there six months, and rumor had it he was leaving for California. On the other side of the room was a stockbroker whom she'd met at David's office Christmas party. He was eating lunch with an overweight elderly woman and a man who looked strikingly like the woman, perhaps her son. She guessed that they were customers.

After he'd ordered, Hunter said, "Well. Will you stay with us?"

"What do you mean?"

"You're it," he said. "You're the only person at the magazine with any kind of name."

"I'm not exactly Walter Cronkite," Liz said. "I had a kind of quiet time in New York, and all I do here is the lightweight stuff. Warren Barnes is a good investigative reporter by anyone's standards. Amy Monroe can write up anything and make it sound good. Cal discovered her, you know."

"That was great stuff you did on those bombers," Hunter said.

"I don't know how you remember that story," Liz said. "I'll bet you don't remember the series I did on shallots."

She wondered if Cal had given Hunter a copy of the story to convince him that the magazine staff was good. She hadn't been able to figure out why Hunter had invited her to lunch. Now the conversation felt like a setup, as both praise and flattery often did to Liz.

"How did you find those people? When the cops couldn't."

"A friend of mine put me in touch with them."

"Whatever happened to them?"

"Nothing wonderful. One of them turned himself in and pleaded guilty. He's serving a short sentence for the original charges and for jumping bail. The others—they must still be hiding. My father represented the one who turned himself in."

"That's right," Hunter said. "Cal told me your father was a big cheese."

The waiter appeared and brought them beer from the People's Republic. A little while later, the food was served on three oval metal platters.

"Weren't there cops all over you after that story," Hunter asked. He watched as Liz arranged her ivory chopsticks in her hand. "I mean, contact with wanted criminals."

"Not really," Liz said. "The big cheese got rid of them. It seemed so boring to be underground. Like having a secret no one cares about anymore, but still having to keep it to yourself. Boring and frightening. I don't know if I got that across."

"You did," Hunter said. He was turning his fork over in his hand, stroking his palm with the tines. "But it seemed more exciting than what I was doing at the time, and so much more to the point."

"I'm not sure what their point was, after a while. Where were you then?"

"California. I still live in L.A., basically. But I was in San Francisco then, in my brooding-artist phase."

"What kind of artist were you?"

"Not very good. I did steel sculpture. I was the only kid on my block who could afford the equipment. It's amazing how close a thing can look to good art and still be second-rate. I never really liked San Francisco. I wasn't much of an artist, either."

"Which left a clear field for brooding," she said.

"You've got it."

They ate in silence, Liz confining herself to the blandest dish, the chicken and walnuts. The beer made her feel light-headed, as drinking at lunch always did.

"Will you stay," Hunter asked when he'd cleared his plate.

"Of course," Liz said. "There isn't any question of my leaving. I don't want to leave Houston. I'm working freelance for *Spindletop,* so I do a few things for other magazines. But I'm not working very hard right now."

"I want you to do great stories. Just for us," Hunter said. "I want you to travel and write funny stories and serious stories about—stories like the bomber story."

"It's hard to find stories like that," Liz said.

"What are you working on now?"

Liz took a last swallow of beer and set her chopsticks down. The museum director had left long ago, and in his place there were a mother and her small son in shorts and a jacket and tie. The boy fidgeted in the large chair. She wondered what they were doing in the expense-account restaurant and thought it might be their local Chinese place. An older woman joined them, the child's grandmother, and made a more natural picture, a family treat.

"I'm working on an old murder," she said. "I don't know if you were in Houston twenty years ago. . . ."

"In and out of Houston," Hunter said. "I was finding my way in and out of schools."

"You might remember the victim, a woman named Carolyn Sylvan.

She was only twenty or so. She had a little girl. They were living in a house out on West Beach, and someone shot her and ran over the little girl."

"Gruesome," Hunter said. He looked young at that moment, younger than his age, younger than Liz. She found it impossible not to think about his money, even sitting there talking so casually. It was such an absurdly large fortune, too large even to lose. It was a fortune that could buy anything, including time, as the sum she'd inherited from Willy was buying her this year of taking it easy, maybe the next of not working too hard, giving her time to figure things out and not be excited when a publisher said, You're it.

"It was a gruesome murder," Liz agreed, "and also unresolved. They never found the weapon or a clue to the murderer. Her lover was questioned, but there was nothing to charge him with."

"So who did it? It's not a good story unless you know that."

"I don't know who did it. Not that anyone's grieving over it. Carolyn Sylvan didn't have any family or friends here. I've read the Houston papers, and it isn't clear where she was born, who the father of her child was. She brought the little girl to Houston with her. She worked for your father as a clerk, or something."

"Did she?"

"Briefly. That seems to be how she met the man who set her up in Galveston. If he did. I have to check out ownership of the house this week. And check with the coroner. The Galveston paper published stories for a few days, then dropped it. The Houston paper dropped it too. They kept running her picture in a heart-shaped cutout with a matching blank heart next to her face."

"Who assigned this gem to you? Or did you think it up all by yourself?"

"I've had worse ideas. Magazines are hungry monsters, and they have to be fed regularly."

"How did you even know about this incident? Not coming from Houston or Galveston."

"I didn't," Liz said. "Cal Dayton thought it would make a good Bad Old Days. Even to tell it unsolved. He thought it would be good for me to do the story because I'm an outsider. Not a Houstonian." She was making up this justification on the spot. Hunter was frowning and looking past her as if he might be annoyed.

"I was hoping you'd be working on something interesting," he said. "We don't want to waste your talent on unsolved crimes from yesteryear."

"There's always something interesting about an unsolved crime," she said. "It won't take very long to finish this up. Another week. It depends."

"I want the magazine to work," Hunter said. "I want the best writers and editors and art people there are. I don't want people wasting time on stories like this."

"It's only a minor waste, if it's any at all."

"A waste," Hunter said, and he leaned away from the table while the waiter cleared the dishes. "Look. I'm in touch with some very interesting people. In L.A. In New York. They really know what they're doing with magazines. And they could come here and turn *Spindletop* around."

"But they don't know Houston."

"Neither do most of the people who live here. Cal's the only native on the magazine. The trick is to make a magazine that will grab people while they're here. It doesn't matter if there's a deep knowledge of Houston, so long as the magazine can grab the readers."

"How is it supposed to grab them? We've been trying, building it up slowly."

"If I hadn't liked the tries, Liz, I wouldn't be putting more money into it. You don't have to defend the magazine. But the vision's too small. A tabloid on newsprint. I want all that changed. I want it slick. The best design."

"The budget's been too small," she said. "You can't judge the vision of the people here by what's been done so far. Look at the figures: Cal's monthly editorial budget is half of what I'd get for one small story for a national magazine."

"I understand that," Hunter said. He motioned to the waiter and took out his wallet. He fingered an array of plastic credit cards, selecting a gold American Express. "But I don't want to sit around talking about the past. I want the magazine to get big. Fast."

"It will," she said. "The circulation has been growing steadily. We're starting to get some big accounts. It takes a while for people to realize there's a magazine in town."

"Peanuts," Hunter said, and he signed the check. He tapped the tablecloth with his spoon, making an impatient sound. He looked at Liz. Their eyes met and she looked away. He didn't have any idea how the magazine should improve, only an idea of where he wanted it to be in the end. This would make problems for Cal in the meantime. Liz wondered if Hunter knew how anything developed or grew, or if he was always able to buy the equipment, the magazine, then try to force it quickly into whatever shape he could, good or bad.

Hunter slipped his card back in his wallet and said, "Let's go."

On the way back, he drove more slowly and tapped the dashboard in a distracted way, as if he were keeping time to a tune he was singing to himself.

"If you drop me at the magazine," Liz said, "I'll get a ride home from there. Unless that's out of your way."

"Not at all," he said.

They drove past the Blue Bird and the golden hostess office. Liz wondered if Hunter would come into the magazine with her. When they were outside the Carlton, he stopped the car and turned off the engine, staying in the driver's seat. She thought she had displeased him somehow. He seemed absent now, as if her small difference of opinion on the bigger and better magazine had ended his interest in her. Perhaps she had been too quick to reassure him that she would stay with Cal's magazine; once secured, her value had dropped.

"What are you doing tonight?" Hunter asked as Liz moved to open the door.

"Having dinner with David Muse," she said.

"I was wondering if you'd have dinner with me."

"I'm sorry," Liz said. She thought of inviting him to go out with her and David but decided against it. David was in Austin on business for the day, and she didn't know when he was arriving home or if he'd like a surprise. "Thanks for lunch. I enjoyed it."

She opened the door a crack. The sun was bright outside the silver windows. Hunter put his hand on her arm, and Liz said again,

"Thanks." He leaned over, turning Liz toward him, then kissed her on her lips. "Nice lunch," he said.

Liz got out of the car, clicking the door shut behind her. She watched Hunter drive away. He kissed like a confident adolescent who'd rehearsed his moves before a mirror. She thought he must have kissed her automatically, to be sophisticated or friendly. But it had been such a small kiss, almost personal. She walked slowly across the street to the magazine, wondering if anyone had been able to see the kiss through Hunter's silver windows.

Inside, Cal and Graves, the business manager–ad director, were carefully carrying a desk down the stairs. Graves moved backward slowly, at each step calling out, "Whoa," as if Cal and the weight of the desk were a horse he was soothing.

"Hi, Liz," Cal sang out. "Go upstairs when we're past you. If you can find upstairs."

"What's going on?" she asked, and preceded them into the art room. The art department had taken up the whole of the downstairs space, aside from the stairs and Cheryl's reception desk. Now the drawing tables, the light table, and the big layout tables were being moved by Mary Alice and her assistants to the east side of the building, and Cal and Graves were carrying the carved Mexican desk that Liz recognized as Graves's into the emptied side of the room. The desk had girlie calendars taped to the top, which Liz had finally accepted as a joke.

Cheryl was busy on the phone but waved to Liz and pulled a face that expressed alarm and hope. Liz waved and walked upstairs, automatically opening Cal's door.

Harrison, Hunter's aide, was sitting at a new black Formica desk on which large accounting books were open before him. On the wall was a chrome-framed poster of a bathhouse under a crystal roof, with bathers in twenties costumes swimming in the mint green water, poised on the white diving boards. The image reminded her of the lap pool she'd seen out on Post Oak with Hunter. She was surprised that Harrison had chosen the poster, then concluded he probably hadn't.

"May I help you, Miss Gold?"

"I'm sorry I barged in," she said. "I was looking for Cal's office."

"He's just next door," Harrison said, pointing with his mechanical pencil.

Cal's desk had been moved into Graves's office and set in a temporary place on top of Graves's shag rug. Cal's piles of papers, letters, and magazines were arranged all over the floor, tilting precariously. Liz wove her way around them and stood at the window, surveying the damage. Crumpled on the floor was Cheryl's note: *Please clean up your room.* A cardboard ear of corn—an advertisement for fertilizer—which someone had given Cal after the Valentine's Day issue, had been folded in half, perhaps by accident. Cal appeared at the door and said, "Nice, isn't it? It's like having the Mafia move in."

"Hush," Liz said. "You know the acoustics between these offices. How did this happen?"

"Harrison needed an office. And Graves is about to be canned. That much I can tell. It isn't what you would call tactful, but Harrison decided that my office was his size and he took it."

"Did you object? Put up a fight?"

"It was so symbolic," Cal said, frowning. "He was doing it that way and I took it that way. Symbolic fights are so embarrassing. I figured I'd save up my energy for the real thing, like when he tries to fire me."

"I thought you had a contract."

"Hunter can afford to buy me out. They've got all of editorial plus Mary Alice and her people downstairs. Plus Graves, for as long as he lasts. He'll probably go back to that girlie magazine I rescued him from and start making money. The arrangement downstairs should last about two days before they're after each other with X-acto knives. The noise. Between the rock radio the art people like and the checkers and writers on the phone, plus the typewriters. Tower of Babel. And up here it's only me and Harrison, very cozy. Plus the salespeople, who're gone half the time."

"What's the next move? Do you really think he's after you? Hunter was talking at lunch about wunderkinds from L.A. and New York."

"Harrison is keeping an eye on us," Cal said, lowering his voice. "He approves all checks from now on."

"Well, it's Hunter's money."

"I know all about Hunter's money," Cal said irritably. "You don't have to tell me a thing about Hunter's money. He wants a lineup for the next six months. I didn't want him to know we live minute to minute around here."

"Too Zen," Liz said. "He's not the type. Do you need any help?"

"I've got it under control," Cal said. "I always have an idea what I want in advance, I've just never been able to get it, so I haven't wasted paper on it. There hasn't been a minute." He expelled his breath slowly through pursed lips, an exercise he'd learned to control anxiety. "I have the feeling the Trojans must have had when they saw that big wonderful horse."

"I told Hunter that outside people wouldn't know anything about Houston."

"It doesn't matter," Cal said, newly calm. He looked past Liz to the blank wall. "Where did you go for lunch?"

"Uncle Tai's. Would it have meant more if we'd gone to Tony's?"

Cal was relaxed now, and Liz watched him as he moved around the small office, moving piles of papers, setting the chair behind his desk.

"Always these interesting people from far away. Buy a magazine and get pros from out of state. Harvard boys or movie boys or New York hustlers. No one ever believes the hometown people can do it, especially in Houston. Hunter's always thought he can buy everything. I knew he'd try something. I'm not surprised." He looked up at Liz and asked, "Found out any more about Carolyn Sylvan?"

"Not much except that no one seems to have cared about her. I have a friend in Galveston who's going to try to get me the police file on the case. Very illegal, but he's trying. I'm going back to Galveston tomorrow to see if he's got anything. I've got the clips on the case, but it was quieted pretty fast."

"By whom?"

"I don't even know if it was by anyone or if the story just died from lack of information."

"Are you working on anything else?" Cal asked. He sat down behind his desk and folded his hands before him, making a visible effort to stop looking at the piles of papers and to concentrate on Liz.

"Nothing else."

"Then can you get me the finished story in a week?"

"At this rate I can. There's not much to say. I do see a lawyer to-morrow who may be able to help. I went to the house where she was murdered, and a grumpy caretaker told me to see this lawyer for information. Kelly Kilgore. Do you know him?"

"By reputation only," Cal said.

"What are you up to tonight," she asked.

"I have a late date."

"Anyone promising?"

"They're all promising, all these bums I pick up. By the way, Liz." Cal stood up and threaded his way around the piles to the door where she stood, her hand on the knob. "I'd be careful with Hunter Corrigan."

"What do you mean?"

"Long lunches at Uncle Tai's and all. He's used to life in the fast lane. Nasty games with tough boys."

"Boys? Literally?"

"That's the word. He's not above an occasional woman, but that's the way I hear it."

"It doesn't matter," Liz said. "Remember David?"

"Good," Cal said.

Once she was outside the Carlton, Liz remembered that she didn't have her car with her. She thought of going back in and asking someone to drive her home, then decided she'd walk, something she rarely did in Houston. She crossed the street and walked toward the freeway underpass. Out of the sun, under the eight elevated lanes, it was suddenly dark and there was a damp nasty smell in the air. Tin cans and paper bags lay on the ground, and the remains of a barbecued chicken. Liz hurried on, thinking this was the right place to get mugged, though there was no one in front of her and—she checked quickly—no one behind.

She picked up her pace once she was on West Alabama, and the sun was so warm she considered taking off her jacket. She had dressed up for lunch with Hunter; she'd worn Lucy's silk shirt and raw silk trousers, a linen jacket over them. She wished she'd worn walking shoes instead of heels.

Liz looked at her watch. It was two-thirty. If she got home by three—which she could, easily—she could drive back in the direction of the restaurant, out to Galleria or Saks. She could shop for three or four hours and sit out the rush hour, then slide home in the dark. Liz imagined the elegant stores with copper fittings and smooth gray carpeting, and the smell of new clothing that was somewhere between paper and cloth. She rarely bought clothing at full price. She went to stores when there were sales. But she'd come to understand that she never got quite what she wanted by shopping that way. Sometimes, particularly after a fruitless visit to the Blue Bird, Liz thought how nice it would be to buy everything new and never to look at the price tag. She thought of Hunter's clothing and wondered where he got it, unable to imagine him in a store, putting up with other shoppers or with overeager or inattentive salesmen. Salesmen, she thought, would never be inattentive to Hunter.

When she reached the Blue Bird, she stopped and looked up at the shiny plastic bird poised above the street, forever gliding on a good wind. The parking lot was nearly empty, only a little more than an hour before closing time. Inside there were few customers. Two men in the clothing section: a young man leafing through the ties, an older fat man holding up suits to his girth. A young blond woman in jeans and a tight yellow T-shirt marked *Cancún* was talking to a girl of about three. She let go the child's hand and the girl walked over to Women's Shoes, where she started to try on giant pumps, staggering over to the mirror to stand and consider her reflection. Her mother looked through the rack of children's clothing as slowly and with as much concentration as if each garment were a priceless etching. There was only one woman— in her seventies, three sizes larger than Liz—over in the women's clothing on the other side of the Blue Bird. Liz felt the relief and gratitude she did when she found herself alone in a museum or gallery.

The Blue Bird smelled the same, mothballs and lavender. Liz started at Better Dresses and slowly, patiently, made her rounds in the dresses; then, turning with the ease of a square dancer who knows the next call, she looked through the sweaters and jackets hanging on the wall racks near the front windows. The windows were already decorated for Easter. She wondered if the Blue Bird ladies stored the fake grass and dented plastic bunnies year to year. If she squinted, the blue-and-white-checked suit the headless mannequin wore wasn't as ugly as it looked at first. It was only old and used up.

Liz found a brown Harris tweed jacket that looked perfect until she discovered a cigarette burn on the right lapel. If she were in New York, she'd know where to take it for repair. Clarice would know where to take it in Houston. The thought of Clarice gave her a vague twinge. She'd still not called to apologize for missing her on Monday. Liz replaced the jacket on the rack. Farther down, in the large sizes, Liz found a pink jacket with red zigzag trim. It was cut from a thick wool material, flat as felt. Liz held the jacket up to her, then carried it over to the mirrors by the dressing rooms, pausing a moment by the rack of evening dresses. The sequins and feathers rustled as she passed.

Liz held the pink jacket up to her, then took it off the hanger, replaced it with her wrinkled linen jacket, and tried it on. She rolled the sleeves up and adjusted the collar, up and down, to see if the jacket could be made to look like something.

On someone taller, she thought, or a blonde, or on herself with another color hair in another life.

She returned it to the rack and noticed a hunting jacket with an English label, nipped waist, and a flared skirt. This she carried back to the mirror and held up, then she tried it on. It fit perfectly and, though old, was mellowed rather than worn out. She turned and held out her arms to test the fit. She could think of three pairs of trousers it would go with and a skirt, plus her dungarees. Liz felt the combination of exaltation and fear that she often did at the Blue Bird. She had been led there and given a gift; she might as easily have missed it. She might be in her car at this moment, driving to Saks, hoping she wouldn't spend too much money or buy something awful.

She looked steadily at her reflection in the stylish jacket. Her weakness, really, was in this consistency of taste. Anyone who knew her could go to any reasonable store and find something—a crewneck sweater, a cotton shirt—and say, This looks just like Liz. She had done it often enough in thrift shops and department stores, in antiques shops and flea markets. She'd salvaged souvenirs for her friends. She'd found Cal's favorite tie that way, and a pale gray cashmere scarf David always wore on his trips north, though he said he hated thrift shops.

She remembered Hunter saying that the underground life sounded exciting. The only excitement Liz had been able to detect or to envy was that they had all changed their identities.

Vanity went first, one of the women had told her. Disguises were easy if you were willing to wear an unflattering haircut or ugly eyeglasses or clothing you wouldn't have been caught dead in.

Not that the regulation politico costume was flattering, Liz had said.

No, the woman had agreed, but it was socially approved by them and it had been something else to give up, along with family and friends, their past lives. It was their modus vivendi, to be changed, to be hidden.

She thought of her consistency of taste—white oxford-cloth shirts, a black glass pyramid paperweight on her writing desk, a tiny crystal bud vase that sat dusty on the windowsill of her bedroom. Seeing the consistency was seeing herself grow old and seeing her path until death as the slow ascent of a single person on an old escalator, one that was rising above a crowded department store three days before Christmas. It was impossible to reverse the moving staircase. Worse than fingerprints. She could be found. She could be traced. She could be caught.

Liz returned the hunting jacket to the rack and took the pink wool jacket from its hanger. On her way out of the shop—four o'clock, time for closing—she saw a paisley suitcase by the hat and handbag shelves. The suitcase was cheap-looking, a plastic brocade. It was nothing like her, and quickly she took the pink jacket and the suitcase to the wrapping counter and watched the silver-haired Blue Bird volunteer clip the price tags, fold and then wrap the jacket in a paper bag, and attach the tags for both items to the paper bag.

The suitcase beside her, the bag in her hand, Liz took her place in the cashier's line. She was standing behind the young mother, who'd found a pair of high-heeled sequin shoes for herself and a pink party dress with bunnies all over for her child. The little girl leaned against the glass exit door, pressing to get out into the world. Liz thought of going back and getting the hunting jacket too; then it was her turn at the cashier. She paid and left the Blue Bird, still feeling regret for the hunting jacket.

She had been in the apartment for an hour when David called from Austin. She'd put the jacket into the suitcase, then put the suitcase at the back of the hall closet. She was typing her notes on the Sylvan story and was up to the visit to the house and the meeting with the caretaker.

"It's beautiful in this city. Everything's a reasonable size. The legislature doesn't spend enough time here to mess things up. Every time I come I wonder why we don't live here."

"Don't make any decisions right now, I'm just getting used to Houston. When's your plane? Should we meet somewhere for dinner?"

"I'm sorry, Liz. I have to stay here overnight. There's a man I couldn't get to see today, and he can only meet me early in the morning. It doesn't make any sense to fly in and fly back so soon."

"Okay," she said. The pen she kept by the telephone table was rolling, and Liz watched until it reached the edge, then set it at its starting place again. "You have to see a man about a horse?"

"About a land deal for a client. Where will you be? Is Cal free?"

"I'll figure something out," Liz said. "I think Cal's going a little nuts. It looks as though Hunter's about to give everyone the ax, and Cal's powerless."

"You know the old saying: You lie down with dogs, you get fleas. Cal knew what he was getting into, didn't he?"

"I guess. I wanted to see you tonight," she said. "I miss you when you're away."

"You act like I'm always away, Liz. Some men travel regularly—five days a week."

"Okay, okay," she said.

"He doesn't have to fire Cal. He can fire everyone but Cal, then surround him with people he can't work with. Then Cal will quit. Peace in the family. It's the publisher's prerogative, isn't it?"

"But Cal's the editor. Everyone has to work together to get a magazine out."

"You make it sound like London in the Blitz," David said. "Hunter can carry a loss to get rid of Cal, if that's what he wants. He may not want to. He may not even know what he wants."

She thought of saying, We had lunch today and he wants to see me tonight. David was waiting for her to say something. He would be back in the morning, then continue on to New York, returning to Houston on Saturday. It wasn't worth it to keep talking. The pressure of the phone against her ear troubled her. She took down the number of his hotel in Austin and told him she wished she could see him that night. She thought of flying to Austin but didn't even suggest it. She had to be fifty miles south of Houston the next day, bright and early, in time to see the Galveston lawyer. She told him she loved him, and they hung up.

Liz finished typing her notes and came up with ten pages. She had little hard information that couldn't have been pulled from the newspaper accounts. Her only hope was Jeff, whom she'd been trying to reach since she got back from the Blue Bird. She tried again and this time connected with him.

"You're a lucky woman," he announced. "If you didn't have me as a friend, you wouldn't even see a page of this stuff."

"But since we're friends?"

"A Xerox of the whole thing. If you ever tell anyone, anyone, where you got it, I'll have you fitted for a pair of cement shoes."

"Nice talk," Liz said. "Can I buy you lunch tomorrow? I have an early appointment, then I'm free. Pick the best place in town."

"I'll be awake all night trying to pick it. Why are you working on this story anyway? I thought *Spindletop* was getting all positive and giving even more advice about where to get your thighs waxed."

"This isn't exactly breaking news. But where did you hear that?"

"We hear things," Jeff said. "I've got to run. Tomorrow. Come to the office when you get into town."

Liz made a sandwich and ate it standing up in the kitchen on Graustark, watching the TV news and an early rerun of a situation comedy. She called the magazine, looking for Cal or for someone to have a drink with, and when Harrison answered the phone, she asked him where Hunter was staying. She called him at the Warwick, expecting him to be out, but he was there, asleep, he said, with the TV on. She changed into a red silk shirt and clean dungarees, and he picked her up at Graustark and took her to a fern bar twenty stories up, on top of the tallest building in Montrose. A woman singer stood under a bright orange light in the corner, her pianist and drummer banging enthusiastically as she sang loud lyrics and sounds, throwing scraps of recognizable tunes into random runs of notes.

"Let's sit outside," Liz said. "Until we get cold."

"All right," Hunter said, and he whispered into the hostess's ear. Seeing him lean down close to the other woman—a thin blonde in a black cocktail dress—made Liz momentarily angry; then the feeling was gone. Hunter took Liz's elbow and guided her through the crowded room toward the terrace door.

The dark terrace was unoccupied, and Hunter and Liz chose, from the white wrought-iron tables, one that was in the far corner, close to the terrace wall. They didn't speak until a waitress came and took their orders. Looking east, they saw the familiar skyline of downtown. It rose from nothing and ended abruptly, forming a clump of skyscrapers above the ground-level endless lights of the freeways and shopping centers. They could look in the opposite direction as well and see, to the west, another city, the new hotels and fancy stores of Galleria. It was an inaccurate mirror image, Liz decided, and she wished that there were only one such city rising in the distance. If the prosperity kept up, the view from the terrace might one day be ringed by these independent skylines.

When the waitress had come and taken their drink orders, Hunter said, "What happened to your husband? The muse abandoned you?"

"He's not my husband," Liz said. "He had to stay in Austin on business."

Hunter looked only mildly interested in her answer and lapsed into a pleased silence.

"Why are you staying in a hotel," Liz asked. "Is your father's house gone?"

"I have a house of my own," Hunter said. "The other was sold when my father died. Mine's being redecorated. I'll show it to you sometime. Tonight, if you like."

"Okay," she said.

"It's nearby. It's not much yet."

"Did you grow up in Houston?"

"Until a certain point. Then I started making the rounds of the boarding schools, trying to find one that I could stay in. That would keep me." He turned his gaze from the downtown skyline to Liz and said, "I don't think I was dumb. Disturbed would cover it."

"Most people were disturbed when they were teenagers," Liz said. She waited for a reply or an example of Hunter's disturbance. She might have given him examples of her own: smoking marijuana in Washington Square Park; making out on thin mattresses with boys she didn't know in apartments she couldn't locate to save her life; walking the dark Manhattan streets alone on her way home to her parents' sleeping apartment, wishing she were going somewhere else. Willy had appeared at the end of it, and at seventeen he'd given her the next place to go.

The waitress brought their drinks, and Liz touched the icy glass. She raised it in front of her, saying, "I'm glad you're here." She didn't mean much by the toast, only the wish that Hunter would relax and look at her, talk to her, stop jiggling his leg against the brick terrace wall. To her surprise, he turned at the words and graced her with a sudden and warm smile unlike any other expression she'd seen on his face.

"Thanks," he said. "No one else bothered. They're too busy being scared of me."

He touched her glass to his, lightly as a caress, so that a second later, his smile gone, her drink at her lips, Liz wasn't sure there had been contact.

"So you didn't spend much time in Houston," she said. "When you were a child."

"I lived here until my mother died. Then the old man and I met wherever he happened to be."

"You mean on vacations?"

He hunched into his chair and sighed. Liz thought he might not answer.

"First I'd go and find him wherever he was—New York, Geneva—and then I'd wait around until he had time to see me. We'd have dinner. Or lunch. Then I'd fly back here to Houston. I had an aunt here but she's dead now. I'd stay with her. My mother's sister. If it was a good year, I'd have a friend in Houston and I'd go over there. Once I was old enough to drive, I'd come back and see people I used to know or Texans I met in the East."

"Were you alone in the house? When your father was away?"

"The servants were there," Hunter said. "I was a young man, my father considered. And he was always just leaving or just coming back. A man in motion."

"Did you resent it," she asked, "being left that way?"

He looked at her, and one corner of his mouth turned up in an expression that wasn't quite a smile or a sneer but was closer to expressing contempt than another emotion.

"I waited for him like he was the sunrise. That was the only time I cared for, when he had just returned or he had a little extra time and we'd go somewhere together, do something. Just ride around. He didn't like the way I drove, you see—I was imitating him, not the way he told me to drive but the way he did—so he'd take the wheel and we'd go driving, stop in some little chicken-fried joint, and drink beer. Then we'd come home, get cleaned up, and he'd take me out somewhere. But he always left. Or when he was in town he wasn't around much. Then later it got to be what you could call normal—father and son at breakfast, that picture. I used to wait up for him sometimes, but sometimes he didn't come home."

"Where was he," Liz asked. She thought of her mother, reading until late by her bedside light, and when Liz asked where her father was, she'd answer that he was at a meeting and what a late meeting it was getting to be, how tired he'd be when he got home.

Hunter looked at Liz from his half-closed lids.

"He was out. Out somewhere. So I learned not to stay up all night waiting, but I gave up by inches—one, two, three o'clock in the morning. And then . . ."

"Then you were up too," Liz guessed. "Out all night?"

"Something like that," Hunter said. He leaned toward her and asked, "Another drink?" The waitress was at the door, waiting for a signal from Hunter. Liz thought of the morning appointment she had in Galveston with Kelly Kilgore, but she said, "Okay. One more," and Hunter waved a V-sign to the waitress.

After the second drink came, Liz got up to go to the bathroom, and stopped on the way to say hello to Mary Alice, the magazine's art director, who sat listening to the jazz singer with her boyfriend. Mary Alice said how weird it was at the magazine with the furniture being moved around, then, "We're thinking of moving to Dallas, Liz. It's a great media market. Don't tell Cal. I don't know why I just told you." Liz said she wouldn't tell and went on to the bathroom, which was down a staircase by the side of the elevator. When she came out, she saw

Hunter on the landing, talking on the pay phone, one hand over his ear, straining to hear above the music. She smiled at him as she went by. The smile stayed too long on her face, making her feel foolish when she got to the empty terrace.

When Hunter returned to the table, she said, "Time to go. I have to work in the morning." The breeze was blowing colder, and Liz felt at a loss to say anything more. Whom had Hunter called? Harrison? Was Hunter a man who needed to be at a phone at all times?

"What do you people do for fun around here," Hunter asked. "I thought this was an all-night town."

"You're the one from Houston," Liz said. "I don't know what we people do. What do you do?"

"Whatever I can," he said. "Let's drive somewhere. I'll show you my house."

Going down in the elevator—an office elevator that reminded Liz to worry about the morning, the lawyer—they didn't speak. When they reached the street, Hunter took her arm again; Liz wondered if he touched everyone he was with. He led her to his car and held open the door for her. The weather had turned again, this time to cold, and Liz had to remind herself that it had been only that afternoon that she'd walked to the Blue Bird and thought of taking off her linen jacket.

He drove down Montrose and turned on Westheimer. The strip was bright, light flashing, the biggest street crowd in Houston. Between the nude dancing joints for tourists and the gay bars and hookers, it was a lively street, one Liz and David avoided as she'd avoided Times Square in New York. Hunter turned abruptly and turned again, passing through open gates to a one-block street, Courtlandt Place, where Liz had once gone to a party with David. It was a relic of an older Houston, an enclave of fat lawns and wide, gracious houses. Hunter stopped in front of a large house with a Palladian window and a veranda with an elaborate stone railing. The uncurtained windows looked like pools of dark water.

"That's it," he said. "Home sweet home."

"It's big. Do we go inside?"

"It's all torn up. If you like."

"I like torn-up houses," Liz said as they walked up the path to the front door. "It's the ones that are all done up and full of whatever people want to show off—the ones you see when you're looking at real estate. Words of a non-owner."

Hunter unlocked the door and swung it open for her, reaching around on the wall for a switch.

"Power's off," he said. "Let me go first."

He walked in and she listened to his steps, one at a time, slowly shuffling away until there was silence. He might have been very far off or standing near. Why had he gone? Liz wondered, and for a moment was afraid to be standing outside in the dark, something she rarely did in the city; and she was only rarely in the country. The darkness and Hunter's silence reminded her of Willy's place and the snow on the fields, persistent and enveloping. She thought of leaving, but there was no way to get home without a car. She could walk, she thought, and imagined the familiar streets between Courtlandt Place and Graustark dark and populated with strange figures.

"Here." She heard Hunter's voice and saw a small light. "Just walk straight ahead and it'll be fine."

"Where are you?" she asked, but she walked straight on, one foot ahead of the other as if she were walking a plank. "Is it very far?"

"Just keep on," he said. She couldn't tell if he was very near, the light was so small. "There," Hunter said when she was close to him. She could smell his wool jacket and the faint odor of his sweat. He reached out a hand and pulled her toward him gently, then turned her around so that her back was against him. "Watch closely," he said, and he played the light of his pencil flashlight over the walls and scroll molding, over a fireplace that seemed to take up half the room they were standing in, the floor they stood on, parquet, now dusty from the construction work; the windows, beveled like David's on Graustark but always belonging to this house.

"Hard to tell, isn't it," Hunter said. His voice was close to her ear, and she thought of leaning her weight into him.

"Let's come back some other time," Liz said. "It's too hard to see." She moved away and turned around to face Hunter. The thin shaft of light fell to the floor and moved to her shoes, her legs, up to her face.

"Whatever you like," he said.

"Don't play FBI," Liz said. "Get that light out of my eyes."

"Whatever," he said, and Liz thought for a moment that Hunter would leave her in the dark house or shut her in, but instead there was again his gesture of protection, his hand at her elbow. He took her outside to the air that smelled like sulfur and coffee, the wind from the east, but a relief. It was Houston again.

She assumed he was driving her home but instead he continued up Montrose, past the museums and around the spotlighted Mecom Fountain—a glance up Main Street to the live oaks of Rice and Shadyside—to the driveway of the Warwick Hotel. Hunter left the car key for the black man in the Hollywood-blue footman's uniform and white curled wig. He held the door open for them, but Liz hesitated on the steps.

"I have to get up early tomorrow."

"Oh, come on," Hunter said. "I have insomnia. Just a little while."

The hotel lobby was filled with antiques that looked fake even when they were real. And that raised the question, Liz told Hunter, of real what; they were probably manufactured in the eighteenth century for a provincial hotel lobby. In the wood-paneled elevator she heard a couple speak German, and a scrap of Arabic between two businessmen. She tried to recall the identity of the man in the white jumpsuit whom she'd seen in the lobby. He looked almost familiar, and as they reached Hunter's suite, Liz remembered that he was an actor who used to be in Westerns, a face from late-night TV.

The suite was powder blue and gray. The sitting room was furnished with the same unknown-vintage French antiques as the lobby—gilded chairs, brocade seats. In the sitting room, the furniture looked more than ever like extras from someone's attic. A glance into the bedroom showed twin beds, the covers of the far bed pulled back for the night, a mint on the night table, the bedside lamp lit. With her back to Hunter and the room, Liz looked out over the treetops of Hermann Park and beyond. Houston looked like a city of trees and lights, lush and mysterious rather than suburban or rough.

She turned back to the room and sat on a baby-blue velvet loveseat, across a mirrored coffee table from Hunter. He sat on the edge of an overstuffed armchair, methodically laying out rows of cocaine. When he'd finished making the rows, neat as corn, Hunter held out a new, tightly rolled twenty-dollar bill to Liz.

"Thanks," she said. "So this is what you do. Wherever you are. New York? L.A.?"

"Wherever I am," he said.

"I guess that's the nice thing about being rich."

"Can't your boyfriend afford a little snort?"

"He can," she said. "I can't. He doesn't," and she bent over, careful not to brush the powder with her sleeve or her breath. Hunter ingested expertly, not wasting a speck, and he smiled brilliantly when he was finished. She smiled back at him, letting the drug do what it always did— open her up to every possibility, give her a feeling of power, a sense of the grace of the present extended moment. Liz looked around the room and was glad to be there. It was anonymous and comfortable. It didn't matter if it was pompous. She lost her sense of time pressing on her to sleep, to wake for the morning appointment.

"We could be anywhere," she said.

"All hotels get to look the same. I like it," Hunter said.

"Are you one of those people who likes Holiday Inns because they're exactly the same all over?"

"Surely not Holiday Inns," he said. "I like having my own houses everywhere. Though it's a drag setting them up."

"Ah," she said. "Your scale of things."

The phone rang and Hunter took the call in the bedroom, leaving the door ajar. He sat on the edge of the turned-down covers, his hand cupped over the receiver. Liz wondered again: Harrison? A girl friend? A lover?

"Why did you get involved in the magazine?" she asked when Hunter returned.

"Why does everyone think I did?"

"To make a name for yourself. Though I suppose you already have a perfectly good one."

"You mean so I could do something right for a change," he said. He was mild, not offended. "I've done most things ass backwards, I'll admit, and it hasn't gone unnoticed."

He reminded Liz of Willy saying that he was glad they would be divorced so they could be friends—there was the same attempt to see losses as the path to gains.

"What is it?" he asked.

"You're like my husband. Something you said."

"I thought you weren't married."

"Not anymore," she said, not volunteering that Willy was dead, and Hunter didn't ask, the one question the whole of his curiosity.

"Do you want a drink?" he asked, and he picked up the phone by his chair.

"Just some kind of water," she said, thinking she should leave but feeling as if something that was meant to happen was about to take place, and if she just held on and kept still it would all come out right. But when the drinks of sparkling water had been delivered and she and Hunter were finished with them, this feeling of expectation had worn off. She was tired, and the next day seemed more important and pressing than being there.

"Take me home, Hunter," she said. "Please."

"Don't you want to spend the night," he asked. He sounded indifferent and looked tired. He came around the coffee table and sat next to her on the loveseat, putting an arm around her shoulders, touching her gingerly or tenderly, she couldn't tell which.

"No," she said. "I live with someone. I told you. And anyway"— then he kissed her and moved his hand to her neck—"and anyway," she said. She moved away, touching his cheek, tracing a line from his nose down around his mouth. "We don't know each other, and I'm too old for this."

He laughed and released her. "Maybe I am too. Let's just drive around."

"Like you did with your father?"

Hunter stopped looking relaxed and stood up, stretching his arms above his head. "No. Not like that."

When they left the hotel lobby, she felt a small regret that she had not done what she would have five or ten years before—given in to the logic that it was one night and why not, why not try everything at least once—but when Hunter stopped his car in front of the stockade fence on Graustark, Liz was glad to be going in alone. "Thanks," she said. "It was nice."

"We'll have dinner sometime," Hunter said politely. "I'd like to meet your muse."

He waited until she had closed the fence gate behind her, until she turned on the light inside the house, before driving away. Later, in bed, she remembered him talking about his father and their car rides. She wondered if they spoke or only rode on small Texas roads, glancing into the houses of the poor people who never got to be away from each other, watching up ahead for something that would entertain them and make their time together go more quickly.

VI

In the off-season morning light, the cast-iron buildings along the Strand looked capable of enduring many more cycles of destruction and restoration. When she had seen the street before, it had been summer. Then the restored buildings had been a backdrop for the music and the beer-drinking crowd. Now she was alone on the broad street. Only an occasional car passed by. She noticed the careful attention the stern battered buildings had received. There was a historic marker outside the building where Kelly Kilgore had his offices: THOMAS JEFFERSON LEAGUE BUILDING (1874). She read that the Strand—named for the London street—was the Wall Street of the Southwest, and Galveston the Queen City, until in 1900 a hurricane nearly leveled the prosperous island. The count of the dead stopped at six thousand. There was no way of counting how many more had been swept away. It was the beginning of the end of commerce in Galveston on its previous scale, the beginning of disrepair for its buildings. The Strand was preserved as a souvenir of better times, or perhaps only times before the storm. The 1900 storm was the point from which Galveston Island life continued; it was the point of reference to which the island would always look back.

The offices of Smith, Day, Kilgore & Lord were at the top of the three-story cream-painted atrium building. On the ground floor was a fancy restaurant Liz glanced into as she went to the stairs. There were bouquets on each table, and linen tablecloths. The napkins were folded to look like flowers. She passed by the offices of a travel agent, an accountant, a public-relations firm. Through the thick wood doors she heard the occasional scrape of furniture against bare floors, the click of a typewriter, the ring of a phone. Above, the skylight gleamed and the ceiling fans along the hallways turned slowly, keeping the heat circulating in the big open vertical space. She felt as if she were climbing inside a wedding cake, the creamy light flowing like icing through the banisters, coating the dark wood stairs.

The receptionist sat at a carved oak desk. Her room was painted lemon yellow with white trim, and she was dressed also in stripes of yellow and white that made her red lips and fingernails, her auburn beehive, look as though they were suspended in the air like a Cheshire cat. At her left breast, she wore a gold pin that spelled out *Joan.*

"How are you today. May I help you?" Her voice was husky and deep. They were probably the same age, Liz thought, but the other woman's hair and makeup made her look older.

"I'm Liz Gold. I have an appointment with Mr. Kilgore."

"Down on your left," Joan said, and gestured toward the inner hallway. "Mr. Kilgore's expecting you. He said to send you right in."

Kilgore's door was ajar and he was at his desk, talking on the phone. He motioned for Liz to sit down in one of the brown leather chairs. His office was Old West: a deer's head on one rough plaster wall, a Remington reproduction next to it. A Longhorn skull hung between the white-shuttered floor-to-ceiling windows. The deep green carpeting was almost too soft to walk on comfortably, and Liz slid down involuntarily in the slick leather chair. She took out her tape recorder and note pad, then considered Kilgore. He was a plain-looking man, gray-haired, in a pale blue three-piece suit. He could be a drinker, she thought, noting his red nose and the glow on his cheeks from the fine network of broken blood vessels. His gray eyes were set close together beneath his narrow forehead, giving him a worried look.

"Sorry about that," he said when he replaced the receiver on the phone. Liz wondered why he'd had her sent right in. Perhaps having her wait while he spoke on the phone was the point of the exercise.

"I know how busy you must be," she said.

"Keeping alive. Just about. What can I do for you, Miss Gold. I want you to know I was a charter subscriber to your magazine, and I certainly enjoy it. It's a look at a whole other side of life. My wife enjoys it too, and she doesn't read very much of anything."

"That's always nice to hear," Liz said. "I'll pass along the compliment to my editor."

"You mentioned the house on West Beach?"

"Yes. The caretaker, Mr. Cordell, told me to call you for information on the place. I was out there looking at it."

"I was wondering when *Spindletop* would get around to Galveston. I'll be pleased to help you. I've been here all my life, except for my law-school years. BOI, born on the island."

"The article's not on Galveston per se. It's about the Carolyn Sylvan murders. In that house. You remember. . . ."

"It would be damn hard to forget. Not that much of that kind of thing happens around Galveston. We get mostly run-of-the-mill barfight, convenience-store murders. Domestic disturbances. And we used to have a lot of gambling action. Everything. Then it was all closed down and it's a quieter place now. But mysterious ladies getting themselves killed. Not much of that. People know one another on the island."

"I don't understand what she was doing here to start with," Liz said. "To tell you the truth. Why would a young woman want to be so far away from everything, alone with her little girl on a desolate part of the island?"

Kilgore leaned back in his chair and Liz thought that he looked shrewder than she'd seen at first; no, it was only his sad pleading eyes, at odds with a shrewd expression. His chair creaked as he moved.

"Is that what your article's going to be based on—speculation?"

"I hope not," she said. "Did you know Carolyn Sylvan?"

"I met her once, over twenty years ago. During a business transaction."

"Who owns the house, Mr. Kilgore? And who owned it when she was there? Was it Osborne?"

"In this state, Miss Gold, ownership of property is a matter of public record. All land transactions."

"I'm aware of that," she said. She'd made a mistake. She should have gone to the county office first and come to him with the information in hand. "Naturally, any information you or anyone else gives me on this or any other story will be verified with records before we publish the story. But I came to you because of your connection with the house now."

"I was attorney in a transaction concerning the house. That's my sole connection."

"I'm not accusing you of any other," Liz said. "Or implying—"

"As attorney, with that as my sole connection, I'm certainly not at liberty to disclose any information to you. I hate to put it so baldly, but that's it. Cut and dried."

"This is hardly a confidential matter," she said. "If it's on public record."

"I'd be glad to help you on anything else," Kilgore said. He tilted his chair forward and leaned toward Liz. "I'm a member of the county historical society. I have lots of ideas for stories about this island."

"What would you suggest?"

"We spend so much time in our lives moaning about the wrong and the bad. Forget it, Miss Gold. Pass it by. Pass it by. It's been so long since that Sylvan mess."

"There's no statute of limitations on murder," Liz said. "The length of time doesn't matter."

"Time's one thing. Proof's another. You know, Miss Gold, to be able to make a murder charge stand up in court, you need a weapon. No weapon was ever found. Even if someone came in begging for judgment—no weapon, no proof. You need hard evidence to link a crime to a murderer. Without hard physical evidence or that weapon, it's all circumstantial, and that doesn't hold up in court, less likely than ever after so long a time. You have to think of the court, Miss Gold. Possible motive. Possible presence. Forget it."

"I'm not going to court," she said.

"You need to think like you are; otherwise you might end up with a libel suit. And libel law—that's another swamp you don't want to walk in." He sounded like a benevolent guide.

How stupid she had been, she thought, to come here unarmed with facts, expecting this lawyer to write her story for her. She sat still, trying to think of something to say that would pry the information from him, make it seem to his advantage to talk to her.

Kilgore rose, extending his hand. Liz slowly gathered her purse and notebook, her recorder and pad. Then she took his hand.

"What's the problem, Mr. Kilgore?" she asked. "Why won't you talk to me?" His palm was dry, no sign of nervousness. He smiled as if they were having a pleasant talk.

"That's just what no one ever gets from me—a problem. Good day to you, Miss Gold. And good luck with that magazine."

Up Tremont Street, away from the Strand, Liz found a pay phone and called Jeff, who told her he'd meet her at noon in the same luncheonette from which she'd called him two days before.

"It isn't all clogged up with atmosphere," he said.

"Whatever. Jeff, how would you go about finding out who owned a place? A piece of real estate?"

"Tax records, first of all. Then, if it's owned by a corporation rather than an individual, the corporation is listed in the county courthouse."

"Would it be clear who's behind the corporation?"

"Not necessarily," Jeff said. "All the county requires is the name of the agent of record. And that could be the person paying taxes for the real owner. Is someone hiding?"

"Could be."

"You may have to truck up to Austin," Jeff said. "Officers of corporations are listed with the secretary of state."

"I don't want to go to Austin," Liz said. "It's early yet. I'll go to the courthouse and see what I can find."

She tried to shake off the feeling that she'd been caught out by Kilgore, that she hadn't done her homework and wasn't very good at this kind of story; worse, that she would never find out who Kilgore's client was. She thought her luck might be changing when she spotted the Chamber of Commerce office a few doors up and got a yellow map of Warm & Friendly Galveston Island, showing the location of the county courthouse. It was a short walk, and Liz followed the map, cutting through a shopping mall that had once been a through street and was presently blocked by cement planters of stunted trees, crumpled cigarette packs, and beer cans.

In front of a drugstore, a legless black man sat in a wheelchair watching the people pass. He wore a black felt alpine hat with a small red feather in the band. Other people lingered before the shop windows, alone or in groups of two or three. Many of them were old and looked borderline to poor, or as if they'd just been released from some type of confinement. It was hard to tell if the people in the mall were shopping or loitering. The stores too had an ambivalent air; they might have been closing, opening, or having sales. At the corner of the mall, a short, deeply tanned man wearing tinted aviator glasses, with a mustache, hair wet or greasy, jeans torn at one knee, and a blue, tightly fitting football shirt that read *Finally I've got it all together,* stood talking to a tall woman in a shapeless white shift. Her short-cropped hair was bright yellow. He motioned to her with his left arm, which was held bent in a fresh white cast. He motioned repeatedly, as if he had to convince her of what he was saying. Her head was crooked to one side and bobbed involuntarily, like a Japanese doll.

"Politicians and doctors," Liz heard the man say as she passed. "They're all a son-of-a-bitch, I tell you." The back of his shirt read *Melinda.*

The county courthouse—modern glass from the fifties, in front of it a park of palm trees, benches, and plaques commemorating past Galvestonians—had yielded the information that the taxes on the house and land were paid by Kelly Kilgore, who was the agent of record. The house was owned by a for-profit corporation, the Brazos Land Company, whose purpose was listed as the buying and selling of property. Kilgore was the agent of record for the corporation.

There was no one else around asking questions, and the clerk, a woman a few years older than Liz, whose short graying hair was curled and set with firmness around her face, was obliging. She'd found the deed for the house. Kilgore had bought the house and four hundred acres in 1957 from Clyde Long of Texas City. Four months before her death, Kilgore conveyed ownership to Carolyn Sylvan—again as agent—and at her death the property had reverted to ownership by the Brazos Land Company, Kelly Kilgore, agent of record. The property had then been conveyed to William Osborne. At his death, it had gone to Virginia Osborne, Virginia of the vague recollections of Carolyn Sylvan.

She got to the restaurant before Jeff and sat in a round padded booth across the room from the other booths. The huge models of crayons that were suspended from the ceiling moved in the breeze. The restaurant was deserted except for the slim black-haired waiter and a friend, a frowzy, slightly overweight woman. They sat in a booth across the room from Liz, doing a crossword puzzle.

Liz didn't blame herself any longer because she'd been slow to see the deliberateness of the silence about Carolyn Sylvan's brief presence and quick death. The conspiracy, which was what it amounted to, had been going on far longer than she'd been at work on this minor story. Whoever was involved was working harder at it than Liz had at her story. Unless Kilgore himself had been Sylvan's lover, unless he himself had killed her in jealousy over Osborne or for another unlikely and unknown reason, then he had been deliberately employed by someone else, first to find a hideaway, then to give it to Carolyn Sylvan in order to secure her loyalty and her consent to be put out to pasture in Galveston, then—after her death—to get it back and give it to William Osborne, for some other purpose. That must have had to do with Osborne's coming out on the night of the murder. Whose voice would Osborne have obeyed, for whom would he drive fifty miles in the middle of the night?

Liz looked at the clock over the bar. It was still before noon. She went to the pay phone in the hall at the back of the restaurant and tried to get an address for the Brazos Land Company in Austin, Dallas, Houston, Galveston. Then she called David's office in Houston and asked if there was a number for him in Austin.

David sounded surprised to hear from her.

"I'm glad you got me," he said. "I was just coming back to Houston. I found out I have to leave for New York this evening."

"I thought you were finished up there."

"So did I. But something's come up. It could mean a lot of work later on. The younger members of the family are talking about setting up their own foundation. To avoid these long arguments every year, for one thing. They're free now to talk, and everyone's in place but me. So."

"Well," she said, "I guess you have to go then." She wished she hadn't said anything or had expressed concern for him: clean shirts? what a bother to travel so much? "I was calling because I wondered if you'd have time to do something for me. Now I guess you don't. I'm trying to save myself a trip up to Austin."

"What for?"

"Could you think of someone to get the names of the officers of a corporation? The Brazos Land Company. They aren't listed in any cities so far, so I can't just ask them directly. It's a long story, but it could be something. It's the first new thing I've found on the Sylvan piece."

"I know a legislative aide who might do it. Or someone in a law office up here."

"This is stupid," Liz said. "I can't ask someone I don't even know to do my work. I'll fly up there tomorrow."

"You really want me to do it?"

"Only out of laziness," she said. "And I don't know how to do it—but it's wrong."

"There's worse," David said. "You're not asking for anything expensive or illegal. I'll try. If it takes too long I'll let you know. I'll leave a message with Cheryl or on the machine either way. Did you fix the tape?"

"No," she said. "But Cheryl's at the magazine."

"I'll be at the Plaza tonight," he said, "if all else fails. Cheer up, Liz. You sound beat."

"I wish you'd be here tonight," she said, but when they hung up she regretted that. If she stayed with him, maybe she would learn to gauge when to ask for help and when to just be there, when to say she loved him and when to let it go.

Liz returned to the booth and ordered a glass of white wine. She was halfway through it when Jeff turned up. He was as tall as David, blond, and with a chubby pink face. His front teeth protruded slightly, giving him a sweet rabbit look that made him seem more vulnerable and trustworthy than he was. He carried a manila envelope and stood at the door surveying the room before he saw Liz. She tried to remember if he had one child or two. When they'd covered the trial together in the fall, they'd mostly compared notes on work, exchanging autobiographies in the tersest way possible.

"You're a lucky woman," Jeff said when he sat in the booth. "I mean really lucky."

"Is this it?" Liz asked, reaching for the manila envelope he'd laid on the table in front of her.

"There's not much to the file," he said. "But if you ever let anyone know where you got it, we're all in trouble. Big trouble."

"My lips are sealed. I promise. How did you get it?"

"I have my ways," Jeff said. He looked mysterious and she thought he would tell her—a cousin in the department, his brother-in-law on the city council—but he just shook his head again and said, "Never mind. What you don't know can't hurt you. It's an open case, so legally you shouldn't have this. But big deal. The DA's report is in there. The guy was okay. Not a complete moron. But he didn't have a thing. It's a masterpiece of dead ends."

"But this is it," Liz said. "If I read this, then I know everything the police saw and heard and knew."

"As much as they'd write down. They don't write down suspicions. You probably know now as much as anyone knew about the murder. Cops may not be geniuses and they don't know how to spell—you'll see that. But they know procedure. What they think of the victim isn't relevant—the girl might have been trouble, but that isn't their official business. The police didn't follow this down every gopher hole, but they proceeded. There wasn't anything."

"Thank you," she said. She took the envelope and set it on the slippery banquette next to her. "I don't know how to thank you, really. Can *Spindletop* buy you a melted cheese and steamed vegetables on whole-wheat pita bread?"

Jeff looked across the room at the menu on the blackboard near the bar.

"How about a beer and a hamburger," he said. "Sometime, Liz, I'll be asking you for something more serious. Like a recommendation to Cal Dayton to take me on at *Spindletop*. We may want to get off this island."

"Kilgore taught me a new term this morning," Liz said. "BOI."

"Well, the causeway works both ways. Not right now. We don't want to move right now. It's hard to remember in winter what this place gets like in summer. Now the beaches are clear. The weather's perfect."

"What happens in summer? Heat?"

"Tourists," Jeff said.

The slim waiter came to take their orders and when he'd gone, Jeff said, "This BOI business. It's really important to people around here. It stuck in people's throats, the child being killed with Carolyn Sylvan, but—"

"They were strangers, weren't they?"

"Yes. It's hard to explain. It isn't as heartless as it must look to you. It's a funny place. Did you notice those huge red stone mansions as you drive down Broadway? The esplanade with the giant palms? Well, one of those belongs to the richest lady in town. It's the family mansion and this is their island. But the Dairy Queen's right next door. Now what can anyone say about that?"

She rode back easily to Houston, driving quickly in the gap between the morning and afternoon rush hours. When she got back to the apartment, she called Cheryl, who spelled out a message from David: "The incorporators are Dale Lord, L-O-R-D, Trudy Landers, L-A-N-D-E-R-S, and Joan Blackwell, B-L-A-C-K-W-E-L-L. And he said he'd talk to you tonight."

Galveston information had too many Landerses and no Trudy or Gertrude listed. Dale Lord was obviously Kilgore's partner in Smith, Day, Kilgore & Lord. Liz had better luck with Joan Blackwell, who lived on Bonita Street.

The phone rang at Joan Blackwell's six times before a child answered.

"Hello," Liz said. "I'd like to speak with Joan Blackwell."

"Mama," Liz heard. "Mama. The phone's for you."

"Hello." An adult voice. "May I help you?"

Liz recognized the husky voice of the receptionist at Kilgore's.

"This is Liz Gold, Mrs. Blackwell. I came in this morning to see Mr. Kilgore, and I wonder if you'd answer a few questions."

"What kind of questions?"

"Are you the Joan Blackwell who's an official incorporator of the Brazos Land Company?"

"Yes," she said. "It's all legal, you know. There's not a thing wrong."

"I'm not saying there is anything wrong, Mrs. Blackwell. Trudy Landers—does she work for the firm also?"

"She sure does. She's Mr. Dale Lord's secretary. He's semiretired."

"You never really had anything to do with this land company, did you? Except to sign the papers. I mean, I'll bet you don't know anything about it."

"You're right, Miss Gold. We have to sign things all the time in that office." Liz was silent, waiting for Joan Blackwell to explain or start chatting about the office, but she thought it unlikely. "Is there anything else? I have to get my little girl's supper on the table."

"No," Liz said. "Nothing. Thanks for your time."

She cleared the papers off the bed and lay down.

If it had been cash or diamonds or drugs, then the bribe—if it was a bribe—would have been hard to trace. Property was so clumsy. The houses Clarice had dragged her and David in and out of had taught Liz that. Looking at real estate was like being a judge at a sad beauty pageant. Everything showed, the ambition of the owners or the lack of it; their faith in their future or desire to cut their losses and be rid of the house and each other, then move on. Liz hesitated, thinking she was only involving herself in something unpleasant, and dialed Clarice's number. She hoped Jessie or Maria would answer.

"I'm so pleased," Clarice said. "I was beginning to think—now did I do something wrong last week at dinner? Sometimes I say awful things and people don't tell me. Some do. I don't know what's worse."

"Oh, Clarice. Of course you didn't say anything wrong." In a group where most people sent thank-you notes after a dinner party, Liz must certainly have set Clarice's teeth on edge, not phoning, not answering messages. "I've been horribly rude. It was a wonderful dinner. But I got involved in a story."

"Oh, I understand." Clarice was always respectful of Liz's writing, which embarrassed Liz, who took what she considered to be a realistic view of her career.

"In fact, Clarice, would you have a moment to answer a question for me? To help on a story?"

"I'd be delighted. If it's real complicated, you might try Helen. She's the boss."

"Well, I'll try you. Say there was an old house on the west end of Galveston, near Pirate's Beach. A really nice old house in good shape. Way off the road with mature trees. And land. Four hundred acres."

"It's out of your bracket," Clarice said. "I speak with confidence on that. I'd value it—ballpark—at well over a million. It's all potential until it's developed, but the owner could use it as collateral. It's a real valuable property, Liz. A lot of money. A Galveston person would be able to tell you more."

Part of it had already been sold, for Lafitte's Acres, Liz thought. It was enough money, then, to keep Mrs. Osborne going, especially if Osborne had left her with anything else. Liz waited for Clarice to offer to show her a house or to tell her that the house in Shallow River Oaks was gone, sold for an admirably low price.

"Thanks," Liz said. "That puts it in perspective. I wonder if you could tell me one more thing. . . ."

"Anything, Liz."

"This isn't any of my business, but I was thinking about Helen. Does she live off the real-estate business? Or does she have something else?"

"Well, she worked for Corrigan forever. And he paid her very well. Then he left her a bunch of Corrigan stock in trust and she could live off the income of that. It was about a hundred and fifty thousand, when he died. It's probably worth a lot more now."

"I was just wondering," Liz said. "I went to talk to her the other day."

"She mentioned it," Clarice said.

"Well, send my love to Doug," Liz said. "And thanks again."

"Love to David. Glad to be of help."

They hung up and Liz thought, I've finally managed to alienate Clarice. She'll never show us anything again. We'll have to buy Walden.

Liz took the envelope Jeff had given her and settled down on the white wicker couch to read the homicide file. She read through once quickly, then sorted through the documents and categorized them: the reports from the FBI and the county medical examiner on physical evidence; the police and witness reports; the DA's summary.

The medical examiner had found Carolyn Sylvan to be a well-developed, well-nourished white female measuring sixty-seven inches and weighing an estimated one hundred and fifteen pounds. He noted an old scar on her right knee, possibly from childhood, and an appendectomy scar.

The clothing submitted with the body was a full-length blue cotton dress.

The bullet had entered the body beneath the left scapula. It had traveled through the lower lobe of the left lung, through the stomach and aorta, and through the liver. There was no exit wound in the front of the body.

Carolyn Sylvan had died as a result of exsanguination, itself the result of a gunshot wound.

Then he took her apart. Part by part—hair, skin, teeth, heart, lungs, spleen; her cavities and genitalia; her liver, gallbladder, biliary ducts, and pancreas; gastrointestinal tract, adrenals and kidney, urinary bladder; aorta and arteries, veins; her skeletal system; her skull and brain— all revealed that aside from the gunshot wound, Carolyn Sylvan had been a sturdy, symmetrical, and healthy young woman to whose body life had done nothing more than leave the traces of childbirth, a possible fall on the knee during her childhood, and an incipient and untended cavity in a tooth that might have given her trouble in time.

The child's body—Rose's body—had been similarly measured and weighed and had come out sounding like the same kind of solved jigsaw puzzle. She had no scars. She was normal in all her tissues and her organs. She had died from being crushed. Marks of the tire were on her small chest. Comparing the measured width of the chest with the width of a tire, Liz thought it might have been an equal match.

She stopped reading and went to the window, thinking she'd like a drink or something to eat. Her refrigerator was bare. She'd go the next day and get food for the apartment. She looked back at the wicker couch, at the pile of papers there, and thought of going back to Graustark, where there was leftover roast and cold potatoes, beer and fruit.

The FBI report wasn't much help. None of the samples of fingerprints from two adult females, two adult males, and one child yielded any criminal records. Everything that had been sent to the FBI had been meticulously labeled and listed: Q6 eleven cigarette butts, Q20 a child's knit shirt. K18 was described as a partial matchbook cover, showing a shield divided into three parts; a star on the upper left, a black swan on the upper right. Across the bottom sector was lettering Liz could just make out. The words were Latin: *In hoc cygno refugies.* The prints on the matchbook fragment had been too smudged for the FBI to check.

There were two supplementary offense reports from the Galveston police department, and homicide anatomy forms, showing on one side of the page a standing male, front and back; on the other side a female. The female was drawn with a sagging stomach and heavy breasts. The male was in better condition. On the sheet marked *Complainant Carolyn Sylvan* there was an X on the back. On the sheet for *Complainant Rose Sylvan,* a large X covered the midsection of the body.

The officer on duty the night of the murders was Sergeant Richard Battle. He had been called at 11:10 P.M. by a man who identified himself as William Osborne of Houston. He was reporting two deaths on West Beach. When the sergeant and the ambulance arrived at 11:30 P.M., they found a child sprawled on the half-circle driveway and, inside the entrance to the house, a woman dead of an apparent gunshot wound. There was a Chevrolet convertible in the garage; in the driveway, a Cadillac—Texas plate TGV 395, registered to William Osborne. It was parked at one end of the driveway, far from the child.

The woman and the child were photographed in place and eventually taken to the Broadway Funeral Home to await the medical examiner. Fingerprints were taken in the house; a search warrant was applied for for the house, the Cadillac, and the Chevrolet convertible. Battle waited until dawn in the house, until the bodies were taken away and the search warrant had come through. The rest of the force was busy on the Seawall with a three-car collision.

Frank Bone, the DA, made his summary three weeks later. It recapitulated police action from the moment of arrival at the scene of the crime through interrogation of the one witness—William Osborne—and dealings with the house, bodies, and cars.

Bone mentioned that the day after the murder, a neighbor had come forth and volunteered that two cars had been to Sylvan's house the night of the murders. One had come and gone. The other had come to the house and stayed. The DA noted that it grew dark early that time of year; the woman had no idea what kind of cars these were, or if they had actually gone to the Sylvan house or perhaps continued on. Therefore, her statement was useless.

Liz noted that Osborne's statement and the DA's matched in each detail. Osborne listed his address and occupation, age and phone number. His statement had been typed the day after the murders.

According to Osborne:

> At nine-thirty on the 6th of April 1959 I received a phone call at my home. It was a voice I couldn't identify even as to man woman or child. But it told me that Carolyn Sylvan—whom I had known previously in Houston—needed me and had asked me to come to the house in Galveston. My wife wasn't home. I left immediately. When I arrived in Galveston after eleven o'clock I saw the body of Carolyn's daughter on the driveway. I backed out my car and drove in the other way. I went over to the child and saw that she was dead. The front door of the house was wide open. I went inside and saw Carolyn on the floor. I took her pulse and saw that she was dead. I called the police and waited for them outside. I tried to be careful not to touch anything in the house.

Osborne was questioned and stayed in Galveston for the remainder of the day and night after the murders. He wasn't arrested at any time.

Fingerprints in the house were identified as Carolyn Sylvan's, her daughter's, Osborne's, and several unknown.

The gun was nowhere to be found, but the bullet identified the weapon as a Beretta, a common hand weapon. Carolyn Sylvan had been shot at close range. The child had been run over once with a car that was neither Osborne's nor Carolyn Sylvan's. The tires were Firestone, a standard type. In the living-room ashtray were cigarette butts and one cigar butt. The DA commented that the scraps of the matchbook cover with the shield were found by the doorway. It wasn't identified as coming from a Galveston club or restaurant.

In the absence of a weapon—none turned up in the bushes or immediate yard of the house—and in the absence of clear motive or evidence, Osborne was released by the Galveston police. Physical examination of his hands showed he hadn't fired a gun that night. When people on the West End were questioned about the activities of Carolyn Sylvan and her daughter, they could say only that sometimes there was a big dark fancy car there at night, but no one was able to identify Osborne's Cadillac as that car. Osborne was open about his close relationship with Carolyn Sylvan.

The DA was scrupulous, and he wrote that he and Osborne drank a lot of coffee the day of the murder. He noted when they ate anything. He ordered doughnuts for them, which they shared with Sergeant Battle when he came on duty the next evening.

Osborne made one phone call. He spoke with his wife for some time, indicating that something terrible had happened, that he'd been called out to the house in Galveston and had found Carolyn Sylvan and her child dead. He sounded agitated during the conversation and said in a loud voice that he could handle himself. Mrs. Osborne had just arrived back from a trip to Georgia to see her father. When Osborne was told he could go home, he seemed at a loss. Bone offered to find him a hotel room in Galveston, if he was too tired to make the drive back to Houston. After he had signed his statement, Osborne left.

The investigation had lasted a few weeks, dragging into May, when Bone's report was written. It all added up to nothing. No one came to claim the bodies. They were buried in the county cemetery.

Liz stayed the night at her apartment, reluctant to drive the few blocks to Graustark. The bedroom in the apartment overlooked the back yard and the parking lot. A live oak that repeated the angle of its curving trunk in every branch tapped at the window in the night. One or two more nights, it would be cold enough to sleep with blankets; then it would be spring, with weeks of keeping the windows open, then shutting them for months against the summer. It would be air conditioning, another form of hibernation. The oak was too close to her window. Liz had watched it during squalls and wondered if it would fall into her room, yet she hadn't moved the bed away from the window. Sometimes at night when she couldn't sleep, Liz reviewed the layers between her and the world—paint, plaster, lath, brick, paint.

What had happened in that house the night of the murders? Had the little girl been running away? Why had Carolyn Sylvan been shot in the back—was she running also? Did the murderer stand at the door, and did she recognize him or her, then start to run and falter when she was shot? Did the child feel very much, out there on the shell and sand driveway, dying under the big trees and the ocean sky? To be taken apart, piece by piece, to be weighed, measured, examined, and to be summed up as healthy except for being dead; both of them, healthy, young, mysteries. To die without disease or natural causes—that was what Liz remembered about the war, that they kept sending in healthy young men and producing dead or mangled bodies; that the war was a machine that consumed bodies.

Liz turned and tried lying on one side, then her other side, then her back, looking again at the shadow of the tree through her blind. To change her vision, so as not to dream of the sagging woman in the police outline, X marking her spot, Liz tried to recall Hunter's face. She only managed to see men's faces that reminded her of his, models for jeans or cologne.

She thought of streets in Manhattan where she'd walked after high school, unwilling to go home and face her parents and homework, to arrive for the cocktail hour when they sat with drinks and she sat with them. She thought of Madison Avenue and tried walking from Fifty-third to Fifty-seventh; she imagined a British men's clothing shop, a five and ten, fancy button store, Chock Full O' Nuts, and Hunter walked in front of her. The avenue was dark and deserted. She imagined standing on the corner of Fifty-seventh and Madison on a sunny Saturday afternoon, looking for someone, peering into each face for the familiar, the awaited.

Home at six-thirty, her parents would be sitting in the living room, discussing the day. They reported to each other, she often thought, proving that their days hadn't been wasted. The most interesting time to Liz—the time she really listened and stopped narrating a private commentary on her parents' behavior—was when one or the other would say, "A funny thing: I bumped into . . ." and then launch into a story about someone from their past, perhaps an old political companion now moved away from New York into prosperity, or still in the city but nonpolitical, a schlemiel, but a nice guy, always was. These stories gave her parents' relationship so much more depth than the daily reporting. It reached back to a time before the war, before Liz, when they must have loved each other.

When she first began going on demonstrations her name was recognized, or perhaps others saw something of her father in her face. He was small and dark and looked wise. His professional boldness, his ethical stance, his shrewdness as a lawyer committed to civil liberties went perfectly with his lined, concerned, intelligent face. He was blue-eyed and handsome, and would have been completely content if he'd been six inches taller, or so Liz guessed from the stories he told about tall girls he dated in college.

She'd not thought much about her parents' marriage until she met people in the peace movement who knew them. Few of her friends' parents were divorced or separated. When they did divorce, it was a stigma for the child to bear. Her mother and father were so often together and joined so seamlessly in their opinions and their efforts to keep life running smoothly that Liz never connected the possibility of divorce with her home. But she learned through rumor and pretended to have known it all along: her father was known on the left as a ladies' man. There hadn't been one affair but many.

She had always been urged to bring reason rather than emotion to problems, so Liz fell into the habit of walking home from school and meetings and of using that time to think about her parents. How did it balance—their careful scruples and this hypocritical marriage? If her mother knew about the women, she hadn't talked about them with Liz and would resent her daughter for bringing them up. If she didn't know, how could Liz be the one to tell her? If her father wanted a divorce or a separation, a new marriage with one of the women—Liz imagined first Rosa Luxemburg, then the small blond mother of a friend, a woman active in raising money for the civil rights summers in the South—her father would do it if his daughter liked it or not. People were free, her mother had taught her; there were no chains on their feet, or shouldn't be. Even the best marriage was only a social agreement, a pact to be honored so long as it was just. Her mother was taller than her father, with short wavy brown hair and button eyes that made her look Chinese. She wore her clothes like a uniform and lived her life in a fury of organization against the chance that she would lose time, miss out, or—worst of all—waste energy, food, time, opportunity.

And so Liz kept silent and learned not to listen to gossip. What did she know, after all, about marriage? She was only recently a child, without an idea in her head. When she met Willy, short years later, she told him about her father. Willy told her that the only really bad thing her father had done was to keep his real life a secret from her, and Liz felt free and mature. Now, in Houston, she thought her father should have been better at keeping secrets, and that the real crime was that she'd ever found out.

What did she know about marriage still? Her parents had the most enduring marriage she knew. Liz thought of the intimacy of those daily times at cocktail hour, when they gave over versions of their days. Perhaps her mother left out more personal news as well.

She was out of it now, she had escaped to Texas, but at times like this, in the dark, sleepless and alone, Liz could have been anywhere. She remembered a postcard she'd sent her father when she first arrived: the picture of a small boy in a cowboy suit, who stood by a Model-T. The caption: *The sun has riz/The sun has set/And here I is/In Texas yet.* She wondered now—had she been here too long, was she too involved, would she work it all out and make it as airless as home? She thought of her dizziness at street corners, looking at the ugliness of Houston and the clean expansive sky. This disorientation too could become memory, and then she would only be at home, in Houston, in Texas, with David.

Around ten o'clock, Liz went to the phone, first dialing Cal's number and listening to it ring, imagining the sound in the pine-paneled cottage, the chintz pillows absorbing the small noise. She thought Cal might worry if he came home and she wasn't there, no note left for him. David might have been trying her on Graustark. She dialed the Plaza and listened to the phone ring in his room. She called back immediately and left a message that she'd called. She didn't want him worrying about her, she thought, and more than that she wanted to be right, never to be the guilty one. She gave up on David, but still wanted to talk to someone and couldn't think who it would be. She was friends with Cal and David. She knew Clarice and Doug, Doc, and the people at the magazine. If she lost David, she would be losing everything again, leaving the biggest hole in her life. Whom had Carolyn Sylvan known and whom could she have counted on? Perhaps she was another woman who could count her friends on one hand—Helen Dayton, William Osborne, Gus Corrigan.

In the morning, Liz drove across to the Village, an old shopping center with low yellow-brick buildings, and ate breakfast at One's A Meal. She liked the biscuits there. She was earlier than the lunch crowd and past the breakfast working crowd. She felt as if she'd fallen into a safe crack in time. The smell of eggs and coffee was like nourishing sleep to her, as she considered what to do with the day ahead. There was only one piece of material evidence unexplained in the file; perhaps the DA knew more than he'd included in his report.

When she left One's A Meal, the air outside smelled like vacation mornings at the seaside, salty, with a lingering odor of car exhaust.

"How'd you track me down," Bone asked, "an old retired person like me."

"There aren't many people named Bone in Galveston," Liz said. "I hit it lucky, first try."

"The Sylvan case isn't closed," he said. His voice crackled slightly over the phone. "But I'll answer what questions I can."

"It seems that you didn't have very much to go on. . . ."

"Nothing much."

"Someone mentioned to me . . . something. Part of a matchbook?"

He paused, and she wondered if he would press her for her source, ending the conversation.

"Smart girl," he said. "That was all we had, blurred prints and all. It looked like it dropped out of someone's pocket, right where the killer would have been standing. From that distance, he would have been at the door and gotten the girl when she turned to run. It might have dropped out of his pocket. It was pretty clean. If it had been there long, it would have been saturated with dirt and salt air. So we figured."

"But you never identified where the matchbook was from?"

"Hard to. There wasn't much to it. It's some kind of shield, some official symbol. It wasn't Rice. Wasn't U.T."

"Well, that eliminates some people," Liz said.

"There flat wasn't anything. Nothing to go on."

"Who owned the house, Mr. Bone? She didn't have any money when she worked for Corrigan in Houston. It was transferred to her by Kilgore, and I can't find out who he was acting for."

"Another dead end," Bone said companionably. "That's just the way the case ran, start to finish."

"Did the police really try to find the killer?" Liz asked. "Did you? Was there—I don't mean any offense, but sometimes there's pressure. . . ."

"Sometimes there doesn't have to be pressure," Bone said. It sounded as if his years as DA had inured him to the accusation that he and the police hadn't tried hard enough, or perhaps he had turned philosophical in his retirement. "If a killing is very simple and it's covered up well—let's say a spur-of-the-moment killing—it may never get solved. A police department—and Galveston's is very small—a police department has a lot to take care of besides murders. Something's always going on, and a case can get washed over. There was an effort made to find the killer, Miss Gold. Carolyn Sylvan wasn't what you would call a floater—a guy picked up out of the bay with a set of bullet holes. Maybe we could have done more, but she got what a person of some status would get."

By status, Liz thought, he meant white and living in a big house.

"I guess no one could think of what to do, so they let it drift. It's a long time in the past."

"That makes sense," she said. "If I need to, Mr. Bone, can I call you again?"

"Try your luck," he said. "I'm considering a trip to Florida for Easter. But Easter's a long way off."

Liz cleared her desk of notes and research clips for the last piece she'd written, setting the piles of papers and files on the floor and resolving to sort them out later. She thought of shopping for food for the apartment; the refrigerator on Graustark was full of food, this one was empty. But the trip out of the house would just prolong the agony of getting down to work, so she sat at the desk and began.

She spread out her notes from interviews and her Xeroxes of court records and newspaper stories.

The interviews, as she typed them, came out more coherently than she thought they would, and she was able to start putting together atmosphere notes—color of walls, description of Virginia Osborne, Kelly Kilgore's office. She listened to her tapes, then combined her memory of them with the shorter notes she'd made. When she was finished with an interview, she clipped together the typed pages and put them in a neat pile to one side. Around lunchtime, she was hungry but decided to keep working until she was finished. When she next looked up, it was two o'clock.

She phoned Cal at the magazine.

"Where have you been?" he said. "I tried to get you last night and finally gave up."

"I stayed here," she said. "And I've been working this morning, typing up my notes."

"I'd like to see a copy."

"Why would you want to? I just type them because my handwriting's so bad."

"Humor me," Cal said. "Give me a copy of the notes."

"Okay. Have you had lunch?"

"I ate with Hunter. Sandwiched between his brunch for advertisers and his plane to L.A."

"He's gone again?"

"You didn't expect him to stay in Houston for long, I hope. This isn't his kind of place, cowboy chic aside. He did everything at the brunch but give away cars and have me strip. I hope they were impressed."

"I guess you can't have lunch."

"I guess not. What's up for the weekend? Anything exciting?"

"We're going to Walden," she said. "David wants us to stay there until Monday."

"And am I invited?"

"Why are you so testy?"

"I can't talk now," he said. "It's nothing. There's people around. All I meant was that you and David, of course, may want to be together. Alone. Which I perfectly well understand."

There was something off between her and Cal. She considered the time at Walden with David, time he had requested, and didn't know how to say no to Cal. He was asking to come, after all, and might need the time away from the city or the time with them.

"You're more than welcome," she said. "As always."

"I'm not sure I can make it," he said. "Maybe late on Saturday night. I have things to do in town Saturday and Sunday."

"Do what you want," she said. She felt suddenly close to tears and left out of Cal's life; thinking of the homicide drawings, the sad Xs on them, she wanted to be away from Houston, away from David's return to her. She wanted to be back in New York, in her life as it had been; and she thought of herself alone in her north-lit apartment, looking at Cal's windows and hoping for company. "Bring someone with you," Liz said.

"There isn't anyone to bring," Cal said. "I'll see you late Saturday night. I'll bring marvelous fattening things."

"Okay," Liz said. "That'll be fun." The urge to be elsewhere had passed and she felt only tiredness. "That'll be wonderful. I can't wait."

She wrote a note to herself: *Liz, Cal, extra.* Once the Xeroxes were made, the only unique material for the story was in the cassettes. she put the typed notes into a manila envelope and went downstairs to her car. Late February, and she was smelling the summer odors of cut grass and new flowers. The redbud tree by the side of the yard was blooming. The Arizona ash was budding out. She had learned the names of trees and shrubs studiously, noticing how much she really knew about the East, all the names of trees and flowers, learned by osmosis. Spring would come on suddenly in Houston. There could always be a last norther, Cal had told her, up through April, but in that moment the true warmth seemed solid and permanent to Liz.

The Xerox shop was in the same shopping center as One's A Meal. She dropped the notes off with the Xerox attendant, who looked as if he'd escaped from a rock band that had been on the road since 1970. Then she drove a few blocks to buy food for the apartment.

At a four-way stop, Liz waited for the other three cars to decide which would go first. She hated four-way stops. You were supposed to yield the right of way to the driver on your right, but in a circle someone was always on someone's right, and who was to say who should go first?

The big blue Buick with the side bashed in moved forward, and Liz started to move straight ahead at the moment the white Toyota on her right started to make a left. Liz braked quickly and shrugged at the startled-looking woman driving the white car. The driver of the green pickup wearily waved Liz on.

In the food market, Liz pushed her cart past the fresh produce—the glowing strawberries and tomatoes from Mexico, the tough green broccoli and the tender lettuce—and stood before the frozen food cabinets, trying to decide what to buy. On Graustark, she worried about food for David and took care to make the refrigerator look inviting— vegetables and fruits, juices and mineral water in sparkling bottles, bread and croissants from the bakery, and jams and jellies from France and England. She cared more about the refrigerator than she did about the living room or bedroom. In the apartment refrigerator she kept coffee and milk, until it went off; in the hot months, she tried to remember to buy club soda. Now she selected four packages of Cisco's (formerly Little Juan's) frozen burritos, a few chicken pies, and some cans of orange juice. She rolled her cart toward the cashier, picking up a six-pack of beer, a bag of Tostitos, and a can of refried beans as she went.

Back at the apartment, Liz put a few burritos in the oven and opened a can of beer. She'd had two copies made—one for Cal, one for her, leaving one extra. She couldn't explain the extra copy, which spoke of a caution she couldn't justify. The story was a blank wall, except for the single fact that if the case was unsolved, then the murderer was still free. Or dead also, but that was unknown. Someone had made sure that the loyalty of the Osbornes was set for life. Someone was paying Kelly Kilgore to answer questions. There was nothing to the case—no known motive, weapon, evidence, no circumstances to put anyone on the spot, not even William Osborne, who could have been telling the truth. Thinking backward, Liz decided that the killing had been done for what it accomplished—Carolyn and her child were out of the way; an obstacle was removed to someone's happiness.

She took one copy of the Xeroxed notes, her original handwritten notes, and the tapes and put them in another manila envelope. Then she opened the hall closet and found the paisley suitcase she'd bought at the Blue Bird and put the envelope inside, covering it with some of the dresses and jackets she'd left in the closet when she moved over to Graustark. She put the suitcase at the back of the closet and rearranged the hanging clothes so that they hid it from sight.

The second copy, Liz put in an envelope for Cal. The original, she put in a file marked *Master/Sylvan Story*.

Liz turned on the television in the bedroom and settled down with her burritos and another can of beer to watch a late-afternoon movie about teenage abortion. During the first commercial, Liz went to the kitchen and opened the Tostitos and beans, bringing them back to the bedroom with her. The evening light was dimming, and she sat cross-legged on the bed, surrounded by her food. The movie's background music was Respighi's "The Fountains of Rome," which Liz associated with travelogues about Europe in the spring. She felt lonely and a little strange—in the half-light of the TV and the evening, the bedroom could have been in a welfare hotel—but she was comfortable. David would come home and she would return to the house on Graustark. She'd spend tomorrow getting ready for Walden, buying food, changing sheets on their bed, cleaning the house, washing her hair, shaving her legs. She wished she could perform a miracle of beauty on herself, and when she'd finished eating she went into the bathroom and looked in the cabinet mirror, the only mirror in the apartment. She'd better stay out of the sun, she told herself. Lines were visible that hadn't been in the pale northern light, or perhaps they just hadn't been there. Since Willy's death almost two years before, her mouth had changed shape. She held it so that two small furrows formed on her chin, like someone whose lips want to tremble and who refuses to let them. She liked looking at this small change, as evidence that clichés are true—that wrinkles and white hair come from stirring events.

When she'd first come to Texas, she'd had a hard time in parking garages and large parking lots. She never followed the arrows, indeed drove automatically in the opposite direction. It was a relief to try to do things right, Liz thought, simpler not to question; and as she turned from the mirror, she caught another expression on her face, one she had never seen before Willy's death—closed off, masklike, set.

VII

The house at Walden had been cleaned during the week by a service from the nearby town of Conroe, and on Saturday when Liz and David carried in their suitcases and bags of groceries, the place looked pristine as a hotel room. The posters of Latin miners waited for them, and the baskets on the wall. The glass coffee table had been wiped clean of fingerprints and rings left by cups and glasses. The ashtrays were washed and the piles of magazines straightened. The shag rug lay before the fireplace fluffed and expectant as a puppy.

"I'll carry our stuff upstairs," David said. "Did we bring anything for lunch?"

They'd gotten a late start—David's plane had been late leaving New York, then it had circled the Houston airport for an hour—and now, two o'clock on Saturday afternoon, Liz felt they'd lost the weekend. She had woken up early and packed the car with the groceries and liquor she'd bought on Friday, and she'd reread her notes on the Sylvan story, then waited for David to call from the airport. When he was gone, she missed him; but when the separation was nearly over and David was close to home, the feeling became a burden, akin to anger, unrelieved by his presence.

Liz started unloading the food, filling the refrigerator, pushing in against the pantry shelves yet another roll of paper towels, more cans of peeled tomatoes for emergencies or lazy, unprepared-for nights that never came. He hadn't been annoyed, as she'd feared, when she told him Cal was coming. He'd only shrugged.

"I wish I could get a game of racquetball," David said. He'd changed into dungarees and a T-shirt and began to stretch his back, holding the top of the kitchen doorjamb and letting his weight fall forward. "New York's okay because you walk a lot, but it's nasty there now. Nasty wet weather."

"Don't you know anybody at Walden to play racquetball with?"

Liz thought of David and Lucy, the pair in tennis outfits, healthy and strong, and she regretted that she didn't know how to play tennis or racquetball. The lack made her feel urban and Jewish, mismatched with David, and for a moment she thought again, If this doesn't work, I can always go back to New York.

"You know I don't know anybody here. And in New York ... I don't like doing anything social with those types on the board. I see them enough during the day."

"You could jog," she suggested. "And we could eat when you get back. I'll wait."

"What is there to eat," David asked. "I can't remember if we left anything here."

"What do you think was in those five bags we just carried in? I spent all day yesterday getting food for us. The world keeps spinning when you go to New York. I went to Jamail's and got roast beef and that bleu you like. I got bread at the French bakery and fruit and vegetables from Ed's Market. I went downtown and got wine and beer at Spec's. I got some chickens smoked at Good Company. Pasta—I can make you pasta. I got some fresh at the factory in the Village."

"You know," David said, "what I thought about on the plane was that we'd drive up here and jump straight into bed."

"And now?" Liz felt close to tears, angry with him for not giving her credit for driving miles of Houston, store to store, and feeling foolish for wanting the thanks.

"I guess I don't feel like jogging," he said. "Let's make roast beef sandwiches."

"And me?"

David straightened up and turned toward her. For an instant she thought he might come at her and strike her, but she stood where she was. He came into the room and when he reached her, he put his arms around her and pressed her against him. She relaxed, smelling the airplane on him, cigarettes, plastic, the odor of travel.

"I don't like it when you're gone," Liz said. "It throws me off. I forget."

"Then come with me," he said. "I forget too. I get so hacked with you for not being there with me. I have to go back on Monday. Come with me."

"If we'd been together a long time," she said, "would it be easier when you go away?"

"I don't know," David said. "We haven't been together a long time."

"I can't come to New York," Liz said. She thought of her parents and David together in the living room at cocktail time, of returning to the city's late-winter streets. "You know that. I have a deadline for Cal. This week."

"Then how about a sandwich," he said, releasing her.

"I can manage that."

It was just warm enough to eat outside on the patio overlooking the marina and the country club. They opened beers and put out a tray of condiments—pickles, mustard, olives—the small, half-full jars representing their time at Walden and some left over from their landlord's time there.

"Good bread," David said. "Thanks for dragging around town."

Liz had overpacked her sandwich and was slowly dismantling it to eat it piece by piece.

"I called Clarice while I was up in New York," David said.

"Did you? Why?"

"I wanted to see how the house deal was coming along."

"I had a busy week," Liz said.

"I guess you did. She said she hadn't heard from you."

"I talked to her on Thursday."

"I called her that morning. Did you go look on Thursday? Friday? She said she had a few possibilities lined up."

"Thursday I had to work on the story. Type my notes. Xerox. And

Friday—I was getting ready for the weekend." She held up a piece of rare roast beef as evidence of her activity.

David finished his sandwich and pushed his plate away from him, then took the last swig of beer in the bottle.

"Those are pretty sad excuses," he said.

"My work . . ."

"It's not your work stopping you from looking at houses. We've had all these talks, and we end up back at zero every time."

She put down the piece of roast beef she'd been about to put in her mouth. Her stomach felt tight and her mouth dry. She took a careful sip of beer and looked at David, watching for a sign that he was about to tell her that it had been a mistake with them from the start.

"How do you mean, zero?"

"We look for a house when I drag you to look for a house. If you don't want to invest in a house, that's fine. You don't have all that much. You might want to keep your money liquid. I need to reinvest the profit I made on the house I sold."

"I don't have a job, really. I don't have a salary and I need the money."

"It isn't the money. It's you being so tentative. I don't know how I'm supposed to handle this. If you'll leave me at any minute—I couldn't go through it again. You act like the neighborhood we'll live in doesn't matter, like nothing matters. You'll keep that damn apartment—"

"It's all I've got, David. It's my only place now."

"We live in a place together on Graustark."

"That's your place. It was yours first."

"Then we'll find a place together."

"Okay. I know you're right," she said.

If she disagreed with him, said the wrong words, she might lose him. She looked at him—tall, wiry, sitting across the round patio table from her, his eyes squinted against the sun. He looked just right to her, just like the person she wanted to stay with, with whom she'd fallen in love, who'd surprised her by wanting her.

"But try to understand," she said. "This is new to me. I've never owned a house."

"We must have lived in twenty houses before I was out of high school. I've told you all this. We lived in ugly towns and pretty ones. It's nicer to live in the pretty ones, but it doesn't matter. It's just places, easy come, easy go. But who you're with—that's what counts. That's what you move with you."

"I know," she said. "I know. Can we walk while we talk? Can we?"

They walked through the deserted development, past the empty model houses and townhouses with open curtains that revealed vacant rooms or closed curtains that indicated no more life within than the open ones. There were no boats out on the lake, no sound of motors. It was quiet enough to hear their sneakers scuffling along the macadam and to hear a mockingbird's cry off in the tall pines.

"While you were in New York," Liz said, then stopped, unsure if she wanted to tell him what she'd done or ask what he had.

"While I was in New York," David said, "I went to meetings during the day and at night I ate with one person or another, or I ate alone. That's all I did. That's all I do up there. At night I'm lonely. We could be having a good time up there together."

"There are things to do there. People to see."

"What do you mean?"

"I assume you either see Lucy or you want to."

"This is getting old."

"You were married to her so long," Liz said.

"If I wanted her, I wouldn't be with you, would I? I'm not a glutton for punishment," he said. "I may be loyal, but I'm not that."

"You were married to her and you would have stayed married if she hadn't left. So how can it be over completely?"

"Things end," he said. "Like it or not. When they do, it's best to face it squarely, no matter if it hurts."

"It's so soon," she said. "For you and me."

"Not for me," David said. "Would you be happier if we'd waited a year or two, circling each other? You're the person I want to be with, but . . ."

They were at the marina, at the edge of the water. David stepped onto the dock and kept walking. Liz followed him, trying to hear him in the breeze off the lake.

"You can't think I'm stepping out on you every time I go away," he said. "That isn't what we're doing together, acting that way. You don't know me if you think that."

"I'm not stepping out on you either," she said.

He turned around to face her, took her elbows and held them tightly. "Listen to me, Liz. I don't want to hear about it. Don't involve me in your made-up stories. If you don't want me, say it. But don't make up these fears and reasons."

"You make it sound like an act of will. Maybe you don't know me either. Maybe it can't work."

"It is an act of will," David said. "It's called growing up and accepting what's in front of your face. Living the life we have."

They turned and continued walking the length of the dock, past the shiny wood and plastic boats, the folded sails, the yachts pulling against the moorings.

"I never divorced Willy," she said. "I left him, and maybe that was wrong. It probably was, but I couldn't see anything else to do. We never divorced. We never even discussed it until the last time I saw him and he asked me to get one."

"Maybe he wanted to marry Ruby," David said. "He more than likely had a reason."

"Maybe. But until he asked me, I assumed we would always be married. And when he died—I don't know. It's hard for me to let go of him."

They left the marina and walked back to the house. Liz went inside to change into a fresh shirt and sweater, while David set up the grill for dinner. When she came downstairs, she stood inside, watching David through the glass sliding doors as he scraped patiently at the grill, part of a large and expensive barbecue that had come with the house and hadn't, from the looks of it, ever been cleaned. When she went out on the patio, David said, "Make me a drink?"

"Gin?"

"With tonic. Lime if we've got it."

Liz brought out the drinks and set David's on the ground beside him. She sat at the round white table. In September when they'd rented the place there had been boats drifting by and foolish swimmers fighting the water hyacinths that grew along the shore of the lake. Children's voices had come across the water from the apartments, and the regular little balconies had been festooned with drying towels and bathing suits. Now all was calm and unpeopled. There was only the breeze from the lake, the blue sky, the clipped lawns, and in the background the mournful bell-like tones of halyards clanging on the masts.

"Why does the country club look so much like a synagogue," Liz asked.

"Maybe they hired a Jewish architect," he said.

"The problem," Liz said, "the problem is me."

"That sounds very harsh," he said, "a little down-so-far-you-can't-get-up. Let me tell you something I've been thinking about."

"Sure," she said. She thought they probably looked fine, like any other couple on a Saturday evening by the lake, dressed casually, drinking their first gins in the early spring light. Yet she was full of fear and would have given anything to change the conversation.

"You think there was some wrongdoing, some mischief with Willy's death," he began.

"Mischief? What kind of mischief? There was an autopsy and a coroner's report. The money went through—"

"Jesus, Liz. You've put so much energy into this Carolyn Sylvan deal, someone you never met, someone who's been dead for twenty years. And if I suggest something about Willy . . . look. The way you told me about it, suddenly he died a violent death. The people he was living with disappeared. His mother and cousin, his father—no one did anything, and they benefited from his death."

"For that matter, so did I. Not so much, relatively. No. The question isn't clearly one of *cui bono*. I don't know what it is. Just a feeling that something terrible was going on with him, something extreme, dangerous, and I didn't know it."

"And should have saved him? Liz to the rescue?"

"Yes," she said. "I should have."

David carried his glass over to the table and set it down beside hers, then dragged one of the chairs close to her and sat down.

"Do you think they murdered him for his money? Over something political? Or do you think he killed himself?" David asked. "Is that what bothers you?"

"Yes," Liz said. "Yes, it is."

It was quiet now by the lake, not even the sound of the breeze picking up water and pushing it into small waves.

Liz said, "If he killed himself, it would be worse than him just being dead. It would mean he'd given up on everything. And everyone. I knew he didn't have any use for me. Not after Stockholm. But he kept going, and that meant something to me. He was there. I don't think I could bear it if I knew he'd given up like that."

"I think you could," David said. "You can usually take the truth—most people can; it's the lies that wear you down."

She could see now that David was tired, and in his fatigue thought that she glimpsed his old age, with her or without. She would like to be there, she thought. It was like looking over the border of a country she'd never walk in.

"I think I'm stuck with it," she said.

"Why? We could at least try to find out. Get closer to the truth. Finish the Sylvan story by the end of the week, and we'll go to Vermont—"

"New York State."

"Wherever it is. And we'll find out. Talk to the cops and the coroner. The DA. There's paper on every accidental death. We'll check it out."

It was a good offer, Liz knew, the best anyone could make, but she said, "I don't know. Not right now. Maybe in the summer we could go," thinking that if he agreed to doing something in the summer, it would mean they would be together until then at least.

"Liz, I'm not saying this would be a fun trip to take. But something's got to give, cookie. We can't keep going on like we are. I couldn't stand it again, being left like I was. And I love you but I won't let myself in for it again. It would be intolerable for a while to leave you, but I'd get over it. I don't think I'd try again, but there's other ways to live and lonely isn't the worst way to be. I could be a nice old gent like Doc, live alone. Have Clarice invite me for dinner to round out her table. I can do that. But not this. Not much longer. So you've got to fish or cut bait."

"We'll find a house," Liz said. "I promise I'll look."

"I'm willing to put my life with yours," he said.

"David—"

"I think I'll go lie down," he said.

"I'll go with you."

"No," he said. "Make a fire."

"I don't think I could stand living without you."

"That's a good place to start," David said.

She built a fire in the barbecue from hickory scraps and charcoal briquets, then watched it slowly burn out. David slept on. It grew too cold to stay outside, so she built a fire in the limestone fireplace inside.

She had made accommodations in her affections all along: loved her father in spite of his two-faced life, loved Willy with the thought that at the end of his danger there would be a reward of peace. With David the accommodation would be to peace and convincing herself that she belonged as much as anyone to the world she would live in. She would get more credit cards and follow the arrows in parking lots, making life easier for herself. She would use OUT doors to exit, IN doors to enter. She'd stay with the same haircutter until one of them died or moved away; she'd wait for the white sales each year to replenish her supply of one-hundred-percent cotton sheets. She and David would live in a house with pecan trees out back and a magnolia in front, and in time they'd find land or a place in the country. People would cease asking her how she liked Houston. Her accent would modulate. Already her hair was turning redder. After thirty or forty seasons in the sun her skin would be wrinkled and tanned permanently. She would become a new person.

She had been the same since she was a child, two eyes that looked out and tried to guess what fork the grown-ups use. Married to David, she would be one of the grown-ups.

Without him, there would be an apartment with piles of paper, and there would be friends, still friends, but no one who would cast his lot with hers with such firmness. There would be sympathy but not a true linking.

If she went east with David at the end of the week and even attempted to find out how Willy had died—succeed or fail—she would have to acknowledge that she'd moved past Willy, that he was dead, no longer there to be her guide, her death's head, her first lover.

"Knock, knock." She heard Cal's voice. "Anybody home?"

"Us chickens," she answered.

He was standing at the open front door holding two grocery bags. A black bottle of Spanish champagne stuck out of one.

"I can't believe I left the door unlocked," she said.

"This isn't a high-crime district," Cal said. "By a long shot. You'd have to be on the ten-most-wanted list and shoot up a few condos before you got any attention around here. Where's David?"

"Upstairs. Asleep. I wonder if many of the people who come to Walden are afraid of being kidnapped. Or assassinated."

"Not rich enough," Cal said. "Doctors and lawyers and small-time real estate people. Bankers. All I ever do when I come here is tell the guard I'm coming to see David. He'd let in the Manson family so long as they were white. Where should I put these heavy bags?"

While Cal unpacked the food he'd brought, Liz watched from a seat at the kitchen counter. She noticed that the cutout window through which she was looking had brown shutters, which had never been closed, to her knowledge. Cal had brought croissants, Danish butters, fig preserves, kiwi fruit, champagne, pecan-cured pepper bacon, eggs, and a hunk of creamy blue Camembert.

"I hope this Sylvan thing isn't going to your head," Cal told her as he looked in the refrigerator.

"I can't solve a mystery unless I think mysteriously, can I?"

"Is it so hard to solve?" He turned his bright gaze on her, and she saw his resemblance to Helen. As he grew older he would look more chiseled and beautiful, still more like his marble mother. "No beer?"

"Look behind the milk. It's not hard to find the general motive—she was in someone's way. But whose way was it?"

Cal opened a bottle of beer and Liz followed him into the living room, back to the fire. Cal settled on the sofa with a groan and put up his loafer-shod feet on a stack of magazines on the glass table.

"If people were killed every time they were an inconvenience to someone else, the streets would be running with blood. I can think of a few obstacles I'd gladly see removed."

Liz thought of telling Cal about David's proposal that she go and investigate Willy's death but thought better of it. He'd advised her often to forget Willy, just to shut it off and get on with it, and she couldn't imagine how to tell him why it seemed like a good idea.

"Still, I wonder who wanted her out of the way," Liz said.

"You'll figure it out."

"Do you know? Why don't you just tell me?"

"You're the reporter," he said.

"I'm glad you have such faith in me. I want a big reward when I finish this—dinner out. I might go away with David."

"Whatever you want is fine with me. How's David doing?"

"Fine. Tired of flying back and forth."

Cal smiled at her, then stared into the fire. Liz wondered if he was lonely around them, if he envied her and David. Maybe when the magazine was on its feet, his income more secure and his position clearer, Cal would be able to fall in love and make a life with someone.

"How are things at the magazine?"

"I spent all day yesterday on the cover. Shooting it and reshooting it, then talking it all out again. I'm thinking of using only all-type covers." He stood and walked into the kitchen. "Beer?" he called out. "Drink?"

"Drink," Liz said. "Gin and tonic."

When Cal came back, he sat again on the couch. It had grown dark, and the room was lit only by the kitchen light behind them and the fire before them.

"I went to my psychic today," Cal said. "Have I told you about her?"

"Never."

"She's fabulous. She lives outside the Loop on the Gulf Freeway, in one of those singles complexes. You find the place by the billboards screaming about it for five miles around, but it's okay. There's a swimming pool near her part of the complex. Small. A guy in a wheelchair usually is sitting there reading on warm days. He's the only person I've seen there besides Aileen. Her place isn't bad. The usual motel-type apartment, but the walls are a pretty color. It's very simply finished. Bare."

"And what's Aileen like?"

"A very modest sort of person. She's short. Shorter than you, with reddish hair cut very close to her head and really wide harlequin glasses in clear plastic. She's probably worn them since high school. She doesn't look at though she spends much time worrying about her looks."

"How did you ever hear about her?"

"Oh, Amy was doing an article about magic Houston, and I killed it eventually because there was no story. But I liked what Amy said about Aileen, and I was curious. This was my third time in six months. You sit opposite her on a folding chair, a very ordinary metal chair, and the table is a card table. Couldn't be plainer. No equipment, no cards or charts. You might like it," he said cautiously, "who knows? It's been a help to me. I've had the feeling since I came back to Houston that I don't exist anymore. The magazine lives but I don't. No personal life. I don't mean sex."

"What about me and David?"

"Well, you were my friends separately, but now you're together. It isn't your fault. It's just what happens. I often wondered what would have happened if Helen had remarried. I remember worrying like mad about it until I was in high school."

"We're still your friends," Liz said, then was immediately sorry she had said 'we' instead of 'I'. She took a drink from the glass Cal had brought her and told herself it was the last of the night. She felt sleepy and past hunger or thirst. "What happened in high school?"

"I got busy with other things."

"I was never so desperate in my life as in high school."

"Of course," Cal said, "I was busy then trying to like girls."

"What stopped you?"

"Natural disinclination," Cal said. "Besides, I fell in love with a boy and that was that."

"You never told me about him. Was he in the same high school?"

"No. He was sent away because he was a nuisance. We saw each other for Thanksgiving and Christmas. Easter it was over. My first broken heart," he said, pulling a face.

"What did Aileen have to say today," Liz asked. The house was so quiet, the silence deepened by David's sleep.

"She said there's big changes coming for me, but it's reshifting rather than destruction. Some destruction but not the end of the world. She told me—surprise—I wouldn't always be gay. I told her I sometimes feel that it isn't really true that I'm gay, and sometimes I've thought it would change."

"I didn't know you were discontent."

"I don't have anyone, Liz. It's as simple as that."

"But that's not because you're gay. There are gay couples who last forever."

"Lots who don't last. It's too lonely for me."

"It's lonely for everyone," Liz said. "You'll find someone. I know you will."

"Maybe," he said. He reached into his pocket and took out a thin silver tape recorder. "Would you like to hear her?"

"Sure. But I'd have thought a psychic would rather not have you recording her predictions."

"Oh, don't be a knee-jerk realist," Cal said. He set the small machine on the table. The reproduction was good and the voice of the psychic came through, its tones flat, midwestern, and slightly husky.

"You're an impulsive person, Cal, but you've learned to control yourself. We've talked about this before. You've learned self-control. You've learned to make plans and follow through on them. Now you're coming to fruition, aren't you. But hold on, Cal, and be firm. An old enemy appears. Or maybe he's on the scene now. I'm not that good about time. This may have happened already or it may be just about to happen. I see . . . do you know who I'm talking about?"

"I know exactly who you're talking about," Cal's voice replied.

"You have to be careful. You think you can defend yourself, but he's more powerful than you are—"

"Isn't this great," Cal said. "I mean, people pay thousands for less in therapy." He flicked off the recorder and put the silver machine back in his pocket.

"I can see the attraction," Liz said. "Is that true about the old enemy?"

"I'm not saying." Cal finished his beer. "I'll tell you one dark night when we're all alone."

Liz and Cal made sandwiches, ate them, and drank more beer. They decided to take a walk but found once they were outside that the night had turned cool, so they came back inside and said good night. When she went into her dark bedroom, Liz felt around in her suitcase for her toilet kit and came upon the manila envelope with the Xerox for Cal of her notes. She took the envelope out to the hall, propped it against Cal's bedroom door, and went back to her own room. She washed quickly and got into the king-sized bed with David, wondering whether she should wake him and talk. The large bed afforded her a lot of absence in proximity. David stirred and reached toward her, then turned away. He must be very tired, she thought, to be sleeping this way. He didn't see Lucy in New York, she believed. He wanted to be with her. Liz turned away from David and tried for sleep.

Perhaps she would go to Cal's adviser and ask: was she in danger, should she marry, were her enemies friends and friends enemies? Sometimes advice came from unexpected people.

The night after she got the news that Willy was dead, she'd cooked dinner for a reporter who was supposed to be a speed freak and a little crazy. They'd made the plan the week before and Liz hadn't bothered to break it, not knowing what else to do. During dinner he'd bored her with a story about his long divorce and what a toad his ex-wife was. The phone rang, a college friend of Liz and Willy's, calling to give condolences. She sounded drunk. When the phone call was over, Liz returned to the table. The reporter laid his knife and fork over his barely touched food.

"Why didn't you tell me?" he asked.

"I don't know," Liz said. "I can't talk about it yet." Besides, she hardly knew him.

"You have to trust someone sometime," the man said. "You can't stay self-contained forever. I don't know if I can stay here any longer. I feel as if you've been making fun of me the whole time."

They did continue eating, though the conversation was over and the atmosphere strained.

The doorbell rang. It was nine-thirty. Liz wasn't expecting anybody, but she excused herself and went to the door. She opened it and saw a very tall redheaded man she didn't know. He looked at Liz and past her into the apartment.

"I'm looking for Susan Winterbottom," he said.

"She doesn't live here."

"Apartment Ten-A?"

"This is Eleven-A."

The man apologized and left, still glancing past her into the apartment.

When Liz returned to the table, she remarked that she would never have opened the door if she'd been alone in the apartment. Still, it was a foolish thing to have done. The man could have been anyone; he could easily have slipped past the doorman.

"Do you know if there's even a Susan Winterbottom in the building," the reporter asked. "You should be more careful."

"You're right," she said. "I'll check in the morning."

She never did check, for she knew she'd opened the door to prove to him that she could trust people, and that the proof had worked.

Sunday morning was warm and bright, and Cal carried a tray of croissants, butter, preserves, eggs, bacon, and coffee out to the patio to Liz and David. He said, "I forgot the most important thing." When the door had slid shut behind Cal, David asked, "Did you sleep okay? You were gone when I woke up."

"Okay. Not great."

"What time did Cal get here?"

"Late. It didn't seem worthwhile to wake you."

"I don't know if you could have if you'd tried."

"Surprise," Cal said. He had walked around the side of the house, carrying a camera. He pressed a button, waited, and said, "Fast photos. Great color. So the salesman said." A color photo of Liz and David, heads together, emerged from the black box. Cal took another of David alone, then of Liz, then David took one of Cal and Liz holding coffee cups up to the camera. The condominiums across the inlet formed the background. They looked more than ever like a North European resort, and Liz and Cal looked like American tourists with jaws set in determined merrymaking.

"How about a sail today?" David asked Cal when they were eating.

"I have to get back to Houston right after breakfast."

"Not fair. You and Liz stay up all night yakking, then you go."

"Circumstances beyond me. Hunter wants a full staff meeting when he gets back from L.A. tomorrow. And then he lets us know how he likes the editorial lineup. I want the place cleaned up. All my ducks in place."

"What if he doesn't like your ideas?" David asked.

"Well, the staff is expecting either to have their salaries raised to a reasonable level or to get canned."

"You look calm enough," Liz said.

"A profile in courage." But he looked simply unruffled, almost unconcerned.

"How's Hunter fitting in over there," David asked.

"He's never been big on palling around," Cal said.

"Did you know him when you were kids," Liz asked.

"Not really," Cal said. He folded his napkin carefully, replacing it next to his empty plate. "I'll see you back in Houtex. David—when you get back, give me a call, okay?"

When she thought he was gone, Cal came back out on the patio to say, "Your deadline, Liz. Don't forget."

Liz started to clear the table. David reached across and took her hand, saying, "Truce?"

She held his hand to her face for a moment and said, "I hate it when we don't get along."

"I'm not trying to make you unhappy."

"I know," she said. She stacked the plates and silver on top of the tray. "I know you're right. I have the feeling we just failed Cal. He came with all his toys and he left so quickly."

"Don't make too much of it."

"He was so breezy. It was spooky."

"He's a breezy guy," David said. "Didn't seem much different to me. It may be hard—spending so much time with us. It must make him lonely."

"I guess," she said.

They went off to different corners of the house and read. In late afternoon, they took a walk, and when they returned, they made love and fell asleep afterward. When it was dark, David got up and went downstairs to start the fire in the barbecue, and Liz went to the kitchen to prepare the Rock Cornish hens she'd thawed that morning. They ate inside—it was cool again that night—and afterward went up to bed and read side by side, like an old couple, Liz thought, comfortable together. As she was drifting off to sleep, Liz remembered that she hadn't Xeroxed the drawing of the matchbook scrap from the police file, and that she'd forgotten to bring the copy of it from the file up to Walden. She'd wanted Cal to look at it, to see if it reminded him of anything from the old days. But she would see him the next day. She would go to the magazine and see if Cal would help her.

VIII

They left Walden in the early morning. The fog was still fighting the light through the pines, but only miles down I-45, that fog and light seemed far away as night. The sun was warm and they were surrounded by cars rushing toward the city. Liz left David at the airport terminal and waited until he'd walked through the double glass doors and disappeared from sight. Then she joined the stream of traffic into Houston. The radio reported the names of the streets to avoid, where the major accidents and bottlenecks were, where the eighteen-wheelers lay overturned and no one was hurt but rubberneckers slowed the flow, where cars were stalled on the left lane or right lane. There was a roll call of streets with names like Fernwood, Woodglen, Wildwood, Brazos, Quail Hollow, Post Oak—arcadian names that saddened Liz.

She tried to keep in the middle lane and tried to think what she would do with her day. There was no one to interview and no more research to do. There was nothing to do but think and write. Still, the thought of returning to the apartment and facing the typewriter made her feel trapped. She looked around at the surrounding lanes of funereally paced traffic. There was the scrap of shield and Cal, but Cal had enough to do that morning. There was always the Blue Bird, she thought. She could be there in no time. She could rest there and then get back to the story. And once the story was done, there would be David to consider.

Liz started at Dresses and looked over the sturdy, indestructible costumes with limp collars and stained underarms, the low-necked cocktail outfits that hung awkwardly from wire hangers, and the pleated polyester numbers with dropped waists and long sleeves to cover a woman for work. She took a white chiffon off the rack and held it up to her. She imagined a younger Helen Dayton in a soft white dress, so different from the browns and grays she wore to work. She might have worn such a surprising bright dress to a holiday party given for special employees by Gus Corrigan. She might have been considered a kind of hostess. Carolyn Sylvan didn't look like the type for chiffon or white. Liz remembered her first day at elementary school, when her mother dressed her in a stiff plaid taffeta dress which had a big bow at the collar. The bow rubbed a sore spot on the underside of Liz's chin by the end of the day. She felt like an overdressed bunny in the taffeta and had envied the children whose mothers had sent them into the world in dark skirts and white shirts that were inconspicuous. She wondered whether her first-day dress had gone to a thrift shop or to her younger cousins in Brooklyn.

The Blue Bird ladies talked among themselves and laughed a little louder than they would later when there were more customers. Early in the day, the shop smelled better than later, when the fixed smell of mothballs, lavender, and cleaning fluid would combine with the colognes of the women who'd passed through, and with the sweaty and soapy odors of the bodies that had struggled in and out of garments too big, too small, too worn out for purchase. Even triumph must leave a scent, Liz thought, and she recalled times when she thought she'd caught a garment that had some life. Now, in the morning, the air was neutral and promising.

Liz passed by the women's sweaters, and their winter weight reminded her of walking down Broadway with Cal, only blocks from their apartment house, when the salt-melted snow crept up into her boots. Cal was receding from her, and it was natural; he'd said so himself. David was there. But it wasn't right. Cal was going away from her and she felt afraid for a moment, as if she were standing alone in the world, without a friend. How could he be seeing a psychic and never have told her? She would find something for him, she thought, something beautiful and odd, and they'd go to lunch somewhere fancy or to the Cajun place with loud music and hot food, and she'd tell him everything she could think of, and he would tell her what he thought of it.

The men's clothing was all the way across the Blue Bird from the ladies', and another customer, a thin dark Mexican, was looking methodically through the rack of shirts, holding up those he liked to his chest, replacing them carefully where he'd found them. Liz went to the corner, past the tuxedos and sport jackets, past the men's dressing rooms. The smell here was hair tonic, shaving lotion, and sweat. In the dark corner was a rack of ties, hundreds of ties tucked onto a wooden rack meant for twenty. There were slanting wide stripes in colors that hated each other, greasy knits with pearlescent sheen, a silk tie with a peaceful design of sitting ducks, some spotted bow ties too far gone for cleaning. Liz looked up to see if the man had left the shirts. He was still there, so she looked back to the ties and found a white knit that looked less dirty and used than the others and a navy blue tie that caught her eye. There was a design across the widest part, a shield divided into three parts, star and swan on the upper portions, on the bottom lettering that she could barely read but which she knew: *In hoc cygno refugies.*

Liz looked quickly through the rest of the ties to see if there was another one; then she looked through the belts. The tie she held was the only one with that design. It had a 75-cent price tag on it.

At the wrapping counter, Liz asked the Blue Bird volunteer if there was any way to trace the donor of the tie.

"Oh, honey. We first of all just never give out that information. And second. Ties come in sacks usually and we price them and put them out. We only give inventory numbers to the larger items. Are you taking this tie? My, what a pretty bird."

She drove straight down Alabama to the magazine, impatient at the stop signs, driving quickly under the Southwest Freeway and over toward the Carlton. She would show the tie to Cal and see if he agreed that it matched the scrap in the homicide file. He might know where the crest came from and what the swan and star meant. As she turned onto Winbern, she saw that every parking space on the block was filled. Hunter's silver car waited by the front door, poised for an easy escape, she thought. Liz drove past the Carlton, pausing at the stop sign at the corner, then drove back the way she'd come, more slowly this time.

She laid the tie out on her desk. It might take hours or days in the library to identify the shield, if it was listed anywhere. In the meantime, she would record the design. She looked in the closet and found some tissues she'd used for wrapping Christmas presents. She laid the tissue on top of the tie and with her softest pencil traced the design. She made three copies of the pattern—then hid the suitcase again at the back of the closet. She rolled the tie as tightly as she could and put it in her pocketbook.

Liz dialed Frank Bone's number in Galveston and let it ring. He picked up after fifteen rings, sounding sleepy.

"Mr. Bone? This is Liz Gold again. I hope I'm not disturbing you?"

"Gold?"

"We talked the other day," she said. "I'm from *Spindletop* magazine. I was asking some questions about Carolyn Sylvan."

"You caught me napping, Miss Gold."

"If this isn't a good time . . . but I have just one more question."

"Fire away. I'm up now."

"The shield, Mr. Bone. The design on the matchbook. I wonder how far you pressed that lead. If you tried. . . . Did you check Osborne's school or club?"

"Our prime and only suspect? You bet we did. There was nothing there."

"And Gus Corrigan?"

"Sorry. That dog won't hunt. His secretary looked at it for us; he was away. It was Eastertime and he'd gone away on a trip with his boy. She said it certainly wasn't from any of his clubs, nor from Rice."

"And when Corrigan came back to Houston, did you question him about it directly? Did you show him the matchbook?"

In every interview she'd done, Liz had noticed that—no matter how trivial the subject of the story—she would hit on something the other person didn't want mentioned or discussed. She'd decided that the power of her kind of press was the power of plain embarrassment.

"Was he too rich," she asked quietly when Bone didn't answer. "Did you go to the clubs all over Houston?"

"I'm under no obligation to talk to you."

"I know," she said. "I appreciate your giving me the time. It could be important. And it all happened so long ago."

"I may be retired, miss, but I'm not dead. You might think we let this slide—fancy Houston people—or maybe that we had our fingers in the cookie jar."

"Did you check Corrigan at all? Beyond talking to Helen Dayton. He could have been Carolyn Sylvan's lover and Osborne could have been covering for him. It was a natural. Osborne was Corrigan's flack. Corrigan was his main business. The house and land out on the West End are owned now by Mrs. Osborne. It all fits together."

"We didn't find a thing that would stand up in court. That's our standard of judging what fits."

"And that was all right with you? And the police? This was two people dead."

"I don't throw myself against brick walls to see if it hurts. There were crimes perpetrated in Galveston just at that time that we could solve. That means we could get criminals into a courtroom and be sure they'd get to see the inside of a jail."

"I'm not trying to badger you," Liz said. "I'm trying to understand."

"Let me know if I can help you further," Bone said.

"I wasn't expecting you, Liz. But come in."

"I should have called, I know."

Through the open kitchen door, Liz could see the remains of Helen Dayton's lunch on the counter: lettuce and tomato resting on a blue glass plate, a glass of melted ice and a slice of lemon. A newspaper was folded by the plate, a napkin crumpled on top of it.

"I'm sorry. I interrupted your lunch."

"I was just finishing," Helen said. She led Liz into the Wedgwood-green living room, indicating that Liz should sit on the couch. She chose one of the brocade armchairs and sat well forward on it, her long thin legs crossed at the ankles. Helen wasn't happy to see her, Liz could tell. She wondered if Helen had ever liked her or if Liz had mistaken good manners for a real welcome. Helen could have been on her way out, or perhaps she just didn't want to talk. She was wearing a seal brown dress with a silver crocheted collar, dark stockings, and white leather bedroom slippers with frothy feathers across the toes. They were very frivolous, private slippers.

"I was on my way downtown," Liz said. "To the library. And it occurred to me you might be able to save me a few days there." She took the tie from her pocketbook, unrolled it, and handed it over to Helen. "I'm trying to identify the shield. Does it look at all familiar?"

"Where on earth did you get this tie, Liz?"

Helen held the tie away from her, and Liz caught the familiar odor of the Blue Bird.

"Serendipity," Liz said. "The tie's not important. Have you ever seen the shield before?"

Helen considered the tie again, then looked at Liz and smiled, as if, Liz thought, a child had shown her something amusing.

"Are those geese? Ducks? Where should I have seen it?"

"I don't know," Liz said. "I'm asking because it matches up with something else I came across. It's related to the Carolyn Sylvan story."

"Well, I'm sorry to let you down. I've just never seen this before. But surely there's a guide to such things in the public library. I'm sorry not to be of any help." Helen laid the tie on the table, then folded her hands in her lap. Her thin gold wedding band and matching engagement sparkler looked as though they'd become too large for her thin hands.

"You were friends with Carolyn Sylvan, weren't you?" Liz asked.

"What gives you that idea?"

"Just a guess, really. You know, Helen," she said, as peaceably as she could manage, "Cal gave me this story. I didn't ask for it."

Helen looked sharply at Liz, then returned her gaze to the tie on the table.

"I'm not trying to upset you," Liz said. "I'm trying to write this story for Cal."

"To answer your question," Helen said, "I knew her, but I don't know if I can say we were friends or if I believe women are ever really friends. When she first came to Houston, we used to visit. We were both women alone with children. Of course, Cal was much older than her child—but he was still my son and in my care. Carolyn wasn't prepared for anything. When Cal's father died, I'd been working for the company all along, so I was ready for more work, more time, better money, and I was glad to get the job with Gus Corrigan at the top of the company. But if that hadn't come along, something would have because it had to. But Carolyn—she had no skills. She couldn't type properly, though she tried. She used two fingers. She didn't even know the proper way to answer a business telephone, she just always said hello, like she was at home. When Gus found her, she was waiting tables in some café out in the Panhandle. She told me she didn't mind doing that because she could keep an eye on her baby. They lived right next door. She thought she was lucky, you see, for every little thing that came her way. It sounded dreadful."

"And Mr. Corrigan brought her to Houston?"

"Not right away. He found her a job up there with a subsidiary. Eventually—I don't know how long after—he brought her here and gave her a job."

Helen was talking to her out of loyalty to Cal, Liz thought, and would have preferred to refuse to speak. But the greater loyalty was to Gus, and what a prize he had had in Helen, all the loyalty, admiration, and servitude she'd shown him.

"It wasn't much of a job," Helen said. "She answered some mail, which meant she gave it to me and I sent it along to the right person. She took phone calls—what calls there were, and she usually got something wrong. There wasn't a lot to the job, so it didn't bother anyone."

"She was Gus Corrigan's mistress, wasn't she?"

Helen looked almost relieved, as if the other shoe had finally dropped. She touched her hair with both hands, then resumed her pose, hands in lap, legs crossed.

"I think at first," Helen said, "he really did bring her down here and give her a job purely out of kindness. He did kind things like that just the same way he did cruel things—firing people suddenly, that kind of thing. He liked picking people up who interested him. He had a great distance, a larger vision than most people do, rich or poor."

"He could have married her, couldn't he? He was a widower by then."

"If you'd known him, Liz, you'd see that was out of the question.

Gus Corrigan was a very social figure. He was instrumental in founding the symphony, the museum. With his wife, of course. They belonged to the River Oaks Country Club, for example."

Was that license to kill, Liz thought, or did you have to be a member of the Bayou Club for that? She remembered once asking Cal if he thought Doug and Clarice were happy, and he'd answered dreamily that they were past the hard times. They belonged to the River Oaks Country Club and the Bayou Club, they were on the opera board and other boards, they were set for life.

"I don't understand, Helen. Cal tells me there are plenty of people living in River Oaks who started out in the swamp, so to speak. It's not like Boston or New York society."

"It's one thing to make a lot of money and be able to afford to buy a house in River Oaks, even back when it was easier to buy in River Oaks. It's something else to belong. She wasn't his only mistress," Helen explained, as if Liz were very naive. "There were other women, completely presentable women, with whom he could be seen in public. Some of them, I suppose, he was intimate with. He was a very magnetic personality."

"So it seems."

"Don't judge him by Hunter," Helen said. "They have the same willfulness but that's where the resemblance ends. Hunter gets his way. Gus Corrigan did too, but with more finesse."

"So Mr. Corrigan was the Brazos Land Company. And he gave the place to Carolyn. Was there a provision that it would revert to him on her death?"

"I can't tell you anything about that," Helen said. "That was between Gus and the lawyers. Cal knows I won't say a thing about that."

"Did you help her settle in to the house in Galveston? It was such a big place, I can't imagine how she would have done it."

Liz thought of Carolyn Sylvan struggling with samples for drapes and upholstery, and Helen stepping in to make sure everything coordinated.

"Oh, by that time," Helen said, "Carolyn was much beyond me. She was a quick learner. She figured out how to spend money all by herself."

———

It was past lunchtime and Liz was hungry. On the way to Good Company Barbecue, she stopped at Kinko's and handed her notes from the talk with Helen to the freckle-faced boy who worked there. She got the two extra copies and put them in her pocketbook, then drove slowly through the four-way stops of the village to the barbecue.

Lunch hour was over and the place was nearly empty. The tables and chairs were old, a motley collection from junk sales and auctions. There were enamel-topped tables she recognized from childhood kitchens, and round oak tables with rickety legs. Some of the chairs were bentwood, split only slightly; other had designs stamped into the seats and backs. She got her chopped-beef sandwich and iced tea from the cafeteria line, then sat at a large table in the corner. Old Texas license plates hung on the walls, along with mounted skulls of Longhorns and deer, rodeo posters, pictures of cowboys squinting at the camera, hubcaps of Dodge cars, fading photos from small Texas towns where the main street is straight for hello and goodbye, beginning and ending in one glance.

Liz and Cal had come to Good Company for lunch, the day after Liz and David first made love and spent the night together. She'd felt dreamy and content, listening absently to the Texas Playboys blaring from the giant speakers that hung from the ceiling. She'd told Cal, "It may not work out with David. But something will happen. I've always liked him so much. And I didn't imagine this would happen. I didn't think nice men were in my field of interest."

"Tell me about it," Cal said, and he'd grinned ruefully for them both.

"I just hope . . ."

"What?"

"It's stupid," Liz said. "It shows how limited I am. I hope it lasts through the winter. Just give me the rest of the summer and the fall and the winter."

"Don't count your chickens," Cal said. "You may not get away this time."

"I could fall in love with him," she said, knowing that she was making Cal uncomfortable with her sincerity and her sentimentality. He liked gossip and funny stories about lovers, he'd been fine about Willy; but he couldn't take more than a few phrases of anxious talk about possibilities. "Maybe I have already."

"Another beer?"

"What's the matter, Cal? Am I such a disaster?" Liz said this smiling, feeling radiant. "Am I all wrong for David?"

Cal stood up to refill their beer mugs. He looked down at Liz, saying, "Bright eyes. It isn't you who's wrong for him or him right for you. I don't believe in that stuff. It's just that I mistrust love, and I get all nervous when my friends start talking it up. It's my problem, okay? Not yours."

Traffic was moving slowly along MacGregor Way. When she reached the gate, the white Osborne house looked less impressive to Liz than it had the first time, more like the idea of a house than the real thing. She stopped at the gate and buzzed, and when she identified herself she was buzzed in. The presence of the white horse grazing in front of the house was as startling as before.

Virginia Osborne stood at the front door. She was dressed in soft fawn-colored trousers and a loose white shirt, her faded hair pulled back in a careless ponytail.

"I was driving by," Liz said. "And I wondered if you could answer a few more questions."

"There's nothing I enjoy more than a surprise at the end of the day," Mrs. Osborne said. She beckoned Liz inside the house. "I'll just run up and change into something that doesn't smell like horses. You know your way to the plant room."

Liz walked through the yellow living room, pausing before a small gloomy painting of a rowboat floating on a misty lake. She sat in the plant room, in the same place she'd taken on her first visit. Mrs. Osborne appeared shortly, wearing a similar but less rumpled outfit.

"A drink?" she asked. She walked behind the wicker bar, reaching underneath for glasses.

"All right," Liz said. "Thanks. Gin and ice."

When she'd brought the drinks, Mrs. Osborne sat in the armchair near to the couch, holding her glass of clear cold liquid. Liz took a sip of her gin and said, "It's about the Brazos Land Company, Mrs. Osborne. I've been to Galveston to see Kelly Kilgore."

"Yes." Her face didn't change expression.

"Why didn't you tell me you owned Carolyn Sylvan's house?"

"If I own it, surely it isn't Carolyn Sylvan's. And you never asked, Miss Gold. As it was, I was surprised at myself—I surprise myself this minute—answering your questions."

"You must feel very safe," Liz said. "Secure."

"That house and the land were first of all a gift to my husband. And they were—with this house—about all we salvaged when his public-relations company went under. So I don't feel ghoulish or sorry or guilty, whatever it is you think appropriate."

"I'm not assuming anything about how you feel or how you should feel. Who made the gift of the house to your husband?"

Virginia Osborne tapped her blunt fingernail against her glass. "There's no reason for me to answer that question. It was my husband's property. Now it's mine. It was fairly worthless when we got it. It's chance that it's good development land now. And it's only a coincidence that girl was ever there."

"I spoke to Helen Dayton earlier today," Liz said.

"Mrs. Dayton was an efficient secretary. Gus Corrigan was lucky to have her."

"We had a nice talk," Liz continued. "Your husband never had an affair with Carolyn Sylvan, did he? Or if he did, it wasn't very important to anyone. He was the stand-in, the one who took the heat and made the arrangements. I'm sure he deserved the house and land by the time it was all over. He did a good job. By the time the case faded from the newspapers, his was the only name anyone connected with Carolyn Sylvan."

"Bill wasn't as bad as people made out. Look around you—there are women who've done better, plenty who've done worse. No one expected that I'd get a penny when he died. But we did all right in the end."

"From his public-relations business?"

"It broke even."

Virginia Osborne drained her glass and went to the bar, filling her glass again. She motioned with her head—if Liz wanted more, she should take it. Liz closed both her hands around her still full glass.

"I don't know what Bill expected," Virginia Osborne said. She stood in front of the bar, half leaning on it. "The more you expect the more you're disappointed. We didn't have a really bad time. But Bill died without getting what he wanted. The house and land—Galveston land wasn't worth much then. This was long before NASA and the thousand people a week coming down here. We never used the house. When we went to Galveston, we stayed at the old Galvez Hotel."

"Mrs. Osborne," Liz said, "I'm going to write this story whether you talk to me or not. I'm beginning to have the feeling that I'm the only person in Houston who doesn't know who killed Carolyn Sylvan and her child."

"I hope not," she said.

"If it was Gus Corrigan, why not tell me? He's dead. How can it hurt him?"

"What you don't know won't hurt you." Mrs. Osborne smiled briefly. "You might think about that."

"I'm sorry you won't tell me," Liz said. "I'll find out from someone else, and the outcome will be the same." Yet, she thought, what reason did Mrs. Osborne have for tolerating her presence and why should she answer questions? What reason did anyone ever have for answering questions from reporters? On the glass table there was a neat stack of *Southern Living* magazines and the latest issue of *Spindletop*. Liz set her drink down and stood. "Thanks for the drink, Mrs. Osborne."

"You haven't touched it.

"I don't mean to tell you your business, Miss Gold," she said when they were at the front door, "but I'd steer clear of this story. It's all over. Everyone's dead and gone."

"No one seems to care about Carolyn Sylvan," Liz said. "There was never an arrest. The crime's still unsolved, so the case is open—but no one does anything about it. What about her child? She never had a chance."

"They've both been dead a long time. It was a terrible thing. It was shocking. The kind of thing you read about in the papers and then you turn the page quicker to get past it." She looked out over the bayou. "If they solved the murder, she'd be just as dead. What difference would it make except to you at the magazine. You'd put it in between some story on what to wear or what to eat or who's doing what to whom. And there it would be. You'll have to convince your readers it's even worth reading about."

"It has to be," Liz said.

"I wish you luck, Miss Gold. I really do." Mrs. Osborne stepped back into the open doorway. "Goodbye," she said, and closed her big solid door.

There were only a few cars at the Carlton—Amy's ancient dull-blue Delta 88, Cheryl's gold-sprayed VW Bug, a black Mercedes sports car Liz didn't recognize.

She thought when she went inside that Cheryl must have gone for the day; then she saw that Cheryl was down behind her desk, looking in a deep side drawer. On top of the desk, beside the switchboard, the message racks for staff and freelancers, a calendar, and a limestone ashtray in the shape of Texas, were several bottles of nail polish in shades of brilliant to deep red, a box of Kleenex, pencils, miniature bottles of Southern Comfort and gin, a green plastic soapbox, facial astringent, and a towel.

"Cleaning up?" Liz asked.

"Cleaning out. Boy, you missed Black Monday around here. It's a good thing you're not on the staff full-time, you'd probably be fired now. Or maybe you wouldn't be."

"Who's been fired?"

"Everyone. Little Lord Hunter is going to have to run the next issue off on the Xerox machine. Unless he kicks that out too. He fired Graves—"

"Cal said that was coming."

"Sure. He replaced him with Harrison. But Amy? Not that you aren't a great writer, Liz, and everything, but Amy's so *great.*"

"Pride of the fleet. Anyone else?"

"Mary Alice and all the art people. He said he didn't like the way the magazine looked and he didn't find anything interesting to read in it. *Everyone.* I told you."

"Where's Cal?"

Cheryl made a face and bent again to rummage in the desk drawer. She spoke but the answer was muffled, and when she sat up, Cheryl said again, "It wasn't Cal's fault. I'm sure."

"What wasn't his fault? Spit it out, Cheryl. Don't be shy."

"Cal was the only one *not* to get fired. The only one. I mean, the scenario's all wrong. The courageous talented editor should get canned by the creepy owner, then the staff walks out or not. Whatever they want. But this is the other way around."

"You're not fired," Amy said from the doorway. "Hi, Liz. You've heard the news?"

"I sure did. Didn't Hunter explain anything?"

"Some of us may be rehired. But Hunter wanted to clear the decks. In Harrison's words. To start afresh." She walked over and cleared a corner of Cheryl's desk, then sat down. "Cheryl, you don't have to leave. She didn't get fired," Amy explained to Liz. "But she's being loyal. I think she's looking for an excuse to go back to Racine."

"Very amusing," Cheryl said. "It was an insult not to get fired. It showed how low I am on the totem pole. So I'm going to quit. Come with us for a drink, Liz. We're going to get drunk and read the want ads."

"I'd better not," Liz said. "I have to talk to Cal. Where is he?"

"He went somewhere to think," said Cheryl.

"Maybe Mexico," Amy said. "He didn't mention where. I think he wanted to be alone. At least he didn't feel up to talking to any of us."

"It couldn't have been his fault," Cheryl said. "He wouldn't want us fired. He practically invented us."

"Oh, Cheryl, you make it sound like he's Walt Disney and we're the Mouseketeers or something," Amy said. "You don't know whose fault it was or whose decision. We were sitting there, Liz, waiting for Hunter with our lists of story ideas. I spent the whole weekend trying to think up-market. We knew he was in the building because his car was lurking outside. The time for the meeting came and went. Then around noon, Harrison appears and tell us to go home. I mean, it was humiliating enough to be sitting there trying to impress him—Hunter's practically a cretin as far as I can tell and knows squat about magazines. Or about anything except being rich. By the time Harrison was finished with us, Hunter's car was gone from the front of the building. What a coward. And to be fired and to have to fold up those lists . . . when I think of it I could scream."

"What happened for the rest of the day? Did everyone just file out quietly?"

"Cal told us he was going to have to think things over. He left fast. Then everyone started clearing their desks and we went out to lunch and kept wondering what had just happened. Are you coming with us or not? I want to get out of this place."

"Don't quit, Cheryl," Liz said. "Amy's right. And Hunter may re-hire everyone. Wait it out."

"But it's my friends, Liz. It's business with you and Cal. With me, it's my friends."

"That's unfair to Cal," Liz said. "This magazine is what he's always wanted and dreamed about—"

"Spare us," Amy said. "I just want to know what he had to do to keep his job. And what you'll put up with to keep working for him." Amy turned and walked back into the editorial office.

"Don't mind her," Cheryl said. "She's upset."

"I don't mind her much," Liz said. "I don't blame her. Call me. Let me know before you do anything rash." She was at the door when the buzzer sounded on the switchboard. Liz heard Cheryl say, "She's just left. I'll see if I can catch her." She put down the phone and said, "Will you see Harrison? I could say you're gone."

"I might as well," Liz said. "To see what he has to say. They can't fire me. I never got hired."

Harrison sat at the black Formica desk, the bathhouse poster behind him an image of green coolness and leisure. He wrote a dark blue shirt, sleeves rolled up to the elbow, and a maroon tie whose knot was loos-ened. There was a coffee cup on his desk and an ashtray full of cigarette butts. He was lighting a cigarette with a gold lighter when Liz walked in.

"Miss Gold," Harrison said. His voice was gentle and invited her confidence. "Please sit down. If you have a minute. I have a message for you."

Liz stood by the door and nodded. He smiled at her refusal to sit and he stood, stretching out his heavy muscular arms.

"This story you've been working on, the Sylvan story."

"Yes."

"*Spindletop*'s not interested in this story. It's been suggested that you turn your talents to something more worthy."

"Why isn't the magazine interested? The magazine was very interested two weeks ago when I got the assignment. I'm almost finished. A few final touches—it would be a waste of company time, wouldn't it?"

"It's a whole new ball game. What the old magazine wanted, the new one doesn't. Simple as that."

"I really object to this. Strongly. And to being told in this way."

He looked down at his desk, as if there were something there he wanted to show her, then looked back and said, "You'll get a kill fee, of course."

"A kill fee isn't appropriate. I won't stop working on a story without word from my editor."

Harrison took a piece of paper from the desk and handed it to Liz. It was a memo from Cal, dated Sunday, the day before, addressed to Hunter and canceling the Sylvan story.

"I have to talk to Hunter," Liz said. "And Cal."

"There's no need to talk to them," Harrison said.

"I'm a rigid personality," Liz said. "It's hard for me to adjust to sudden changes. Like being jerked around like this. Where's Hunter? I need to discuss this with him."

"Mr. Corrigan's not here. He may be in tomorrow."

He had a slight smile on his face—amiable or perhaps only smug. He started to sit down again.

"I don't think I want to come back tomorrow," Liz said. "I'll just write him a letter in words of one syllable so he can read it."

The door to Cal's office, next to Harrison's, was open, and Liz went in. The room looked neat. There was a note on the appointment calendar, *Full staff meeting.* A cotton sweater was draped over the back of the desk chair. In front of her on the desk was a pile of letters and résumés which she looked through. They were from all sorts of people—writers, editors, art directors, young people just leaving college who wanted to work on a magazine. Some of the letters were months old, others were recent and referred to meetings with Hunter in Los Angeles and New York and to phone calls with Cal.

Downstairs again, Liz saw that Cheryl was gone. She looked at the editorial and art rooms, which were like Pompeii. The magazine had stopped midswing. Paste-ups were half finished, typewriters still held pieces of papers with attempts at lead paragraphs that hooked and snappy headlines. The phones should have been ringing, Liz thought. The silence was the most unnatural aspect.

When she was outside in her car, Liz looked back at the Carlton. Harrison was inside, moving from room to room, turning out lights as he went.

The house on Graustark did not welcome her. The living room looked like a waiting room, a magazine open on the floor, a book face down beside it. The bedroom reminded her of David's absence, as if he were gone for good and she'd failed him once and for all. The white comforter was crooked on the bed, revealing wrinkled sheets beneath. Bed pillows were flattened and moved out of place. The mirror over the dresser was tilted, and a tie of David's, flung over it, looked abandoned rather than jaunty. She wished he were with her. He would know what she should do next—some obvious, sensible path to take. Her father had often told her when she presented him with quandaries, When in doubt, do the right thing. Liz had listened to him so earnestly, it had been years before she saw the joke.

She washed her face and changed into clean dungarees and a white shirt and tied a red sweater over her shoulders. She would have to get her hair trimmed soon, she thought, looking in the dresser mirror. Small groups of hair struck out in back, and a feathery fringe was appearing around her ears. It was a good thing for her that Tito had decided to stay in Houston.

Downstairs in the kitchen, Liz started water for tea. She stood by the window while the water was heating and looked across the unkempt yard at Cal's. It was seven and dark outside. The light was on over his doorway but the cottage was black. His car hadn't been on the street when she came in. Liz looked at the brass hook by the door where she and David kept extra sets of keys for their cars, Walden, their house, and Cal's cottage. Cal had keys for their house and for Walden. She'd never used his keys without permission, Liz thought, nor had she in New York, where they'd also exchanged keys for convenience, in case one or the other was locked out or wanted a friend let in. She'd gone into Cal's cottage when he wasn't home only when he'd asked her to as a favor. Would she see if he'd turned the oven off before he left?

Would she bring the envelope on the pine table to the magazine when she came over?

Liz turned off the flame underneath the kettle and opened the back door. The high dead grass in the yard below looked forbidding. The small area where they'd made late and lazy attempts at a fall garden looked grotesque, like a miniature graveyard.

His door was locked with only one of the keys. She turned on the overhead light and stepped into the cottage.

Cal's living room was neat. Once she was inside, she couldn't see why she'd bothered to come. It was reassuringly the same, it was Cal's place, an odd knotty-pine cottage above their jungle yard. His fat chintz armchair sat cozy by the gas heater, and the bamboo couch with matching chintz cushions was placed near it for company. On the other side of the room, near the tiny kitchen, was a pine picnic table that seated six. Cal had had it built so that a grown man could sit on the attached seats and dangle his feet. He said it reminded him of being a child.

Liz crossed the dark bedroom to switch on the light by the double bed. The room looked as abandoned as hers, and she wondered where Cal had been sleeping. Still, it reflected Cal's customary order—there were no stacks of bills to be paid or letters to be answered on the painted boudoir desk in the corner, only the photo portrait of Helen Dayton as a young woman in the mirrored frame. The Polaroid of David and Liz at Walden was lying on the desk. As Liz looked more closely at the young Helen's face, she noticed an ashtray on the desk marked SOUVENIR OF GALVESTON, TEXAS. It was ceramic with a decal of palm trees at the center. In the ashtray was a book of matches. *Swan Club* was written in raised green Gothic letters on the back. On the front was a shield with a swan, a star, and the familiar motto. Liz closed her hand around the book of matches, then dropped them. She couldn't recall having seen them in Cal's bedroom before, yet they might have been there all along. She left the bedroom, turning out the light, glancing back to check if she had left any evidence of her visit. She walked to the front door and paused by the coat closet in which Cal had built shelves for linen, liquor, and cigarettes. His white sheets and towels were folded perfectly, the terrycloth fluffy as toy pandas who waited for Cal to return home, the only companions of an only child.

She returned to the house and replaced Cal's keys on the hook. Upstairs in the bedroom, she took a nylon bag from her closet and quickly packed it with a few shirts and pairs of jeans and socks. She paused as she was going out through the living room and switched on a light above the sofa, a signal for burglars that the house was occupied. Then she left, locking the door behind her. On the street, she heard the stiff magnolia leaves knocking into each other in the wind.

Liz drove the few blocks to her apartment and parked in front of the building. The weather felt as though it could turn cold—colder and damper, the last blow of winter. She left the bag of clothing in the car and carried her Xeroxes upstairs. She unlocked the door and went in, going straight to the back door to see that it was locked and that the chain was on. Then she double-locked the front door.

Liz turned on all the lights in the apartment, then opened the closet and took out the paisley suitcase, adding to it one copy of the Xeroxes of her notes on Helen Dayton. Then she put the suitcase at the back of the closet and shut the door. The other set of Xeroxes she added to the master file on her desk. She had an extra set of notes, she realized, one she'd made automatically for Cal. She pushed the master file and extra notes to a far corner of the desk and began typing up her interview with Virginia Osborne.

Liz had worked steadily for twenty minutes when she heard a noise. Sometimes the trees out back beat against the bedroom windows, making a sound uncannily like knocking. She returned to her typing but stopped when she heard the noise again. Someone was at the door, knocking in a gentle but persistent rhythm, softly, as if to attract only her attention, not her neighbors'. Liz took the page she'd been typing and stuck it under a stack of files on the desk. She put a new sheet of paper in the typewriter and typed *Dear Mother and Daddy.* She waited until she heard the knocking again, went to the door, and asked, "Who's there?"

"It's me."

"Cal?" It didn't sound like Cal but she hoped it was he. "Cal?"

"No. It's Hunter Corrigan."

When she opened the door, Hunter was standing up straight and re-laxed, not at all like a man who'd been knocking unacknowledged at a strange door. He was wearing a trench coat, a sports jacket, and a gray cashmere turtleneck sweater over camel's-hair trousers. Liz smelled a faintly powdery cologne and, behind it, his sweat.

"I was about to try the old American Express card trick," he said, unfolding his palm and showing her his gold card. In his other hand he held a silver metal attaché case.

"Is that like a Sears card trick?" Liz asked. "Breaking and entering?"

"Are you going to invite me in? It's started raining and I'm dressed for another climate."

Liz stepped back from the door and Hunter walked past her into the apartment. She closed the door behind him and took the damp coat he handed her, opening the closet for a hanger, then carrying the coat and hanger to the bathroom. She glanced at herself in the mirror—her mouth was tense and her eyes looked plain and tired. She considered putting on makeup but thought better of it.

Hunter was sitting on the wicker couch in the living room, the silver case flat on the table before him.

"I wanted to celebrate," he said when she stood in the doorway looking at him. "Then I got my equipment together and realized I was short on friends. I can't find Cal anywhere. Harrison's a little sobering, if you see what I mean. All my oldest friends want to borrow money from me or talk business—"

"How do you know I don't want to borrow money?"

"True. You could be deciding to open a shopping center or to develop fifty acres between here and Victoria. But maybe not. Probably not."

He snapped open the clasps of the case and Liz went near him to look inside. A bottle of champagne wrapped in corrugated cardboard to keep it cool. A pack of cigarettes. A plastic bag of white powder, along with a mirror, silver straws, and a gold single-edged blade.

"Got any sandwiches in there," Liz asked. "I haven't had any dinner."

"Neither have I," Hunter said. "Do you keep glasses in this place?"

Liz went into the kitchen and found two jelly jars that looked clean enough and didn't have chips in them. She set them in front of Hunter and sat next to him on the couch.

"What are you celebrating?" she asked. "Causing an employment crisis in Montrose?"

"It's the start of a new and better magazine. Don't worry. You'll be in on it."

Hunter took the champagne bottle from the case and set it upright on the table, removing the wrapper. Liz reached out and touched the bottle. Sweat was forming on the shiny dark surface.

"What will you ask of me, if I'm in on it?"

He removed the foil from the neck of the bottle, then looked over at Liz. She met his eyes, then looked down at his hands on the dark bottle. His gold ring shone dully against his skin. He resembled Willy, not physically as she'd thought at first but only in his sadness. Something in his care for the bottle and his kit for having fun made Liz think of Willy, who'd had so little fun himself. It was hard to give up on sad ones, she thought, though it didn't do to stay with them.

"We'll ask you to write wonderful articles and drink a lot of champagne. Fair enough?"

"All right," Liz said. "We can start now."

Hunter uncorked the wine expertly. The cork slid out obediently, the champagne waited patiently to be poured. Liz and Hunter sat silently for a moment. She was embarrassed to be with him, and silence was more intimate than talk. Then he smiled at her, filled their glasses, and said, "To *Spindletop.*"

She touched her jelly glass to his and drank. The champagne was cool and dry, the cleanest wine she'd ever tasted.

"Do you always travel with an attaché case full of champagne and controlled substances?"

"Harrison won't let me. But this is a special occasion."

"Have you spoken to Harrison recently?"

"For permission?"

"For anything."

"I took the bit in my teeth," Hunter said. "Made my own decision this time."

Liz moved to the armchair by the couch.

"I went to the magazine this evening," she said. "I talked to Cheryl and Amy. They were the last ones there. Besides Harrison. I even talked to Harrison."

"And what did they have to say, Liz?"

"They were very unhappy. Not Harrison, of course. They felt that they'd been treated unfairly and arbitrarily. They've worked hard without much pay because they believed in *Spindletop*. Why did you have to dump them so fast? You don't even know the quality of their work under good conditions."

"They must have neglected to mention the severance pay they're getting. Ah. I can see that's true. Amy gets six months' salary. That's enough for sentiment, isn't it? Everyone starts somewhere. I'll rehire some of them so fast they'll forget they were fired. Don't get all twisted around by those people, Liz. They're just employees. I thought you were a brighter girl than that."

"That's all I am, Hunter. Work for hire. Piecework. You can't even fire me, right?"

"Don't be stupid," he said. "Think of what you and Cal will do with a big budget. He can hire anyone he wants, and he wants you. Be happy."

"Good for Cal," Liz said. She took a drink and felt that she was sounding sullen, arguing with him and drinking his champagne. "I mean it. Good for Cal."

"How about turning down this light in back of me?" Hunter squinted at her. "It's too bright to see very well."

Liz learned over the couch and turned off the bright reading light behind him. Orange street light filtered through the white gauze curtains. It was raining, a wet haze to start with, then a sudden heavy downpour that she knew would subside as quickly as it had come, leaving rivers in the streets. Hunter touched the hand Liz put on the back of the couch for balance.

"Sit down," he said. "Don't be so mad at me."

"You remind me so much—"

"Have some more champagne," Hunter said. "Maybe I'll look more like him."

Liz went to the armchair and sat down, then held out her glass. When Hunter had refilled it, she asked, "Have you ever heard of something called the Swan Club?"

"Sure," he said. "Everyone knows about it."

"Everyone?"

"Old Houstonians. My dad and some of his cronies helped Wade Swan and his brother Walt start the thing. They wanted to call it Swan Brothers, but Gus thought they'd do better calling it the Swan Club."

"Was it a nightclub?"

"Not at all. It was a private club, a retreat, a place to go and do mild exercise, weights, punching bag. No tennis or swimming pool, but there was a steam room and a massage table. Walt was the front man. He'd book people in, greet you at the door, help you to whatever you needed. He treated everyone of every age as if they were eighty-five and about to meet their maker. Tenderly. The club was in a house on Sunset that someone's painted beige now and put a big fence in front of. Walt would greet you at the door. Then you'd change into sweats or shorts, or if you only wanted steam and massage, he'd wrap you in a big white towel, more like a sheet than a towel. Walt had charm. He'd remember people who'd been there only once, as guests. Call them by name."

"Was it only for men?"

"Of course," Hunter said. "But Wade Swan was the one. He'd worked for Gus forever and that's how Gus knew he could massage that well. After my mother died, Gus had the idea to make this club. It only lasted two or three years."

"Who belonged to it?"

"Rich folks," Hunter said. "Businessmen like my father, with clients from out of town. Less than a hundred memberships were ever given out, but boys my age came, sons of members. After the exercise or massage you'd retire to the bar and sit. Drink a beer or a brandy. Have a cigar, if you cared to. There was a little kitchen and always something hot to eat, always sandwiches. It was the perfect home, and you could leave anytime you liked. Did Cal tell you about the Swan Club?"

"Cal?"

"I used to take him there with me all the time when I was home for vacations. He was just about my only friend in Houston. But you know Cal—he was company enough."

Liz set the glass on the table and walked to the window. She parted the curtains. The rain had stopped. A bearded man walked by with a little boy in a bright yellow slicker and red boots. A fat black mutt followed them. The man carried a newspaper and a paper bag.

"So you and Cal were good friends."

"Fairly good friends. I wasn't around much. My father and Helen Dayton sent me to one school after another—but I've already bored you with the story of my education."

Hunter was leaning his head against the back of the couch, looking tired and used up.

"Come and sit down," he said. "You'll give me a crick in my neck looking at you."

"In a minute," Liz said. "This time of night, my neighbors walk to the U-Totem around the corner for a paper. Beer. I like to watch them. Last September when it rained so hard—you weren't here, were you?—my car was parked right where it is now, out front, and I watched until the water rose up to the exhaust pipe. Then I went and moved it to higher ground."

"Cal must have talked to you about the Swan Club," Hunter said.

"No. I just happened on it. In my travels."

"I wonder," Hunter said. He sat up and reached for the champagne. "Let's finish this now," and he refilled the glasses. "I feel overcome with something. . . ."

"Champagne?"

"Maybe. I don't sleep very well. Maybe it's fatigue. Would you mind if I stretched out on that rug? And you might move those pillows. We could finish the champagne on the floor, like a picnic."

"Why not," Liz said, though while she moved the pillows, carried her glass to the rug by the window, and sat next to Hunter, who reclined like a sultan, she knew very well why not. But she'd drunk so much of the good champagne, and, she reasoned, she might now have the courage to talk to him. Everything seemed possible and for a moment she felt that she was strong and upright, beyond the possibility of harm. She might do everything she had to and come through it whole. It was important that nothing be excluded. Hunter reached for her and kissed her, even more gently than he had in his car, slowly and long enough for Liz to taste the champagne on his breath. He let go of her, leaned away, and smiled.

"Do you and Cal have pajama parties," he asked. "You're such good friends. I miss Cal. We used to be good friends, so close. We've done terrific things together, been to great places. Now we barely get along, in some ways. He doesn't trust me anymore, he says. Well, not that he really says it. But I can tell with Cal."

"It happens with old friends," Liz said. "Distance and time."

"I wouldn't know," Hunter said. "Cal was my only friend. Besides Wade and Walt Swan, and they weren't precisely friends."

"I've seen Wade Swan," Liz said. "At the Buccaneer Club in Galveston. Cal—"

"I wouldn't know," Hunter said. "I lose track of people."

He reached for Liz, pulling her so that she was lying down beside him. He kissed her again and started to work the buttons on her white shirt, awkwardly at first, then with more ease. Never impatiently, she thought. When the buttons were undone, Hunter leaned back and smoothed his gold ring up and down her rib cage, circling her breasts.

He said, "Let's take off your shirt." Liz allowed him to pull the shirt off her and lay it on the rug next to her. She leaned back, cold now in the unheated room. From the floor, the white walls and ceilings looked like the boundaries of a snow cave. It was warmer by Hunter, warm against his soft sweater, against his body. They kissed again, a longer kiss, and Hunter touched the waistband of her jeans.

"Hunter," she said, "this is silly. Let's—"

"Why silly?" He smiled at her and released her. "I'm here and you're here. You want me, I know. I could see it from the first."

"No," she said.

"Now, Liz. He's not here. I am. And we both . . . you want it," he said, "and . . ."

She imagined a completion—I want you—that wouldn't ever come. How close to Hunter she felt, lying there still as sleep, feeling his breath and the golden ring against her naked chest. He touched her breast with his ring, then took her nipple between his fingers. He tried to shift her so that she would be lying on top of him, and Liz imagined that also, as a luxury of movement, imagined that she could stretch her legs to the length of his, kiss him, make him smile. But slowly as she could, as if she might disappear and he would never notice, Liz moved away until she was sitting up. Once she could no longer feel his warmth, once his hands were no longer on her, she felt rumpled and foolishly naked. The cold air coated her back and her breasts, and she crossed her arms over her chest to cover herself. She was afraid to reach for her shirt. If she moved, she thought, anything could happen. A look crossed his face like the look on Willy's face before she left him in Sweden, the look before he told her to go into the world if she wanted it so. Then it had let her know that she had hurt him as much as he had ever hurt her. But it was brief in Hunter and turned back into his look of calm boredom, which released her. She could now be simply afraid of him. She held her pose, as if a change might crack her into pieces, and said, "You'd better go now, Hunter. The game's over."

"I don't think so," he said.

"Really," she said, thinking it would be over soon and she might never have to face him again and would never want him if she never saw him. "It won't—" She wanted to say that if they made love it wouldn't go anywhere, but of course it wouldn't. She thought it would be too crude to do what she wanted, invoke David's name, and she looked to the phone, as if it might bring him into the room.

Hunter moved away from Liz, standing up, straightening his clothes, leaving her on the rug. He took a cigarette from the pack in the attaché case, and for a moment she thought he would close the case and leave her. Instead, cigarette in his mouth, smoke rising in a thin blue plume, one eye closed against the smoke, Hunter sat on the couch and began unloading his equipment—mirror, straws, razor, powder. Liz reached for her shirt and put it on.

"So you and Cal are friends," Hunter said. "He told me all about you when we shared our summer place in East Hampton. You never came out to see us."

"I was never invited," she said. "I didn't know—"

"Did he ever tell you about my spring vacation when I was sweet sixteen and so was he?"

"No," she said.

"I figured," Hunter said, "Cal had told you everything when he sicked you on me. Of course I assumed he was lying when he told me he was sending you out blind."

"I'm not sure what you mean," Liz said. He was bending over the mirror, chopping the fine powder with the gold blade.

"He's such a loyal person, Cal. All these years, I believe he's never betrayed me. In a certain way. And that's all you can expect from a person. More than I would expect. It's gone on so long." He looked at Liz and shrugged. "And yet . . . I've told you, haven't I, about my father taking me for drives? That started when my mother was in the hospital, and it went on after she died. I'd come home for a few weeks' holiday and there we'd be, stuck together in the house. I think he might have invented the Swan Club as a place for me to go—if I flattered myself that he worried about me."

Hunter gave Liz a quick look, then bent his head, birdlike, and breathed in two lines of coke through the straw.

"He did know that I like Wade and Walt. He knew I liked Cal, but that was different. I think he may have suspected how different but we never discussed it. The Swan Club made his life easier and so did Cal. So did the automobile. We'd eat somewhere, the Confederate House, usually." He looked at her, checking her again.

"I know the place," she said.

"That's right. Deep blue walls and portraits of Confederate generals. Gus loved that stuff. Then we'd drive."

She wasn't sure now how much more she wanted to hear from Hunter. "You've told me some of this," she said, as casually as she could, as if the conversation might be ending and Hunter might be leaving.

"I stowed away once or twice," Hunter said, oblivious to the interruption. "My father would drop me back home after dinner. Tell me he was going out for a drive to think. He needed time alone, he said. Ever since, I've known when someone says that, Watch out. Isn't that right, Liz?"

"I suppose," she said. "We've all done that."

"I'll bet you have," Hunter said. "So independent."

She was startled by the bitterness in his voice. It had nothing to do with her, she thought. He hardly knew her.

"You stowed away," she prompted.

"Once or twice," he said. "The first time he only went to the Swan Club. It was past closing time but the light was on and he banged on the door. Walt let him in. That time I walked home, all the way to River Oaks."

"That's a good walk. A few miles, at least."

"I got in long before Gus did." Hunter smiled at the memory. He stood and walked to the living-room door, his back to Liz, and stared into the kitchen. Then he turned and spoke again.

"The next time, it was a long, hot drive. I was crouching in the back of his Lincoln, my nose against the carpet on the floor, smelling my father's cigar. I could hear him singing along with the swing station he always tuned to."

"I think I know—"

"Don't be sure what you know." He came toward Liz, to where she still sat on the rug, and offered her his hand. She took his hand and he led her to the armchair and returned to his place on the couch.

"It took time for Gus to reach Galveston. He took the freeway—it was just built—but he drove real leisurely. I was afraid to look at my watch, afraid I'd make a noise and Gus would find me. I didn't know where we were going, of course, but the longer the trip took, the more hope there was that I had the goods on him. I'd find out where he went all those times he left me home.

"We got there finally. Gus pulled into the driveway—I could feel the curve of it—and got out and slammed the car door. Then I heard a door open to a house and a woman's voice called out to him, not very loudly. Then I could hear nothing but the cicadas, and sometimes a gull. I looked at my watch. We'd driven for over an hour. I waited, crouched, thinking he might be back out anytime. But I finally got up my courage and stretched out in the back seat. I had the idea he might come out and find me asleep and he'd feel guilty. I don't know what. Apologize. Have a change of heart.

"But I got bored with that. I sat up and looked at the house. Columns. Columns out there on that mosquito-riddled flat. I climbed into the front seat, and for lack of anything better to do, I went through the glove compartment. It was locked, of course, but Gus had left the keys in the ignition. There were maps—Texas, Louisiana, Arkansas—maps of cities like Dallas, Austin, Corpus, what you'd expect. Nothing surprising. Then I happened on the Beretta. What do you know about guns, Liz?"

"Nothing," she said. "I thought a biretta was a priest's hat."

"It's a pretty handgun," Hunter said. "My father had one. Most of his friends too. It was the fashion then. I checked the gun—my father taught me all about guns—and saw it was loaded. I guess he kept it there just in case, the way people do.

"Lights went on upstairs in the house and I heard voices. It was a warm evening, the big old windows were open, and I heard some music, a child's song about a bunny. I put the gun in my pocket."

Hunter reached out to touch his metal case. He looked at Liz, his face wrinkled into a new expression of worry, then he smiled, erasing it.

"Why did you put the gun in your pocket?" she asked.

Her throat was dry and her voice cracked as she spoke, but she was afraid to get up and get a glass of water, afraid to interrupt.

"It just happened to be in my hand at the moment I decided to leave the car. No reason. Well, it might have been my trained hand. I used to sneak cigars and spare change from the top of my father's dresser, just a little at a time so he wouldn't notice.

"I slipped the gun in my pocket and walked to the front windows. The ceiling fans were turning slowly, rustling the magazines and the slipcovers on the furniture. There were toys on the floor and next to the armchairs two drinks with ice melting in them. Chintzy old armchairs, real stuffed and comfortable-looking. On the floor there was a big oval rag rug."

That had been clever of Carolyn Sylvan, Liz thought, not to try to make the house into anything fancy but to create a place for him to come and play home with her: comfortable overstuffed furniture, his favorite liquor, pretty Carolyn and her baby. It was ordinary domesticity with no strings attached.

"The noise stopped upstairs. I heard footsteps on the stairs, and I went down low and watched Gus come down the stairs first and then Carolyn Sylvan. I'd seen her only once before, at the office. Helen told me she was helping out there.

"They settled into the armchairs and sipped at their drinks. Then she got up and laughed, and she went over to Gus and sat on his lap. He was a big man, far bigger than I, and she was a good-sized girl, slim but not small. She looked small in his lap. They started laughing and talking, kissing each other. I think they must have been half high already. They must have had some drinks before they put the little girl to sleep upstairs. She was calling him Peachy, her big ripe Peachy. She was his Little Baby. Then they started talking more baby talk, about each other. About making love. He was touching her breasts and undressing her. She was laughing and saying things about fruit and peaches and her baby bunny, leaning back in the chair against him, spreading herself out for him and laughing softly, as if she was enjoying it all."

Hunter looked toward the window, then at Liz and her hastily buttoned shirt, her hair not quite in place.

"I must have made a noise," he said sadly. "Stepped on something that was out on the veranda, because suddenly she was up, standing and saying, 'What was that? You hear something?' and Gus was coming to the door, looking out and saying, real manly, 'Who's there. Come show yourself.' And so I did.

"I walked to the door. Right up to my father. I was wearing a new white suit that night, but now it was all creased and dirty. I had my hands in the pockets of the jacket. He always told me not to do that, it stretched the jacket and made me look like a hoodlum. 'What are you doing here,' he asked me, and I could tell he was getting ready to hit me a good one. She was standing behind him in the foyer. I could see her clearly. She was smiling. I thought maybe she was relieved it was only me, not something worse.

"Or else—maybe this is the truth—she might have been waiting for a chance to push herself further into his life, get something worth something, and here I'd given her an opportunity on a platter.

"Gus said, 'What do you have in that pocket?' and he reached for me. He twisted one arm behind my back and got the other hand out of my pocket. He found the gun, of course, and took it from me. He looked at me real hard, and I told him it wasn't what he was thinking. I went for him, meaning to put my arms around him and make him look at me straight, but I ended up shoving him. I startled him, bumped him, something. The gun went off. The safety must have been off the whole time. And when I grabbed him like that, the gun fired straight at her. It happened fast. But she was fast. She started turning away as soon as she saw Gus take the gun from me. That's how she got the bullet in her back."

"My God."

"Gus told me to get out of there, to get out to the car, and so I did. I sat in the driver's seat, waiting for him. He was kneeling by her, touching her. I could see him through the front door."

"And the little girl?"

Hunter looked up at Liz's question. She would hear it all from him, she thought, and then she never wanted to see him again. She could feel the imprint of the wool rug against her flesh, his fingers on her breast.

"The little girl woke up from the noise. Maybe she'd never gone to sleep. She came downstairs to see what was going on. When she saw her mother and Gus beside her, she started screaming. This is what Gus told me. He reached for her——"

"Why?"

"To calm her. To stop her from screaming. But she wriggled away and was running across the yard to the road, still screaming. I didn't know a child could scream and not stop. Gus yelled to me, 'Get her. Stop her.' By then she was past me, behind me in the dark. I started the car to go out to the road to find her. I was backing up to straighten out the car when the bumper knocked her down. You'd think I wouldn't have been able to feel it," he said, meeting Liz's eyes until she dropped her gaze. "Such a big car and such a little girl. I must have kept going over her. I felt the resistance of her body and then not.

"Gus had seen the whole thing. I think he would have gladly killed me too but he couldn't bring himself to do it. When I got back to the house, he told me not to touch anything, to wait outside on the veranda, no matter how long it took. I stood at the door and kind of leaned against it and didn't know where to look."

Hunter must have torn the matchbook as he stood at the door, she thought. He must have been nervous, caught between the two bodies. Liz would have given anything for some heat or for her sweater, which was across the room, too far away.

"And Osborne?" she asked. "Where does he come in?"

"Gus called him and told him to get out there," Hunter said.

"Why Osborne? Why would he jump like that when your father said so?"

"It was his job," Hunter said. "He knew how to keep things quiet. Gus told me Osborne would handle the situation. We waited until he got there, and Gus told Osborne that there had been some accidents. That Osborne would be taken care of and to leave him out of it."

"And what about you?"

"I was hiding in the car. Osborne never knew I'd been there."

"I wonder what he thought happened."

"Who cares," Hunter said. "He did what he had to. And Gus was right to call him—if there hadn't been someone there, the police would have investigated thoroughly and probably have gotten to Gus, at least."

"That leaves the gun, Hunter. What happened to the gun? Or was that left for Osborne to take care of also?"

"Don't be silly," he said. "Hand him the only evidence? We drove straight to the bay and threw the gun as far out as we could, and it hasn't ever washed up."

He stood, slowly, and went to Liz, then knelt by her. She wanted to move away from him and could smell a new kind of bitter sweat through his clothing.

"Now you know everything," he said. "What do you think you'll do now?"

Get out of here, Liz thought. And if I do, I'll hide forever.

"Why did you tell me?" she asked. "Why in the world?"

"You wanted your story," he said. "You were close to it. I thought I'd just give it to you. You're wondering why I would put myself in your hands this way, that's the real question. You might be thinking, A confession. But it's invalid. I could be telling you any drivel I wanted—it won't stand up in court, I can assure you. I've told you the circumstances of the case, in detail; some people are murder buffs. The gun is gone, the car is gone, Osborne's gone, my father is gone."

"The land," she said. "The house. The gift to Osborne. Why did your father give a gift of such value to Osborne unless—"

"A whim. He gave a quarter of a million dollars' worth of stock to Helen Dayton along the way. He rewarded loyal employees." He took Liz's wrist in his and laid her hand on his shoulder. "Touch me, Liz. I'm no different. You wanted to touch me, didn't you?"

She withdrew her hand and said, "Why did you tell me? So that I'd feel sorry for you?"

He laughed and stood up. He went to the coffee table and began packing up the mirror and cocaine, setting them carefully in place in his case.

"I don't care how you feel about me," Hunter said, "or what you feel for me. This isn't personal. I told Cal. I told him he made a big mistake involving you. He can't do anything and you can't do anything. You have nothing to go on."

"The logic of the thing. Certain clues. Hints."

"I congratulate you if you find an editor to publish this story. All you have are interviews with old ladies. I have enough money to keep litigation alive long after the publication is dead. Editors don't fool with libel suits gladly."

But someone, Liz thought, there must be someone who could help her construct a version of the story that would pass through the sifter.

"You don't have anything. Nothing material. Forget it, Liz. I've consulted the best criminal lawyer around and he's assured me as he assured my father: we're safe, my father and I. But you and Cal, you're in trouble."

Like a salesman finished with his spiel, Hunter clicked the metal case shut. He crossed the room to the rug, picked up her red sweater, and tossed it to her. She caught it, wishing she could refuse it.

Hunter walked to the front door, carrying the metal case. Liz looked at the phone, the window. When he leaves, she thought, I will lock the door, double-lock the door, and I'll never open it again.

He opened the door and leaned out, looking down the stairwell. "It's all right," he called out. Liz heard the sound of footsteps coming up the stairs.

Harrison appeared at the door, wearing a trench coat that was an imitation of Hunter's. He walked into the apartment, glanced briefly at Liz, and said to Hunter, "Are you ready?"

He must have been there the whole time, Liz thought. Was that his idea or Harrison's? Hunter was standing in back of Harrison. He watched her with no particular expression on his face, the lack of interest shown by spectators at an unexciting rear-end collision.

"Liz, " Harrison said. "Keep this to yourself. No one's interested in this or in you. There are car crashes. Untimely drug arrests. Fires and household accidents. Is this clear?"

"Yes," she answered.

"The notes," Hunter said impatiently. He walked past Liz to the bathroom and reappeared, his coat over his arm.

"Your file on the story," Harrison said. "We want it."

They let her walk to the desk. She looked through her piles of papers for the file marked *Master*. When she turned to give it to Hunter, he was gone.

"Here it is," she said, handing it to Harrison. "All I have."

"We know you have a good memory," he said.

"Not particularly."

"Things happen to memories," he said, as if she hadn't spoken. "Things can happen to your boyfriend. Even to your friend Cal. Remember us."

He turned and left, as noiselessly as Hunter. Liz stood looking at the open door, listening to the sound of his footsteps, the slam of the car door, a car departing. Then she locked the door of the apartment and leaned against it with all her weight.

Liz looked around and wondered if there was a way—when her back was turned, her attention elsewhere—that Hunter or Harrison might have planted drugs in the apartment. Or if there was a way—her eyes to the corners of the room, up and down from floor to ceiling—that photographs might have been taken of her and Hunter. She could take the place apart, bit by bit, polish every surface, dust every edge and corner, sift through the papers and clothing and junk dishes. But it was too late, she thought. She didn't have much time left there, and she had to use it well.

She went first to the telephone and looked through the pile of airplane tickets that lay on the telephone table. She selected one, still valid, for New York, then paused a moment, thinking of people hiding in places like Tucson and Albuquerque, new identities taken on and clung to. Was it tempting for her, she thought, could she even do what the others had done? Hide forever or, more precisely, shed herself as a snake sheds skin? It was a temptation, for Liz saw a road ahead, pink sand, white road, a child's vision of running away. Then she tore the tickets one by one, put the ticket for New York in her pocketbook, and went to the hall closet.

There, behind the magazines and thrift-shop mistakes, was the paisley suitcase, looking more unsuitable and innocent as ever. She took it from the closet and opened it, setting aside the pink jacket. Her copies of the notes were there as well as her tapes. Liz went to the desk and uncovered the notes from that day's interviews with Helen Dayton and Virginia Osborne. She put them in the suitcase with the tapes and notes, then zipped up the suitcase once again.

In the car, she decided that she needed a place somewhere outside of Houston where she could sit and figure her next move. She could go straight to the airport, of course, but before she saw David she needed time alone to get her story straight—what David should learn from her, what he shouldn't know.

And Cal? Was he home or at Clarice's? Was he in a bar or taking comfort from his mother in the soft green living room? She could look for him, but she wouldn't. If they saw each other now, what would there be to say? She needed to be calm, she thought. She would be better off at Walden. It would be a chance to breathe. That's all it had ever been, she thought, a place to go in order to be somewhere else.

There wasn't much traffic on I-45 North. The road stretched ahead, promising emptiness soon, the dark pines of East Texas and the land beyond, rolling farmland, the road would take the willing driver anywhere.

Liz put the radio on a country station. The whining domestic stories bothered her at first, then joined with the sound of her tires on the highway, the force of the air when a big truck passed, and the momentary music that came from other cars whose drivers were riding with their windows down. Liz hoped the other cars were going home, not just heading out as she was, trying to get past the cheap motels and surplus warehouses, the neon signs as big as buildings, and the shopping centers that were the town squares for Houstonians who lived in this sprawl.

She felt dizzy for a moment when she was past the airport turnoff. It was the vertigo of a stranger who recognizes the lack of landmarks. A rust-colored Cadillac Seville passed her, driven by a man no more than ten years her senior. He had white hair and wore a cowboy shirt. In his rear window, she could see his palomino-colored Stetson, and she smiled, she didn't know why, and felt relieved. Thus located, she sat back and slowed her pace to the speed limit. She was only twenty minutes from Walden.

The house waited, cleaned since she and David had left it in the early morning. The magazines were in place on the low glass table. The posters and baskets on the wall hung at decorous angles. Liz switched on all the downstairs lights, then climbed the stairs and switched on the lights there too—her bedroom, Cal's, both bathrooms. For a moment she felt foolish, alone in the house. It seemed a long way to have come, but, walking downstairs, seeing the edge of the black-watered lake and the faintly lit country club beyond it, Liz was glad to be there. She made a pot of coffee and took a cup outside, sitting at the patio table, listening to the wind. When the coffee cup stopped warming her hands, she went inside to the couch, put her feet up on the table, onto a stack of magazines. Then she leaned back.

She didn't have long to wait. In the hushed resort, the arrival of one car sounded like the approach of an army. The tires crunched the pavement coming down the hill, around the curve, and, at the second Liz thought the car might pass, stopped at her door. Liz didn't move. There was the sound of a key at the door and she turned to see Cal.

He was empty-handed, wearing jeans and a dark sweater, white sneakers and socks. He stood in the doorway, quickly looking over the kitchen, as if he'd expected to see her there, then upstairs for David. He looked at the couch and at Liz.

"I didn't know where you were," Cal said. "I figured you were either here or—"

"Gone," she said. "You know me well. I'm here now and soon I'll be gone."

"How about a drink?" Cal asked. "Before you go."

"Help yourself," she said. "You know where everything is."

She listened to him at the glass cabinet, the refrigerator and wet bar, then turned as he came toward her, his drink in his hand.

"I've been thinking about you all day," he said. "I tried calling you. You weren't home."

"I was busy," Liz said. "Running around. Talking to people."

"Anyone interesting?"

"All very interesting," she said. "This is such an interesting place you've brought me to. And such a wonderful assignment you gave me."

"It's late in the day to blame me for Houston. You came here of your own free will."

"I'm not saying anything about Houston."

In his sigh, she heard the signal that she was being difficult. It was hard, even at that moment, not to change the subject and try to find something pleasing to say.

"Traveling light," said Cal. "I don't see any luggage."

"I won't be gone long," Liz said. "I'm just meeting David in New York for a few days."

"I thought you might be doing that." Cal sipped at his drink, then looked up at her. "I didn't come just to say goodbye."

"No? Did you come to explain why you set me up for your murderous boyfriend?"

"No," Cal said quietly. "Not for that. I came for the tapes."

"What tapes?"

"You always tape your interviews, Liz."

"Just goes to show," Liz said, and she gave a quick smile that surprised her. "You think you know a person, everything about them, and then you find out they've changed on you. I took notes this time. You have my notes."

"Bull," Cal said. "You do both. I want both."

"I'd forget it if I were you," Liz said. "You have two copies of everything, don't you? Yours. Hunter's. Harrison came and got the master set. So you've got it all now." She stood and went over to the couch that was set at right angles to the one Cal rested on. "But what do the notes matter, Cal? You don't have anything on your pal. I'm sure he's given you the legal rundown. How can you, Cal? How can you go on with him?"

"I don't want *you* thinking you have anything on him, Liz," Cal said patiently, as if he were explicating a fine point of a game he was teaching her. "I know you. You're thinking you'll take the tapes to your father. Or to the police. The Justice Department. Just to see if there's a case, and—"

"I'm flattered," she said. "Do you really think I'm so courageous? Would I take these imaginary tapes and go up against Hunter Corrigan?"

He looked at her in silence, calculating.

"I didn't do anything for Willy," she said. "I took my check. I made a settlement."

"Willy—"

"Willy was my husband. So why would I do anything for Carolyn Sylvan or her little girl? Strangers. People I never met."

"You always tape. I know you have the tapes. And I want them," Cal said. "I don't want you making this worse, trying to do something grandstand with them, something stupid. Something that might endanger you and David."

"I appreciate the concern," she said, "but I got this speech from Harrison. You probably are concerned, but don't be. Don't bother."

She went to the kitchen for more coffee, and when she returned to the living room, she asked, "Why did you have to set me up like that? Why not tell me about it, trust me. Or if you couldn't do that, why not assign the story to someone else, someone you weren't friends with?"

"Someone else might have used the knowledge for himself. It's because we were friends," he said, "that you were the logical one. I didn't think you'd get this far, frankly. It isn't your kind of story. You're not such a great reporter. So I thought I could guide you through it and then stop you at a certain time, short of your finding out anything definitive. Just to prove my point to Hunter."

"Well, that was logical. Not flattering, but logical. Of course, other things went wrong for you too. Hunter told me everything, Cal. I guess you didn't count on that either."

Cal lit a cigarette and moved the Venetian glass ashtray closer, then set his glass carefully on a stack of magazines.

"I doubt he told you everything," he said.

"He told me about the night he and his father killed them. About William Osborne and the gun in Galveston Bay. What else is there?"

"Other versions," Cal said. "Baroque stories developed over the years." He drew in on his cigarette and expelled the smoke slowly.

"Sometimes Gus did it alone. And Hunter's been protecting his daddy's reputation. Sometimes Osborne was there all along with Gus."

"Ah," said Liz. "I see who's doing the protecting. You're telling me Hunter Corrigan is unreliable. That he's been spreading this story around for years, and I shouldn't think I've found out anything special. Or that he's told me something important."

"Something like that," Cal said. "It's useless information. For any public use. There's corners to that boy we don't know."

"Maybe," she said. "Where were you going to stop me on the story? What was your cut-off point? I mean, what on earth did you expect to gain from this?"

"I never thought Hunter would take the magazine seriously enough to actually come back to Houston and try to be a publisher. I thought at first when he said he wanted his ownership out in the open, that it would be all right. More exciting. More money for the magazine. But I saw that he was planning to move in on this thing I've worked on so hard. He could get rid of me. Destroy the magazine. Then move along. I would have killed the story as soon as you got close to thinking Gus Corrigan did it. It had to be you—you're the only one loyal enough to me to keep you mouth shut. I swear, Liz. It would have been a lesson to Hunter—that anyone who cared to could get to him. I needed to re-mind him of what I knew and the power of that knowledge."

"What a dangerous lesson," Liz said. "But he fooled you, didn't he? He cut you off at the pass by telling me everything—and don't tell me he was lying to me. He wasn't."

"I almost lost the magazine," Cal said.

"And me? How could you do this to me?" Her voice was shaking and tears blurred her vision. Cal sat still. "We were such friends. I trusted you, Cal. I would have done anything for you."

He leaned toward Liz, and she thought he might try to comfort her with a touch, and that she'd hit him if he did.

"I'm very sorry," he said quietly. "I had to make a choice."

"But I was your friend. Doesn't that count for anything?"

"It's been a luxury in my life," Cal said. "It's been a lot."

"But what has it been, if you've known everything about me and I haven't known about you and Hunter. I always thought you were soli-tary, looking for someone—"

"When you love someone," Cal said, "you take the circumstances as they come. You'll beg, borrow, steal, cheat—"

"Kill?"

"It hasn't arisen."

"I see it differently," she said.

"I don't know the way it is with other people," Cal said. "It's always been a secret with us, ever since it started. We talk on the phone all the time. We fly places to see each other. If this works out—the magazine—we'll be together more than we have in years. The night he took you for a drink, showed you his house? We had a late date, and he told me he liked you. I started to hope it could work out so that we could all be friends, out in the open. But it's always been secret, and if it has to stay that way, that's okay too."

"Aren't you afraid of him?" Liz asked. "Maybe one morning he'll decide he doesn't like the pattern of your eyebrows or that you know too much for his comfort—"

"We go through that," Cal said, with a small smile that indicated that Liz didn't know what they went through, not half. "It always starts again. Hunter is what I have in my life. Hunter and the magazine. I thought I could make him nervous, if you were getting close to the truth. I thought he would see that his safety lies with me. But don't tell me what he might do to me. I wrote the book. You have David. I've had no one but Hunter for so long, and you know him a little now, don't you? Use your head, Liz. He keeps me occupied."

"And the other lovers?"

"Just other lovers. Nobody important."

"Sandy?"

A quiet came over them in a parody of talks by this fireplace and in other rooms.

"Did he confess to you," Liz asked. "How did you find out about Carolyn Sylvan?"

"He didn't confess. He didn't have to. I was waiting for him when he and his father drove back from Galveston that night. We'd had a date and when he stood me up, I went to his house and waited for him. I hid in back where I wouldn't be seen. Once Hunter was inside, I signaled at his bedroom window. He let me in. He didn't tell me what happened. Not that night. He was restless. Scared or angry. He woke up in the middle of the night in a sweat. I left before daylight. I always did. But I knew something was wrong."

"His father must have loved Hunter after all, to cover up for him."

"Gus was in it over his head," Cal said. "Not to mention the scandal."

Liz thought of her parents, who had defended so many difficult causes. It wouldn't have occurred to her that scandal would be a factor in protecting an only child.

"He changed after the murder. We were really close before. It was sex, of course," Cal said. "But it was more, as if we were two parts of the same boy, and that loving each other made it as if we were from another planet. Some fabulous place. All our own. We knew things other people didn't. We thought what we were doing had never been done before."

It made Liz uncomfortable to see a look of nostalgia on Cal's face, a softness she hadn't seen before.

"And after the murder," she said, "how did they get along once Carolyn Sylvan was out of the way?"

"Hunter told me they never talked about it again. They went to a criminal lawyer, and he told them they were clean. They never talked about anything much anyway. You still don't get it, do you? This thing happened in outer space. The only connection between her and Gus was that she worked for him briefly. No one bothered to push it. There was no reason to."

The sound of the restless boats in the marina came across the water. What an inconvenient person Carolyn Sylvan had been, Liz thought, and how unlucky. Helen had watched her take Gus. Cal had seen her divert Hunter's attention. For Gus, she had been there and was gone. Liz wondered if Gus had found Harrison for Hunter, to keep him in line. She thought of all the times she'd talked to Cal about love and he'd said, one way or another, "I mistrust love, that's all." She must have sounded so foolish to him.

"Do me a favor," Cal said. "Not the tapes. I'm not going to force them from you. I'll just warn you—forget it. The favor is David. Don't tell David about all this."

She looked into Cal's blue eyes and asked, "Our secret? You want me to keep a secret from David?"

"There's no need for him to know. Never mind calling it a secret."

"I have to tell him, Cal. It's just as you said—I have to make a choice."

"That's the end of it then," he said. "I'll be okay. Don't worry."

"I'm not really worried, Cal," she said. "I'm not really worrying about you."

He nodded absently, as if he'd stopped listening to her. He was figuring something out, she could tell, counting his loss, weighing the gain. It had seemed to Liz for a long time that Cal lived on the edge of an unnamed danger, in an icy mysterious place that had its own excitements; or maybe it was that he had seemed to her freer than herself, without her burdensome considerations. Now she knew this wasn't true. Early in his life he had given himself over to Hunter, and his complete gift had been worn the same as freedom.

Cal walked slowly toward the door, then turned back to look at Liz. Before he could speak, she said, "Don't think you can try to talk to me ever again. Or that we'll patch this up," and Cal nodded, as if he'd anticipated that too. He stood twenty feet away, removed from Liz, and they looked at each other.

"Destroy the tapes," he said. "I would if I were you."

When she didn't say anything, he turned and went out, shutting the front door quietly behind him.

For a split second, Liz wanted to run and get Cal back. She listened without moving to the slam of the car door, to the sound of the car starting and pulling away. When the noise had died down, she went to the phone on the kitchen wall and dialed the number of David's hotel.

The phone rang ten times. A busy night, she thought, and she imagined the bright fountain in front of the Plaza, dancing for strangers. It would be cold in New York, colder still upstate. The hotel operator rang David's room. Liz didn't expect him to be there, but he answered on the fourth ring.

"Hi," she said. "It's me. The Gimp."

"I was going to call you in a minute. How's the story going?"

"Finished," she said.

"That was quick work. How did Cal like it?"

"Not very much," she said. "It wasn't what he expected. But it'll work out. David. I'm thinking I'll get on a plane. Right now. I'm ready to come to New York. I need help with a few last things, and I thought, Well, I know a smart lawyer up there."

"You probably know two or three," he said. "Do you want me to meet you at the airport?"

"Oh, no," she said. "Stay right where you are. Wait for me."

"I could easily get a cab. No trouble."

"It's a long ride," she said. "Just wait for me."

"Whatever you like," he said. "Have a good flight."

After they'd hung up, Liz stayed for a few minutes by the phone, her hand on the receiver, then she began straightening up the house. She turned out the upstairs lights and washed Cal's glass and her cup, emptied the coffeepot and washed it. She didn't know if David would help her, but she hoped he would. It was possible, she thought, that she would find a way through this, and much more likely that she would have to find a way to live with what she knew.

She turned out the last light and went outside, locking the door behind her. She listened to the night sounds at Walden for a moment— the water, the frogs. For now, she thought, she would drive south on 45 back toward Houston, to the airport. She would play her car radio loud in the Texas night, and she would fill her lungs with air. Then, quiet, she would fly to David.

Printed in the United States
66604LVS00002B/271